MORE ADVANCE PRAISE FOR *More Than Moody:*

"Dr. Koplewicz once more proves himself to be a teacher and champion for families with children who suffer from mental illness. I recommend this book as required reading for the entire lay public."

—MARILYN BENOIT, M.D., President, American Academy of Child and Adolescent Psychiatry

"More Than Moody is highly readable and offers a wealth of information and much practical advice. This book will certainly be of great value to parents, but it will also become an important resource for professionals."

—STANLEY TURECKI, M.D., author of *The Difficult Child* and *Normal Children Have Problems, Too*

"More Than Moody presents moving and convincing stories about depression in adolescents. I recommend it to all those who have ever wondered how seriously to take their child's mood."

—JUDITH RAPOPORT, M.D., Chief, Child Psychiatry Branch, National Institute of Mental Health, and author of *The Boy Who Couldn't Stop Washing*

"Young people have no better friend than Dr. Koplewicz. This is a superb guide to adolescent depression."

—DONNA E. SHALALA, President, University of Miami and former Secretary of Health and Human Services

"More Than Moody is a terrific book. The use of case studies that include extensive interviews with individuals suffering from major depression before, during, and several years after their diagnosis is powerful."

—RICK BIRKEL, Executive Director, National Alliance for the Mentally Ill

"For too long we have not paid enough attention to the presence of diagnosable and treatable depression in our adolescents, sometimes with tragic results. That is why this book from Dr. Koplewicz is so important. Everyone needs to know more about how to recognize the signs of adolescent depression. This book, written with knowledge and compassion, will become an important resource for families and anyone with teenagers."

—ROSALYNN CARTER, former First Lady

"'A person who saves one life, it is as though that human being has saved the world,' says the Talmud. More Than Moody is a fantastic book that every parent and grandparent must read. Dr. Harold Koplewicz, one of the world's most prominent child and adoles-

cent psychiatrists, has written a compelling page-turner and an essential guide for anyone who has a teenager."

—DR. RUTH WESTHEIMER, world-renowned psychosexual therapist

"Dr. Koplewicz skillfully navigates describing the symptoms of depression, its impact on the adolescent and the family, and the diversity of treatments available. Through case examples and scientific discourse, he provides parents with an excellent and very readable primer on depression."

—TIMOTHY E. WILENS, M.D., associate professor of psychiatry, Harvard Medical School

"A leading child and adolescent psychiatrist, Dr. Harold Koplewicz presents an authoritative guide to this relatively common but emotionally devastating illness."

—JAMES F. LECKMAN, M.D., Yale Child Study Center

"This is an outstanding book, which takes an informed and compassionate look at the very real problem of major depression and other serious mood disturbances in adolescents."

—BENNETT L. LEVENTHAL, M.D., professor of psychiatry and pediatrics, and Director, Child and Adolescent Psychiatry, University of Chicago

"The best investment any concerned parent can make."

—DONALD F. KLEIN, M.D., professor of psychiatry, Columbia University

"How can you tell the difference between the predictable mood swings of adolescence and a life-threatening depression? As parents, we have all anguished over this question. Dr. Koplewicz's book brings sanity and sunlight to our understanding of our children at the most vulnerable time of their lives."

—ERICA JONG, bestselling author

"More Than Moody offers compassion and, more important, solutions for any reader looking to help young people learn from and ultimately transcend depression."

—JONATHAN MOONEY, international lecturer, activist, and author of Learning Outside the Lines

"Adolescent depression is common and life-disrupting, and may lead to suicide—and adolescent depression is usually undiagnosed. This book clearly describes the symptoms of the disorder and enables the reader to recognize the first warning signs. Valuable, highly recommended."

—PAUL H. WENDER, M.D., Distinguished Professor Emeritus of Psychiatry, University of Utah School of Medicine

"Must reading for any parent or teacher helping teens to navigate their adolescence."

—JAMES T. McCRACKEN, M.D., professor and Director, Division of Child & Adolescent Psychiatry, UCLA Neuropsychiatric Institute

MORE THAN MOODY

Also by Harold S. Koplewicz, M.D.

*It's Nobody's Fault: New Hope and
Help for Difficult Children*

Depression in Children & Adolescents

*Childhood Revealed: Art Expressing
Pain, Discovery & Hope*

*Turbulent Times/Prophetic Dreams: Art from
Israeli and Palestinian Children*

MORE THAN MOODY

RECOGNIZING AND TREATING
ADOLESCENT DEPRESSION

Harold S. Koplewicz, M.D.

G. P. PUTNAM'S SONS   NEW YORK

All names and identifying characteristics have been changed to protect the privacy of individual patients.

Every effort has been made to ensure that the information contained in this book is complete and accurate. However, neither the publisher nor the author is engaged in rendering professional advice or services to the individual reader. The ideas, procedures, and suggestions contained in this book are not intended as a substitute for consulting with your physician. All matters regarding your health require medical supervision. Neither the author nor the publisher shall be liable or responsible for any loss, injury, or damage allegedly arising from any information or suggestion in this book.

G. P. Putnam's Sons
Publishers Since 1838
a member of
Penguin Putnam Inc.
375 Hudson Street
New York, NY 10014

Library of Congress Cataloging-in-Publication Data

Koplewicz, Harold S.
More than moody : recognizing and treating
adolescent depression / Harold S. Koplewicz.
p.   cm.
Includes bibliographical references and index.
ISBN 0-399-14918-X
1. Depression in adolescence.   2. Teenagers—Mental health.   I. Title.
RJ506.D4 K67   2002
616.85'27'00835—dc21   2002068379

Printed in the United States of America
1   3   5   7   9   10   8   6   4   2

This book is printed on acid-free paper. ∞

Book design by Meighan Cavanaugh

To my parents, Roma and Joseph Koplewicz—models of strength and optimism. They lost their families and innocence in the Holocaust but kept and shared their values and joy of life first with my sister and me and now with their grandsons.

CONTENTS

MORE THAN MOODY

MORE THAN MOODY:
AN INTRODUCTION

I first met Jesse Altman on a cold day in late January, when he came to my office with his mother and father and a story of trouble not easily unraveled. He was 16 and already very accomplished—not very surprising, considering that he was the son of a doctor and a lawyer. He was near the top of his class academically, was the first-string pitcher on the baseball team, and played both the violin and the guitar superbly. He was considered one of the stars of his school.

But a few weeks earlier, right after school had resumed following the Christmas break, Jesse had stunned his tenth-grade English teacher by bursting into tears after a discussion of the classic adolescent novel *The Catcher in the Rye*. It was the triggering episode, the ostensible reason why he and his parents were sitting in my office now. But there was a history here, a saga that reached back to when Jesse was a first-grader who talked about shooting himself. Now it was a decade later, and I found before me a lanky teenager with piercing emerald green eyes, olive skin, jet-black hair, and not a clue as to what it was that was making him so unhappy.

When I shifted my eyes to his parents, I saw fear. Earlier, they had told me that the incident in the English class was only the most dramatic manifestation of Jesse's troubles. "He's much more irritable, really hypersensitive," his mother told me. Of course, "irritable" and "hypersensitive" could describe most teenagers walking the earth at any given moment, but Jesse's parents had noticed a change. The touchiness was more pronounced, and it was becoming chronic. His parents found him more and more difficult to be around; they felt tremendous guilt to be thinking that they couldn't stand their son. Most days he would come home from school, go directly to his room, and sleep through dinner. Then he would be up for most of the night, going to bed at about three in the morning and unable to wake up for school. The whole thing was baffling to his parents. There was no question that he was very unhappy. But was he "just being a teenager," as his mother hoped? Or was it something more serious, as his father suspected?

It would be months before Jesse would allow his entire story to be uncovered and explored, but as we began to know each other, his unhappiness became more and more palpable. I learned that he had been in therapy with a psychoanalyst when he was in first grade, and was now seeing that doctor again. "I'm not on the program," he said.

"What do you mean, 'on the program'?" I asked.

"Society," he said, invoking the teenager's catchall word for the universe beyond his own skin. "The world is pushing me to do the right thing, but nothing changes. I just want to feel better, but I can't. If someone handed me a gun and loaded the gun and took the safety off, I'd stick it in my mouth. If someone gave me an axe, I'd chop my own head off." I was taken by the passivity of the image—to say nothing of the impracticality of it—but of course I was concerned. Jesse saw that I was nervous, and he raised his hands slightly. "Listen," he said, "we don't have a gun in the house, and we don't have an axe."

I wasn't quite reassured.

Jesse was in real trouble, as you will see later. His grades were slipping, and he didn't care very much about how he looked. He was avoiding his friends and sleeping away the weekends; he was increasingly pessimistic about the future; and he wanted as little as possible to do with his family. Jesse was more than moody. He had major depressive disorder—MDD—commonly known as depression.

·

When I began practicing child and adolescent psychiatric medicine, I hardly expected to be treating depression. Young people, it was widely believed, had neither sufficiently formed egos nor the brain development to cause the kind of chemical imbalance that is at the root of clinical depression. Indeed, twenty years ago depression in adults was often misdiagnosed, mistreated, and stigmatized. If the public, and even the medical world, couldn't entirely accept depression as a disease in adults, certainly innocent children had to be immune. Unhappily, we now know that this isn't the case. Not only does major depressive disorder exist in adolescents and, more rarely, in children, but the syndrome is in many ways clinically equivalent to the spiral of depression in adulthood. We also—and I say this with great caution—know how to treat it.

I couldn't have imagined the response I would receive to the one short chapter on depression in my first book, *It's Nobody's Fault: New Hope and Help for Difficult Children,* which was published in 1996. The media was quick to wonder whether depression was an explanation for adolescents on murder sprees, for teenage mothers callously killing their newborns, for all the "children without a conscience" who made up the collage on the cover of *People* magazine. Parents who had read the book or heard about it wondered if the surliness, listlessness, hopelessness, and despair their children were experiencing could be caused by something medical, something more than simply the natural—and not unhealthy—volatility of adolescence. Pediatricians, teachers, social workers, seemingly everyone whose lives brought them in contact with young people suddenly had in mind some child or teenager they felt was at risk. No doubt, many *are* at risk.

This is no exaggeration. Upwards of 40 million Americans suffer from depression, and approximately 3.5 million of them are children and teenagers, according to a 1999 report by the United States Surgeon General. The studies indicate that as you read this, between 10 and 15 percent of the child and adolescent population have some signs of depression. It is still relatively rare among preteens and young children, so the vast majority of those affected are teenagers. But one reason there are ten times more depressed adults than teenagers is simply that there are that many more adults. Significantly, studies estimate that in a given year as many as 8.3 percent of the adolescent population will begin exhibiting signs of major depression—compared with only 5.3 percent for adults. And while adults are much more apt to recognize their depression and be treated, most teenagers—for reasons I will discuss in the coming chapters—will not receive the help they need.

As a group, perhaps the most affected are college students. Studies suggest that significant percentages of them have bouts of depression in which they feel hopeless and even suicidal. On the other hand, the widespread use of antidepressants such as Prozac means that some young people who might have been too debilitated to go to college in earlier years can now attend and succeed. In either case, parents today need to be especially alert to what depression in adolescents looks and feels like, and to be capable of helping their children, perhaps long-distance.

Young people with depression don't suffer every day, or all their lives, or with the same intensity with each episode, but they do suffer. Whether they are entering middle school or finishing college, the pain of depression can seriously erode their capacity for joy and curiosity and for facing the developmental hurdles they must overcome to take their places as happy, productive adults. And at its worst, depression can lead to severe isolation and even suicide or violence toward others. In 2002, some 2,000 teenagers in the United States will kill themselves. That's more kids than will die from all other illnesses—from cancer to AIDS—combined. Only traffic accidents and homicides take more adolescents than suicide. What's perhaps even more frightening are studies suggesting that every single day, in every single high school in America, teenagers are thinking about suicide or making actual attempts. The most recent survey on youth risk behavior from the Centers for Disease Control reports that annually, 3 million teenagers, or 19 percent of all U.S. high-schoolers, had thoughts of suicide, and more than 2 million of them made plans to carry it out. And some 400,000 made actual suicide attempts requiring medical attention. That comes to an average of more than 1,000 attempts a day nationwide, every day of the year. I can say with a reasonable degree of confidence that depression plays at least some role in most of them. It's a cliché by now to say, "We had no indication at all. Everything seemed fine." But, of course, everything was not fine. And even those with recognized problems invariably leave devastated family and friends thinking, "I never thought he would go that far."

Like Jesse Altman, many of the patients I've treated have been brought to me by parents stricken by profound worry. Their children may or may not have histories of a mental disorder, but their recent behavior indicates something more serious than teenage angst. But for every one of those my colleagues and I have treated, there are countless others who never get the help they need. The problem is that adolescent depression is terribly underdiagnosed in this country. That statement applies to every socioeconomic group, though members of minority groups are the most neglected, as is the case in health care in general. It is in large part because major depression can be insidious that it is so often unrecognized and untreated. Depression starts silently and slowly in most cases, and it is usually only when the symptoms become severe that others begin to take note. The costs are enormous. An adolescent with depression not only suffers at this crucial stage in his development, but he is at much higher risk of having depression as an adult.

Consider that some 20 percent of teenagers—one in five—report that they have had a major depressive episode that went untreated during their adolescence, according to a study by Dr. Peter Lewinsohn from the University of Oregon. That's a striking number, and it may help explain why there are so many depressed adults. Recently, a friend of mine was seated at a dinner table with a man who described his vivid memories of being depressed during college. "I was so tired, I didn't know what was going on," he recalled. "At the end of my freshman year, my brother literally had to carry me home. I thought maybe I had mono. I went to my doctor, who said I didn't have mono and sent me to a psychiatrist. I went into therapy and eventually came out of it, but it was one of the darkest periods of my life." Now his own daughter has an anxiety disorder, and she is a reminder to him of those years. Is her anxiety a precursor to depression? Clearly, there are too many teenagers suffering from more than moodiness. And though we can't prove it yet—studies are now underway looking at long-term effects—it also seems logical that many adults might be spared if we get better at spotting and treating the disease during adolescence.

"Depressed" is perhaps the most overused word in the English language—especially by teenagers. *I'm so depressed,* they say—even when they mean they're just upset about something. They don't say, "I'm so demoralized," which would be a more accurate word. You never walk by a bunch of teenagers hanging out and hear any of them say: "God, I'm so dispirited." But despite this semantic abuse, there are many more teenagers who truly are depressed but who don't *say* they are—because they don't know that's what's wrong with them. Their parents, meanwhile, will be just as much in the dark. Maybe you are one such parent. If that's the case, I hope this book will shed light.

Through the stories of some of the patients I have treated over the years, along with those of some other adolescents and their parents I've met in the course of writing this book, I hope to offer a window into the challenges of diagnosing depression—of determining when a teenager is truly depressed versus when she is feeling down because of a major setback, sad over a divorce or death, or even just struggling to cope with the ups and downs of being a modern teenager. Mallory is absolutely crushed when her boyfriend breaks up with her, but it lasts only a few days or a couple of weeks. She bounces back. But if the sadness persists— if Mallory has become a different person, if she's lost her sense of humor, if her sleeping and eating habits are disturbed, and if she's become socially isolated and is suddenly having trouble keeping up with school-work—it may be that the breakup was the triggering event of an under-lying depression that needs to be treated.

Treatment itself is a delicate and controversial matter. Much has been written and said about kids and pills, and I believe a good deal of the consternation has to do with a simple misconception: many people don't believe children can become psychiatrically ill. At the same time, hard questions need to be addressed: Are we changing our children's personal-ities with these medications? Is it right to set them on a course where they might have to take medicine, at least intermittently, for the rest of their lives? Is there a better way? Are HMOs, to say nothing of the phar-maceutical companies themselves, encouraging the use of medicines in-stead of psychotherapy for the sake of expedience or profit? The truth is that while we know what works best for most adults, we're still address-ing that question for adolescents. There is abundant clinical evidence that antidepressants work for teenagers. But do they work better than cognitive behavioral therapy? Or is a combination of medicine and ther-apy best?

What we think is that most teenagers who respond to antidepressants for a first episode of depression will need to take the medication for about 6 to 12 months. Only those teens who have recurrent episodes of depression should take medication for the long-term.

Very important, too, is the understanding, support, and cooperation of the child's parents, who will need to recognize that they can't use a "pull-yourself-together" or "kindness first" approach to a disorder that will not respond to either discipline or sympathy any more than cancer or diabetes can be cured by a willed change of attitude. Not only are many parents guilt-ridden over the diagnosis ("If my child is so unhappy, I must be doing something very wrong"), they are also loath to submit to the news that their child might have to be on medication for many months, or even years, even if that medication will treat the illness effec-tively. More often than might be expected, coming to grips with a child's disease serves as a different kind of catalyst for parents: many come to understand that they, too, have suffered depression at some point or even throughout their lives and they, too, may need treatment. Thus, understanding and helping families to work more effectively is always a part of the treatment. MDD is rarely a disease that pops up once, is treated, then goes away for good.

When I was a kid, children weren't permitted to get depressed. In fact, I remember well that when I complained about feeling sad or upset, my mother instructed me to knock my head against the wall; when I stopped, I would know happiness. No one has ever argued that this is an effective method, but it does represent, if somewhat ludicrously, earlier attitudes not only by the public but also by mental health professionals, who believed that children were not sufficiently mature to experience depression. Meanwhile, parents have generally presumed that most young people have nothing to be depressed about—especially those who have had the good fortune to be born into affluence.

As any parent can attest, moodiness is practically a trademark of adolescence. Virtually all teenagers have swings in temperament during these years when they are gradually trying to accomplish many developmental tasks—adjusting to the physical changes of puberty, separating from parents, focusing educational or vocational goals. The noted psychologist G. Stanley Hall called adolescence the period of "storm and stress." Teenagers can be irritable and sensitive—especially where their parents are concerned. Millions of parents with teenage kids feel as though they are walking on eggshells: one minute their children might be perfectly pleasant, the next they're ready to bite their parents' heads off. These parents may think this is just the way it's going to be for a while, and they might be right. After all, they may ask, what teenager *doesn't* drive her parents crazy? But some others may have children with a serious illness that requires identification, diagnosis, and treatment. Which ones are which? That, of course, is the $64,000 question.

We used to believe that all moodiness, or "affective dysregulation," as we say in psychiatry, was normal for teenagers—that adolescence was simply an adjustment period marked by all sorts of fluctuations in mood as one struggled to grasp one's identity. Anna Freud said that affective fluctuations or moodiness in adolescence merely *resembled* illness or psychopathology. She believed, as did the field, that adolescents who *didn't* exhibit depressive or sad periods were actually abnormal—that they had an inability to cope with internal struggles. Therefore, a *lack* of unrest in teenagers was a sign that had to be taken seriously. Freud claimed at the time that these teenagers were "excessively defended" and hadn't achieved the psychological development necessary to proceed to adulthood. Today we know that these views may have been a case of wishful thinking. Depression in adolescence is real, and it is not trivial: left untreated it can lead to school failure, social isolation, family breakdown, and even sometimes psychosis or suicide.

It's not too difficult to spot a depressed adult. There is a pronounced change in mood, one that is clearly noticed by a spouse, and this change doesn't lift after a few weeks. But for the parent of a moody teenager, the baseline is already pretty high: *Michael gets angry about things I don't think are all that important—but that's what teenagers do.* Is he depressed, or is he just being a teenager? Moreover, whereas a depressed adult's mood typically will be consistently low and not reactive to events in her daily life, a depressed teenager can have periods when he seems fine. As one confused parent told me, "It seems like he decides if he's going to be in a good mood or bad mood. He went to a party and was fine, having a good time. Then at home he was impossible to be around. What's going on?" What's going on is that a depressed kid, unlike most depressed adults, can feel good if something good happens to him. This is called "atypical depression," and a teenager with this form of the disorder—probably the most common in adolescence—can fool his parents into thinking he is just being a moody teenager and that he has control over the situation. He doesn't. In fact, it is a rare instance when a depressed teenager cannot experience any pleasure. That's what makes diagnosing teenage depression challenging—and why untold numbers of teenagers are not being treated.

As parents, we all have memories of adolescence, some of them painful, and we want our children to have an easier time of it. But we filter their lives through the lens of our own experience. Of course, we cannot help but empathize, but we shouldn't necessarily apply our memories to our children's lives. When a child is depressed, perhaps falling apart right before our eyes, it's all the worse because we feel it with her. We'd like to think that we can somehow fix everything for our kids. But then we find that an illness like MDD seems beyond our control. When they were smaller, we used to lift up our kids and support them. We could protect them and have a real impact on their happiness. But as they've become teenagers, we've reluctantly begun to cede influence to their peers and other social forces outside the cocoon of the home. But we've also begun to realize that the more questions we ask our children and their teachers, the better able we will be to grasp any potential problems.

In the coming pages, you will meet some teenagers and their parents who have experienced what you and your child may be going through now. Some of these adolescents are current or recent patients who are still battling depression. Others portrayed have since become adults and graciously offered their perspectives, hoping it might help the next generation. I have changed their names and some identifying details to protect their privacy. Through these stories, and through my own and my colleagues' experiences, I hope you will come away with a better understanding of adolescent depression, and the warning signs to look for that may help you improve or even save your child's life.

Part of the process is recognizing what is *not* depression. My own son, the eldest of my three boys, once went through a period of listlessness that I feared could be depression. It turned out to be Lyme disease. Later, he went through all the normal teenage behavior that drives parents crazy. Dealing with this so routinely in my professional life, I couldn't help but consider depression yet again. But it turned out to be nothing that an acceptance letter from his first choice of colleges couldn't cure.

Just as I had to grapple with my own son's moodiness, mental health professionals face the challenge of discerning depression in adolescents every day. Diagnosing and treating depression in adults is a relatively simple task: the patient usually acknowledges the problem, has some insight into it, and is motivated to fix it. With adolescents, the process is much more difficult. A young person rarely asks to go see a psychiatrist; it's almost always his parents who have to suggest, cajole, and sometimes force him to get professional help. The clinician must carefully interview the young person, who is apt to deny the problem or shade the truth— if he offers much at all in the way of insight. Parents and perhaps teachers or a school psychologist or counselor must be interviewed. There are questionnaires and rating scales to administer and assess and sometimes stacks of records from other doctors as well as school reports to review. It's as close to detective work as a psychiatrist can get.

That said, you will notice that the young people whose lives I discuss in this book have in most cases been seen by other professionals. That has been the nature of my practice over the past decade or so; I see about 200 new children and teenagers every year for diagnostic evaluations, and in almost all cases I am a second, third, or even fourth opinion. That these young people have lived in pain for months or even years, overwhelmed by troubles whose true nature has eluded previous clinicians, is less a commentary on these colleagues' competence than on how difficult diagnosing adolescent depression can be. I also have the benefit of finding out what has not worked in past evaluations and treatment.

Across the country there are excellent centers that specialize in treating depressed young people, and the field is fortunate to have so many dedicated and truly gifted researchers working to unlock the mysteries that remain. These people are saving teenagers' lives and advancing knowledge. But it's also true that over the last quarter century, one of the most widely acknowledged shortages in medicine has been in the field of child and adolescent mental health. While 10 million children and adolescents have a diagnosable psychiatric disorder right now, there are only 7,000 board-certified child and adolescent psychiatrists in the United States and fewer than 6,000 child psychologists. The overwhelming majority recognize that treatment is driven by diagnosis, but the fact that so many young people are brought in for help after having debilitating symptoms for many years means that we are failing at early identification and intervention. We wouldn't think of letting children with physical symptoms go without seeking treatment, dismissing the complaints with the timeworn words, "It's just a phase."

Sometimes it *is* a phase. Sometimes a teenager is just moody. I hope this book will make you better equipped to recognize when it is more than that—when it is an illness crying out to be treated.

1

DIAGNOSIS: DEPRESSION

What a pain Jasmine's become. She's sullen, she's nasty to her parents and siblings, and she's generally very anxious. She's doing poorly in school and brings new meaning to the concept "lazy teenager." Forget cleaning up her room; Jasmine isn't even bothering to brush her hair. She's so irritable that when her mother asked at dinner one night if she was going out later, she threw a roll at her and stormed out, screaming, "I can't talk to you! I can't stand being in the same room with you!" Jasmine's parents wonder: Is she just being an unbearable adolescent? Or is this something else?

The fact that Jasmine's mom and dad are even asking the question is a good sign. But the answer is a double-edged sword. On one hand, they want to see their daughter as a normal teenager—even if it means putting up with all her atrocious behavior. They feel a little guilty because they confide in each other: "I can't stand her." Although they love her, they truly do not like their child right now. But there's comfort in the thought that they're not the only ones going through this—that millions and millions of other parents have survived adolescence (including their own parents) and they will, too.

On the other hand, as with any other medical condition, there can also be relief in finding out that what's going on is *not* normal—as long as it's followed immediately by an assurance that something can be done about it. If Jasmine is in fact depressed, her parents want to know what's wrong, and they want to know what can be done to help her—and they want to know it *now*. I have sat with countless parents who are thrilled to hear that there is an explanation for their children's low moods and difficult behavior, and that there is a way to treat it. That teenagers can suffer severe depression still seems counterintuitive to many people—even physicians, who might be reluctant to prematurely "brand" a young patient with a mental illness diagnosis. But we've known for some time that, as was first reported in 1989 in the *Journal of the American Medical Association,* depression seems to be occurring earlier in life than ever before.

I'm not ready to declare that kids are more depressed than ever—we may just be more *aware* of it—but the fact is that reported depression rates are actually higher for adolescents than adults. This would no doubt be a big surprise to Jasmine's parents. But they would probably find it comforting to know that their daughter isn't the only one suffering—nor are they the only parents.

So what, exactly, is depression—what does this common word really mean? It is actually a broad term that covers four distinct varieties of illness:

- *Major Depressive Disorder (MDD).* This is a serious depression that in adolescence lasts on average from seven to nine months. It has many similarities to adult depression—sadness, pessimism, sleep and appetite disturbance, decrease in concentration and sex drive—but in other ways it is distinct. For instance, anxiety symptoms and irritability are more common in depressed teenagers than adults. Adolescents frequently have the "atypical" form of MDD. This is characterized by being overly sensitive to the environment and responding to perceived negative interactions, with symptoms opposite of the classic picture. Eating and sleeping too much, for instance, rather than not enough.

- *Dysthymic Disorder.* A milder but more chronic depression. Also called dysthymia, it is a low-level depression that is felt most of the day, on most days, and continues for years. In adolescents, the average duration is four years, meaning that they spend virtually their entire adolescence depressed. A low mood for so long a time during such a crucial period of development is likely to affect a person's mental state as an adult.
- *Double Depression.* A combination of major depression and dysthymia—a depression that is both serious and chronic.
- *Bipolar Disorder.* Also known as manic-depression, this is characterized by unusual shifts in mood and energy. Though there is debate about how prevalent it is in young people, the condition frequently begins with a depressive episode during adolescence. Research has also shown that anywhere from 20 to 40 percent of adolescents with major depression develop bipolar disorder within five years.
- *Reactive Depression.* The most common form of mood problem in children and adolescents, but the least serious. This is a depressed state brought on by difficulty adjusting to a disturbing experience—something as serious as the loss of a parent or as relatively inconsequential as a rejection or a slight. It usually lasts anywhere from a few hours to a couple of weeks and is not considered a mental disorder.

Most of these terms and definitions apply generally, no matter a person's age. Clearly, though, there are differences between depression in adolescence and in adulthood—sometimes subtle distinctions that parents need to understand in order to know when it's time to pick up the phone and make an appointment for an evaluation. The good news is that there is a fairly straightforward list of symptoms that can go a long way in distinguishing between normal teenage moodiness and real depression. Some of these symptoms are similar to those that characterize adult depression. Like adults, young people with depression are likely to be lethargic, indecisive, and to lose interest in activities they enjoy. They may be self-critical and feel unloved and pessimistic about the future. But there are also some important differences—largely because adults and adolescents are, physiologically and emotionally, very different animals.

Unfortunately, little can be said about diagnosis that is hard and fast. There is no gold-standard medical test for depression or, for that matter, any other mental illness. That's the Holy Grail of psychiatry. Many parents have asked me to do a brain scan on a child to determine what's wrong. Today we can do any number of scans and lab tests to diagnose cancer, heart disease, diabetes, and other physical illnesses. We haven't gotten there yet for mental illness. Compared with, say, cardiology, psychiatry is an immature field, and a much more complicated one. The brain is by far the most complex and mysterious of the body's organs, and the growing brain is even more so. The fact is that we barely understand the mature brain, much less the developing one. So we have to diagnose by talking to people. No matter how good a psychiatrist or psychologist is at it, it's still not a great way to make a medical diagnosis. But for now it's all we have.

With those caveats, there are some pretty reliable differences between adult and adolescent depression. For instance, whereas depressed adults tend to be quietly sad—you can *feel* their depression—teenagers are more likely to be angry, irritable (or more irritable than usual), or to act out. It's not that there is a different quality to the irritability when a teenager is depressed, but that it is more easily triggered, lasts longer, and comes with other symptoms. That there is a closer relationship between irritability and depression in young people than in adults is partly due to the fact that, to begin with, virtually all teenagers are irritable. But it's also because teenagers often have trouble verbalizing their emotions, so instead of expressing how bad they feel, they lash out. Parents and educators, in turn, might misinterpret this suddenly aggressive behavior as a conduct problem. It's no surprise that parents do very poorly at identifying major depression in their children.

There are other differences. While sad adults are apt to have trouble sleeping and lose their appetites, teenagers are likely to sleep and eat *more.* Depressed young people are more likely to have an anxiety disorder—fear of separation from parents or a reluctance to meet and socialize with peers—than adults with depression. Also more common for teenagers are "somatic symptoms"—general aches and pains, stomach aches, headaches. And while depressed adults tend to lose their sex drive, teenagers will still likely have an interest. They may be masturbating or responsive to someone else's sexual interest. But they tend not to *pursue* sex (or the idea of it) as they might have before they became depressed.

Perhaps the biggest difference is the instability of adolescent depression. While a 40-year-old is going to stay glum until the depression lifts, you can't count on a teenager to stay depressed 24/7. She has an ability to snap out of it, even if it's just for a few hours when she goes out with her friends, before falling back into the depression. A friend with a teenager remarked to me, "I never know who I'm going home to. She can be sweet and charming, but there are days when she's Cruella DeVil." I remember my mother calling my sister "Dr. Jekyll and Miss Hyde." My father, coming home late, tired, and oblivious, called her "Princess."

Here is a glance at typical differences between adult and adolescent depression.

ADULTS	ADOLESCENTS
Depressed mood or loss of interest or pleasure in nearly all activities	Depressed mood, irritability, or loss of pleasure in daily activities
Decrease in appetite or weight	Overeating, increased weight
Decrease in sleep	Increase in sleep
Change in activity, either lethargy or agitation	Lethargy, decreased energy
Decrease in libido	Little sexual impairment
Social environment plays small role	Reactive to social environment

I must repeat that—as you will see—the rub is that none of this is etched in stone. Many teenagers experience depression in ways very similar to adults—being more sullen than irritable, for instance, or having trouble eating and sleeping. And, of course, whether it's school or work, a person of any age going through a depression will find it difficult, if not impossible, to concentrate. So a marked drop in performance in school is one of the primary indicators that a teenager is more than moody. But the fact that depression doesn't always look the same—and that it comes at a time of life that can be inscrutable anyway—confuses parents: *What do you mean he's depressed? He's kissing his girlfriend, and as soon as she leaves he becomes surly with me. Isn't that just being a teenager?* Parents often don't recognize that this is a biological disorder with consequences that can be much more serious than when it happens to an adult. One sobering piece of evidence is that rates of completed suicides have increased dramatically in adolescents over the past 40 years. We know that a large percentage of suicide victims suffer from depression.

But even if it never comes to that extreme and irrevocable step, the teenager can find herself falling behind in life in ways that can be hard to recover from. An adult can manage to tread water at work and eventually regain her footing without losing much ground. But a 15-year-old who falls into a depression can lose an entire year or more of school, as well as become socially impaired. In later chapters you will meet several young people whose depressions have put them on such a detour that it will take years for them to recover—not so much from the depression itself but from what they lost during their struggles to overcome it. Recent research has demonstrated that depression that comes on in adolescence is particularly insidious. It often follows the onset of other mental disorders, such as an anxiety disorder or disruptive or antisocial behavior, raising the possibility that the depression is a response to those problems. Depression in teenagers is also closely associated with substance abuse. In all, some two-thirds of young people with major depressive disorder (MDD) have another mental disorder. (This is discussed in chapter 3.)

The good news is that the recovery rate from a single episode is quite high. The bad news is that each episode increases the risk of having another one and that the condition might continue into adulthood. So young people with severe depressions can find themselves in a serious hole—especially if their illness goes unrecognized and untreated. When their peers are graduating from college and getting ready to become productive, independent adults, they are still living at home, struggling to get on track. A generation ago, my generation, this was sometimes known as "finding yourself." I would venture to say that some of these young people who were said to be finding themselves were actually suffering from MDD. The message: it's vital to recognize depression early and to take aggressive steps to treat it.

What, exactly, is "mood"? It can be defined as a way of characterizing how someone feels in the broadest sense, and how he or she expresses that feeling. Mood, in either direction, can be affected by external events.

In the case of adolescents, this can be anything from acing a big test to getting dumped by a boyfriend. Whether they are up or down, most people, of any age, return to their "normal" moods—whatever that happens to be—after a short period. Not getting to go on a date or to a movie might cause a teenager to be *dispirited*. Being rejected by a boyfriend might cause her to become *demoralized*.

One way to distinguish between being dispirited and feeling demoralized is to think of weather versus climate. Being dispirited is like the weather: it's raining today, and it may rain tomorrow, but the sun will be out the next day. Being demoralized is like climate. It's broader, more defining, more all-encompassing. Florida has a tropical climate; you can count on it being hot and humid a lot of the time. Semantics aside, the real issues are how bad a young person feels and how easily he bounces back. An adolescent who is demoralized may be able to snap out of it momentarily—if something good occurs, he may be able to enjoy it—but it might not last. If it doesn't—if feeling bad becomes the new climate—then we're talking about depression. Dysthymia, meanwhile, a form of depression that may be less severe than major depressive disorder, is chronic, and the treatment is the same. Clinical studies on adults have shown that antidepressants are successful at treating both dysthymia and depression.

Adolescence is demoralizing almost by definition. So how do parents decide if their children may be depressed and need an evaluation? Here is a list of signs that may be associated with depression in adolescents, compiled by the National Institute of Mental Health:

- Persistently sad or irritable mood
- Loss of interest in activities once enjoyed
- Significant change in sleeping patterns or appetite—sleeping or eating too much or too little
- Loss of energy
- Feelings of worthlessness or inappropriate guilt
- Difficulty concentrating
- Recurrent thoughts of suicide

- Frequent vague, unspecific physical complaints—headaches, muscle aches, fatigue
- Frequent absences from school, cutting classes, or a drop in academic performance
- Outbursts of shouting, complaining, unexplained irritability, or crying; increased anger or hostility
- Excessive boredom
- Social isolation: lack of interest in friends and poor communication
- Alcohol or drug abuse
- Fear of death
- Extreme sensitivity to rejection or failure
- Reckless behavior

All of us experience some of the feelings and behaviors on this long list at one time or another. I've been bored. I've had low energy. I've feared death. But it takes more to make a diagnosis of major depressive disorder. There has to be a significant change in mood overriding these feelings that lasts at least a few weeks. "Significant" is the operative word, because with teenagers a mood can last 30 seconds. Simply put, a significant change in mood for an adolescent means going from fine to miserable and staying there for more than a couple of weeks. Of course, what makes the diagnosis difficult in teenagers is that it's not uncommon for them to feel some of the things on the list and to have a period of moodiness as well—and still not be clinically depressed. It's the duration of the symptoms that tell us if a teenager has crossed the line into depression.

It can also be tough to distinguish between some associated conditions. For instance, people who are socially anxious can look sad or withdrawn, especially if they are in a public situation. Someone with separation anxiety might very well look depressed when not in the company of her parents. These young people may have an anxiety disorder alone, or they may have both anxiety and depression. Consider also grief and bereavement. A reaction to a sudden and powerful loss—whether it's a personal tragedy or a more communal one, such as the September 11 terrorist attacks, can make anyone depressed. Again, the key is how long it lasts.

Meanwhile, physical illnesses always have to be ruled out before a diagnosis of major depression can be made. A parasitic illness such as Lyme disease or a virus such as the one that causes mononucleosis can lead to symptoms suggestive of depression. Meanwhile, various diseases of the brain have strong associations with depression. For example, there is evidence that lesions of the left frontal lobe frequently cause major depressive disorder. Similarly, diseases such as Parkinson's also seem to be associated with depression. Virtually all this research, however, is based on studies of adults. With adolescents, there is emerging evidence that various forms of allergic disorders, chronic infections, and immunological diseases may show specific associations with depression.

It's critical for parents to understand how the teenage years are different from any other period of life, and to make certain adjustments in their perceptions of their children. For instance, many parents remark (either wistfully or with bemusement) that their kids no longer want to be around them. This is not only normal, it's healthy. Separating is an important part of the journey to adult independence.

If it's possible to scientifically document that parents move from center stage of a child's life to somewhere off to the side, Dr. Reed Larson at the University of Illinois has done it. The psychologist conducted several studies with large samples of normal, middle-class teenagers in the Chicago area in an effort to find out how they really spend their time. He gave them pagers, then beeped them systematically and asked them to write down what they were doing at that moment. Over time, he found, kids spend less and less time with their families—from 35 percent of their time in fifth grade to 14 percent by the time they are high school seniors. He found no difference between boys and girls. But at the same time, Dr. Larson found that the time children spend alone with their parents, one-on-one, doesn't decline. It seems they are just more selective with the time they spend with their families—and this suggests that, in the end, parents are still their biggest influence.

Another reason for hope is that it appears adolescents eventually learn to value their families again. Dr. Larson's studies have found that ages 13 and 14 are the peak period for teenagers to be down on their families and to feel bad when they are with them. Things improve dramatically by the time they are 17 and 18—so at least they can go off to college on good terms. As Mark Twain said, "When I was a boy of 14, my father was so ignorant I could hardly stand to have the old man around. But when I got to be 21, I was astonished at how much he had learned in seven years."

Parents might be surprised to learn that they aren't the only ones being pushed away. Teenagers distance themselves even from their friends. Sometimes, they just want to be alone. Some parents might see this newfound preference as a possible symptom of depression. In fact, it's perfectly normal for a teenager to go up to his room and not be heard from for hours. (It's important to note that this kind of isolation *by choice* is different from social isolation, in which the teenager doesn't have the energy for or interest in a social life.) Dr. Larson concluded from his studies in Chicago that not only is spending time alone normal, it often has a therapeutic effect. After spending a brief period of time alone, teenagers who were feeling down often rebounded. But as is often the case, it's a question of degree. Dr. Larson found that teenagers who spent *a lot* of time alone (approximately six hours or more on a school day) were more likely to have mood problems. The message of all this is that it's important to look at the big picture, to go beyond one small behavior. How's his appetite and sleeping pattern? Is she still playing tennis? Have his grades dropped? These and others are the questions that have to be asked.

For all the increasing awareness of teenage depression in the last decade or so, we are only now starting to give it as much attention as we have to adult depression. Research on adults and depression is vast, and famous depressives are part of the culture: such celebrities as Mike Wallace, William Styron, and Barbara Bush have helped bring depression out of the closet. But only in the last few years have clinicians and researchers turned their attention to young people and become more skilled at understanding how depression feels to them and how it looks to us. We have become more focused on asking *specific* questions of both adolescents and their parents that target the symptoms of depression.

Previously, it was common to talk only to the teenagers themselves, and ask only general and open-ended questions—"How do you feel?" "How's school going?" That would not provide the clues that would lead to a correct diagnosis. What's needed are pointed questions that will yield helpful information: *How many hours did you sleep last night? How about the night before? How long does it take you to get to sleep? How's your appetite? Have you noticed any changes in your ability to concentrate and your capacity to do schoolwork? How often do you see your friends? Do you call them? How often? What do you do on weekends?* Even now, questions like these are not always asked, increasing the possibility that the teenager will fail to be properly diagnosed.

Similarly, parents should be asked specific questions about their observations. On the following page are some that Doctors Adrian Angold and Elizabeth J. Costello of Duke University compiled into a "Mood and Feelings Questionnaire." There is a similar one for the teenagers themselves. The questions refer to how the teen has felt in the previous two weeks. Marking TRUE means the statement is true about the child most of the time.

In developing this questionnaire, Doctors Angold and Costello did not intend for it to be a litmus test for depression. There is no scoring system with a magic number that identifies depression. However, it can be a useful checklist for parents who have concerns about a change in their child's mood and behavior. Of course, knowing the answers to some of these questions about your teenager's internal thoughts and perceptions is difficult for any parent. But being able to observe changes in his or her behavior, and being able to help your teenagers through demoralizing experiences and perhaps depression, means talking to him or her. That can be a daunting task, especially if there's isn't a solid foundation of dialogue from the child's earlier years. But it's vital to do. Just as parents struggle with how to talk with their kids about things like sex

MOOD AND FEELINGS QUESTIONNAIRE

	TRUE	SOMETIMES	NOT TRUE
1. S/he felt miserable or unhappy.	____	____	____
2. S/he didn't enjoy anything at all.	____	____	____
3. S/he felt so tired that s/he just sat around and did nothing.	____	____	____
4. S/he was very restless.	____	____	____
5. S/he felt s/he was no good anymore.	____	____	____
6. S/he cried a lot.	____	____	____
7. S/he found it hard to think properly or concentrate.	____	____	____
8. S/he hated him/herself.	____	____	____
9. S/he felt s/he was a bad person.	____	____	____
10. S/he felt lonely.	____	____	____
11. S/he thought nobody really loved him/her.	____	____	____
12. S/he thought s/he could never be as good as other kids.	____	____	____
13. S/he felt s/he did everything wrong.	____	____	____

and drugs, they must be ready to discuss how their sons and daughters are feeling emotionally. That's why waiting until a child is 14 to start talking to him or her about important emotional matters is a very bad idea. When they are young, we talk to them about brushing their teeth and hygiene; we take them to the pediatrician on a regular basis. Mental health is no different. If there is a significant change in a teenager's mood, it's incumbent on parents to take note and take action. To ignore it is to be neglectful. It conveys to the child that the parents are insensitive, unaware, or uncaring.

JASMINE'S SECLUSION

Let's return to Jasmine's story. She is a 15-year-old African-American girl, bright and creative, with a mischievous smile and three earrings in her left earlobe and two in her right. When I met her she was dressed in tight jeans and a light blue sweater that exposed her midriff. Jasmine had been under the care of a colleague at the NYU Child Study Center, and had been taking Prozac for four months. She already seemed to be feeling better, so I talked with her and with her father about her depression from a retrospective point of view. For my purposes this was good, because Jasmine was engaging, insightful, and articulate—things she would not likely have been when she first came in for treatment.

I spoke first to Jasmine's father, Dennis, a tall, dignified man who had come directly from his office at a bank. He was dressed impeccably and had a reserved way about him. He said that Jasmine's problems seemed to start in eighth grade. She had always been a happy, caring child, but something happened. "It was like there was no emotion in her," Dennis said. "We have a difficult situation with our son, who has autism. And it seemed like Jasmine didn't care, like she had water inside her, not blood. It was very frustrating for us, because she was never like that before."

The following year, when Jasmine reached high school, her grades took a precipitous drop. Dennis and his wife, Sonya, didn't think it was merely a problem of adjusting to a new school—it was an all-girls Catholic high school—because it was accompanied by behavior they had never seen previously. When Dennis offered to give Jasmine extra help in math, "she looked at me like she didn't know what I was talking about."

When they tried to talk to Jasmine about it, she opened up a little. She said she didn't feel accepted at school—and that became a regular refrain. It became hard to be around Jasmine. She was easily offended, overly sensitive. And though she was sleeping fine, she had very little energy. She'd always been a good student, very talented, a big reader. Lately, she had become drawn to books with dark themes that would affect her deeply. She read *The Diary of Anne Frank* and became very preoccupied with the cruelties of the Holocaust. As she sank more deeply, she paid less and less attention to how she looked. Jasmine had never been much for dressing up, but now she wasn't even showering.

I asked Jasmine's father about any family history of depression or other mental illness. He said his wife had had two episodes of depression, and her grandfather had committed suicide years ago.

When Jasmine came in and plopped herself down in the corner of my couch, she struck me immediately as someone with an air of intelligence. I asked her a question that I frequently use to break the ice with young patients I'm meeting for the first time. "Everybody worries about something. What do you worry about?"

"What do I worry about?" Jasmine repeated. "I'm always living in the past or living in the future, never the present."

"What does that mean?"

"Things that happened in the past, any little incident, can still affect me. I also think a lot about things that can happen to me in the future. So I don't think about what's happening to me in the present."

"Tell me about the past."

"I had a very horrible childhood, actually," Jasmine said matter-of-factly. "I remember the first day of school, kicking and screaming. A lot of kids were pretty mean to me. They said I was different. I didn't know what they meant. Later on, I found out. For one thing, I'm very quiet. I don't talk a lot. That's one of the things that caught their attention. They wanted to make me talk, so they provoked me, picked on me. Once they pushed me down the stairs, I guess just to get a reaction out of me. I used to be a tomboy. I was a fighter, and they would tease me a lot. I'm so involved in the past, things that happened to me. I'm like, I don't know, an outcast. I totally forget who I am sometimes. I'm like two people. I actually have two e-mail addresses. One is Vanessa, the outcast. The other is Jasmine. She's responsibility, reality, pain, anger. There's always one oddball in the family. The outcast. That's me. My sister is more normal, and she's my mother's favorite."

I imagined that Jasmine's earlier years were no picnic, but I also sensed that her description of a "very horrible childhood" was the product of the drama of adolescence. It was like the soundtrack of her life.

I asked Jasmine to tell me about her mother.

"My mother. Well, let's see. I can't talk to her. I've felt rejected by her. She confessed to me, a couple of years ago, when she was really, really angry, she said, 'I never loved you.' And one thing about my mother, she never, never lies to me."

"I understand she, too, has had depression," I said. "Could that be why she would say something like that?"

"I don't know."

"What's been going on lately? How have you been fitting in at school?"

"Eighth grade was the worst. They had this stupid little dance thing. I said, 'I'm not gonna go, I'm not gonna waste my time with these people who made my life so impossible.' The principal said, 'Oh, c'mon, you'll have the time of your life.' A lot of kids are very sexually active. I'm not. I'm very passive. Also, drugs are a big thing. I wouldn't touch that stuff. Although this year I kind of got in the drinking thing."

What about friends? "I never had a very, very close friend," she said. "I still don't know who my friends are."

"Do you have a boyfriend?"

"*Nooooo!* I mostly have guy friends. Girl friends, I hate them, they're impossible. I found out this year that guy friends are much better than girl friends. I feel much more comfortable with them. I'm like a geek. They call me the 'pentalingual schizophrenic lesbian.'"

"Wow. Why do they call you that?"

"I take a lot of languages. I'm good at it. I speak Spanish, some Russian. We had Russian neighbors and I picked it up."

"Some kids worry about what other people think of them. Do you ever worry about that?"

"I used to be very self-conscious. I used to think I was stupid. But that's changed."

"Why do you think that's changed?"

"I got used to it. I just didn't care. That's when I stopped taking care of myself. I wouldn't brush my hair, wouldn't brush my teeth, wouldn't take showers at all. My mom was very worried about me. There would be like dirty clothes, french fries on the floor in my room. I didn't even care."

"What about sleeping?"

"You know how they say that your body might rest, but your mind never does? I have like so many running thoughts, things just popping into my head like telepathy. I would think for hours about my life. I was very tense, very nervous. I didn't eat much. There were so many people telling me I'm garbage. I forgot who I was."

"Who was telling you that you were garbage?"

"Well, my biology teacher told me I'm smart, she couldn't believe this was happening to me."

"That doesn't sound like she was calling you garbage. It sounds like you're a little tough on yourself. Tell me what triggered your trying to get help. Why, all of a sudden, couldn't you take it anymore?"

"Well, ninth grade was the peak. That was my first suicide attempt."

Jasmine said she swallowed half a bottle of Excedrin. "All that happened was I got sick and started throwing up," she said, rather nonchalantly. "Then I did it again, this time I slashed my wrists." She hesitantly revealed to me three dark, raised scars from gashes on her left arm. "I really wanted to die. I thought, 'If I don't even care about myself, then why am I here?' I was very, very morbid. I felt like nothing was fun anymore, not even things I used to love, like drawing and creative writing. They weren't fun anymore. Everything was so boring, so dull. I had nobody to talk to. My mother, I don't talk to her. My father is at work all day and comes home late. The one way I can describe depression is any bad thing that happens becomes magnified, like a hundred times bigger, and that makes you feel even worse. We're like extra-sensitive people. And this is my childhood. Imagine what my adult life could be—why don't I just end it?"

Cutting herself—in the bathroom at school—turned things around for Jasmine. It finally made her parents sit up and take notice. They knew Jasmine was doing poorly in school; they knew she had no energy, low self-esteem; yet it took a dramatic incident for them to seek help. This is the way Jasmine describes the events that led her to treatment:

"My grades were dropping. Even my best subjects, I didn't give a damn about. I didn't care about anything. I felt like I had no energy inside me. I'd come home and not feel like doing anything. I'd sleep like the dead, just drift off. I would think of so many things that I would like to do but something was holding me back. I looked at my room. It was a mess and I wouldn't do anything about it. I looked at myself. My hair was all dirty. Pimples. It wasn't even funny. Mrs. Gaynes, my guidance counselor, she just looked at me and she said, 'Child, you're depressed.' I'm like, 'How do *you* know?' She said, 'Lose the attitude. I want you to go see someone.' She's the only one I told about my suicide attempts. She told my parents. I was so mad—I told her it was just between us. She said, 'I *had* to tell your parents—this is your *life* we're talking about.'"

Three cheers for Mrs. Gaynes. She came to Jasmine's rescue. Ironically, one of the reasons her depression wasn't recognized at home during the previous couple of years was that Jasmine's mother was also depressed. She viewed it as an adult problem, and overlooked the symptoms in her daughter. Her father, too, was unaware. Significantly, the first I heard about the suicide attempts was from Jasmine. Her father never even mentioned them.

Jasmine perceived that when her parents heard about the suicide attempts, they were "mad at me." But also worried. Initially, she resisted going to a doctor but eventually relented. After an evaluation that confirmed a diagnosis of major depression, Prozac was prescribed, but she was initially reluctant to follow the course of treatment. "I never liked pills," she said. "Even if it was something to take away acne. I think it has to do with an incident when I was young. I thought it was candy and choked on it." But she agreed to take the medicine, and began feeling much better within three months.

"I feel much more confidence," she said, her face brightening. "My schoolwork is better."

"Your hygiene is fine," I noted.

"Yeah, I care about myself. Even my pimples are gone."

"That's amazing! Prozac makes pimples go away!" I said as we both laughed.

Jasmine told me she has a website, where she posts her own artwork and poetry. She wants to become a graphic designer, but has been concentrating more on her writing lately. "I write about myself, I write about my friends," she told me. "I post them on my Internet site." Jasmine recently won a poetry contest run by the local library. I asked her to describe her writing. The first thing she said was: "I always kill my characters. I never let them reach their goals." So her life wasn't all sweetness and light. But that wasn't depression; it was just Jasmine. Among other things, she told me she doesn't cry, doesn't like the word "love," and hates romance. "I like blood and gore; that's why I get along better with boys. Sex and romance—please don't talk about it." She was not without a sense of humor about it. "I like Japanese comics because they're bloody. I'm kind of morbid."

Despite such dark thoughts, Jasmine was clearly in a better place than just a few months before. "If you could have any three wishes in the world, what would they be?" I asked. "Except for more wishes."

Jasmine thought for a few seconds. "One, I'd like to see myself fulfilled as a person. Two, I would like people to know who I really am. I'm not the person I was when this started. I'm recuperating from this monster, depression."

"And three?"

"That my parents will have a long life."

Jasmine took medicine for six months. She wasn't perfect. Her father described her as "lazy and disobedient."

In other words, she was back to being a typical teenager. But she wasn't depressed.

2

THE TEENAGE BRAIN

Anna Freud was half right. It would be abnormal—maybe even impossible—for a teenager to breeze through adolescence on an even emotional keel. Being moody and crabby are as much a part of the territory as pimples and proms. To a certain degree, they can't help themselves: it's virtually a biological necessity. Where Freud was wrong was in her assertion that there's something wrong if a teenager *doesn't* get depressed—and that no matter how moody she gets, no matter how sad she becomes, it's all more or less normal and it doesn't constitute any kind of mental illness.

In adults as well as younger people, brief unhappiness is indeed a normal human condition, sometimes triggered by a disturbing event. But when that depression doesn't go away, when it lasts more than a few days or weeks and interferes with a person's ability to function—that's when it crosses into the category of biological disease. Depression among adults is very common and well documented. Studies suggest that one woman in five and one man in ten can expect to develop it during their lives. With the advent of medications that mysteriously rebalance brain chemicals that regulate mood, treatment of depression has been revolutionized in the past decade. In the memorable phrase of Elizabeth Wurtzel that served as the title of her book about her own youthful depression, we are a Prozac Nation. Yet depression is often not thought of as a real disease, especially in the case of children and adolescents.

The whole idea of depression in young people has evolved in psychiatry over the last century, particularly in the last two decades. Earlier generations believed that adult-style depression could not exist in children because they didn't have the emotional or cognitive maturity of adults. What began to change the perception of adolescent depression from a myth to a real disorder were studies showing that while depression among the young has some distinct features, many of its symptoms and effects are similar to what adults experience. Moreover, it was found that even after recovering from the depths of a depression, many adolescents continue to have residual effects and are much more likely to have depression as adults. Eventually, clinical research found that treatments that work for adults—from antidepressant medications for serious depressions to cognitive behavioral therapy for milder cases—also work in adolescents.

These realizations were enough to convince the field that adolescent depression could not be dismissed as a normal, even necessary, passage. Now we know that the opposite is true: serious depression is the most common mental illness among teenagers, and research is starting to give us clues as to why. As if just being a teenager—or a parent of one—wasn't enough to worry about, it appears there may be solid biological reasons why adolescents as a group are especially vulnerable to depression during these critical years.

Every parent has to have wondered what on earth goes on in the head of a teenager. The answer is: a lot. Adolescence is nothing if not transition. Puberty changes everything from boys' voices to girls' self-image.

We know all about those raging hormones. But there is a growing body of scientific evidence that the physiological changes of adolescence may be most dramatic in the chemistry and circuitry of the brain. Much has been said and written in recent years about the brain development that occurs in babies, from birth to age three. But there is fascinating new research showing that brain "remodeling" is nearly as dramatic during the teen years.

One researcher, Jay Giedd of the National Institute of Mental Health, has used a technique called Structural Magnetic Resonance Imaging (SMRI) to show changes in the shape and size of the brain during the early to mid-teen years. Studies have shown that the brain's gray matter—where the higher intellectual functions are carried out—thins out with age. Giedd found that the gray matter thickens until age 11 in girls and 12 in boys. Unlike in infancy, when millions of new brain cells are constantly being created, what happens in later childhood is not the formation of new brain cells but an increase in the number of synaptic connections between the cells already there. In fact, that's what might make the gray matter denser. But just before adolescence, and continuing until about age 25, the gray matter is gradually "pruned," in a natural chemical process that clears out unused brain-cell connections to make the brain more efficient. It's analogous to driving in the country. There are plenty of roads to take, dozens of them, but they're not good roads. Eventually you come to a multilane superhighway. You leave behind the meandering and abundant dirt and gravel roads for the smooth, efficient pavement of the highway. In terms of cognitive development, it is the "use it or lose it" principle. As the brain prunes, a person gradually becomes more specialized in his abilities. That's why learning languages is relatively easy for children. They can learn just about anything, though depth comes only later. Their learning abilities are a mile wide and an inch deep.

Giedd's key finding was that the highest rate of pruning occurs from 14 to 17—as much as four times as high as during any other period. This means that there is a lot more structural change in the brain than was earlier thought. This burst of brain maturation occurs at a time when rates of major psychiatric disorders, including depression, increase markedly. The significance of the changes in the brain during adolescence can't be overstated. But at the same time, the jury is still out on the question of how or even whether these are associated with the release of sex hormones—testosterone, estrogen, and progesterone—all of which have an effect on mood. In fact, Dr. Adrian Angold, one of the nation's leading child psychiatric researchers, suspects that hormones associated with puberty turn on genes that make some young people more vulnerable to the development of depression and/or anxiety.

The eruption of brain development may be the reason normal adolescents are not only moody but also often grandiose, and why they are risk-takers. And it may very well play a role in the development of depression during adolescence. The spike in depression rates—in the same years when the brain is pruning at its highest rate—seems to have more to do with the onset of puberty than with strict chronological age. So the reasonable speculation is that there may be understandable biological reasons for an increased susceptibility to depression during adolescence.

Also intriguing are studies conducted with teenagers who had attempted suicide and volunteered to undergo spinal taps for research. The tests revealed that they tended to have very low levels of serotonin, a compound that is widely distributed in tissue and is involved in many different aspects of our bodies' functioning, including sleep, blood-clotting, and digestion, as well as mood and aggression. Though we're not ready to use the spinal tap as a diagnostic tool, the studies on suicidal teenagers are another piece of evidence that the level of serotonin is important in depression, and that Selective Serotonin Reuptake Inhibitors (SSRIs), the new generation of antidepressants, are an important part of treatment. While giving someone pure serotonin won't work because of the barrier between blood and the brain, the SSRIs—Prozac, Zoloft, Paxil, Luvox, and Celexa—slow down the use of serotonin in the body, allowing it to be more available in the brain for a longer period. At the same time, it is not clear whether the lower serotonin is a cause or an effect of the illness.

All this research suggests that we are on the verge of uncovering biological "markers" for depression. As we become better able to measure neurochemicals such as serotonin in noninvasive ways, we will be better able to make diagnoses with confidence. One thing parents often ask is whether there is a blood test for depression. There isn't one now, but in time there will be improved measures that indicate physiological risks of depression, and perhaps even whether someone is depressed or not. This is not as easy as tracking how blood-glucose levels of diabetics improve with insulin or how cholesterol changes with diet and medication. The changes in depression take place inside some of the cells of the brain, and those signals are lost in the flood of other messages from other parts of the body. For example, although we know that serotonin is important to the regulation of mood, among other things, we also know that 95 percent of the body's serotonin is released in the gastrointestinal tract.

Even with these new advances, we still don't know why some young people are vulnerable to depression and others are not, or why some have a more difficult time meeting the challenges of adolescence. Familial or genetic risks seem to be part of the answer, but early life experiences and stresses are also important. An important clue with implications for treatment is the observation that major depression in both adults and teens is often associated with a certain set of "cognitive distortions" that both define current symptoms and predict later ones—in other words, how they think. Adolescents who are very pessimistic about how others view them and the way they view themselves—they think they're ugly or stupid and that people don't like them—are more at risk. If it's true that thinking determines mood, depression may be treated or even prevented by intervening in a child's distorted thinking patterns before they become embedded in the brain.

Though much of the relevant research is highly preliminary, the clear implication is the provocative notion that adolescent turmoil is the result of both environment and physiology. For at the very time that the brain is going through its most intense shaking-out period, a typical teenager is deep into her own sorting-out process. These years are an extremely salient time for experience. Disappointments and failures and embar-rassments—all the classic confidence-busters—emerge in sharp relief on the bridge between childhood and young adulthood. They may not per-ceive it—and neither may their parents—but the life of teenagers is all about accomplishing several specific developmental tasks:

- First, of course, they must adjust to the physical changes of pu-berty. Their faces and bodies are changing, and this isn't always easy to accept ("I'm so ugly"). Raging hormones, meanwhile, are putting sex front and center in their lives—an exciting, but jar-ring, new preoccupation. Actually having sex is almost beside the point. Simple consciousness is enough. Boys are becoming aroused and girls are beginning their menstrual cycles. They're not kids anymore.

- They must separate from their parents. Teenagers are famous for experimenting with ideas about everything from music to clothes to drugs to politics as a way of challenging or being different from Mom and Dad. They're not doing this just to drive us crazy; they're doing it because they have to. As parents, we need to think of ourselves as booster rockets who will fall away as a necessary part of the process. When kids rebel or push limits, they are doing what is required so that by the time adolescence is over, they can be healthy and independent individuals. They don't need to call their parents three times a day—or have to keep a safe thousand miles away.

- They must develop a social network. This is the period when young people build their first true friendships and intimacies—those based on similar interests and values rather than on mere convenience. In these years, they develop the concept of loyalty and the ability to accept people, flaws and all. It means spending years negotiating the twists and turns of social relationships, inevitably getting hurt or inflicting hurt on someone else along the way.

- They must begin to focus their vocational and educational objec-tives. At 12 it might be art or algebra, but at 19 or 20 it might be looking ahead to a professional career in business, law, medicine, or the arts, so that by 22 or so, they have a clearer sense of their life goals and needs.

- They must realize and come to terms with their sexual orientation. Even if they are not sexually active, young people should, by the end of adolescence, know what attracts them.

Overriding all these developmental tasks is an emerging sense of ethics. In pulling away from their parents' influence, teenagers are deciding how they are going to live their lives, even on a subconscious level. All this is a lot to expect from a young person who really just wants to get rid of those damn pimples and get through another day at school without feeling humiliated.

As major depression is a disorder of abnormal regulation of stress, there is a clear link between depression and these developmental challenges. Studies of animals have demonstrated that stress has a significant effect on the parts of the brain that are involved in the regulation and control of emotion. These studies have also shown that events that occur during key developmental periods have an enduring impact on many of these same brain systems. So it's no wonder that in humans, stressful events during adolescence are among the strongest precipitants of initial episodes of major depression.

In the wake of the September 11 tragedy, I became involved in efforts in New York City to care for the emotional well-being of the children of the victims as well as those who lived near the World Trade Center. This horrific event put kids at significantly higher risk for depression, and it brought home the important role that parents play in moderating stressful events in the lives of their adolescents. That's why I recommended that parents turn off the TV and take care of themselves. If they felt okay, their kids would feel okay. And in protecting against stress, they might even be protecting their children's brains.

Allison, 14, has always been an uptight kid. Her homework's always done on time, and long-term projects are finished early. But she also has a pit in her stomach before her weekly math test, and even before her

Saturday soccer games. Her parents have always recognized that she's a very sensitive kid and a worrier. But she manages to do well in school, have lots of friends, and still be affectionate with her parents. After 9/11, her mother, Linda, saw that even though they lived more than a hundred miles from New York City, Allison was deeply affected, worried about the safety and the future of her family. She became addicted to CNN and seemed more upset after each report she watched. Linda knew her daughter, and made the decision to limit the television to half an hour at seven o'clock in the evening, and she and her husband made a conscious effort to keep the discussion of 9/11 to a minimum. They also reassured Allison and her sister and brother that they believed that the government was taking action that would make flying safer and the country more secure. And through their own behavior—for instance, making sure the whole family attended Allison's soccer game that Saturday—they demonstrated that life was getting back to normal.

·

With all the psychological and social stressors that teenagers face, combined with the burst in their brain-cell activity and all their other physiological changes, it's no wonder teenagers sometimes seem like creatures from another planet. And it's no wonder they themselves think their lives are in turmoil. It's because they are. And that's why depression is so often mistaken for normal adolescent angst, overlooked or dismissed as a passing phase.

Fill up your high school auditorium, look out across the sea of young faces, and you are not likely to find very many who haven't gone through periods of feeling bad about themselves. In fact, for many teens, inadequacy is the salient sentiment of these years. I speak from personal experience. I'll never forget entering junior high school and discovering that I had to change into a uniform for gym and shower after class. I remember the first day vividly: taking off my clothes, standing next to a boy in my grade, and feeling ridiculous. He was only a few months older than me but six inches taller and as developed as my father. I felt like a little boy in comparison. Who knew (or cared) that adolescents develop at different rates? All I knew was that I felt bad about myself. Years later, I read an unsurprising University of California study that found that early-developing boys have more self-esteem than those who develop at more typical rates or are late bloomers. Peers and even teachers treat them with greater respect. The study didn't address girls, but in my experience I've found that the reverse can sometimes be true for girls. It's part of teenage-girl culture to want to be in step with the pack, so developing too *soon* can make a girl feel different when all she wants to be is the same as everyone else. Back in junior high, while I was embarrassed and feeling lousy about the seemingly slow pace of my pubertal development, there were two girls on the other side of the locker room wall who were feeling bad for the opposite reason. They were not only the subject of lurid talk among the boys, but were scorned by the girls. For these two girls, it was one more stressor on top of all the others that they and their classmates were dealing with.

These kinds of demoralizing blows to the ego are part of the adolescent experience. It's the teenager who has trouble handling the stress induced by these setbacks who might be a little more vulnerable to depression than his classmates and friends. As will become evident throughout this book, depression is a function of stress management. So parents should be especially watchful for any emotional challenges above and beyond those usually confronted by all teenagers. And one of the things they should keep in mind is that jolts to their child's ego don't have to make him feel diminished. Part of our job as parents is to show our children how *not* to feel defeated by their shortcomings, whether it is a learning disability, social awkwardness, limited ability in athletics, imperfections in their physical appearance, or anything else. We need to give our sons and daughters protective armor—not only to help them get through adolescence but also to help them accept and like themselves when they become adults. It's a matter of complimenting their assets and joining them in facing their deficits head-on.

This doesn't mean giving false praise, or denying the obvious. It would have done no good if my father had said to me: "What do you mean you're not developed? You're as developed as anyone!" Rather, empathy and support are what's needed. It would have been better for him to show compassion for my situation and point out that the other boy was older than I was, that everyone develops at his own pace, and lots of my classmates were as hairless and undeveloped as I was. All of us would grow up before we knew it—and I might even wind up taller than that kid towering over me. For a young person who is self-conscious about his athletic ability, there's no reason why his parents can't work on it with him or simply guide him toward what he *is* good at. Good parents know their kids, and they take steps to keep life from getting their children down. They don't always succeed, of course—if they did, there would be no need for this book—but they look for ways to make their kids' lives better. And part of this is showing empathy, understanding who their children are and what they're going through, and not seeing their teenager's less-than-perfect behavior (their response to the stresses they are feeling) as an insult to *them*.

WARNING SIGNS

How can parents recognize if their teenager is not managing one of the key developmental tasks I outlined earlier and so might be vulnerable to depression? Here are some things to look for.

ADAPTING TO THE PHYSICAL CHANGES OF PUBERTY

Is she overreacting to the onset of the menstrual cycle? For instance, is she pretending it's not happening? It's normal to become upset, even very upset about acne, but is she consumed by the emergence of every pimple or the shape of her nose? Again, dishonesty and denial—saying everything's fine—doesn't work. Being compassionate, supportive, and helpful in a practical way does. But if your teenager is avoiding social situations or becomes convinced that she must have plastic surgery, this indicates that she is not managing the stress of her physical changes. If the problem is out of control and does not pass, if she is spending an inordinate amount of time—several hours a day—looking in the mirror and obsessing about her imperfections, professional help may be necessary.

SEPARATING FROM MOM AND DAD AND DEVELOPING A PEER GROUP

Kids who are excessively clingy and would rather be with their parents than peers, as well as those who are so angry at their parents that they don't want to be with them any time or any place, are not effectively handling this developmental passage. Clearly, teenagers who don't want to separate from their parents are in the minority. But these young people need to be encouraged to reach out and cross whatever barrier is keeping them tied to the nest. One factor may be social phobia, which is discussed in depth in the next chapter. Another possibility is simple immaturity. A teenager who is not comfortable with what is expected of him can be nudged toward the door. Parents can arrange family dinners with people who have kids of similar age. They can take trips with other families or get involved in church or synagogue activities that might involve more social interaction. But it's paramount to keep from making the child feel like a failure for not being social.

Much more common is the teenager who is all too ready to flee the nest. While teenagers naturally spend more time alone, they still manage to make room for family time—and though it may be hard to see, some do appreciate it. One approach for parents whose children don't want any part of them is to be sensitive in the language they use with their teens, and to keep reminding themselves that this is probably just a transitory situation. Don't take the rejection personally. Try not to set up situations that will only lead to more alienation. For instance, if your daughter doesn't want to wear a dress to a college interview, don't shout in frustration: "Go naked for all I care!" Parents can be more provocative than they realize. Sometimes it's a good idea to use others as a buffer, whether it's a grandparent or a favorite teacher. Deferring to people who know and care about your teenager and can offer constructive criticism without carrying your emotional baggage can be very helpful.

When a child reaches adolescence, her peer group becomes more important and influential than ever before, even though her parents remain the most significant people in her life. There are two problematic reactions that the teenager may have to this natural gravitation to her peer group: one is becoming so attached to the group that it seems that she thinks nobody else exists in her life. She only wants to wear the clothes the girls in her group wear and only wants to do what they do. The problem with this is it creates a loss of independence—or worse, if it's a "bad" group of kids, some of whom may also be depressed. The other extreme is being unable to crack a social network. For instance, the peer group that the teenager wants to be in doesn't want her. An inability to be social might mean an anxiety disorder is at play.

FOCUSING EDUCATIONAL AND VOCATIONAL GOALS

A sign of trouble is having a teenager who has absolutely no interest in any educational pursuit, can't complete tasks, and is constantly lost. School is work for adolescents. It should be challenging, but also rewarding. A teen who never talks about school and has no motivation may have a learning disability, attentional problems, or boring teachers. A 22-year-old who says he has no idea what he wants to do in life may be immature. But for either one of them to be paralyzed by their lack of motivation or interest might be a sign of depression. Parents have to know what's going on at school. You may not be as involved on a day-to-day basis as when your child was in elementary school, but you should know and have a genuine interest in what your child is studying, what books he's reading, and how he's doing.

SEXUALITY AND SIGNIFICANT RELATIONSHIPS

Somewhere between the early teen years and the early twenties, an adolescent comes to terms with his sexual identity and begins having sexual relationships. This doesn't mean teenagers are or should be having intercourse. They may be engaging in other activities, including, most commonly, masturbation. The sexual images that accompany masturbation will tell them what their orientation is. If it is homosexuality, it's important for the individual to adjust to it and accept it by the age of 22. This is the most difficult of the developmental stages for parents to know about, unless they have a very open relationship with their child. Even today, discussions of sex are the biggest for parents and teenagers. The young person's struggle with his or her sexuality hasn't gotten any easier. In the teenager's life, it may be the most profound stressor of all. If by 22 a person hasn't had a boyfriend or a girlfriend, it may—*may*—be a signal that this is an issue. The discomfort of not accepting one's own sexuality is stressful and could be a trigger for depression. It's not the homosexuality itself that is the stressor but the difficulty in coming to terms with it and dealing with the stigma imposed by peers and society.

For all of these developmental tasks, it's important to remember that there is a lot of variability in the "normal" time for them to be accomplished. Adolescence stretches a decade or more. That means there is no single right time. Parents shouldn't push too hard, nor should they worry too easily. But they should be cognizant of signs that their child may be having a particularly hard time. With depression, the real issue is the effects of the struggle. Just as difficulty managing the stress of these developmental tasks can be a precursor for depression, the converse is also true: when you're depressed, it's hard to accomplish these fundamental goals.

Whether or not depression is in the picture, parents of teenagers would be well advised to pick their battles. Don't waste time fighting about clothes and other matters that are ultimately trivial. In whatever way feels right to you, either explicitly or implicitly, let your child know you understand he's changing and moving away, but that you stand behind him, and are there for him if he needs you—just as you were literally behind him as he took his first steps 15 years ago.

Carly's Room

Eighth-grader Carly Eckel had always been a happy child who did well in everything, whether it was playing viola in the school chamber ensemble or catcher on her Little League softball team. She was responsible academically, and always liked school; if she didn't finish her homework because of a game or concert, or because it was Halloween, she would wake up at five o'clock the next morning to do it. She didn't need her parents to drag her out of bed. She set her alarm and got up on her own. This year she had even been taking two high school–level courses and doing well in them.

Smiles had always come easily to Carly, and she was known for her agreeable disposition. With her straight black hair and dark eyes, she reminded her friends' parents of a young Cher. Her friends thought she looked more like Alanis Morissette. She wasn't lazy, learning disabled, inattentive, disorganized, or oppositional. So the last thing Carly's parents expected to be doing was driving their daughter to a psychiatrist's office to figure out why her academic work had suddenly taken a nosedive and she had all but stopped going to school.

Through the first five months of the year, Carly had missed 36 days of school—an average of two absences a week. "She feels she can't do her homework and puts it off," Carly's mother, Sue, explained, as she tensely shifted in her chair and interlocked her fingers. "Then she gets too tired to do it. Then she says she can't go to school unprepared, so she stays home."

Some days, Carly's parents managed to get her to go to school anyway—her absences numbered nearly 50—but they were finding it harder and harder to break the pattern.

"What do you do when you stay home?" I asked Carly.

"I stay in my room and read," she said. Her voice was soft, and she tended to swallow her words. "Or watch TV."

"She wasn't much of a TV watcher before this," Sue said.

"What happens when it's homework time?" I asked Carly.

"I don't know. I just don't feel like doing it."

"Motivation was never your problem before."

"No. I can't get myself going. I don't feel like doing anything."

"The only time she does any work is when I force her to and stay in the room with her," Mom added.

"Do you argue about it?"

Carly and both her parents smiled faintly. "Oh, we argue," her father, Alan, replied curtly.

"What happens?"

"We have huge power struggles," her mother said. "Sometimes there's shouting."

"And sometimes you grab me," Carly added.

"What's become of your social life?"

"I'm not allowed to go out if I missed school. But I don't really feel like going out anyway. I just stay in my room."

"She eats there," Mom said.

I wasn't Carly's first stop. As things got worse and she was missing more and more school, the administrators put increasing pressure on her parents to get her to school, or to get an evaluation to see why she wasn't going. This made Carly shut down even more. She refused to keep appointments her mother made, refused to go anywhere or talk to anyone about what was happening. "There's nothing wrong!" she would yell, and become even more irritable. At one point, the school had arranged for Carly to be admitted to a hospital for an evaluation, and her parents somehow managed to get her to at least come and talk to a doctor and social worker prior to the admission. Mr. and Mrs. Eckel were shocked at the response by the professionals—as was a colleague of mine who later saw the family and referred them to me.

"The hospital staff were totally at sea as to why a child who was not going to school, not going out, eating only in her room, refusing to be evaluated by anyone on an outpatient basis, should possibly need to be hospitalized," she wrote to me, so annoyed that she lapsed into unusual sarcasm. "After all, in today's very intelligent mental health system, the only possible important mental health problem is suicide. Normal functioning would appear to be a totally irrelevant goal."

Carly's mother thought her withdrawal was related to her grandfather's sudden illness and death. He had lived with the family, and he and Carly had been extremely close. He had been diagnosed with cancer in January and died in August, just before the beginning of the school year. Mrs. Eckel said Carly's school absences had begun around the time her grandfather became ill.

But while her grandfather's decline could have been a contributing factor, a trigger, Carly's problems could not be seen as isolated from other aspects of her life, particularly several important personality traits that suggested a history of anxiety. Carly had always been a rigid kid, perfectionistic about some things. "She always needed things to be the way you said they were going to be, even as a small child," Alan explained. "Like if you said you were going to go somewhere at a certain time, she would get very uptight if we didn't do that. We were always telling her to chill out."

"Even now," Sue added, "she insists I say things a certain way. If she asks what's for dinner and I say, 'I don't know, maybe steak, maybe pasta,' Carly will say, 'No, Mom! You don't understand. You have to say, "We're having steak. Be specific!" But that sounded to me more like an intolerance for ambiguity than an obsessive need to simply hear things said a certain way.

There was also a lot of family history at play. Alan, a high school geology teacher, had had a six-month episode of agoraphobia—a fear of being in open spaces—after the death of his mother when Carly was two. And his father—the grandparent who had lived with the family until his recent death—had been treated for 30 years for what his son described as "a very bad depression" that was first triggered when he lost his job. Carly's mother had also had a bout of depression following the death of her father about 20 years earlier. "I put a blanket over my head and didn't eat for three months," she recalled. "I was down to 85 pounds." Her mother (Carly's grandmother) had also had occasional periods of depression. So there was a very strong family history of depression.

In the verbal and written ratings my colleague gave her, Carly acknowledged behavior consistent with generalized anxiety disorder. "I try to stay near my mom and dad," she said. "I try not to upset anyone. I try not to think about things that might upset me. I don't like to speak in public. I get nervous. I try to do everything exactly right, and I check to make sure that things are safe." When she talked about her grandfather, she described how she watched him get "sicker and sicker" and take debilitating chemotherapy that didn't help.

When she was asked if she felt depressed, Carly said no—a common response from depressed teenagers. That's partly because they might feel embarrassed by the idea of anything that smacks of being "mentally ill." But it's also because they don't really know what depression is, or how it's different from the way they are supposed to feel. But when my colleague described some of the symptoms of depression—irritability, poor concentration, anxiety, disinterest—Carly's eyes misted over. "I think I could have reduced her to tears without much trouble," my colleague told me later. It was clear to her how frightened Carly was about not being able to function in school. "For someone whose identity has been her brains, she's being crippled in a very important way," she said. "And she's fearful of letting people down."

Carly met all the criteria for major depressive disorder, as well as generalized anxiety disorder. She began taking the antidepressant Luvox, which got both under control, and started a course of cognitive behavioral therapy to change her negative way of thinking. For many teenagers, as I will discuss later, this type of therapy is a more difficult task, but ultimately one that can be life-changing.

3

MORE THAN DEPRESSION

When I see a new patient, I go back to the beginning—all the way back. This is because I need to know all about the child's life, not just what's been going on lately. In adolescents especially, depression is often accompanied or preceded by something else. And that only complicates the elusive art of diagnosis and treatment. Has the child displayed or been diagnosed with attention deficit hyperactivity disorder (ADHD)? Has she a history of being socially isolated, fearful of separation from her parents, or generally anxious? In the case of an older teenager, have there been any episodes of psychosis that might suggest a more serious mental illness such as schizophrenia?

Adult depression is usually just that: depression. This is not necessarily the case with adolescents. Their diagnoses are often tied up with any number of other childhood mental illnesses that can confuse even the best clinicians. This combination of disorders is called comorbidity. Anxiety is one of the most common disorders comorbid with depression. Gather a roomful of teenagers who have clinical depression, and nearly half of them will have an accompanying anxiety disorder—social phobia (pathological self-consciousness), separation anxiety disorder (marked by fears about the well-being of the family), or generalized anxiety disorder (a fear of the future and constant worries about one's performance). Significantly, of those who have both anxiety and depression, research indicates that 85 percent experience the anxiety first. One study by my colleague at the New York University Child Study Center, research psychologist Rachel Klein, found that among children with anxiety disorders as preadolescents, 30 percent went on to have depression later on, either as adolescents or adults. Does treating a younger child with anxiety disorders decrease that child's chances of having depression as a teenager and, later, as an adult? Experience tells me the answer is probably yes, but research on depression in children is scant, so for now it remains an open question.

·

Among the anxiety disorders that are commonly associated with depression are social anxiety and generalized anxiety disorder (GAD). In the case of the former, a strong component is social *failure,* which may or may not be a real consequence of social anxiety. Danny Pine, M.D., a top researcher in mood and anxiety disorders in children at the National Institute of Mental Health and Research Professor of Psychiatry at the NYU Child Study Center, concludes that the nature of peer relationships is a predictive factor in adolescent depression—not so much anxiety about relating with one's friends but about whether they *have* friendships. "There are a lot of people who are extremely nervous about having friends, but they have a lot of friends," he says. "And those kids do okay. There are other kids who aren't nervous about friends but they just don't have any. Those kids don't do okay." Kids who are ostracized by their peers are more likely to be depressed. That's no surprise. But it is more complicated than you might think.

People who are socially engaging feel comfortable with themselves. They like themselves, see themselves in a positive light, and feel they have something to offer other people. They listen to others and are able to engage them by finding out what interests them or learning what hobbies or pursuits they share. Individuals who have excellent social skills are not supersensitive. They have an ability to go with the flow. Little things aren't going to throw them off.

People who fail socially, meanwhile, don't feel comfortable with themselves. They see themselves as defective and inadequate, and they tend to exaggerate their flaws. Since they feel so bad about themselves, it's very difficult for them to empathize with others, and they are apt to say the wrong thing at the wrong time. They are not good listeners and are hypersensitive, overreacting to criticism, never forgetting slights. They try to hide their own weaknesses, yet can be cruel to others. Sometimes this is to make themselves feel better; other times it is because they are simply oblivious to their own social ineptitude. It becomes a self-fulfilling prophecy. Once a teenager is considered a "loser" by his peers, it's very hard to change that. Though such labels may be cast off in the movies—see *Revenge of the Nerds,* among countless others—it rarely happens for teens in real life. Where adults can reinvent themselves by changing careers or moving away, teenagers are usually stuck in their little world, essentially staying with the same people they've been with since kindergarten. The stress of not being able to create a social network makes life more complicated and can be a trigger for depression. In such a case, however, the social problems can remain even after the depression has been addressed.

What, then, can a parent do to help a child with poor social skills? First, it's important to recognize that social skills need to be fostered. They have to be encouraged and modeled, just like language. We're not born with vocabulary and the ability to communicate verbally. One of the obligations of parenthood is teaching children how to speak and behave with other people, mainly through modeling. They are lessons that have to start early.

If your child seems shy or uncomfortable and less talkative in family gatherings, don't dismiss it as a phase or, "That's Billy; he's just shy. I was the same way." Without your intervention, the effects of social phobia can be toxic. Helping is not impossible. Take as an analogy the clumsy child who can't catch a baseball. You could avoid the baseball field, or you could go into the backyard with him and work on his skills. When teaching social skills to your child, start easily: *When you talk to someone look them in the eye. If you feel nervous about meeting someone, think of three things to talk about beforehand.* Rehearse with the child—the laboratory is close friends and family—and compliment her when she does well. Make it fun, not critical. Practice at home during dinnertime.

Some children are so socially phobic that they have physiological reactions such as blushing and even vomiting when they are confronted with some situations. Relaxation techniques can help, but the only thing that is really effective is exposure—practicing in groups that might include both other socially phobic kids and volunteer stand-ins. By putting them into situations they fear and teaching them how to cope, a therapist can help a patient identify how he thinks and feels in those circumstances, and how the anxieties can be confronted and overcome. The first step might simply be joining the group. Next time, the assignment might be to say two words. And then five, and then ten. It's a reciprocal process of learning social skills while desensitizing the child to the social situation he fears.

ADAM'S SELF-IMAGE

Adam Bates was a 19-year-old college sophomore who had dropped out of school a month before coming to see me. He had always been an outstanding student with serious social problems. Unlike the vast majority of parents of teenagers, Adam's mom and dad would have been thrilled if he spent a Saturday night just hanging out with friends when he was in high school. Though he was a member of the debate team and tennis team, they had to beg him to socialize.

Adam was shy as a child and had daily stomach aches, indicative of a school phobia, when he was in second and third grade. He told me that he began feeling very socially ill at ease around the time he hit puberty. He was uncomfortable urinating in front of others, and he became extremely self-conscious about his appearance. He was particularly bothered by the hair on his legs and began shaving it. He excelled academically and was accepted into an Ivy League college. His parents saw some signs of hope when he began socializing a little shortly before graduating high school.

Continuing his pattern, Adam's adjustment to college was difficult socially but not academically. He had problems living in a dormitory because he didn't like to be naked in front of others and had the idea that he had offensive body odor. Soon he became self-conscious about the way he walked. All of this was ironic because Adam was exceptionally good-looking. When I first met him I thought he was reminiscent of John F. Kennedy Jr. This was in October of his sophomore year, after Adam had called his parents in tears and told them he felt his whole life was unraveling. He told them he was uncomfortable everywhere, that he was constantly afraid of looking foolish. He had stopped going to classes, was sleeping all day, and was feeling hopeless and suicidal. Now he was back home, sleeping the days away in his parents' basement. He had no appetite.

From talking with Adam and his parents, both separately and together, it was clear that he had a long-standing social phobia that was now accompanied by major depression. The first step was getting Adam out of the basement, sleeping at night rather than during the day, and getting him to accept help. I told him during our first meeting that he had a certain medical diagnosis, that other people his age had similar problems, and that there was a way to treat it. He agreed to take Prozac. He told me a few years later (when I talked to him for this book) that it was these initial assurances that allowed him to comply with treatment.

The medication worked swiftly. Within four weeks, Adam's appetite and normal sleep returned, and he became increasingly optimistic. But if treating Adam's depression was relatively straightforward, his social anxiety was considerably more challenging. I had prescribed a higher-than-usual dosage of Prozac, hoping to attack the anxiety symptoms, and I had sent him to a colleague who conducted cognitive behavioral group therapy (CBT), a specialized approach that seeks to change a patient's distorted way of thinking. (It's described in detail in chapter 12.) Adam agreed to try it, but he was reluctant, and then resistant, because, he said, CBT left too much up to him. This was part of a pattern in which he deflected responsibility. During his sessions he articulated his feelings about his peers. "I'm pissed at girls for making me feel inadequate," he said. "I'm mad at my friends for being able to enjoy college when I'm not able to."

But Adam did continue with the CBT group, and found that he benefited from the sessions. If being relaxed among his peers at school was impossible, he found that practicing being himself in front of a group of kids with similar problems was not so hard. In the real world, he said, he felt that people put demands on him, and doing well—being able to "perform"—was important to him. In the group, it didn't really matter. And that was a relief. When he went back to school, Adam still had social phobia about dating and sexual interactions. He began using a deep-breathing exercise to relax, and tried to employ some of the behavioral skills he learned in therapy, such as reframing how he thought in a particular situation or asking himself, "What's the worst thing that can happen?" His social anxiety looked to be a long-term struggle, but for now his depression had resolved.

In the other anxiety disorder that is associated with depression, generalized anxiety disorder (GAD), a person worries constantly about the future, her own performance, and what people think about her: *I'm going to fail, I can't manage things, I'm not smart enough, I didn't study enough.* These worries are often related to the depression symptoms. So the first step is to treat the depression; only when it's under control will a patient be able to begin attacking the anxiety. Fortunately, the SSRI antidepressants treat both disorders, so it's possible to reduce or eliminate the symptoms of both disorders at once.

Anxiety, like depression, is referred to as an "internalizing disorder," and it's quite possible that one neurotransmitter—serotonin—is involved in a number of these behaviors. For instance, SSRI medications, that are effective at treating depression are also excellent anti-anxiety drugs. (Though Paxil is marketed as an anxiety medication, it's virtually the same medicine as Prozac.) Clearly, the two disorders are close relatives.

Successful treatment of depression is more apt to diminish the performance anxieties of GAD than the symptoms of social anxiety disorder. We can speculate that this is because individuals with social anxiety start to avoid social situations and this further reinforces the symptoms. Therefore, medicine alone is less likely to resolve the symptoms, and needs to be supplemented with psychotherapy that includes deconditioning.

Another condition that is frequently comorbid with depression in young people is conduct disorder—what we once called juvenile delinquency. But the relationship between the two is the source of some controversy. While anxiety comes first in the overwhelming number of cases in which teenagers have both anxiety and depression, there is a real question about whether this is true in the case of conduct disorder. Is a teenager depressed because he's been caught doing something illegal or improper and is now facing the consequences? Or is he depressed or demoralized about life, and this in turn leads to outrageous, illegal, or oppositional-defiant conduct? There is an old theory that conduct disorder is masked depression, but there is no evidence to back it up. More likely is that some young people simply have both disorders at the same time.

Posttraumatic stress disorder (PTSD) also has an association with depression. This occurs when a person witnesses or experiences a traumatic, fatal, or life-threatening event and later relives it, either in his thoughts or dreams. The response can bring extreme distress—intense fear, agitated behavior, flashbacks, and even physical reactions that might include reexperiencing smells. A person suffering from PTSD might be jumpy, has trouble sleeping, and will take pains to avoid anything associated with the trauma.

Traumatic events can cause both PTSD and depression, either alone or in combination. After the events of September 11, children who lost a parent or who were physically close to the event were at increased risk of both PTSD and depression. Those with a preexisting depression or depression and anxiety symptoms were most vulnerable.

Finally, and least clear, is substance abuse. There is little argument that substance abuse is associated with depression. Questions come about concerning the direction of this association. Some people feel that depressed adults "medicate" themselves with drugs and alcohol, and that the same holds true for teenagers. For some teenagers, this may be true; however, the relationship between substance abuse and depression is more complicated in other adolescents. For example, some adolescents may become depressed after they have been using alcohol or other substances. Finally, other disorders may be associated with substance abuse and depression, and this may explain the relationship. Two such disorders are conduct disorder and social phobia. For instance, socially phobic young people are more likely to use and abuse alcohol and illegal drugs than the general population, apparently because the substances have an immediate, calming effect. They tell us that they feel better when they smoke marijuana—less tense, less conscious of themselves, less upset. It sounds as though they *are* treating themselves. Whether that's actually the case hasn't been established. The only way to know would be to treat the anxiety symptoms and see if the drug abuse goes away. Such a study hasn't yet been done.

LORI'S WORRIES

Since we all experience worry, and we remember our own adolescence as being stressful at times, parents often fail to recognize how serious social anxiety disorder and generalized anxiety disorder can be—and how commonly they are tied to depression. The public has recently become more informed about social anxiety disorder, largely because of a recent television campaign advertising Paxil for the treatment of this disorder. But the commercials in many ways minimize the severity and the pain experienced by those with the disorder. Social anxiety disorder is more than feeling uncomfortable at a cocktail party or, in the case of a teenager, getting sweaty palms and weak knees at a school dance or going blank when called on in class. These events can happen to anyone. But when it happens frequently and in many different social situations, it can completely contaminate one's life, affecting a teen's ability to attend school, participate in sports and other extracurricular activities, and go to parties or family events.

Generalized anxiety disorder is also a misunderstood condition. Everyone at times worries about the future or their performance at school or work. Even experienced actors have butterflies before they go on stage. Teenagers with GAD waste a lot of energy worrying about how they will do on a test, how they *are doing* on a test, and how they did on the test. Some parents might say, "What's the problem? I wish my kid worried a little bit more about how he did on a test." But GAD is worry without purpose. It's worrying about anything—a moving target of uncontrollable anxieties about everything from crossing a bridge to get to a soccer game, to how you'll do in the game, how your performance will affect your place on the team, and how your place on the team will affect your college aspirations. It seems ridiculous, but saying to a person with GAD "Stop worrying!" or "Get over it!" has no effect. If anything, it makes him feel even more inadequate, because now he is worrying that his worrying is a serious problem.

Since half the teenagers who become depressed also have an anxiety disorder, this is not an uncommon presentation. Unfortunately, anxiety symptoms are often insidious, minimized by parents and the world— "She's just shy"; "He's a worrywart, but he'll grow out of it"—but by the time it develops into a full-blown disorder, it can be impairing and even devastating to the life of the teenager and the family.

Lori Connelly was adopted when she was 16 days old. Her parents, Mark and Cece, had tried eleven in vitro fertilizations before finally giving up and contracting with an adoption agency in Georgia. They are a Catholic couple and leaped at the opportunity to adopt a baby whose biological mother was Irish Catholic. They didn't know about the father. The biological mother was 30 and unmarried at the time, and had dabbled in a variety of occupations, everything from driving a bus to working as a disc jockey at a radio station. "She was intelligent and did very well in school," Cece said. "Her father was an engineer, and her brother is extremely intellectual."

"So you know something about half the gene pool," I said.

"Right. But who knows what *my* gene pool is really like?"

The Connellys were seeing me for a consultation while their daughter was in the middle of her second hospitalization for depression. They had taken her out on a pass to see me, with the permission of her treating physician. As they sat in my office with their daughter, the Connellys appeared to be a close couple. In fact, they actually looked alike. They were big and friendly, and both had thick red hair. Throughout the session, they held hands.

Lori was petite and blond. She sat on the other side of her mom on the sofa. I wondered what kind of role adoption had played in Lori's life. "It was really only an issue once, when she was in kindergarten," Cece said. "For preschool, she had gone to a Y where there was maybe 30 percent of kids who were adopted, and a whole bunch of parents were already adopting their second kids. So it was a very normal thing. But then Lori gets to kindergarten and she tells the world she's adopted, and lo and behold they're telling her, 'Oh, you were an orphan, your mom's not your real mom.' It was the first time she sort of got a sense of 'Hey, wait a minute, I'm different.' The kids would go home and tell their parents and the parents would come and say to me, 'Oh, I didn't know Lori was adopted.' Or, 'Wasn't that so nice of you to do that?' So Lori started learning that sometimes you have to keep information to yourself." Cece didn't see it that way: it wasn't that she was nice for adopting Lori, but that she was lucky to have her.

That year it became apparent that Lori didn't have natural social skills. Cece continued, "I remember we had 12 or 15 kids to her birthday party, and only half of them invited her to their parties. As the years went on, she was invited to fewer and fewer parties."

"She started to become very sensitive to this, and felt that people were slighting her," added Mark. "To the point that even if something was not intended she would feel as if it were." Once when the family was at an airport, across the concourse a group of people were talking. At one point, they erupted in laughter. Lori leaned over to her mother and asked, "Why are they laughing at me?"

What Cece and Mark were describing was classic social phobia. Lori was pathologically self-conscious—overly worried about being embarrassed, mired in a belief that she did not measure up to her peers, even a little paranoid (I'm using that word colloquially, not clinically).

Lori also seemed to have a hint of generalized anxiety disorder, a tendency to be nervous and to worry about many things. Kids with GAD frequently ruminate: "What if I flunk this test, what if I don't have enough money when I get older, what if I don't get into the right college?" They think over and over again about all the bad things that could happen. No surprise that this disorder may be a risk factor for later depression.

Lori's social anxiety didn't extend to going to school—no Monday morning flu—but once she was in class, a form of it took hold. "Every report from every teacher has always been that she's very good academically, she loves to read, but she never raises her hand and participates," Lori's mom said.

I asked what she thought made Lori so reticent. "Well, she's reluctant to ever express herself. I think she's worried about being embarrassed if she says something wrong. She doesn't have confidence that her opinion either has value, is correct, or whatever. She's afraid of taking that risk in front of her peers."

Cece's observation was a textbook description of the plight of teens with social phobia. It's true that most parents would report that they themselves experienced this during their adolescence, and that their children have expressed similar concerns at one point or another. The difference for Lori was in the intensity, duration, and relentlessness of her symptoms.

I asked Cece if Lori had any other anxieties or phobias. Cece said that Lori had a tendency toward hypochondria. If someone in her class had strep throat, Lori would invariably come home and say her throat hurt. Or if someone near her was sick, she would worry that she might get sick. "I got so tired of it," Cece said, "that now I just take her right over to the pediatrician's office and let him tell her that nothing is wrong. For instance, I took her for a strep test and he told her, 'You don't have strep,' and I didn't hear about it again." Some parents might be critical of Cece for "giving in" to Lori's incessant fears. But understandably, the all-consuming nature of dealing with her complaints led Cece to do the expedient thing.

"What about fears about *your* health?" I asked Lori's parents. "Does she have any fear of you two dying? How is she when you go out on a Saturday night and she's home?"

"Lately," Mark said, "she's begun to call us on our cell phone and ask why we aren't home yet." This was interesting, given that at the same time, Lori's relationship with her parents had become much more acrimonious, to the point of Lori claiming she was being "abused." While it seems illogical, Lori had mild separation anxiety worries about her parents as well. It shows that anxiety isn't logical.

For Lori, all the brewing anxieties of her early childhood took a serious turn when she was in fifth grade. One day, Cece was cleaning Lori's dresser drawers and found a piece of paper on which Lori had written: "I hate my life." Cece wasn't shocked. She knew that Lori was unhappy. She had always been seen as a nerdy kid, but that year, by the luck of the draw, she happened to be in a class with more than the usual number of obnoxious kids who picked on her. She constantly complained about kids not liking her. When Cece went to pick her up from school, she saw that all the other kids were laughing, talking, goofing around with their classmates. Lori was always by herself. It struck Cece that Lori had virtually no social life—unlike her younger daughter, ten-year-old Jenny, who was much more socially adept. The kids Lori was friendly with in earlier years all seemed to have become best friends with other people, which was devastating to her. She couldn't understand why they weren't her friends anymore. She couldn't grasp the idea that people, especially kids, move around in relationships. Meanwhile, she saw that Jenny (who was also adopted) was surrounded by friends. The resentment boiled over.

Finally, Cece and Mark took Lori to see a psychiatrist. But rather than make a diagnosis of either social phobia or depression, she focused on Lori's relationship with her sister. This may have been partly because Cece's presentation of daily life was so dominated by the fighting between her daughters. It was such a difficult part of their environment that it sidetracked the psychiatrist, who saw the main problem as "sibling rivalry."

It was true that Jenny was much more outgoing and socially engaging. At a restaurant, a waiter would get extra goodies for Jenny and not Lori because Lori wasn't very responsive. It was also true that Lori felt picked on by her parents. Where Jenny recovered easily from setbacks, Lori seemed unable to put the social problem of the day behind her. Mark admitted: "If you've got one child who's bubbling about her day and her experiences and the other who's constantly complaining, I imagine from her perspective maybe we did sort of focus our attention on Jenny."

"Actually, we spend a lot more time and effort on Lori," Cece said. "If you add up the hours and the discussions of Lori versus Jenny, Jenny always gets shortchanged. Lori's just a high-maintenance kid. Nothing's easy. With Jenny, she runs over to you, she gives you a hug. She'll cry her eyes out when she's upset, but she'll snap out of it in three seconds and be giggly and happy. She's fine with life again. But Lori . . ."

So one seemed to be cruising through childhood, while the other felt every bump in the road. But to make it about sibling rivalry wasn't going to do Lori any good at all. Or her parents. All children have rivalries, and there are very few brothers and sisters who don't fight with each other. The missing ingredient from this evaluation was a diagnosis, without which there could be no treatment.

I asked the Connellys if they ever considered Lori happy at any point in her life. "Can you remember an image in your head? You just talked about Jenny. I have an image of her in my head, without even knowing her. I see her laughing and running down the stairs at school, or just engaging the waiter in conversation. Give me an image in your head of when you thought Lori was happy."

Cece and Mark thought a moment. "Really happy?" Mark asked. "I remember coming back from a very long trip overseas. I came to the door and I got the warmest hug. She wouldn't leave me alone for hours."

"But do you have a memory of going to a movie or having an ice cream and she's smiling and just happy?"

"She likes to go to Serendipity and have a hot fudge sundae."

"But is she smiling, giggling? Do you giggle with her?"

"We tell jokes sometimes, and she starts to giggle," Cece said.

"I understand what you're driving at," Mark said. "We're always trying to manufacture happiness for her."

"She loves our puppies," Cece offered.

Mark's observation about "manufacturing happiness" was an echo of something I've heard many times from parents of depressed teenagers. They recognize that their kids can experience happiness at times, but they feel the burden of helping create situations to help them experience joy. So the image the public has of a depressed adolescent—sullen, defeated, virtually unable to smile—is incomplete and misleading. There are times when they can experience pleasure and enjoy life, but it's intermittent and infrequent.

Lori's anxieties didn't prevent her from going away to summer camp and having a reasonably good time. The first year, the summer before fifth grade, she became friends with another girl who had social problems, "a hypochondriac weird kind of child," Cece said, fully aware that she was describing her own daughter as well. Lori's letters home always mentioned something about a kid bothering her or the fact that she had few friends, but she always wanted to go back the next summer. "The third year, I went up for a mother-daughter weekend," Cece recalled. "And I could count on two hands the number of words she said to any other camper there that weekend. I was dumbfounded. Many of the kids had been in her group for three years. I figured we would have to do something different for the next summer, but she insisted she wanted to go back. And she wanted her sister to come, too."

The Connellys were wary of this idea. The psychiatrist's words about sibling rivalry were ringing in their ears. But they decided to go ahead and send Lori and Jenny to camp together for the first time. "In my gut I knew Jenny shouldn't go to that camp," Cece said. "They shouldn't go together because the kids at camp were going to like Jenny, and Lori was going to feel even more isolated. And that's exactly what happened. The kids in her bunk were playing with Jenny and not Lori."

Cece and Mark went up for visiting weekend, and found Lori hysterical. "I can't stand it here!" she cried. "I have to go home."

If Jenny hadn't been so young, and if this hadn't been her first year at camp, Cece would have taken Lori home. But she didn't want to compound the problem by pulling Lori out and having Jenny unhappy because she would miss her sister and become homesick. Desperate, Cece told Lori that she would get something special if she finished the summer. "What do you want?" she asked.

"A puppy," Lori said, though the family already had a dog.

When they came home at the end of the summer the girls were greeted by a new puppy. What might appear as Lori being manipulative and Cece bribing her was actually a picture of parents feeling trapped by a seemingly impossible problem.

"She was truly happy," Mark said. "The puppy's still just about the only thing that puts a smile on her face."

That's why Cece thought of the puppy when Mark mentioned "manufacturing happiness." But she reminded her husband that even the puppy brought Lori only transitory pleasure. "Even when we first got the puppy," Cece said, "Lori was happy for five minutes and then went off to her room and closed the door."

They've tried other things. Lori wanted to wear makeup, which Cece saw as a good sign. She took her to the makeup counter at Macy's, and had her taught by a professional. "That was fine for that day," Cece continued, her voice filled with exasperation. "The problem is there's no payback. We put so much energy into trying to get her to be happy, and then you say to yourself, 'Now what?' I said to Lori, 'I don't know what more you want from me. Except for my blood, I have nothing more to give you.'"

When Lori was in seventh grade, her social problems were making her feel lower and lower, and her parents began looking for a different school for her. Lori had exceptional musical talent. She was taking guitar lessons and doing wonderfully. Her teacher said she had a fantastic ear and was probably the best student he'd ever had. Though she didn't play the piano, she could sit at the keyboard and figure out a song. So she applied and was accepted into a private school with a good music program. She handled the transition surprisingly well, and for the first time was feeling socially successful. Kids were talking to her, and she was responding. But by Christmas, they were withdrawing. Lori expressed herself most vividly in writing. "Dry and tasteless, they treat me like a crumb," she wrote in her journal. "I hate myself and the world. Everything would go on without me, no one would care when I'm gone."

Lori was invited to a bar mitzvah, and it was a torturous affair. In the car, Lori mentioned—not for the first time—a TV commercial she had seen for Paxil, one of the new generation of Selective Serotonin Reuptake Inhibitors (SSRIs). It's an antidepressant that has been marketed to highlight its effectiveness in also treating anxiety. "Are you afraid of social situations?" the narrator in the commercial asks. Lori said she needed that. "She was almost shaking as she got out of the car," her father said. "You could see the panic." She wound up hiding in the bathroom. "I felt like I was crawling out of my skin," Lori told me.

Lori was also struggling academically for the first time. She had been an A student in elementary school, where she was required to do a lot of memorization, which she was good at. But in her new school the emphasis was on assimilating information, not memorizing it, and that exposed her weakness in organizational skills. She was better at remembering what year the Stamp Act was enacted than at understanding why it was important.

Throughout this time, Cece felt that Lori might have depression, but couldn't get anyone to agree. A psychologist they started seeing was reluctant to make that diagnosis. In therapy, she focused instead on Lori's social problems and her relationship with her parents. She would meet with all three of them and make up contracts—make her agree to go to bed by ten o'clock, for instance, or to do her homework before dinner rather than after. As Cece explained, "It takes her a long time to do things anyway. Her mind wanders. If she has twenty math problems, she'll be dreaming and you'll find her on the computer doing something else." That was a hint of an attention problem, which seemed to have been exacerbated by the style of the school she was attending—less structure, more long-term assignments. Lori started complaining that she was miserable and wanted to change schools again. She wanted a fresh start. "Lori, we can't keep having new starts," her mother told her.

After a while, the sessions with the psychologist weren't helping. Meanwhile, the frustrations were building, to the point of screaming, and even physical contact. "Cece is a very organized person," Mark said. "Lori's not. Cece would suggest, 'Why don't you set your notebook up this way?' 'No, Mom.' And it would escalate into this shouting match. And then, I would say, 'Lori, go to your room,' and she would refuse. And I'd actually have to drag her, lift her, and then she would scream even more."

Cece realized that she needed help with her own life frustrations, which she felt had an impact on how she handled Lori's problems. "My frustrations have to do with the fact that my dad died 12 years ago and my mother is beyond a pain in the ass," Cece said, sighing. "So I would say things that were wrong. I would get so frustrated that Lori was doing her *ninth* hour of homework. And there would be a fight. Then I would feel bad and try to explain that nobody's family is like *Ozzie and Harriet*—I didn't use that reference because she wouldn't understand it. But I gave her the example of a friend of mine who had a fight with her daughter and she said, 'You need another mother, go get another mother.' Families say things like that. But if I said that to Lori, I'd be crucified."

Clearly, the Connellys felt guilty and were concerned that somehow their behavior was causing or at least contributing to their daughter's worsening psychiatric condition. They both had trouble coping with Lori, who was not shy about telling me (as she had other professionals before) that her parents were emotionally and physically abusive. I asked Cece if she thought it was that she and Mark had simply reached their limit, or that Lori was getting more difficult.

"No question, she's getting more irritable," Mark said.

"She's so frustrated with life at this point," Cece added. "And, yes, we're reaching our limits." In fact, that's what motivated them to start seeing a family therapist to help them work on their self-control with their daughter.

Recently, Lori had told her parents that she had been trying to hurt herself. Last summer at camp, she said, she went on a swing, as high as she could go, and jumped off, hoping she would get hurt. And lately, in her room, she had been cutting herself with scissors. "Since then, she's become pretty much nonfunctioning," Cece said. Until that point, she had recounted her daughter's travails with composure. But then her voice started to break, and her neck and face became flushed. "We don't know what it is or what to do," she said. "Is it suicidal thoughts? We don't really know. Earlier this year, I saw lines on her wrists. I asked what it was from. She said one of the puppies scratched her. It was only recently that she admitted she has been cutting herself. She told the psychologist, who told us. And then she started to cut much more. She said it was to 'get through the day.' She calls me from school. She says she feels terrible, she's going to hurt herself, can I come get her?"

Cece gave me a copy of poem Lori had written and shared with her at the time:

Doom

The only visible light
Into darkness
The only relief is
Cut into my flesh
As deep as sadness
As red as blood
Pain passes away
But I will be left with the scars
From the past

I hear vividly the sounds
The screams.
I am but a bug
Invisible to life
Picked on when sought.
Pain is an addiction
The only life I've known.

Blood returns me to life
But at any mistake may turn me away
Sadness is but a dream,
Supplied by the haunted past.
Shame upon the head
Grows older into endless time.
Until the next time
I wait in endless time
For the end.

The poem made it obvious how insignificant Lori felt: how the numbness, the detachment, and the sense of being alone—like a bug—was her way of surviving. Her cutting, meanwhile, was both an act of desperation and a way of helping her feel alive, if in a perverse way. She was playing at the precipice of suicide, scratching herself rather than slashing, and it gave her some sense of relief—so much so that it became addictive, a compulsion. This kind of behavior has been reported to be on the increase among girls. Like suicide, which is known to be "contagious" to susceptible adolescents, cutting and other self-abusing behavior can become an accepted practice in some teenage circles.

The cutting convinced Lori's psychologist that there was a bigger problem here than sibling rivalry, and she referred her to a psychiatrist, who immediately diagnosed depression and put her on Zoloft. Nonetheless, the cutting got much worse. And because it generally takes four to six weeks for an antidepressant medication like Zoloft to work, the psychiatrist, as a precaution, thought it would be a good idea for Lori to be hospitalized. After interviews and examinations at the hospital, the head of psychology wrote: "This patient appears to be severely depressed and is likely to be at acutely increased risk of suicidal behaviors. Her depressed mood appears to be accompanied by anxiety that may represent a separate syndrome, may be secondary to her depressed mood, or may be a more chronic feature of her personality. . . . This young woman is likely to suffer from chronic feelings of inadequacy and difficulties in social interactions that may well have contributed to her current episode of depression."

The psychologist's report was right on target. He described Lori as a teenager who had social phobia as well as (comorbid) major depressive disorder. What made it more difficult to treat Lori was the fact that she stated that she didn't like doctors and therapists. In fact, she believed that people shouldn't discuss their personal problems with others, which makes sense in light of the pathological self-consciousness she experienced because of her social phobia.

The hospital staff persisted, and her psychiatrist increased Lori's Zoloft dosage and arranged for a comprehensive inpatient treatment program. This program included teaching Lori deep, progressive muscle relaxation techniques along with other specialized anxiety management skills. In addition, Lori's therapist prescribed depression–specific CBT to address her negative thoughts. (See chapter 12 for further discussion of this therapy.) There were also weekly family therapy sessions with her parents, in which all of them worked on what they acknowledged were difficulties that they had had accepting each other's personality differences, resolving conflicts, building trust, and maintaining "normal" family life in spite of Lori's illness.

After two weeks in the hospital, Lori came home. A few weeks later—long enough for the Zoloft to have had an effect—Lori was still depressed. Her doctor decided to stop the Zoloft and put her on Paxil. But when she returned to school, Lori went back to cutting herself—and started doing it in class. She was clearly more anxious now that she had the social pressure of school. She was spending more and more of the day in the nurse's office, and she began dropping courses, one at a time. One day she told the nurse that she felt she would be better off dead. That was the end of Lori's school year. While she wasn't acutely suicidal, it was understandable that school officials felt they couldn't be responsible for what might happen if she acted on her thoughts. The next day, Lori was back in the hospital.

Lori was asked to write something describing her life. Here's some of what she wrote:

> Everybody is hurt sometime in his or her life. For me it started with my parents. But let me start further back. I was adopted in 1986 by my parents. In [elementary] school, people were not very nice to me. They spread rumors about me that I was a lesbian, which by the way, I'm not. Anyway, I had very few friends and was what they call a nerd or a dork. I did not know fashion, and I did not know "anything" that was cool. So this girl decided to do a makeover on me which was not a total success. On a more serious note, home wasn't going too well either. I was being abused both mentally and physically. My dad would grab me and cover my mouth so I couldn't scream and hit me and my mom yelled at me. It was hell. I decided to deal with my school problem by changing schools. There I did well in the beginning but my grades began to drop as I got more depressed. Soon the abuse got worse, my temper got worse, and I got serious depression. I began going to a child psychiatrist who finally

got my dad to stop physically abusing me but up until a few months ago, my mom mentally abused me. School life went downhill. I began to get very depressed and stopped talking to a lot of people so they stopped talking to me so I lost many of my friends. My grades also dropped. Eventually I started cutting myself to relieve myself of the emotional pain. It became an addiction. When I finally told my parents and psychiatrist they sent me to a hospital. I made many friends and got better. But they discharged me too fast. I got sick again. Now I'm sick and I'm still cutting myself and I can't stop. I also tried overdosing but I spit it out. That's my life.

It's not unusual, of course, for a young person to be uncomfortable and uncommunicative when she is brought to an office and asked to share her most personal thoughts with a complete stranger. But when the Connellys visited with Lori one day, she was the picture of social anxiety disorder. She looked down, her arms folded. Her head made involuntary movements, and she began to bite her fingernails. Still, Lori was able to articulate some of what she was feeling. I asked her what kinds of things made her worry, and the first thing she thought of was when she was a little girl. "I wouldn't eat my lunch in school because I was afraid I'd throw up."

I asked Lori why she cut herself. "It's an addiction," she said. "It relieves stress. I don't know . . . I just need to do it. It's kind of like smoking. Cutting is a stupid thing to do, but I have to do it."

"What are you feeling when you have the urge to cut?"

"Like I don't want to go on living. Like a really bad person. One girl in the hospital said I was evil. Inside my head I talk to myself."

"What do you tell yourself?" I asked.

" 'You suck. You're ugly. You're stupid. You don't deserve to live.' "

Lori's case points out how commonly depression comes in different kinds of packaging. She has social phobia and major depressive disorder. It was once believed that diagnoses were exclusive. For instance, you couldn't have both anxiety and ADHD: one caused cautiousness, the other impulsivity. But that turned out not to be true. Some people have both. Today we know that social phobia should be seen as a red flag for depression. It's often a precursor.

Unfortunately, patients with depression, whether adults or teenagers, do not always respond to the first or even second antidepressant. Since Zoloft and Paxil had not worked, I recommended that Lori's physician at the hospital try a different class of antidepressant: a monoamineoxidase inhibitor (MAOI), which is indicated for "atypical" depression. Because they require dietary restrictions to prevent potential side effects, MAOIs are not first-line medicines. Lori was started on Parnate and discharged from the hospital at the end of the summer.

At Christmastime, I called the Connellys to see how Lori was doing. Cece sounded significantly more upbeat since the last time I had seen the family. Lori had started ninth grade in the fall, and appeared to be calmer and managing well at school. Her parents still had a sick child—Lori slipped back into cutting and fretted about "the answer to things"—but her mother told me that at least it was now livable. Lori didn't dread school, was passing her classes, and was more socially accepted. She was seeing a psychiatrist weekly, and her parents were going to a family therapist who was working with them on both keeping firm limits and keeping the house calm.

As hard as it was for her to say, Lori's mom told me, "We have a child with a serious illness. But she's in remission and we go from week to week. We're in a better place now than I ever thought was possible."

While 3.5 million children and teenagers suffer from major depressive disorder, with the overwhelming majority of them adolescents, not all of them will remain depressed into adulthood. The hope is that early identification and effective treatment will lessen the risk of these young people having recurrent episodes and a chronic condition. What we hope never happens is for basic depression to develop into something more serious. But sometimes it does.

One percent of the adult population suffers from a serious psychiatric illness that is classified as psychosis, with the two most common types being bipolar disorder and schizophrenia. These disorders most frequently emerge during late adolescence. In some cases, a teenager initially meets the diagnostic criteria of anxiety or depression before his condition evolves into a more severe and perplexing disorder. Fortunately, this is a rare occurrence. But when it does happen, the ordeal for patients and their families becomes a lifelong battle demanding enormous emotional and material resources.

HENRY'S WORLD

Henry Siff's mother brought him in because he was having serious social problems. She reported that he was less mature than most adolescents—both physically and emotionally—and had trouble gaining his peers' acceptance. Socially timid and self-conscious about his short stature, Henry had anxieties that extended to his being uncomfortable going into a public lavatory. By middle school, he was no longer being invited to parties out of obligation. Meanwhile, he was reluctant to pick up the phone and call a friend. Many of his social engagements were made by his mother. "I knew he should be doing this on his own," she said. "But it just wasn't something that came naturally to him. He's more of a loner."

Henry's mom, Christina, thought he was immature. She felt that just as some toddlers are slow to walk or talk, Henry was slow to socialize. She remembered that when he was very young, "he was very clingy." She would sit with him on the floor for two or three hours at a clip, reading or teaching him something. But when he was separated from her, he would often vomit. He was less close with his father, and after his parents divorced when Henry was nine, he and his father were even more distant. Christina brought both Henry and his brother to a child psychologist to help them get through the transition. Christina recognized that the divorce was going to be difficult for the whole family, but especially for her more sensitive child.

As he grew older, Henry did extremely well in school, but he remained socially awkward, sometimes saying inappropriate things without understanding why they got him in trouble. He would make fun of a teacher's baldness right in front of him, and he gained a reputation as a wise guy. But Henry really wasn't a wise guy; at least he didn't mean to be. His inappropriate remarks were an odd aspect of his personality, a paradoxical counterpoint to his general lack of assertiveness in situations with peers. Henry was anxious about how to behave in front of others, especially with those in his peer group. But even with me, in a one-on-one, nonthreatening setting, he seemed to lack a sense of social awareness and appropriateness. His method of engaging was awkward. Within seconds of our first meeting, he asked, "How much did that shirt cost?"

Like Lori, Henry had clear symptoms of generalized anxiety disorder. He was worried about the future and worried about the health of his father's business—even though he resented him for never seeming very involved in their relationship, even before the divorce.

When he was 16, Henry came home unhappy from a "teen tour" summer camp. From that point on, he started locking himself in his room and listening to music for hours—not an unusual thing for a teenager, of course, but disquieting to Henry's mother because it was followed by a drop in Henry's performance in school. He told her he felt "out of it" and started bringing home Bs instead of As. And then, seemingly out of nowhere, Henry began getting into fistfights with his younger brother, and he even became physical with his mother. He threw things, spit, and cursed. What seemed to trigger these episodes was when he had a test coming or a paper due, and didn't feel he had prepared enough and had run out of time.

At one point, Christina received a phone call from the high school art teacher, saying Henry had been provocative with her in class and had refused to do his work. She gave him a D for that marking period, putting his college aspirations in jeopardy. At another point, during the winter of his junior year, he became so overwhelmed with schoolwork that he stormed out of his house with a blanket and sat down on a neighbor's lawn and cried.

It was in the midst of these struggles that Henry's mother brought him to see me and gave me the history I've just described. When I spoke to Henry alone, he acknowledged that he had problems relating to the people in his life, and that he had many symptoms of both anxiety and depression: difficulty falling asleep, poor concentration, worries about his future, and concerns about his social competence, his athletic ability, and his physique. He admitted that he was rude to his mother, though he couldn't say why. He said that he had been optimistic about the future until about a year earlier, that he was sad and irritable most of the time, and that his performance in school had declined. His lack of insight about his social abilities was especially noteworthy. Henry was very thin and gangly, with unkempt black curly hair, and acne on his forehead. He walked with a loping gait. Henry came off as goofy and odd, but he considered himself cool and stylish and presented himself in a cocky manner. (Think of Steve Martin and Dan Aykroyd as the wild and crazy guys in *Saturday Night Live*.) But it was all in his head. There was a fragility to his social persona, as if he could be knocked over by the slightest rejection. The paradox was that this swaggering teenager was actually pathologically self-conscious. His unrealistic assessment of which peers, particularly girls, would be interested in him proved to be an important early symptom of his disorder.

From the history, it was evident that this was a boy with poor social skills and both social and generalized anxiety disorders throughout his childhood. Now, he also had depression. I started Henry on Celexa, an SSRI, and arranged for him to begin cognitive behavioral therapy. His response was remarkable. His sleep improved, he was significantly less irritable, and his grades went back up. But his social life remained unfulfilling. Much like Lori, he was jealous of his younger sibling, who, while not a strong student was socially at ease, athletic, and popular. Christina told me she felt as though she was living in a different house now, but that she still had concerns about her son's social isolation. Henry graduated high school and, in spite of all the struggles, was accepted to the University of Pennsylvania, his first choice.

As I will discuss in chapter 10, college is a challenging and stressful time for all adolescents, especially when they leave home. For Henry, the social demands became impossible, and his social deficits became glaring. He decided to try to get into a fraternity. As with any institution, college fraternities and sororities have fixed rituals for gaining entry. Students who are interested in joining a frat house participate in "Rush Week," in which they are entertained by various fraternities, tour the houses, and meet the members. At the same time, the members are evaluating the prospective fraternity brothers, and deciding which ones they will invite to pledge. Most freshman don't expect automatic entry and so rush several houses, hoping their first choice will want them. Henry, though, rushed only the most popular and exclusive fraternity, without making any attempt to elicit the essential support of individual members. After he failed to get an invitation to pledge, he was despondent. He couldn't understand what he had done wrong and became very agitated and angry. He was convinced it was a mistake; after all, he thought, he was one of the brightest and coolest freshmen.

Henry quickly spiraled downward. He stopped taking his medicine, stopped sleeping at night, stopped going to classes, and stopped showering. His erratic sleep and terrible hygiene led his roommate to move out, leaving Henry alone. That triggered a call from the campus mental health professional to whom I had referred Henry before he left for school. Henry had seen this psychologist the first week of school but never went back, despite several phone calls from this caring clinician. When the psychologist reached him after his roommate moved out, Henry promised to come in.

The psychologist found Henry disheveled, agitated, grandiose, and lacking judgment or insight into his problem. Henry felt he didn't need to attend classes, that he could take his midterms without difficulty. Reading the textbooks, he felt, was unnecessary and even beneath him.

He told the psychologist his roommate was "childish and conventional" in his need to go to sleep at a reasonable time and to have an orderly room. "What's the big deal—we're in college," he said. "Aren't we supposed to stay up late and live in mess?" He told the psychologist that he had bought a remote control for the television in the dorm lounge and that it was his right to select the programs and change the channel no matter who else was in the lounge. He couldn't understand why his dormmates were bothered by this, or why no one wanted to socialize or eat with him. He dismissed them as immature and petty.

Henry's behavior, attitude, and lack of judgment led the psychologist to make a tentative diagnosis of bipolar disorder. He called Henry's mother, who in turn called me. Told by the college psychologist that he would be expelled if he didn't withdraw from his classes and take a medical leave of absence, Henry reluctantly left school and came home. When I saw him, I agreed with the diagnosis. With Henry's willingness and his mother's active supervision, we were able to treat him as an outpatient. Henry's response to lithium, in combination with a return to Celexa, was excellent. Within weeks his sleep, concentration, and judgment were dramatically improved. He transferred to a local college, lived at home, and eventually became an active participant in therapy with a very gifted and experienced therapist. She not only helped Henry with his social difficulties, but also taught him about his disease and about how to be an active participant in its management, including the importance of taking medication.

Adolescence is a time of change. More often than not, the change is good. Ask most parents to assess their kids after the first semester of college, and they will say that they seem more comfortable with themselves, which translates into less irritability and a greater capacity to listen to their parents' points of view without feeling threatened. This personality shift is not exclusive to the college-age adolescent; it frequently occurs between middle school and high school.

But at the same time, a very small percentage of adolescents—one percent, according to research—undergo a personality change that is caused by psychosis. Both Lori and Henry started off as anxious, socially awkward, peer-rejected children, and evolved into depressed teenagers. But Henry's personality transformation into the tyrant of the TV lounge, a once diligent student who now scoffed at the idea of attending class and taking exams, wasn't a sign of immaturity or a flaw in his character. Nor did it have anything to do with his college experience. It was that his psychotic illness derailed the natural maturation process and affected his behavior. In time, it would have affected his very personality if he had not received the treatment he did.

4

THE ODDS

What puts a young person at risk for depression? That phrase—
at risk—describes how people in medicine and science decide,
based on statistics, what the odds are for groups of people to get a particular disease—whether it's lung cancer, heart disease, schizophrenia, or
anything else. In other words, based on who has gotten it before, it helps
predict who might be susceptible in the future. As Lori Connelly demon-
strates, children who have poor social relationships and/or anxiety disorders
are at greater risk for teenage depression than their peers. This means
that anxiety is not only a disorder that's frequently *comorbid* with depression, but it is also a prime *risk factor* for depression.

Anxiety disorders can be treated with therapy or medication. Thus,
it's a risk factor that can be diminished. But some significant risk factors
can't be changed. One is having a family history of depression. Another

is having had depression before, particularly if it was prior to adolescence. Generally, the earlier the onset of depression, the greater the risk of its being chronic. A third risk factor that can't be controlled is being a girl.

Gender is perhaps the most glaring epidemiological factor in adult depression. Studies show that it is much more common in women than men, and this disparity holds true for teenagers as well. Why this is so is a matter of lively speculation. One leading line of thought holds that in early adolescence, boys and girls adopt personality characteristics regarded as appropriate for their gender, and that those adopted by girls make them more prone to depression. For instance, girls are more socially oriented than boys, and place a greater value on having positive relationships. Teenagers of both sexes have sometimes intense social pressures and tensions, but girls may be more vulnerable than boys to the effects when things go wrong. They also cope differently: girls are thought to dwell more on broken relationships, to become more distressed when they are rejected, and that could make it easier for them to slip into a depression.

There is also a tendency for girls to develop more pervasive negative thoughts about themselves than do boys in early adolescence. This inclination to view oneself negatively, particularly after stressful events, extends to adulthood and predicts a higher risk for depression. Moreover, when bad things happen to women, they are more likely to attribute these events to their own faults, more frequently blaming themselves when things go wrong. A wealth of emerging evidence suggests that these circumstances may make them—and their younger counterparts—more vulnerable to depression.

There may also be biological reasons for the gender disparity. The latest studies show that before puberty, the rate of depression among boys and girls is roughly equal. But after puberty, twice as many girls as boys seem to become depressed. Is it that female hormones that kick in at puberty have a special effect on the mood regulators in the brain? Do social or cultural pressures play a role? The idea that girls react differently from boys to romantic and other social fortunes, and that this could be a trigger for depression, is a hotly debated issue. It has also been widely noted that in the last century the age of onset of puberty has gone steadily down; girls in particular have been maturing earlier. If it's true that more adolescents are getting depressed now than in the past, are those two trends related?

We are only now beginning to address these questions, but one thing we do know is that the peak time for risk of depression is around ages 13 and 14. Some have suggested that this spike is related to social roles—the added pressure of being asked to be more mature, to separate more from parents, to achieve—but if that were the case, depression rates might be expected to keep climbing throughout the teen years, instead of leveling off after 14. Another factor is how boys and girls view the physical changes of puberty. Boys get more muscular and their voices change. Girls tend to gain weight and lose the lithe bodies of prepuberty, the kind they see on magazine covers. But if these factors contribute to the higher rates of depression in girls than boys, they don't explain the same gender disparity in adults.

There are, meanwhile, cultural biases in early adolescence that might make girls more vulnerable to depression. For instance, parents often tend to allow their sons more independence than their daughters, which speaks to a whole range of issues regarding self-image and competence. There is also the issue of sexual abuse. Girls are much more likely to be sexually abused at this age than boys. The resulting feelings of fear, help-lessness, and social stigma can be contributing factors to depression. It seems that girls are more conscious of these challenges of early adolescence than boys are, and more concerned with meeting them. One study asked 703 adolescents how concerned they were about a list of 14 aspects of their lives, from intimate relationships to academic achievement. Girls reported more concern than boys in all categories except doing well in sports. According to psychologists Susan Nolen-Hoeksema of the University of Michigan and Joan S. Girbus of Princeton University, these challenges of adolescence are more likely to lead to depression in girls than boys because social biases are more likely to already put girls at higher risk.

RISK FACTORS FOR DEPRESSION IN ADOLESCENCE

- Having a parent who has had depression

- Having an anxiety disorder, especially in preadolescence, or a childhood history of depression

- Being female

- Having a serious negative life event or an accumulation of damaging experiences (e.g., loss of social support systems, loss of a parent, a childhood history of physical or sexual abuse)

I remember a cartoon in the *New Yorker* that depicted a man saying to his son, "It's okay to be depressed," as the rest of the family sits in the background, each member looking morose. The cartoonist must have known something about the subject. Statistically, children of depressed parents are three times more likely to become depressed themselves than children whose parents do not have depression. Meanwhile, it's been estimated that anywhere from one in six to almost half of the parents of a depressed child or adolescent are or have been depressed. The obvious question is one of nature versus nurture: Is depression genetic, or is it, in effect, contagious? Is it so depressing being around a depressed mom or dad that a child runs the risk of becoming depressed as well? The best evidence is that major depression is too complex to attribute to either factor alone. More likely, it results from the interplay of both genetic and environmental influences.

The idea that depressed people, whether children or adults, owe some of their situation to their surroundings is a relatively recent one. Depression is no longer viewed, as it once was, as an isolated illness detached from the environment. In the course of research about genetic factors in the much more serious illness of schizophrenia, something very interesting was learned about family and depression. In studies of children of parents with schizophrenia, children of depressed parents were used as controls. To the researchers' surprise, they found that these children had as much mental illness as the children of parents with schizophrenia. A research team in 1983 concluded that children of depressed parents are at significant risk, not only for depression but also for a range of other mental health problems. So then the question became: Why? Some suspected that it was the stress of living with a depressed parent. But others have argued, sometimes convincingly, that *both* parents and their children can become depressed as a result of a common family situation—a bad marriage or family discord.

The genetic question remains elusive. Studies thus far (mostly with adults) indicate that both genes and environment contribute to depression, with environmental factors being slightly more important. For instance, studies of twins have shown that if one identical twin has depression, the other twin has a greater chance of having it too—but only a slightly greater chance than fraternal twins. Since identical twins share all their genes, while fraternal twins share only half, this suggests that both environmental and genetic factors are important in depression. Moreover, complex illnesses are not caused by a single gene, but by many genes interacting with many environmental factors. Depression is nothing if not a complex illness. So while family history suggests genetic causes, it can also indicate environmental factors: a child of a depressed parent may be susceptible to the disorder herself not so much because of heredity but because living with a depressed parent can make it difficult to have a positive outlook.

When Columbia University epidemiologist Myrna Weissman followed children of depressed parents, she found they had higher rates of depression themselves. In another study, she found that only depressed children with family histories of the disease went on to have elevated rates of depression as adults. Conversely, depressed parents are much more likely to have kids with major depression—anywhere from twice as likely to ten times more likely than parents who do not have depression.

An important variable in that range is the age at which a parent had his or her first episode. Those who became clinically depressed when they were very young are more likely to have kids who also get depressed at an early age. That may suggest that being depressed has a negative effect on parenting, and on a child's psychological health. On the other hand, it's possible that since genetic influences that are stronger emerge earlier, a parent who had earlier-onset depression is more likely to "pass on" the disease to his or her offspring.

A particularly interesting new finding comes from Dr. Adrian Angold, a child and adolescent psychiatry researcher at Duke University. He has found that rising levels of estrogens and testosterone occurring during puberty were associated with greatly increased rates of depression in girls. This increase in depression occurred particularly in daughters of mothers who were themselves currently depressed.

The important message here is that parents with mood disorders—as well as their spouses—must be especially watchful for any psychological problems in their children. It also highlights the importance of treating adult depression, not only to benefit the patient, but also to protect the children, and particularly teenage daughters. This does not eliminate risk for sons—boys of depressed parents are also at an elevated risk for depression.

The role of family circumstances plays into an analysis of ten countries, including the United States, that demonstrated a steady increase in adolescent depression since World War II, accompanied by a decrease in the age of onset. Some of it is simply a matter of better reporting, but not necessarily all of it. For example, some of the risk factors associated with depression have become more common. There is more family instability and divorce. It doesn't mean kids in such families wouldn't get depression anyway (nor, for that matter, does it mean that they *would*). But if a child has a genetic vulnerability or other risk factor for depression, family upheaval can certainly trigger it. Take hypertension as an analogy. If you have a genetic predisposition to it, and you're in an environment where you're eating a lot of high-salt foods, the probability that you're going to get hypertension is much higher.

EMMA'S RISKS

Emma, at age 15, is a classic case of risk factors. She's a girl, she has a family history of depression, and she has had an anxiety disorder since before puberty. Her mother brought her to a psychologist when she was 12, and she was quickly diagnosed with both separation anxiety disorder and social phobia. Emma was afraid of almost everything. She was afraid to be separated from her parents—she'd rather stay home than go to school, and frequently complained of stomach aches in class—and she was afraid of the future. The terrorist attack of September 11, 2001, affected her deeply. She was 14 then, and while most of her classmates seemed to have no trouble mostly ignoring the anxieties that consumed the country, Emma thought about them constantly. She couldn't shake the fear that she would die, and so would her parents.

Emma's parents had first noticed her anxiety when she was about eight. She didn't like to be left with a babysitter. "What if something happens?" she would ask. Scary movies didn't just give her the creeps; they stayed with her for weeks. She had a hard time sleeping alone.

Emma had an angelic face with straight, shoulder-length blond hair. Her parents, a teacher and a homemaker, described her as an over-achiever. She wasn't the smartest kid in the class, but she tried extremely hard and was a perfectionist. She got into a school for gifted children, but went back to her old school after a year. She was well behaved. If she was angry she would say something under her breath rather than openly talk back.

Emma's mother had depression, and was taking Zoloft, which helped her. She wanted a colleague of mine to prescribe the same thing to ease her daughter's sometimes overwhelming anxieties. But the doctor wanted to try some other things first. He started with a little homework. To deal with Emma's continuing separation anxiety, her parents were to stay with her at night for 30 minutes, and decrease the time in five-minute increments until she slept alone—a method familiar to any parent of a toddler. It worked as well with a 14-year-old as with a 14-

month-old. The doctor also gave her breathing exercises: six deep breaths per minute to decrease hyperventilation and to give Emma something to focus on. Preliminary research suggests that adolescents with separation anxiety disorder and adults with panic disorder are hypersensitive to carbon dioxide, and therefore the slow, deep breathing may also help get rid of the carbon dioxide more efficiently.

These and similar treatments helped. Emma seemed less anxious, and she was finally able to sleep alone, though she was still afraid to stay home alone at night with her nine-year-old brother. But in the meantime, she began having some significant problems with mood. Knowing the close relationship between anxiety disorders and depression, and because her mother responded well to Zoloft, my colleague prescribed the same thing. This type of medicine has been shown to be effective in treating both depression and anxiety disorders in teenagers. Emma thought it helped. A month later she said she was less self-conscious and didn't worry so much. But her parents disagreed. "She's still very inhibited," her mother said. "She's uptight with kids her age. She's very uncomfortable with her appearance, even though she's beautiful."

Over the next few months, Emma seemed to go up and down. At one appointment she said she was feeling more relaxed and self-confident, but after the family moved later that year, she complained she was having trouble making new friends and was "terrified" of being ridiculed. Meanwhile, she confided that her parents were really starting to annoy her. "They're cheap, they're always mad at me. They pick on me. They let my brother get away with everything." Standard teenage fare. In a separate conversation, Emma's father said, "Whenever I tell her she's pretty she gets angry because she doesn't believe it."

The following summer, Emma's anxieties resurfaced in a big way. At first she was very excited because she was going to be attending a performing arts high school. She had aspirations to be an actress. But not too long into the school year, she was saying she would kill herself if she had to stay in that school. She was feeling constantly nervous and uncomfortable, even "humiliated." She felt "terrified" by boys, to the point of avoiding going anyplace where she might run into them. Meanwhile, she was having visions of a dead person in a coffin, and feared that her father would die. "I'm constantly thinking of suicide," she said.

As pitiable as Emma might seem on paper, to her therapist she was manipulative and histrionic. "She has a mood disorder, and it's very hard to pierce through it because of her underlying anxiety as well as a tendency for self-pity," he told me. "She tells me she has mood swings. 'One minute I feel like killing myself, the next I feel great.' She says she's happy when she thinks about a boy she likes. Today she saw him at school and he didn't talk to her and she felt like killing herself. She's also very upset because another boy she likes didn't pay attention to her." While feeling down in those situations is completely normal in adolescence, Emma was overly sensitive to rejection—a characteristic that is not uncommon among adolescents with both anxiety and depression.

Emma's talk of suicide became a regular refrain, but she never came close to an attempt. She had bouts of overeating, though she weighed herself obsessively. She was on Zoloft for a while, but stopped taking it because, she said, "It's so fake to be well on medication."

Emma's family history was a risk factor for depression, but it doesn't mean she was destined to become depressed. She had a sister with the same family history who had no problem with depression. The two most important differences between the girls were Emma's prior history of anxiety and her pessimism. Emma's sister was described by her parents as an optimist. In contrast, Emma's approach to life was generally negative. "That's just the way she is, the way she's always been," her mother said.

Conversely, don't be fooled into thinking that a child *without* a family history of depression is in the clear. Adolescent depression is so common that most teenagers who have major depression do *not* have an immediate relative who also has the disease.

There is a caveat to all this. For some people, family history is a mystery. Many parents have described their own parents or grandparents as having had what, in retrospect, seem like symptoms of depression. In earlier eras, of course, depression was vastly unrecognized, unacknowledged, and, of course, untreated. But does everyone who says he had a depressed parent actually have one? As tempting as it may be, it's hard to diagnose in retrospect. The information may be second- or thirdhand, and even seemingly obvious cases may not be so clear-cut. One patient's uncle—her father's brother—had committed suicide. But the brothers were not close, and without a clinical history it couldn't be said for sure what his symptoms were. Most suicides have depression as a component—but not all of them do. On the other hand, as I mentioned earlier, some parents only realize that they themselves were depressed as teenagers when depression appears in their children.

ZACH'S CLUES

Zach was a 15-year-old who guarded what turned out to be strong indications of depression. Combined with his parents' lack of awareness, it made for a teenager who went nearly a year without being diagnosed or treated. During this time, he later said, he came to view the world as a mundane place and his own future as dreary. But these feelings didn't make him dysfunctional, at least not right away; his grades dropped, but not so low that his parents were concerned about anything other than his work habits—and what parent hasn't worried about that? They figured it was just a matter of maturity: Zach had breezed through middle school but had to realize that now he was in high school and needed to put more effort into his schoolwork.

At home, Zach had the usual issues of adolescent independence. He had had a good relationship with his stepfather—they shared a love for electric trains—but lately they fought about curfews and helping around the house. Throughout that year of ninth grade, Zach became increasingly ill-tempered and touchy. But still, his parents figured, that's just the way teenagers are. They had little idea what was really inside Zach's head. As the year progressed, he was having more and more problems concentrating in school, and he was keeping odd hours. He would often go to bed as soon as he came home from school, then get up at eight and stay up until two or three in the morning. Finally, one Monday afternoon,

Zach slipped off the edge. He later wrote the following story—ostensibly fiction, but obviously based on real life:

> It was 2:00 P.M. and I had just woken up. My head was throbbing, and I felt very sick. I stumbled to the bathroom, and got the feeling that something was missing. I felt as if I had something to do today. But then I realized that today would probably be filled with the same nothingness as every other one before that. My days were not always filled with this waste. Then I quickly forgot those days, as if I was jealous of them. I was in a very disoriented state at this time. I went to the bathroom to clean myself up. I picked up my razor to shave the hair that had just been accumulating on my chin for the past week. As I pressed the razor to my face, I paused and began to think, "What if my hand slipped? What if I cut myself when shaving? If no one saw me, then maybe I could leave the pain." Maybe I could leave all the pain and suffering for good. It would be all over with just one slip of the razor. I prayed for the mistake, not having the courage to do it myself; but it never came.
>
> I washed my face after I finished shaving. I looked at myself in the mirror, thinking about the shattered pieces of my life. All I could do was look in the mirror and pass judgment on my life.

Zach wrote the story during his junior year, imagining himself ten years into the future. Despite these hopeless feelings, he became a willing participant in his treatment, and responded well to a combination of individual psychotherapy, family therapy with a psychologist, and the antidepressant Celexa. But what was perhaps most interesting about this case was how in the dark Zach's parents were about what had been going on with him—and what it meant to his mother. Zach opened up during the family sessions, and his mother realized that she had been through a similar period when she was in high school. It didn't go as far as it did with Zach, and she managed to snap out of it after a few months with only a few conversations with a school counselor. She had never thought of it as *depression,* until now.

But she had been one of the lucky ones. She had not been depressed as an adult—so far. When I spoke to her a couple of years later to check on Zach, she told me that he was doing well. But she herself, at age 45, had had a bout of depression. She was now taking Celexa, and was doing much better. And she was no longer in the dark.

•

By now, if you have a teenage daughter who is excessively shy, and you're divorced, and you or your ex-spouse have a history of depression, you're probably reaching for the phone to make an appointment with a child and adolescent psychiatrist. Hang up the phone.

The previous pages have been all about risk. That means there's a greater chance your child may develop depression than the average person. But certainly there is a greater chance that she won't. That said, if you have a teenager with these risk factors, is there something you can do, or should do, to reduce the chances that she will develop depression? Since depression is a malfunctioning of stress management, it would be wise to address those factors that you can influence. For instance, if your daughter is uncomfortable in social situations, you should help her develop her social skills. (Chapter 6 offers ways that parents can help their children manage stress.)

There is no gene or gene cluster that has been identified as a cause for depression. There is no one environmental factor or a single loss or traumatic event that is the definitive trigger. Nevertheless, parents can't *not* worry about their kids. I'm reminded of a family friend who married a man who was later diagnosed with manic-depressive illness. He was a successful engineer with a secure job in the federal government, and to the outside world, including me, they seemed very happy. After four years of marriage, Marjorie became pregnant, and the birth of their daughter, Gabrielle, triggered his first full-blown manic episode. Apparently the responsibility of becoming a father was too much for him to handle, and he became manic and delusional. He went to a psychiatrist who put him on lithium. But a year after Gabrielle was born, he walked out of the marriage and his baby daughter's life. His condition deteriorated, he lost his job, and he eventually died in a men's shelter. He had almost no contact with his daughter. When he died, Gabrielle was 28, and she hadn't seen her father in 15 years.

Gabrielle was an extraordinary child. Everything seemed to come early and easily to her. She was an organized and gifted student, always popular, with lots of friends and activities. But when she was ten, she asked her mother if mental illness was inherited. Though Marjorie and her second husband knew that it was, they reassured Gabrielle that it was not, and that she shouldn't worry. Gabrielle was so even-tempered that when she got into an occasional funk as a teenager, it rarely lasted more than a few hours or a day. Because there was nothing in Gabrielle's temperament that would suggest that she had inherited her biological father's illness, her parents were determined not to let thoughts about her risk interfere with her life. They joked that the only thing she had inherited from her father was his math ability.

Now Gabrielle has a full and balanced life. She has a doctorate in anthropology, she married a lawyer with whom she spends many weekends windsurfing and skiing, and she is looking forward to motherhood. Gabrielle and her parents might have spent years worrying about whether she had "the gene" and would become bipolar. But Marjorie recognized that though Gabrielle's risk was increased, the odds were still in her favor. She made sure her daughter embraced life. She was determined that the only time Gabrielle would have to worry about being bipolar would be if she *became* bipolar. And she never did.

5

THE ARC OF DEPRESSION

From the moment I met him when he was 16, Jesse Altman had a hundred and one excuses for the way he was feeling and acting: "I'm not depressed," he would say. "I'm just tired and lazy." I've seen countless kids who are tired and lazy and claim not to be depressed. But as I got to know him, what made Jesse's condition, and his denial, so dramatic and frustrating to me was how much good stuff there was inside him.

Jesse was smart and he was creative, and it was clear that there was something like a cancer eating at him. His self-esteem and his ability to be socially assertive were very low, but even in this state there was an inner intensity about him. He could dwell on a remark forever. If I said something, he would question its meaning, question why I looked at him the way I did when I said it. But I could also see glimpses of another person inside, an exceedingly charming and gifted young man. He was tops in his class, starred on both the baseball and tennis teams, became the editor of the school paper, and was a talented violin and guitar player. He was the intellectual high school student who was interested in philosophy, art, and music. He had an irresistible smile and a dreamy expression. He was the son anyone would like to have—except for the overarching pain of his depression.

Jesse is not a recent case. I first saw him back in 1989, when he was 16, and he remains the most memorable, poignant, frustrating, and educational case of adolescent depression I have ever had. Whenever I get into a discussion about how depressed teenagers turn out, I think of Jesse. He's almost 30 now. He's just one person, one case, but when I talked to him and to his parents for this book, I was taken by how instructive their recollections and insights were for me as a psychiatrist. His case is an exquisite example of the arc of depression when it begins during adolescence. How, despite the best efforts of parents and doctors, a teenager can become an adult with a perennial struggle—but a struggle that can be won with a healthy attitude and the right treatment.

After he had broken down following a discussion of *The Catcher in the Rye* in English class, Jesse's parents brought him to the same psychoanalyst who had treated him for an episode of depression when he was just seven years old. Now Dr. Barnes was treating Jesse again with the same "psychodynamic" therapy—a talk treatment based on the theories of Sigmund Freud that holds that early experiences determine a person's unconscious and psychiatric symptoms, including depression. Freud's theory, in a nutshell, was that the patient's feelings toward the therapist—known as transference—reflect his unconscious feelings about his parents, and that dealing with these thoughts, both negative and positive, over time relieves the symptoms. When Jesse was brought to him this time, Dr. Barnes augmented the therapy with traditional antidepressants. But neither the medicine nor the psychotherapy was successful.

"What's it like, going to Dr. Barnes?" I asked Jesse during our first meeting in my office at Schneider Children's Hospital on Long Island that snowy January day in 1989.

"Torture," Jesse said.

"Why?"

"I sit there with him, and he sits there in this big chair. He has a much nicer office than you do, no offense."

"Yeah, I've got to redecorate," I joked. "What do you talk about?"

"He asks me, 'How do you feel?' And then he doesn't say anything. So I just sit there and avoid his glance. Last time, I thought, 'I'm just going to wait for the hand on that clock to go around one more time, one more minute, then I'm just going to walk out.' And then a minute goes by. I'll wait another minute. Another minute goes by. I did this about four times. Just when I'm about to walk out, he says, 'It must be very painful not to be able to speak.'"

Jesse was speaking to me just fine. And what he said was that he didn't feel he was depressed. All the sensitivity his parents described, the tears, the mood changes—it was just part of being a teenager, he said, sounding like any number of adults I've spoken to. But I knew that Jesse's history suggested he was not just being a teenager. His parents had described how as far back as preschool he was, in his father's words, "moody . . . you had to walk on eggshells." Jesse secluded himself in his room, and he was given to outbursts of extreme anger. "He would slam the door, he would kick us and use foul language," his father said. "Sometimes he would push a big piece of paper under the door that said, 'Fuck you.'"

Jesse's parents, Bruce and Carol, were pained and puzzled by this behavior, especially since he didn't have any behavioral problems in school. But at home, he was often a brooding child who talked only to people he knew and liked. Bruce, a physician, had been pushing for professional help since Jesse was four, but the notion that their son was in some way not normal seemed to offend Carol's sensibilities. Though she was well educated and sharp—she was an assistant district attorney—she was unwilling to accept that anything was wrong with him.

It's understandable that parents who have a child who's doing well in the outside world would hesitate to seek professional help. It's the rambunctious, disruptive "ADHD-type" children who tend to get the attention from teachers and friends and relatives. These children suffer from "externalizing" disorders that are hard to ignore. The kids who have "internalizing" disorders such as anxiety and depression, meanwhile, either suffer silently or express their unhappiness only with people they feel very comfortable with. They save the worst for their parents. It's only natural for parents to believe that there must be a defect in their parenting when the problem seems isolated to interactions with the family and at home. So there's typically a lag of up to two years between the onset of anxiety and depressive symptoms and a visit to a mental health professional.

When Jesse was in first grade, he wrote a note saying that if he had a gun he would shoot himself. At that point, Carol agreed to bring Jesse to a psychiatrist. He went to twice-weekly therapy sessions with Dr. Barnes, who did talk and play therapy. Jesse and Dr. Barnes would make drawings, work with clay, and play checkers, and then the doctor would interpret the activities. Jesse saw Dr. Barnes through the end of first grade, and it helped, to a degree. Some of the problem was clearly Jesse's quietly intense personality. He was very hard on himself; he could not understand why he couldn't do some things as well as older kids. In his parents' memories, Jesse was often a prickly, socially withdrawn, and tearful child. For his part, Jesse remembers those years as a mixed bag. "Second grade I remember being pretty good," he told me during a recent conversation. "Overall I was pretty happy through fourth grade, though I had some signs of not being completely happy. Temper tantrum kind of thing. I definitely could get extremely upset. If I didn't do things as well as I expected, I would get very upset, particularly in a public setting."

These were Jesse's early signs and symptoms of an anxiety disorder. Pathological concerns about performance and what other people think are the essential features of social anxiety disorder and generalized anxiety disorder. A childhood anxiety disorder increases the risk of developing depression in adolescence.

As a Little Leaguer, Jesse dreamed of being a big leaguer, a pitcher. His father worked long hours, and his mother wasn't one of those athletic suburban moms. But she would squat down on the lawn and catch for him. Jesse would ask her if she thought he could be a major league pitcher. "Oh, who knows?" she would say, like any parent.

"What do you mean, *who knows?*" Jesse would snap.

His mother would back down. "Okay, well, maybe you can."

It was clear that Jesse wasn't like every other kid who ever dreamed of being a ballplayer. He was in a league of his own.

"In fourth grade there was a big game," Jesse remembered. "It was the last inning, my team was ahead, and someone hit the ball directly to me. I didn't have to take a step. I just stuck out my glove and it hit off it and the other team won the game. I was just a basket case. I went off the field and couldn't be consoled."

Jesse's father told me, "You have no idea how much I hated Little League. If he didn't pitch well, we would have these long, serious, dramatic discussions. If his team lost, there would be hysteria. It was embarrassing. He would be nervous before the game, during the game, after the game. He would replay each of his mistakes. Every inning, it was 'I shouldn't have done this, I shouldn't have done that.' I mean, he was just in *third grade.*"

But he was also very sweet, a very appealing little boy, and these positive qualities gradually became the dominant ones as Jesse grew up and headed into adolescence. He was a stellar performer in school, both in academics and extracurricular activities. He liked to read and he wrote beautifully. He developed a close circle of bright and loyal friends. All in all, his parents later recalled his preadolescent years as fairly peaceful and pleasant. "So the bad stuff from when he was young was only memories," Jesse's father said. "Nightmarish memories, yes. But the person he grew into was a very thoughtful, responsible, mature person who also happened to have moodiness. He had genuine concerns for society and a genuine disinterest in material possessions and measuring success and failure by the money he made or didn't make. That was fairly unusual in our community."

When he was 14, Jesse started sleeping erratically. His parents discovered that he was staying up until three in the morning, reading and playing computer games. He was also eating less, and sometimes the two disrupted patterns merged. Jesse would come home from school and, having slept only a few hours the night before, go up to his room and sleep through the dinner hour. This meant that he would eat dinner late, start his schoolwork late, and then go to bed late again. But he was still motivated to do well, and did what it took to maintain his excellent grades. Meanwhile, though, he was becoming increasingly grumpy. And then came the turning point: the incident in English class when Jesse broke down during a discussion of *The Catcher in the Rye.*

Carol got the call from the school and hurried over. She found Jesse in the nurse's office, sitting in a wheelchair. She tried to talk to him, ask him what was wrong, but he wasn't speaking. She walked him to the car and started for home. It was snowing, and on the way home they saw Jesse's good friend, Zoe. "Pick Zoe up, Mom," Jesse said. "Don't let her walk home." They were the only words he said. Carol was struck by the fact that her son had just left school because of an emotional breakdown and seemed to be in real pain, yet it was evident that he was still the same sweet and caring person. There is no doubt that psychiatric disorder affects one's personality in the same way that a chronic physical illness does. Jesse wasn't a depressed teen; he was a smart, attractive, empathic adolescent who had depression. It's sometimes very difficult for parents to remember this, especially when the symptoms, most notably irritability, seem to define their daily interaction with their child. But buried inside there somewhere is the child they used to know.

Reluctantly, Jesse started going to Dr. Barnes again. But going was all he would do. "It was miserable," Carol recalled. "We would just sit there. Jesse wouldn't talk." Dr. Barnes had helped Jesse when he was very young, though what Carol and Bruce didn't realize was that it wasn't necessarily the therapy that had done the trick. Depression is a self-limiting illness. Given time, it will usually go away on its own. But that may be seven weeks or seven months, or even seven years. It's the bad things that happen during the depression that are the problem: the sleep disturbances, the loss of energy, the drop in self-esteem and inability to experience pleasure, and the sense of hopelessness that increases the risk of suicide. For teenagers more than adults, this can mean delaying or missing precious developmental milestones. But even if the Altmans attributed Jesse's improvement when he was young to Dr. Barnes's techniques, it was clear that they weren't working now.

That was when Jesse's father came to me. He believed that his son was desperately ill and, aware that I was doing research on depressed teenagers, he wanted to know if there was anything new he could try. Actually, there was. But first, of course, I needed to have a chat with Jesse.

After some preliminaries, I cut to the chase and asked Jesse what had disturbed him so much that day when his English class was discussing *The Catcher in the Rye*.

"What made you cry?" I asked.

"I don't know . . . Holden," Jesse said, referring to the novel's protagonist, Holden Caulfield.

"What about Holden?"

"They don't know what it's like," he said cryptically.

"Who? Who doesn't know? Your friends? Your parents?"

Jesse nodded.

"So tell me what it's like," I said.

Jesse shrugged. I asked if he related to Holden, the prototypical disaffected and alienated teenager who flunks out of boarding school and wanders in pain, unable even to express what he's experiencing or to ask for help. Jesse nodded, but couldn't get any words out. What kind of turmoil did this suggest? I was concerned when he told me that if someone gave him a loaded gun "and took the safety off," he'd stick it in his mouth. And if someone gave him an axe, he'd chop his own head off. But the passivity of the images—"if someone gave me a gun"—led me to believe he wasn't in imminent danger of hurting himself.

When I spoke to Jesse's parents after that first session, I told them what he had said about killing himself with a gun or an axe—if somebody helped him. "It's very passive suicide ideation, but it can't be ignored," I said. I wanted to put him on Prozac, but I wasn't sure if the medicine would work. I was also concerned that any antidepressant might energize him, perhaps giving him the motivation to find a gun or an axe. Prozac had just been released; it was the first of the new SSRIs, and there was no research evidence on its effectiveness in children or adolescents. In fact, that very question was at the heart of the research I was conducting with the older, traditional antidepressants, "tricyclics" such as Elavil and Tofranil. Since that time, Prozac and similar SSRIs have been alleged to cause suicidal and even homicidal behavior. However, the research evidence does not bear out this claim.

Jesse's father was willing to have his son try the new medicine, but he was skeptical that it would work any better than the Elavil Jesse had already taken. I hoped this new antidepressant would be different. To make sure he was adjusting well to the new medication, I told Jesse and his parents that I wanted to see him several times a week to start. They agreed, but Jesse thought it was utterly unnecessary—the medicine *and* the visits. There was a sullenness about him, a kind of what's-the-big-deal nonchalance. Still, Jesse's mom later told me that while they had to drag him to see me, he felt energized by the visit and almost anxious for the next one. So on some level he recognized he had a big problem and wanted help.

Meanwhile, Carol had some things she wanted to get out, just for her own peace of mind.

"Could Jesse's problems be the result of certain external experiences?" she asked.

I asked her to explain.

"Well," she said, "Jesse accidentally fell on his head as a baby, and we've always felt guilty about it." Carol wondered if that accident could explain Jesse's chronic mental condition.

I told her not to worry about that. He hadn't lost consciousness. Then she told me that when Jesse was ten he had taken chess lessons from a man who later was arrested for sexually molesting some of his students. But Jesse had never had private lessons, and there was no indication he had been one of the victims. Besides, his problems seemed to have begun well before he was ten. One thing that probably was a factor, however, was that there was a family history of depression. Jesse's father had fought the disease, and so had an uncle.

I saw Jesse over the next few months, though at times during our meetings I felt like a dentist: I had to pry words from him. When he spoke, it was about how overwhelmed he felt. He was always behind in his schoolwork, and for the first time he couldn't seem to get motivated and on top of it. When he thought about it, he became intensely tired. But after a few weeks, he said he was feeling a little better. His suicidal thoughts had lessened and he was sleeping better. However, he spent a good deal of time describing the world's condition as hopeless—a lot of somber intellectualizing about the state of modern society. Still, it seemed that Jesse had come to regard our sessions in a positive light, and his parents reported that the medication was improving his mood. He was less irritable and more friendly. They weren't sure exactly how this was being accomplished, but they had made a decision that they would have minimal involvement. "We're taking you to Dr. Koplewicz, and whatever goes on between you two is not our domain," Carol told her son. She later explained to me, "One of the lessons I took from our experience with Dr. Barnes was that I think Jesse resented us for being intrusive. In fact, Dr. Barnes told us, 'Don't try to get inside his head. It annoys him.'"

So they kept their distance, which Jesse appreciated. Occasionally, Bruce would casually ask, "So how are things going with Dr. Koplewicz?" Of course, they were thinking about it all the time, but didn't want Jesse to know that. He would answer in a few measured words, then make it clear the subject was closed until further notice.

By the fall, about six months after we first met, Jesse was coming in once a week, but he was almost always unhappy about being there. He didn't have much to talk about, except to say that he didn't know why he had to keep coming to see me or why he had to keep taking those damn pills. In fact, throughout his junior year, he would intermittently stop taking them. And each time, his symptoms would return: he would become less motivated, less energetic, less willing to take on challenges.

Depression had an undeniable effect on Jesse's social life, playing havoc with his confidence. He was madly in love with a girl with whom he'd had a long platonic relationship. But he was never able to take it to the next level. Meanwhile, there were always girls who were infatuated with him but who couldn't get *his* attention. There was a certain passivity to all his social relationships, whether with girls or boys. His charm with peers allowed him to be pursued.

At home, Jesse showed none of that charm. To his family, he was moody and serious. "When we see his friends reacting to him we see that he has totally normal, upbeat, enjoyable relationships," Bruce said. "These people are looking forward to seeing him. Whereas with us, he very rarely volunteers conversation." While it's hardly unusual for teenagers to behave differently with their peers than they do with their parents, depression tends to exaggerate the disparity.

In retrospect, Jesse's therapy with me was mostly of a supportive nature. We talked about his life, and I was understanding and made suggestions. However, if a teenager like Jesse came to see me today, besides treating him with medication I would refer him for a different and more effective type of psychotherapy: cognitive behavioral therapy (CBT) or interpersonal therapy (IPT). CBT or IPT would address Jesse's negative distortions about the world, his appearance, and his relationships with his parents and peers, particularly girls. Today, teenagers with Jesse's social anxiety could also benefit from short-term group therapy with other young people with social phobia.

Over the summer between his junior and senior years, Jesse went to a music camp in Russia with 25 other American teenagers. The four-week trip started inauspiciously. It seemed everyone but him was socially at ease. "They jumped right in, having fun," he recalled. "I wasn't quite confident doing that. I started getting worried that the whole trip would go by and I wouldn't be able to be myself. I wouldn't get to know anyone." Jesse's way, when he got in situations like this, was to "feel superior," which never went over well. On the fifth day, Jesse took out his guitar and started playing. He looked up and saw that kids were coming closer, and soon they were surrounding him. The moment changed the summer for him. After that, kids went out of their way to make connections with him. It turned out to be a great summer. He came home with a boost of self-confidence and a new understanding of himself and "my social tendencies."

Buoyed by that experience, Jesse came home for his senior year and started applying to colleges. He stopped taking the Prozac once again, and once again he fell into a negative state. Jesse's erratic compliance with taking the medication, consistently and at the dose prescribed, made it difficult to assess the effectiveness of the treatment. While studies done since then have found that nearly 70 percent of children and teenagers with depression have a positive response to Prozac, the improvement is not instantaneous. It takes anywhere from one to two months for a complete response. Typically an adolescent will stay on the medication for six months before the physician will gradually discontinue it. More than half of patients will only need a single six-month course. With Jesse, it was unclear whether he failed to have a complete recovery because his depression was especially persistent or because of his tendency to stop taking the medication prematurely, after a brief period of feeling better.

I convinced Jesse to go back on the medication—it wasn't easy—and once again the medicine brought him back to life, so that by the time he was interviewed for admission to his top two choices, Princeton and Duke, he was looking, sounding, and feeling great. He came into my office in December and said very matter-of-factly, "I got in to Princeton." Three months later, he was also accepted by Duke.

For six weeks, Jesse obsessed over which school to go to. The more he thought about it, the worse his obsession became. "There really is no downside to this," I told him. "Whether you go to Duke or Princeton, you win. But I'll make it easy for you." I took a quarter out of my pants pocket. "Heads you go to Princeton, tails it's Duke." I flipped the coin and it came up heads—Princeton. "Two out of three," Jesse said, making his gut feeling obvious. I flipped the coin five times more before Duke finally came in the winner.

Before Jesse left for school that fall, I met with his parents to discuss his care at Duke. I recommended a psychiatrist there who could monitor his medication, encourage his compliance, and be alert to the warning signs of Jesse's depression should it return. By now, it seemed to be a chronic condition that he very likely would have to battle into adulthood, and I thought it was vital that Jesse adapt to that fact. His parents agreed to arrange an appointment with the psychiatrist, but Jesse refused. "I like *you,*" he told me. "I'll just keep coming to see you." I reminded him that no, actually, he didn't like coming to see me, and even if he did, it wouldn't be very convenient to keep seeing someone 500 miles away. But we negotiated and compromised—this was by now the central dynamic of our relationship—and he agreed to speak to me on the telephone if he felt he was getting into trouble, and he would come in to see me on the school break.

During his first visit at Thanksgiving, Jesse looked awful. He was disheveled, and he actually smelled. He had stopped taking his medication, as I suspected he would, but insisted he didn't need it. He told me he was having trouble sleeping and he hadn't made any friends. College was harder than he had expected, and he was considering dropping a course. But, as before, he insisted he wasn't depressed. He thought he was just lazy, disorganized, and weak-willed.

"You haven't kept your end of the bargain," I said. "You've obviously been having problems, and you didn't call me. You're going to have to see a doctor in Durham."

"I *won't* do that," Jesse said, raising his voice. Then he slouched back in his chair. "But I *will* take the pills again."

When I saw him a month later, during the Christmas break, Jesse was a different person. He looked bright and optimistic, and reported that he was now doing well academically. But I had seen this before, and indeed, when spring break came, he was down once more. His parents told me he had refused to continue taking his medication and would not see me or anyone else. He was extremely irritable, and they were as concerned as ever about his ability to function, especially under the high pressure of an elite college.

At the beginning of May, I was awakened by a phone call at four in the morning. It was a doctor calling from the emergency room at Duke Medical Center in Durham. It seemed that Jesse, overwhelmed while studying for finals, hadn't slept for days, and in a state of extreme agitation about his inability to concentrate, had thrown his computer out the window of his first-floor dormitory room, then jumped out. He only sprained an ankle, but then he ran and lay down in the middle of the road. Campus police found him and took him to the emergency room.

When Jesse got on the phone with me, he admitted he'd stopped taking his medication once again, but insisted he hadn't tried to kill himself when he jumped out his dormitory window. "It was just the first floor," he said.

"What about lying down in the middle of the road?" I replied.

"It's Durham at two o'clock in the morning. There's no traffic."

"I'm glad you still have your sense of humor," I said, relieved that Jesse seemed to have recovered his bearings by the time we spoke.

"*Please* don't put me in the hospital," he pleaded. "I'll have my parents come down and get me. I promise I won't do anything crazy."

Clearly, though Jesse was lucid, even making light of the situation, he was a young man in serious trouble. I began to think of the first time I had met him, some two and a half years earlier, when he had talked about suicide in the most passive of terms. Now I felt that his suicidal ideation had progressed to a more serious stage. It was hard to say whether his actions constituted actual attempts to take his own life or if he was overwhelmed and desperate. But clearly events were going in the wrong direction.

The next afternoon, Jesse walked into my office accompanied by his parents. He looked exhausted, unkempt, and defeated. His feet had been cut up by the jagged glass of his dormitory window. He was arguing, once again, that he was not depressed. "It's just school," he said listlessly. "There's nothing wrong with me."

But as before, his parents and I persuaded him to resume the Prozac—it was pointed out to him how well he had done on the medicine, and how poorly he had done without it—and he agreed to come see me on a daily basis for the next week or two. Within weeks, Jesse was better, and he agreed to be treated by a psychiatrist in Durham; that was also the condition set by the university for his return to campus. He saw this doctor for a few months, and then he once again started trailing off on the Prozac.

Soon after, Jesse's father came to me, very upset. He sat in my office in his white lab coat, close to tears. "I don't understand it," he said. "We give patients medicine that they need to live all the time. So why can't we get Jesse to understand that without this medicine, he doesn't have a life worth living? He loses everything." He began to cry softly. Though he knew I was trying my best, he needed to vent his frustrations. It pained him deeply that it was Jesse who couldn't accept that he was really sick. This was more than adolescence. This was a real illness, one that he might have for life—one that could even kill him. Why couldn't he see that?

It took Jesse nearly six years to graduate from Duke. Intellectually, he was capable of doing it in three. But he kept dropping courses, stopping medication, stopping treatment. There were times when his depression was so deep and his concentration so disturbed that he couldn't read three sentences in a row. But he showed some pretty remarkable persistence, and managed to graduate. After he left college, he moved out to Seattle and became a software developer. I heard about this when I ran into his mother in a museum, and she told me that Jesse—now 29—no longer saw a psychiatrist, but that his internist had prescribed another SSRI antidepressant, Zoloft. "He's doing well at work and seems to be enjoying life," she said. "He jokes about his chemical imbalances, but he finally realizes that he needs help, probably for the rest of his life." She seemed wistful as she recalled his teenage years. Depression had hurt him plenty back then. Medicine had helped, but his refusal to accept that he had an illness had kept him back. I thought again of the time Jesse's father came in to see me, so frustrated that he cried, and I felt relief that Jesse was finally facing up to the seriousness of his depression.

I met again with Carol and Bruce Altman one afternoon about a year later. We were like three veterans telling the same war stories, from different perspectives. I remarked that Jesse was one of the most intellectually challenging patients I had ever seen. "I felt like I was always playing with someone who had 20 more verbal IQ points than I had. So he would twist the facts a little bit, turn it so that he could make a very cogent argument. But then it would get distorted by the depression. He would go back and forth on the medicine, and after a while he would see things in black when they were gray, and gray when they were white." On matters of romantic interest, he could be impossible to move. "She doesn't like me," he would say during a discussion of someone he was interested in. "I'm ugly, I'm too skinny." The more depressed he was, the more unattractive he felt he was. As much as anything else, that was the gauge by which his depression could be measured: how inadequate he felt he was in the eyes of girls.

"He was such a perfectionist for as long as I can remember," Carol said. "I remember once, when he was very young, he spilled a bowl of spaghetti and stormed off. He expected perfection of himself. If anything went wrong, if he did *anything* wrong, he would be just devastated."

In the years after Jesse graduated from college and began his life as an adult, his parents had kept after him to get therapy. He was doing well in many ways. "He's a programmer at this very exclusive website," Carol said. "He's very respected in his field, and his previous employer tried very hard to keep him. He has a really terrific circle of friends, interesting, offbeat, just like Jesse. So it's not just that our child has turned into a wonderful person, but that his values that are expressed through his friends are absolutely marvelous." But she and her husband thought there were still a lot of unresolved issues in his life. One by one, his friends were getting married, while Jesse remained unattached, anxious about a series of failed relationships.

His parents mentioned that for the past several years, Jesse had resisted professional help, but he had finally opened the door during a recent conversation with his mother. "The minute he showed some interest, I called a friend in California who had a lifelong problem with depression," Jesse's mom said, though she differed with her husband about how serious an issue depression still was in his life. It echoed the disparity they had expressed in their views when Jesse was a teenager. "Bruce has the view that Jesse is limited by his depression and that we have to consider his life, his relationships, his professional achievements with that in mind. I expect a regular life."

"He will have to attend to this," said Bruce, whose point of view was surely informed by his own battles with depression. "His ability to derive all the pleasures of life will be somewhat limited, I think. And I think this depression will continue to inflict some serious pain on him from time to time. I only hope he is mature enough and aware enough that he will continue to seek adequate help." But at the same time, Bruce had thought a lot about his own response to Jesse's problems over the years. When I asked him at one point what he might have done differently, or if he had any sage advice to parents of depressed teenagers, he answered without hesitation—and in a way that suggested some serious introspection on his part.

"I feel that parents should accept their child and the problem that confronts them, and not always compare or expect," Bruce said. "Their expectations of their child ought to be readjusted. If your child doesn't have depression or any other psychiatric problem and he's gifted like Jesse, you could feel the sky's the limit. You might think you must get him to the best school and that he must get the best job and the best spouse and he must have the best friends. But you should get satisfaction from what he achieves, and not constantly feel sad that he is not trying hard enough. Because with the burden he's carrying, you should feel grateful and be amazed at what he's accomplished. Look at it more positively, rather than have a 'What if?' attitude. I personally feel that it is wonderful that our child has grown into such a first-class person. I'm proud of that. And I don't for a moment feel, 'What if he didn't have this burden?'"

Carol listened intently, and when her husband finished, she said, "I don't have a 'What if?' feeling, but I do differ in that I don't think my expectations are lowered for him. I expect him to be responsible and I hope that he will have the kind of romantic relationship that is as fulfilling as his friendships. I hope that he'll be able to be a parent. I don't expect him to have the highest-paying job; that's not our values. But I don't lower my expectations for the normal satisfactions of life, which are hard work and love."

"And play," I added.

"Is that part of Freud?" Carol asked, smiling.

"The fact that he's neurotic in some ways, that he's hard on himself, some of that is not depression, that's Jesse," I pointed out. "And when you talk about expectations, I would be disappointed if you told me he was an investment banker. And yet you're surrounded by people who think that kind of career is the path to tremendous success. So in spite of everything, he's still the bright, ethical, caring person that you would have wanted him to be. A dream come true."

"Absolutely," Carol said.

"I think depression limits him when he gets out of control," I explained. "It's like asthma. Think of him as not being able to run or go on the treadmill if he doesn't take his inhaler. Keeping depression under wraps doesn't give a kid IQ points, doesn't get him in to Harvard, but it permits him to go if he's capable."

I wondered how much Jesse's parents had talked about Jesse to other parents back when he was a teenager. Was there a stigma to depression in their social circle?

"We didn't advertise it, but when questions arose we did not hide it," Bruce said.

"It was always an issue," Carol said. "I feel it even today, talking to other people about Jesse's situation. On the one hand, you know that it helps other people to bring it into the open, to destigmatize it. On the other hand, it's your child's life. And I don't think you have a right to tell anybody about anything having to do with another person. I just have a very highly developed sense of privacy."

*

A few months after I saw the Altmans, I had plans to be in Seattle. I called Jesse and we made arrangements to meet at my hotel for lunch.

I had gotten in touch with him a few months earlier to ask if it would be all right if I wrote about him in this book. He was happy to help. Almost 30 now, he recognized that his perspective could offer some insight to parents and teenagers. Back when I was treating him, Jesse and I had had some very interesting conversations about his thoughts on the subject of his own mental health. He was always extremely articulate. But now, more than a decade later, I was anxious to hear how things looked to him from the distance of time and experience.

When I saw him in the restaurant—the first time in more than a decade that we had met—Jesse seemed to have aged very little. He still had long, black hair and a warm smile and was in good physical shape. He had the same mild manner I remembered and a certain hesitance as he entered the restaurant that recalled the first time we had met when he was a teenager. Any trepidation I had had melted away immediately. I extended my hand, and he hugged me.

We got caught up. He told me he had come to Seattle for a job, but also as a life move. "I wanted to separate myself from my family, establish myself," he said. He was working for an Internet company, living alone in a nice apartment in a hip part of town. He had a girlfriend, but the relationship was a struggle. As we talked, he admitted that she was right when she complained that he was distant and at times uncommunicative with her. He joked that it was something he had been working on since I'd known him. "I started in therapy about six months ago," he said. "I'm a procrastinator. I've been meaning to do it for years." I asked him if he had been procrastinating or simply avoiding it. He laughed and asked, "Is there a difference?"

I turned the conversation to the years when his depression began to dominate his life. He had vivid memories of the painful day when it all broke out into the open, the day his English class was discussing *The Catcher in the Rye*. "It really struck me hard," Jesse said. "I was feeling that no one was really engaged in the discussion or really appreciated the subject, and I related to the book very strongly. I sort of withdrew. And at the end of the class, when everyone filed out of the room, I just stayed in my seat. Just sort of paralyzed. I wanted the teacher's attention, but I wasn't really sure *why* I wanted it. She asked if I was okay, and I just broke down crying and tried to explain what I was feeling."

One thing I've found when talking to patients and parents about depression that went back a few years is that memories change. Parents and children often have different recollections of events. In some cases, either or both of them leave out significant events, for whatever reason. In Jesse's case, when I interviewed his parents to get their recollections and retrospective insights, their memories were foggy at times, even about something so serious as Jesse's suicidal behavior in college. Jesse's memory, meanwhile, was selectively vivid. He remembered well his response to the idea of taking medicine for his problems.

"I sort of held on to the dumb notion that, 'This is me.' Like, I don't want some sort of external device to change me. I definitely wanted to change, to feel better. But there was, initially, a certain comfort to being depressed. It's a very low-risk proposition to regard the world very darkly. You're not likely to get disappointed, so it's a safe position in that regard. It's like it's easy to be a critic."

"What was it like being depressed? What was going on inside your head that you found comforting on some level?"

"I remember my mind racing. Kind of like spinning its wheels really fast, and just not getting anywhere and being very frustrated about that. I remember writing something like, 'I'm not just sick of things, I'm sick of *being* sick of things. I'm sick of being sick of being sick of things.' That kind of endless thing, and not being able to come up with any compelling answer."

For the most part, Jesse's depression was not debilitating in the sense that he wasn't able to function. After all, he did well enough in school to get into the best colleges. Out in the world, he was able to mask the depression with friends and teachers. At home, with his parents, Jesse didn't bother to make the considerable effort it took to put up a front. "At home, I just didn't want to talk," he said. "I just didn't want to interact with them at all. So every little question was like an intrusion. Even something as mundane as 'What time do you want to have dinner?' I would snap, 'I don't care.' Very nasty." The classic irritability of a depressed teenager.

"When you first came to see me," I asked, "was the depression diagnosis news to you?"

"It was kind of news to put a name on it. But it definitely made sense to me. As much as that thing can make sense. It's sort of like trying on a new piece of clothing and finding it seems to fit. That label fit."

When I first prescribed Prozac for Jesse—and remember, this was way back in 1989, before the name was part of the lexicon—he had already taken a number of other medications: "a whole slew of them," he said.

"I'm not sure if I'm making this up retrospectively," he continued, "but I think I had the sense that the earlier drugs had some effect but nothing very strong. They didn't change me in a way that, you know, freaked me out. But they weren't terribly effective, either. So I wasn't anticipating anything different with Prozac. But it did help. At least in a certain way of looking at it. It helped me sort of get out of the ditch where I was spinning my wheels. I was in a pattern of thinking about the meaninglessness of the universe, that sort of thing, that would grab me and derail me and get me going in circles. Like, my piddling little life was not worth anything, and neither was anyone else's. It was really just a displacement of my immediate, personal paralysis about something. An interest in a girl who didn't have the same interest in me. It was teenage stuff, but I couldn't manage it. It was crippling."

It was fascinating to hear the adult Jesse expressing the emotions of the teenage Jesse. I wondered if he had a different perspective about medication now. Back then, we had endless discussions—debates, really—about the use of medication for depression. *Listening to Prozac,* Peter Kramer's bestselling book exploring the new wave of antidepressants, was published when Jesse was a junior at Duke. It triggered tremendous media coverage about whether these drugs altered personality, and Jesse was firmly in the skeptical camp. As his mother later recalled: "He was convinced these chemicals were up to no good, that they created negative thought processes, which he defined as all processes that were not representative of his innate brain." It was the classic "Is it me or Memorex?" conundrum popularized by Kramer's book.

I remember Jesse telling me that (1) he didn't really need the medicine; (2) if he took the medicine, he wouldn't be himself; and (3) his problem was just a matter of weakness and poor motivation—if he could be a little bit more ambitious everything would be fine. He couldn't accept that the root of his poor motivation was a broader biological imbalance that could be corrected. I also remember discussing this with Jesse's dad, a fellow physician. "If a patient has cancer," I told him, "we have no problem convincing him to take medicine that has really horrific side effects. That's because they know they *have* to take it if they want to live." This may not exactly have been a life-and-death situation (at least at the time), but it seemed to Jesse's father that it shouldn't have been so hard to convince someone to take a medicine that could pull him out of such misery. Now, years later, I faced a Jesse who had been convinced.

Jesse's parents were at one time emblematic of his ambivalence. When the issue of medication first came up, his father was all for it. His mother was not. "I was very aggressive about not wanting my kids to take pills," Carol had recalled during our conversation. "I was on that soapbox. Now I see that it was just very hard to accept my child was so sick that it had a name and that he needed medicine. But having come through that dark tunnel I would say to other parents that this is no different from taking insulin for diabetes. I said that to my kid a million times. And it borders on bad parenting, or worse, to deny your child chemical help if it can make his life so much better."

The fight to support Jesse's mental and emotional well-being had been a marathon for his parents. Here they had a child who was terrific in so many ways—a stellar student, creative, and a really sweet person. Yet they had to see past the idea that his depression was somehow insurmountable and would be the cause of lifelong agony. With the right treatment and accepting his depression, Jesse was now great—despite all the bumps in the road.

I wondered about that night in college when Jesse jumped through his dormitory window and wound up in the hospital. He recalled that he had been drinking and that the incident was precipitated by jealousy. "A friend of mine was dancing with a girl I was interested in, and she was enjoying it," he said. "It didn't have to go much further than that to upset me." This was a big surprise to me because at the time all Jesse had said was that he was overwhelmed by school. "I wandered off from the group," he continued. "I was really drunk at this point but I remember I was furious. I went back to the dorm and kind of just blew past my roommates. I locked the door, picked up my printer, tore it off the desk, and hurled it through the window, then climbed out. It was just a little jump—it was a first-floor room. Then I proceeded to wander, not sure what I wanted to do with myself. Suicide was up there on the menu. I toyed with it. The building went to five stories. I went up and went to the ledge and looked down. I was very hesitant. I wanted everybody to stop, I wanted the pain to stop, but much more pragmatically I thought of the pain of smashing on the pavement."

This was all a shock to me. Nobody had ever known about these moments. I asked Jesse if he really came close to jumping. "Hard to say," he said. "If someone truly, truly wants to end their life it's not hard to do. I didn't do it, but I was definitely struggling with the question. I was just overwhelmed with school and really wanted everything to just *stop*. But I couldn't quite bring myself to kill myself. So I wandered aimlessly, and I finally lay down in the middle of a road, hoping someone wouldn't see me and run over me. I heard a car coming, and I braced myself. But then the driver got out. I was polite. I apologized. I was very passive. I wanted to slough off the responsibility and have someone do it for me."

So was the episode any kind of turning point? "I guess I became more respectful of how things could go awry," he reflected. "So I tried to get a little better at managing my feelings and keeping myself out of situations likely to set me off, like getting really drunk. But overall there was no major progress through the rest of college."

That Jesse has depression as an adult is not a surprise. There have been long-term ("longitudinal") studies that tracked depressed adolescents into adulthood and found that the problem was likely to stay with them. In one study, 31 percent of those who had depression as adolescents went on to have depression as adults. In contrast, only 8 percent of the normal comparison group—those who had not been depressed as teenagers—later developed depression.

I asked Jesse how connected he felt to what he went through when he was younger. "I feel like it's both a disconnected part of my life and yet still with me," he said. "I have a sense of being a different person now, but I have similar issues. Self-esteem, managing my time well, ability to focus. Working on relationships is still a pretty huge issue. I definitely have depression as an adult. Seeing a psychiatrist has helped. This is the first time I really initiated getting psychiatric treatment. Not that I was ever forced into it, but it was always other people saying I ought to do it. And I think I have a more comfortable understanding of the place for medicine. I'm taking Paxil now. It's like a stabilizer. It doesn't resolve your issues but puts you on a better footing. Now, I won't feel like a failure if I wind up having to do this the rest of my life."

It took Jesse a decade to accept that he had an illness that needed his attention and active treatment. That represents so much lost—lost experiences, lost relationships, lost joy. And for someone so gifted, lost accomplishments. As I sat with him at lunch in Seattle, I couldn't help but feel a little sad. Still, I had to believe that although it was late, he still was the same exceptional person he always was and that the sky could still be the limit.

Not everyone has Jesse's gifts, or his support system. But if there's one lesson that can be drawn from his battle, it's that depression is a great equalizer. Whether she is first in her class or last, any teenager can succumb. And intelligence is no guarantee of recovery. No matter how gifted she is, a teenager has to have the ability to accept that she is ill and that she can be helped. The alternative is to risk losing time, experiences, and perhaps even one's life to an illness that is surely treatable.

6

THE STRESS TRIGGER

There are no other words for depression. If you look it up in a thesaurus, you will find a bunch of entries: despondency, melancholy, gloom, deflation. But these are all really symptoms of, not synonyms for, depression. However, if you look up "demoralized," you will find any number of interchangeable words: disheartened, dispirited, dejected. That makes sense, because while only some people become depressed, *everyone* is demoralized at one time or another. Teenagers? It's virtually a rite of passage.

For an adolescent, just about anything can do it, from a romantic rejection to getting cut from the football team to, of course, something serious like a death or divorce. Whatever the trigger, being down for a few days or even weeks because of a disappointment or misfortune is not depression—just as crying over "nothing" or wanting to be alone are not symptoms of it. Parents tend to worry about such reactions, and might even try to do something about them. Usually it's an unnecessary and ultimately futile exercise. At the same time, though, serious reactions to serious problems should never be ignored.

Since depression is a disorder of abnormal stress regulation, our emotional makeup—how we respond to events—is a critical factor in distinguishing a person who is vulnerable to becoming depressed from someone who is resistant. Everyone experiences stressful events, but how they react to them varies widely. Some young people lose someone close, or live in tense or even traumatic home environments, and become depressed. Others experience the same loss or environment and stay stable. The difference is in their biological constitutions: how well equipped they are to respond to emotional challenges and strains.

Bad things happen more often in children's lives than we would like to think. Half of American families go through divorce, and one quarter of American women report having been sexually abused. Parents and siblings die. The overwhelming majority of young people are remarkably resilient. But for some, particularly the relatively small percentage who have risk factors that predispose them to anxiety and depression, these bad events will often precipitate a full-blown episode. In adolescence, stressful events are among the strongest triggers of an initial episode of major depression.

It's been established that genetic makeup can make an adolescent either more or less vulnerable to stress. A recent study by Dr. Ken Kendler of Virginia Commonwealth University found that individuals at high genetic risk for depression were more likely to develop depression following stressful life events than were those at low genetic risk. Thus, if Jennifer next door has a strong family history of depression, she will be more sensitive than most to the stress of an unsettling event, whether it is a breakup with a boyfriend, her adjustment to college, or the death of her mother. Therefore, Jennifer is more likely to have a depressive episode than her friend Lisa, who has no history of depression in her family.

Some of the most recent and compelling evidence of the role stress plays in depression comes from animal research. In studies by several investigators who used mice, rats, or monkeys, stress early in life—maternal deprivation, social isolation, and maltreatment—caused changes in the structure and function of different areas of the brain, similar to those seen in adult humans with depression. Moreover, when the animals were given nurturing caregivers, these brain changes were modified. Amazingly, some of the changes were reversed and even prevented by pharmacological agents, including Dilantin, an antiseizure medication; Tofranil, a traditional, tricyclic antidepressant; and Paxil, an SSRI; as well as by electroconvulsive therapy (ECT). In addition, magnetic resonance imaging (MRI) studies have shown that men and women with depression have deterioration in a specific area of the brain, the hippocampus, that is related to mood. The degree of deterioration correlates with the cumulative duration of depression. This raises important questions: Is depression caused by this damage, or the other way around? And if depression does cause this deterioration, does each episode worsen the damage? If each depressive episode does indeed cause further erosion of the hippocampus, it might explain why each additional episode of depression puts a person, particularly a young person, at increased risk for yet another one.

These are very preliminary studies, but they are very exciting. They give us insights into how specific neurochemicals are affected by stress, which may lead to the development of a new class of antidepressants. Conceivably, with further investigation, this line of research could even make it possible to prevent depression in genetically high-risk teenagers by giving them medications prophylactically. For instance, sometime in the future, perhaps a teenager like Jennifer with high genetic risk for depression could be given this hypothetical new type of antidepressant immediately after a stressful event. It might prevent the onset of depression and the damage to her brain that could in turn put her at risk for further depressions. Maybe such an endless and incapacitating chain could be broken. This is admittedly something of a leap at the moment, and it might even sound like something from Aldous Huxley's *Brave New World*. But I am not talking about tranquilizing teenagers with *soma*, à la

Huxley's novel. I'm talking about the hope that we might be able to lessen the risk of a young person's developing a debilitating and potentially lethal mental illness that causes damage to the brain.

At the National Institutes of Health, Phil Gold, George Chrousos, and their colleagues have studied the stress response for years, building on the basic knowledge that stress is an essential component of living, and that survival depends on mounting a sufficient hormonal response to it. But our bodies were designed to handle relatively brief stresses, even those that are severe. Gold and Chrousos's work has explored how stress hormones function in a complex system that regulates itself. This phenomenon is called "negative feedback," and it is the same mechanism by which a thermostat keeps a room at the right temperature. Once the room is too warm, the heat is turned off temporarily. But in many people, chronic stress changes the system from negative feedback to one that produces "positive" feedback. Positive feedback sounds like a good thing, but in this context it is nothing but a malfunction and a vicious cycle. Imagine how insufferable a house would be if the thermostat made the furnace work *harder* whenever the temperature inside climbed. The house would eventually have to burst into flames. Many people with depression describe this sort of extreme internal agitation, with their anxiety and ruminations chasing each other until they are paralyzed on the outside but trembling with unimaginably intense, distressing feelings on the inside. Remarkably, all effective antidepressant treatment reverses this positive feedback system in the emotion- and mood-regulation circuits of the brain. However, when the underlying depression system remains in place, stopping medication prematurely simply allows the symptoms to return, as patients like Jesse Altman find out. We don't know why some people have one of these episodes and never have a recurrence, while others have them over and over again. We know that statistically, those who have had three separate episodes of depression are at much greater risk of eventual relapse and should consider long-term treatment.

For now, what can be said with certainty is that stress can be toxic. Perhaps no event illustrates the point more painfully than the massive tragedy that occurred on September 11, 2001, in the city where I live and work. In the wake of the terrorists' attacks on the World Trade Center, I was called upon to advise the New York City Board of Education and to speak to the media about the psychological impact of the attacks on children and adolescents. Two things struck me. First, I became profoundly aware of a disparity in responses by both young people and adults to the tragedy itself. And then, there was the national reaction of fear and anxiety that followed. Individuals who are predisposed to anxiety and depression tend to ruminate and dwell on negative thoughts and expectations, and many of us were doing that immediately after September 11, glued to the television, watching the same images over and over. But while most of us could turn off the TV and eventually recover our balance, people with anxiety and/or depression have a much harder time turning off these worry cycles.

A colleague of mine told me about two friends whose responses were opposite to what he might have expected. One of the friends was working right next to the World Trade Center when it collapsed, and was one of the people seen running on television. She was physically fine, but had gone through an incredible trauma. She also lost her job because her company no longer existed. "I talked to her every day after 9/11, and she was like a rock," my colleague recounted. "No symptoms of any anxiety or depression, to the point where after two weeks she asked me if she should go to a psychiatrist to make sure she wasn't just burying it. And I have another friend who totally flipped out because she saw the attack on TV." Each person's response reflects who they are. Some people are more sensitive to stress than others, and some are better at repelling it, as if they have a suit of armor.

Kids are the same way. Some rolled with September 11—not because they are uncaring, clueless teenagers but because they are constitutionally well equipped to handle stressors. But others refused to go to school and had difficult discussions with their parents about all the bad things that might happen: "What if they bomb my school?" These young people are more at risk for depression. The September 11 ordeal and its aftermath illustrate that parents can crucially impact the way their children respond to high-stress events. They must help their kids handle the sadness and fear that is part of everyday life, whether it's a horrific act such as the terrorist attacks or a more routine difficulty in adjusting to a school transition. In the case of September 11, of course, children who lost parents in the attack were at the highest risk. Those who attended school or lived near the World Trade Center and witnessed either the attacks or their aftermath might also have been traumatized. But even those who had no direct connection to the event might also have been at risk if they were biologically prone to anxiety or depression, or did not manage stress well. Parents could help them by doing things to reassure them: limiting television or turning it off (so they weren't being constantly bombarded with traumatic images and news about terrorism) and talking to them, in language appropriate for their age group. The message should be loud and clear: this is a horrible, frightening event, but we are not helpless or hopeless, and there are things being done and that *we* can do to improve the situation. Explain that we have a democratic government that works; that the President and his advisers are taking actions to protect us and make our country safe; and that we can help by donating time and money to relief efforts. Even beyond the immediate need, this can be an opportunity to teach that helping others—whether it's giving blood, volunteering at a soup kitchen, or any kind of community service—makes us feel better. Finally, it's very important that parents take care of themselves and remain calm, so that the children feel better.

Fortunately, September 11 was an extraordinary event and one that we pray will never be repeated. But it doesn't take an earth-shattering international tragedy to trigger depression. Most often, it is a private one.

We know that depression rates for girls are higher than for boys, and one of the reasons is thought to be that upsetting life events—the stuff of adolescence—have stronger effects on the way that girls think. This gets back to cognitive distortion, the negative style of thinking adopted by people who are pessimistic and generally see the world as a lousy place. This is not at all to say that girls are more negative than boys. Rather, the theory is that girls have more of these stressful life events, or at least more experiences that they view as upsetting life events. And they are more likely to respond to this stress by adopting negative thoughts, perhaps to the point of distorting reality.

Regardless of gender, there are many different kinds of stressful life events. The way they are managed will determine whether a young person will be at risk for depression. There are "loss events" (death, divorce, relationship breakup) and events that affect self-esteem (rejection, poor performance in something important). Within those categories are two more. "Dependent life events" are those that come about because of something you did. (A breakup with a boyfriend is such an event, even if he was the one who did the breaking up; it may be that you did certain things that contributed to the breakup.) "Independent life events," on the other hand, are disappointments or misfortunes that you did nothing to cause. Dependent life events are considered more potent risk factors for depression. But then the question is: *Which* of these events are most important? This is a highly subjective question and depends on the individual. For instance, one person may view a breakup as just about the most important event that can happen, while another may place more importance on academic or athletic failure. Moreover, a breakup may be equally important to two people, but it's how their brains process and respond to the stress of the event that determines whether one, both, or neither will become depressed. Here's where risk factors increase the odds. A teenager with a family history of depression, a previous or present anxiety disorder, or a prior episode of depression, is obviously much more vulnerable to depression following any significantly stressful life event.

Stressors don't come in isolation. Rather, there is usually a cascade of events that, in accumulation, can increase the risk of depression. Take, for example, the common event of divorce. Typically, family finances become strained because now there are two households being supported with the same income. This puts added stress on the custodial parent, usually the mother. Perhaps she will have to get a second job, putting further stress on her and possibly putting her at risk for depression herself. This could lead to any number of consequences for the teenager. Her mom, trying to hold things together, might become neglectful—too depressed, distracted, or busy to supervise her children properly. The financial and day-to-day stressors might mean the mother is short-tempered, even abusive. Later, she might bring men into the home, and if she does not choose her mates well there is the possibility she will be exposing her child to a negative influence or even sexual assault. That, in turn, could have its own disastrous effects on the teenage girl, including the potential for depression.

Plenty of divorced families struggle through this difficult period and do fine, of course. But this scenario does illustrate how the domino effects of negative events can lead to depression. Another situation is domestic violence or neglect. Rather than a cascade of events, the better analogy is a cycle. People who abuse or neglect their children are more likely to be depressed, and we know that a child who is abused is more likely to be violent in school and, later, to abuse his own children. Another common stressor, poverty, leads to a teenager having a higher likelihood of living in a single-parent home with higher risk for inadequate supervision, and a greater chance of dropping out of school, becoming pregnant (or getting a girl pregnant), and having less opportunity to climb out of this socio-economic situation. The accumulation of these negative events and situations puts a teenager at higher risk of depression.

And then there is the psychological stressor of living with a parent who is depressed and not being treated. Such a parent is likely to be inattentive, neglectful, and generally impaired in carrying out his or her parental responsibilities. The children will look to others for attachment, putting themselves at risk for the consequences of early sex: pregnancy, sexually transmitted disease, and dropping out of school. If that happens, the depressed parent is not likely to be of much help. So it's not only genetics that put a teenager of a depressed parent at risk herself. It's also the environment created by the depressed parent.

There is strong opinion in the field that girls are generally more susceptible to the effects of all these life events than boys are. But it certainly doesn't mean that boys are immune.

Rick's Rejection

Rick was always a quiet kid, a good-looking and athletic boy who was popular with the guys but shy with girls. He had a strong sex drive, masturbating at least twice a day, but he was virtually paralyzed when it came to dating. He left for boarding school with some trepidation when he was fifteen and was homesick for the first few months. But by Thanksgiving of his freshman year, he had adjusted well and was succeeding academically.

As before, Rick had no difficulty making a good set of male friends, and girls flirted with him all the time. But whenever he was around them he was almost speechless, falling over his own long legs and becoming as goofy as a Jerry Lewis character. Drinking made Rick feel better. He and his roommate got an older classmate with a fake ID to buy huge bottles of cheap vodka. They would then pour the alcohol into small Poland Spring water bottles, and gradually, by their junior year, with their own fake IDs, each of them was drinking a pint of vodka every night.

The summer before his senior year, Rick found his dream girl. He had actually known Kim since they were classmates in elementary school. They ran into each other at a party at a mutual friend's house on the Fourth of July weekend. Kim was very pretty, very popular, and had something of a reputation. They spent ten days together, going to the beach, and to movies and clubs at night. But nothing physical happened. Rick had gotten slightly more comfortable with girls, but still found himself thinking each day, "I'll kiss her tomorrow." But his big move never came. He thought Kim was very flirtatious, but he never got beyond the thoughts in his head.

Kim left to go on a summer teen tour, and by the time she returned, Rick was back at boarding school. They spoke on the phone frequently, but Rick knew that until there was a real kiss, they weren't officially a couple. Once that happened, he fantasized, their clothes would fly off and they would be passionate lovers. He saw Kim again on Labor Day weekend, and once again they spent all their time together. This time, on the Sunday night before he was to go back to school, Rick finally made his big move. But to his dismay, Kim told him she had become involved with a boy on her teen tour, and that she wanted to remain just friends with Rick. Still, Rick perceived—and wanted to believe—that he still had a chance with Kim. And in fact, a few weeks later, Kim started calling him almost every night. They made plans to spend Christmas and New Year's together.

When they saw each other in December, they spent the first few days of the vacation together, and even shared a few passionate kisses. But the day after Christmas, Kim said she didn't want the relationship to go any further. Rick was crestfallen, but still wanted Kim to go with him and his family to a New Year's party at the city museum. Kim agreed to go. But Rick was too embarrassed to tell his parents—who were thrilled to see his anxiety with girls waning—that their relationship hadn't gotten off the ground and that they were going to the party as friends.

On New Year's Eve, Rick had a drink at home with his parents and Kim, and then another as soon as he arrived at the party. He hung around with guy friends at the bar while Kim circulated. After a while, he went looking for her. To his horror he found her in the crowded lobby of the museum, passionately and publicly kissing a young man several years older than her. Among the other people in the entrance area were Rick's shocked parents. Rick, though mortified, didn't want to make a scene. He went over to Kim, who introduced him to the young man, Scott. Rick sheepishly said hello and told Kim they were about to be seated for dinner. She and Rick joined his parents and another family for a painfully awkward meal. After midnight, as they were getting ready to leave, Kim told Rick she was leaving with Scott.

The next day, Rick was so down in the dumps that he stayed in bed until three in the afternoon and wouldn't eat. Neither he nor his parents wanted to discuss the events of the night before. He was relieved to return to school two days later.

The first week of school, Rick's English class returned to reading *Hamlet,* which took on new meaning for him. He ruminated over Hamlet's melancholy and existential angst. And then, a lesson in genetics in his biology class triggered more disturbing thoughts. He became agitated by the idea that everything about him had been predetermined by his DNA. He became almost obsessed with the concept that he was trapped. At the end of the week, he called his parents and told them he was coming home for the weekend, which he had never done in four years at school.

Rick's parents were alarmed when they saw him. He was disheveled, downcast, and had great difficulty speaking. He couldn't sleep. By Sunday, they were desperately making telephone calls to their friends to find a psychiatrist. One of them knew me socially and called me Sunday night and asked if I would speak to the family.

On Monday morning, I found Rick and his parents waiting for me at my office. When I took the family history, I found that Rick's mother and two of her sisters had depression. His maternal grandfather had suffered from alcoholism. And while Rick had never been treated by a physician, it certainly sounded as if his use of alcohol from age fifteen was a way of self-medicating his social anxiety. When I asked him about the recent events, Rick spoke haltingly, with long pauses. He said that he couldn't think clearly, his head was "stuffed," and he felt "strange," "weird," and "not right." His mother described him as "very sad, lethargic, and uncommunicative." His father reported, "This is not my son. He was always self-conscious and reserved. He was always concerned about stupid things like how light his body hair was. But what's going on now is something else. It seems like he can't think. Everything about him has slowed down."

It's hard not to cringe hearing Rick's story. All of us have had social disappointments, rejections, and losses during our adolescences, and we can imagine what it must have been like to see Kim kissing someone else. But it's also easy to see how this is a "dependent" loss, one that resulted from things he did or didn't do. He didn't make his move at the right time—and when he did, it was too late. The romantic relationship with Kim was mostly in his head, and when they went to the New Year's Eve party it was clearly understood that they were going as friends, implying that he and Kim both had the right to hook up with someone else. Anyone would have been upset with Kim's insensitive and inappropriate behavior, and perhaps dismissed her with an expletive. But few of us would have experienced the loss so severely. The relationship had barely started, and yet for Rick it was a devastating loss that incapacitated him and triggered a full-blown episode of depression.

MANDY AND KERRY

As a contrast, I think of Mandy, the 17-year-old daughter of a friend of mine, whose boyfriend of two years went off to college and promptly told her he was breaking up with her and seeing other people. *That's* a stressful breakup. But while she was devastated, and had some dramatic, weepy episodes in her mother's arms, Mandy got back up on her feet before too long. With a little time, and a lot of helpful, supportive words from her mother, Mandy was pretty much back to normal. After a few weeks, she was looking forward to meeting guys at spring break.

The point is that it's not the loss per se that determines whether a negative experience will trigger depression. It is the dynamic between the severity of the loss, the way the individual experiences it, and his personal vulnerability based on whether he is at risk for depression.

Kerry, a tenth-grader, has been struggling for more than a year. Until she was 14, she was a terrific student and a happy child. But that year, something changed. Her grades started to drop and she seemed to lose the lightheartedness that had always marked her personality. Her parents tried to figure out what might be going on. As far as they knew, she had only one bad thing in her life that might be making her unhappy. Ever since she was small, ballet had been her passion. But when she was 13, a serious foot injury forced her to quit.

When her mother tried to get her to talk about what was bothering her, Kerry said, "Nothing." When she asked if it was her inability to dance, she responded, "No."

Kerry's mom spoke to a school counselor, who told her it was common for kids of that age to become both unexplainably moody and less diligent about their schoolwork. He urged her to look after Kerry, make sure she got extra help in classes that were giving her trouble, and keep the lines of communication open. But things didn't improve, and finally the family went together to a therapist. "And in the second session, we found out what was going on," Kerry's dad said. "It turned out that she'd had an unwanted sexual advance from a boy that traumatized her." Kerry said she had been "almost raped," though she never shared what that meant exactly. But the fact that she was finally able to talk about something she had kept bottled up for a year was the release she needed.

For two months, Kerry went to weekly sessions with the psychologist, who validated her feelings that this was a serious and traumatic event and that her reaction was understandable. They worked together on strategies for coping and helping Kerry feel better about herself. From a diagnostic point of view, it seems more likely that Kerry had posttraumatic stress disorder than depression. She did experience a decline in her mood and functioning, which are symptoms of depression. But these symptoms were secondary to the incident itself and its aftershocks, which were both the root cause of the symptoms. Dealing with the episode and developing new coping skills not only helped her get back to her old self, but may have also provided her with tools she could use in dealing with future life stressors.

JEREMY

One of the least clear, most intriguing, and certainly most sensitive questions about depression in adolescence is what role, if any, homosexuality plays. Another aspect of adolescent suicide that has been receiving attention is the question of whether sexual orientation (which is becoming known as "sexual minority status") plays a role. Are gay teenagers more likely to be depressed? The question has been strongly debated in the field. A study cited in a 1989 federal Department of Health and Human Services report estimated that homosexual and bisexual young people account for 30 percent of youth suicides. But others found no scientific support for that data, sparking a number of studies throughout the 1990s aimed at clarifying the controversy. The results indicate there is in fact an association. In 1998, Garofalo and colleagues found that gay and bisexual adolescents were more likely than their peers to have been victimized and threatened, to have used drugs and alcohol, and to have engaged in sexually risky behaviors. In addition, they have more suicidal ideations and have made more suicidal attempts. While there is no evidence that homosexuals are more likely than heterosexuals to attempt suicide as adults, it does appear that younger homosexual or bisexual people, particularly teenage boys, are more likely to participate in high-risk behaviors and this may contribute to their increased risk for suicide.

Many gay people suffer the consequences of prejudice and discrimination, and respond to the stigma imposed by some religious and social institutions by internalizing such negative attitudes. So a young gay person who has not come out may feel shame, hostility, and self-hatred. The consequences have been linked to substance abuse, family problems, violence—and depression and suicidal thinking. Among those most at risk seem to be boys who behave in "gender nonconforming" ways. Those who are especially effeminate and prefer activities that are perceived as being for girls are subject to harassment and violence, and in some cases find themselves being brought to a mental health clinic by their parents—not for depression but for "treatment" of their apparent homosexuality. One study found that this subgroup of gay teenagers is at particularly high risk for anxiety and depression and, perhaps, ultimately for suicide.

Jeremy Block is a 15-year-old boy whose father is a psychology professor. The parents described Jeremy's life as a bumpy road from the beginning. As a newborn, he was nearly impossible to soothe, often arching his back and crying. Jeremy's father was reminded of the work of Dr. Stella Chess, a pioneering child psychiatrist who studied temperament and conceived the idea that a child's temperamental style can be recognized within the first hours of his life. She described three temperaments: "easy," "difficult," and "slow to warm up." Jeremy's dad was convinced that

Dr. Chess would have described his son as being among the 10 percent of newborns who meet the criteria for having a difficult temperament.

According to his parents, when Jeremy was three they noticed that he was not interested in "boy" activities, preferring dress-up games. One of his favorites was to wrap a towel around his waist and put a crown on his head. "It was clear," Jeremy's mom said drolly, "he wasn't pretending to be the king." It didn't upset them. Being tolerant and well-educated people, they encouraged Jeremy to participate in gender-neutral activities like playing with Legos. He resisted them. He loved playing with dolls—which didn't make him unusual at that age—but at five he became mesmerized by the movie *The Little Mermaid.* He saw it again and again and collected dozens of Ariel dolls.

When Jeremy reached first grade, it seemed that the other boys in his school had moved on to athletics and other physical activities favored by boys, and they no longer wanted to play with him. By fourth grade he was being teased and by fifth grade he was being truly bullied. He responded with very difficult behavior at home. He was moody and irritable, and expressed his sadness through tears. He complained that he had no friends, that no one liked him, that he hated school, and that he hated his life. Jeremy's father consulted a colleague of his who suggested taking a wait-and-see approach. At the time, the Blocks agreed with the colleague, who thought that Jeremy's social problems were related solely to his play preferences, and that his moodiness was a phase that would pass. Recognizing that it was unrealistic to expect Jeremy to start liking sports, he suggested that the Blocks enroll him in a chess class, which they did. The following year, Jeremy developed a friendship with two girls and he had a teacher, a grandmotherly woman, who took a special interest in him. His mood improved dramatically. (A development reminiscent of the animal studies in which a nurturing caregiver could reverse the effects of stress.)

The improvement was temporary. When he hit puberty, Jeremy had a full-blown depressive episode. He couldn't sleep through the night, was lethargic, and more irritable. His mother commented that any topic could make him "so touchy and sensitive." His school performance dropped drastically; in eighth grade he brought home his first failing grades. That's when his parents brought him to see me.

Jeremy was a small, somewhat chubby eighth-grader with short brown hair and a surly expression. He avoided eye contact and kept his coat on throughout the conversation. Despite the image that might have been inferred from the history, Jeremy had no effeminate characteristics. He only begrudgingly acknowledged his symptoms, enough for me to make a diagnosis of depression. I recommended that Jeremy start taking Luvox, an SSRI that I thought would treat both his depression and some of the social anxiety symptoms that he seemed to have. I referred him to a colleague whose office was near the Blocks' home, as well as to a psychologist who specialized in cognitive behavioral therapy (described in chapter 12).

The next time I saw Jeremy was two years later, after his parents called and asked me to evaluate how his treatment was going. He was significantly taller, and handsome. But he was still very grumpy, a prickly adolescent who had come back under protest and kept asking why he had to be there. He nodded affirmatively when I asked if he was still taking medicine, but said he had refused to participate in CBT, or in a group that the psychologist recommended for teens with social difficulties.

Jeremy's grades were excellent, and he was singing in a student opera program. But his social life was still limited. And while he had admitted to his parents, and now to me, that he was gay, it was a topic that he refused to discuss. Questions about sexual drive and activity are a standard part of a psychiatric evaluation because changes in libido frequently occur with mood disorders. With teenagers, particularly boys who may not be sexually active, this usually means asking about their desire and frequency of masturbation. I always explain why I am asking and have found that adolescents are usually very candid, despite being a bit embarrassed. Jeremy, however, became defensive and even hostile at the topic—at any mention of his sexuality, in fact. He crossed his arms and refused to speak. He became irritated when I lightly suggested the possibility of joining a support or social group for gay adolescents.

Though Jeremy was doing well in some aspects of his life, I was fairly convinced that he was a teenager who was finding his struggle to become comfortable with his sexual orientation overwhelming. This was impairing his social activity and, ultimately, preventing him from being happy. The question was whether these factors put him at risk for depression. Like many of my colleagues, I take the view that generally speaking a young gay person has stresses in his life that a straight teenager does not. The negative experiences and internal thoughts that can come with grappling with such an intense, life-defining issue should not be minimized. For some, that stress is weighty enough to lead to depression. For others, it's not.

Recently I met a brilliant medical student who was planning a career in psychiatry. At one point I asked him what his parents thought of his choice of specialties, noting the stigma that seems to be attached to psychiatry by some people. I pointed out that I'd heard from many residents over the years that their parents were disappointed—they didn't understand psychiatry and wished their children would go into internal medicine or pediatrics or surgery.

"It was no big deal for me," the student said. "It's nothing compared to their reaction when I told them I was gay." We talked about that, and I asked him how he viewed the controversy about whether gay youths are more at risk for depression and suicide. He suggested that the biggest factor is not whether a person is gay but whether he realizes it and can accept it. "It's easier if you develop later because you're not coming to terms with it at the height of adolescence," he said. Every teenager is struggling with self-identity. Being gay means being different, something relatively few teenagers want to be. "So dealing with it when you're fourteen is a lot harder than when you're twenty-two. I mean, it's not easy then either, but at least you have a little bit more maturity and experience, and you're not working it out at the same time you're working out everything else."

HELPING YOUR TEEN MODERATE
AND MANAGE STRESS

As parents, most of us would love to eliminate as many negative experiences as possible from our children's lives. It's hard to see our kids in pain, and it's only natural to want to keep them out of harm's way, not just physically but emotionally as well. But this is an impossible goal. Stressful things happen all the time in life, and in the case of an adolescent it's all the more inevitable. A slight or an incident that seems innocuous to us may be considered a defining negative moment by a teenager. We can't think and feel for our kids, nor should we want to. But there are important ways we can help them cope with stressful events and perhaps mitigate the chance of their becoming depressed. Here are some of them:

LISTEN

How is your teenager thinking about the negative event? How is she interpreting it? Listen *without judging* and try to understand and appreciate what she's going through. If the negative event involves bad behavior or judgment on her part, it's vital to avoid making matters worse by berating and punishing her without taking constructive action. That's easy to do and sometimes hard to resist. But it offers your child no insight or guidance that might help her avoid a repetition of the episode. While appropriate consequences can be a part of your response, they shouldn't be the only part. At the end of the day, the most important thing is for your child to know that you love her no matter what—that you are on her side.

DON'T MINIMIZE

Our instinct might be to say, "Oh, I went through that when I was your age. You'll be fine." If it's a breakup with a boyfriend or girlfriend, the last thing your teenager wants to hear are things like, "Oh, you're so young. You have your whole life ahead of you." Or the classic, "There are plenty of fish in the sea." Instead, be empathic and open, and always remember that what might be no big deal to you *is* a big deal to them (and vice versa, for that matter). Validate that it's a tough experience they're going through, and that you will help them get through it. It's all right to mention your own experience, but avoid going into the details. This is not the time to relive your own adolescent torture.

Every parent has been faced with a child who feels mistreated. Someone left them out or treated them unfairly. Our knee-jerk response is to not make such a big deal of it, maybe because we want to toughen up our child for an unfair world, especially if we think our child is too sensitive to begin with. But that's breaking some basic rules of parenting: it's not accepting your child with all his assets and deficits. And minimizing the import of their experiences only makes them feel isolated and perhaps hopeless.

BE A REALITY CHECK

The "Don't minimize" rule comes with a caveat. While you don't want to be dismissive of what your teenager is dealing with, neither do you want to let her dwell on unrealistically negative thoughts. She may generalize a setback: "I'm a loser." That's where your perspective can help. Remind her why she's not a loser, and come up with ways of helping her overcome whatever is making her feel like one. Or if your teenager is feeling hopeless or helpless, seeing herself as a victim—"This always happens to me"—be a voice of reason: "Yes, this happened to you," should be your message, "but it didn't happen to you because you're a bad person or a failure." If you have a child who seems to feel excessively sorry for herself, it's important to get her out of the victim role.

These cognitive distortions are very damaging, and they need to be confronted—gently but honestly. Commiserate with your teenager about the real loss or event, but not about the negative distortions that form her response. Instead, think and talk about what you can do together to make it better. If your teenager is having academic problems and says, "I'm hopeless, I'm stupid," you might offer something like: "I understand you feel awful because you got such a bad grade, but the rest of your report card looks pretty good. Is there anything you can do to improve the math grade? How about making an appointment with the teacher and getting extra help? Is there anything I can do?"

GIVE THEM SPACE

As much as you want your teenager to bounce back from a setback or disturbing event, the reality is that a demoralized teenager needs a safe place to feel bad and to express those feelings. As hard as it is to see your child in pain, accept that it's not in your power to take the pain away. Give him time and help him get back on his feet with a "We'll get through this together" approach. One of the ways to do this is to help get his mind off his trouble, even in small ways. Encourage him to get back to normal with things that make him feel good—shopping at the mall, going with friends to the movies, or out to a restaurant. Of course, if symptoms of depression persist for more than a few weeks, it may be time to get professional help.

❖

These guidelines are not only for parents of adolescents. Life is full of land mines at every age, and parents should practice this approach of validating their children's feelings and helping them develop their own coping mechanisms way before they're hit with a major crisis as teenagers.

Kids feel at a loss when they feel overwhelmed. It's our job as parents to help them avoid getting into that position. We shouldn't solve their problems for them; rather, we should give them choices and tools to help them figure out how to cope in ways that are best for them. This should start when they are toddlers and continue through adolescence. The same coping skills can be applied to any aspect of their lives, whether it is family or social relationships, academic challenges, performance in athletic and extracurricular activities, or personal issues such as self-esteem. It's also important to give children balance in their lives, so that if they are under stress in one area, success and comfort in others can cushion the blow.

Teaching adolescents how to cope with disappointment and stress is clearly the best way to help them get through this most difficult developmental passage intact and prepare them for an adulthood that is sure to present them with its own stresses.

7

CRISIS POINTS

It's been said by many parents that raising kids would be so much easier if they came with a set of instructions. I have another fantasy: a detailed map, road signs, and traffic lights to help navigate the most treacherous part of our trip as parents: Adolescence. It would be much easier if every time our teenagers told us something or did something that meant they were veering off the road, red blinking lights would appear. Then we could pull over and fix the problem before getting back on the road. We would recognize a potential crisis and be able to avoid it before it got out of control. And if the problem was too much for us to handle, we could call for assistance.

Unfortunately, there are neither instructions nor maps to help guide us as parents. I am partial to the notion that our mood in general, and our gut feelings, are designed to provide us with warning lights. But the problem of parenting adolescents is figuring out how and when to take the warnings seriously, and when it's best to ignore them. If we misread or fail to see the warning lights, there are places to go for assistance. Across the street and down the block from my office is one such place to go when things break down.

The pediatric emergency room at Bellevue Hospital is a brand-new facility that belies the fact that it is part of the oldest public hospital in the United States. On any given day or night it is filled with physically ill kids—kids wheezing with asthma, kids bleeding from accidents or fights, kids with broken bones and concussions. But there are also, in some of the cubicles in this very busy emergency room, a stream of psychiatric patients, most of them calm but some so aggressive and out of control that a guard stands next to them to restrain them.

The hospital, which established the first child psychiatry inpatient unit in the country in the 1940s, is part of the New York University School of Medicine and is affiliated with the NYU Child Study Center. And over the past few years, the number of psychiatrically ill young people seen in the emergency room has been on the rise. We now see some 120 young psychiatric patients a month in the ER. That number is triple what it was in 1998. And major depression is a factor in most of them.

You can look at this as a sign of trouble—or one of diligence. That teenagers are reaching crisis points that bring them to the emergency room means that adolescent depression is being *both* overlooked for too long and also increasingly recognized. Earlier or more effective intervention might avert any number of these emergencies. On the other hand, for some children that ER visit marked the beginning of recognition and effective treatment.

The emergency room trend is also a sign of what we instinctively know: that for any number of cultural reasons, today's young people are more stressed and more troubled than previous generations, and that there is not enough appropriate treatment available. It is a reflection of the poor state of mental health care for children. Managed care has made it harder to get mental health referrals. And in lower socioeconomic populations, public health clinics that might be expected to handle many of these cases don't have the resources and simply refer them to the hospital. So the ER becomes a kind of walk-in mental health clinic, the last safety net. "Families are desperate, and they don't know where else to turn," Dr. Karen Santucci of Yale–New Haven Hospital's emergency room told ABC News in 2000. True, the more affluent among them are apt to have received some treatment before their arrival at the hospital, but more and more hospital ERs across the country are finding they need to have a psychiatrist, preferably one specializing in children and adolescents, close at hand.

At Bellevue Hospital, we see on average two kids a day coming into the ER for psychiatric reasons. Most are adolescents, and they are about evenly split into two groups: those who have threatened or attempted suicide, and those with severe behavioral problems. In both groups, major depression is often a key ingredient. In these post-Columbine times, when any stated or even perceived threat is taken seriously, many of these patients are referred by their schools. Yes, some don't need to come to the hospital. Dr. Carmen Alonso, a pediatrician and a child psychiatrist who heads the pediatric psychiatric service in the Bellevue emergency room, told me: "We've had many kids who said, 'I'm gonna kill myself' in school and then we find they weren't truly suicidal. It usually turns out that nobody at the school actually sat down with the child and talked about it to find out what happened."

That's because schools and their staffs are worried that their lack of appropriately trained staff may lead to an oversight with a lethal outcome. So they are quick to refer to a hospital any cases involving potential aggressive behavior, whether it's the teen threatening himself or others. And with good reason: according to the National Youth Risk Behavior Surveillance System, a semiannual survey of young people ages 10 to 24 conducted by the Centers for Disease Control and Prevention, nearly 20 percent of young Americans have seriously considered suicide, and nearly 8 percent have made an attempt.

Young people will frequently let someone know about their suicidal potential, and others will use the fleeting thought as a plea for attention. But as we saw in the case of Jesse Altman in chapter 5, the flip side is the adolescent who hides or downplays his suicidal ideation and gestures. Jesse went to the roof of his dormitory and considered jumping, however briefly, but didn't tell anyone about it. He lay down in the middle of a road, and might well have been injured or killed. But he was dismissive of the danger when I asked him about it. Fortunately, he never followed through on any of his suicidal thoughts, which he'd had since he was seven years old. But he was an adolescent who had several crisis points, one of which landed him in the emergency room.

ANGELA'S CRISIS

Not many of the teenagers we see at Bellevue need to be admitted— maybe one or two a week—but for those that are, it can be a life-changing experience. At least we hope it is. When I say this, one of the kids I think of is Angela Perez. She came into the ER one afternoon after she had slit her wrists with an eyebrow shaver right in front of the assistant principal of her school. "He said words that really hurt me," she explained.

This wasn't out of the blue, of course. The assistant principal had had enough of Angela's skipping classes and said some things he shouldn't have. According to Angela, he told her she was worthless, that she would never amount to anything, and that she might as well give up now. Assuming these were his actual words, whether he said them out of frustration or in an attempt at tough love, he should have realized that berating Angela in this manner could not possibly have been helpful, especially given that Angela took rejection more poorly than most people. What he also didn't know was that for the previous few weeks she had been experiencing increasingly serious symptoms of depression. There was a lot more to the young, unsettled life of Angela Perez than cutting classes.

Angela was born in Costa Rica and moved to the United States when she was five; her family moved in with cousins. Angela's father, Reynaldo, was a laborer who would gather with other immigrants at a particular corner on Long Island, where they would wait for contractors to hire them for the day. Angela's mother, Ivet, headed downtown to clean apartments, taking Angela with her.

Within a year of the family's arrival in the United States, Reynaldo took up with another woman, and he and Ivet separated. When Angela was about eight, Reynaldo went back home to Costa Rica, so her mother had to raise Angela and her younger sister by herself. When I later spoke to Angela's mother, she told me that her daughter had always had trouble in school. She remembers getting phone calls from teachers complaining about Angela's behavior. One teacher told her that Angela did not pay attention in class and did not do her homework. In addition, the teacher said she was a smart aleck. She taunted one teacher by erasing what she had just written on the chalkboard. "The teachers would send letters," Ivet said through an interpreter. "But she was smart and she wouldn't give me the letters and actually signed them on my behalf. Then they started calling."

As a young girl, Angela always had a very close, loving relationship with her mom, especially after her dad left. The trouble started when Angela was 12 and began having boyfriends. Ivet told me that she had asked Angela at that point if she was having sex, and Angela said no. But Ivet wasn't sure. Besides, even if Angela wasn't having sex, Ivet didn't like the idea of her daughter being involved with boys at such a young age.

"How is her mood generally?" I asked Ivet. She said that Angela had recently spent a whole school day in bed when she had her period. But as soon as a friend called that afternoon and asked if she wanted to go to McDonald's, Angela seemed fine. She was ready to go. Her mother said no, and Angela exploded. Her mother exploded back. It was typical of the way things had been going. But doesn't that kind of thing go on in a million households? Yes, but what made Angela different was that it didn't end there. She had been hurting herself.

The first major incident had been two years before, when Angela was fourteen. Her mother found out she was lying a lot; she would say she was staying after school for projects, and then Ivet would find out that Angela wasn't where she'd said would be. Like any good parent, Ivet began asking more questions, worried that Angela was getting involved in trouble. Where was she? What was she doing? Who was she with? Was she into drugs? Sex? Eventually, the discussion escalated to the point where Angela tearfully admitted that she was sexually involved with a 17-year-old boy named Eduardo. Hearing that, Ivet became enraged. She started screaming at Angela, ignoring her daughter's pleas for forgiveness.

"I love him!" Angela said. "And he loves me."

At that, Ivet grabbed Angela's wrist and told her they were going to Eduardo's apartment. Angela was horrified—she didn't know what her mother had in mind—but she also figured that Eduardo would defend her. Perhaps naively, she had visions of Eduardo gallantly declaring his own love for her. Instead, when he opened the door and found Angela's seething mother, he indignantly told her that Angela was no virgin. "She's a whore," he said. Ivet told Eduardo not to come near her daughter again. On the way home she told Angela, who was devastated, not to speak to her.

Ivet is a good mom. She saw the red blinking lights and recognized that there was a crisis. Angela had become distant, less open, and she was lying—a significant change in their relationship. And of most immediate concern, of course, was that she had become sexually active, clearly dangerous behavior for a 14-year-old. But while Ivet recognized the crisis point, unfortunately she didn't know how to handle it. As hard as it would be for any parent to stay calm in this situation, that's what is called for. Being critical, judgmental, and furious are instinctive and all too easy. But our role as parents is to respond rationally, to try to understand why our children might be engaging in harmful behavior, and to help them change for the long run. This doesn't mean that parents can't provide their own consequences when they see their teenagers going in the wrong direction. But, ultimately, you want your teen to know that she can come to you when she needs help and that she can count on you.

You can be angry and disappointed, but you still need to be on her side by giving advice, getting assistance, and helping her face the consequences of her actions.

There are at least two possibilities why Angela was sexually active. One, of course, is teenage judgment and adolescent rebellion. The other is that she had poor self-esteem and may have been depressed, and therefore needed the quick fix of having an older boy "love" her—even if it meant the risk of pregnancy or contracting a sexually transmitted disease.

Ivet was right that Eduardo was a predator and a bad influence, but by confronting him in front of Angela and then refusing to speak to her, nothing was gained. Ivet's very sensitive daughter was humiliated and left feeling isolated. She felt worse about herself, but without the benefit of any insight that would change future behavior. The result of this episode was that Angela didn't learn anything and she was left more susceptible to another crisis. It's worth noting that among the findings of ongoing studies of adolescent depression at the Oregon Research Institute is that depressed teenage girls who clash with their parents are at very high risk of having a recurrence of depression.

Ivet did calm down the next morning, confident that she had gotten rid of Eduardo. She told Angela that they were going to get through this. This was a good thing to say, but it was too late. The damage was done. Angela felt betrayed by her mother. At school a teacher found her crying alone in a hallway and brought her to a counselor. Angela told the counselor that she'd had a fight with her mother and that she wanted to die. And she admitted that she had swallowed a small bottle of Tylenol. She was taken to a hospital, but she hadn't taken a toxic dose of the pills—though, presumably, she didn't know that when she took them. She was referred to the psychiatry department, where she received weekly "supportive" therapy as an outpatient for three months. She and her mother saw a therapist who made suggestions about typical parent-child issues. Angela was on the phone too much, for instance, so the counselor suggested a rewards program for good behavior and a designated time for being on the phone, which Angela accepted.

The issue of boys and sex changed their relationship. Before, Angela said, she and her mother were like best friends. Now they argued a lot, sometimes very intensely. Ivet once blurted out, "I wish I never had you!" The words shattered Angela, constantly echoing in her head. Twice more over the next year she took overdoses of pain relievers—once when she thought she was pregnant and another time when a boyfriend broke up with her. Ivet never knew about these attempts. Angela didn't think her mother was on her side, and this made it difficult, if not impossible, for Ivet to recognize the crisis points. Angela had developed a pattern of suicidal attempts whenever she was stressed or rejected. Each episode put her at greater risk of eventually dying, either by accident or on purpose.

Meanwhile, Angela was continuing to have problems at school. She cut classes on a daily basis and was finally called into the assistant principal's office. What came out of that was a contract. Angela was asked to make a commitment to stop cutting classes, and she agreed. But it had little effect. She went back to cutting a few days later. At that point, the assistant principal called her back into his office and told her, "You're gone." He was suspending her. But he didn't stop there. "You're worthless," he told her, according to Angela. "You're not gonna be anything."

Angela began to cry. She later told me that it was an echo of her mother's terrible remark, that she wished Angela had never been born. At that moment Angela felt as though a shock went through her body.

". . . I've had enough of you," she heard the assistant principal say.

In despair, she took out an eyebrow shaver and began to cut her wrist. Blood spilled on the floor of the assistant principal's office.

*

I met Angela on the adolescent unit at Bellevue Hospital a week later. She was an adorable, spunky teenager. Her attire was not standard hospital issue: She wore black spandex pants and an oversized pink T-shirt with Enrique Iglesias's face emblazoned across it. The first thing I wanted to talk to her about was the incident that had brought her there. "I understand the assistant principal said some upsetting things," I said.

"Yeah."

"It sounds like he was frustrated that you were cutting so many classes."

"He was basically saying things my mother had said before. He said words that really hurt me. He said, 'Now I understand why your mother's tired of you, because you're worthless, just like your friends.' And that hurt me because my mother has said words that hurt me." Angela was getting more upset as she spoke. "I don't want to hear that from anybody but I believe that she's the only person that can tell me things that will hurt me, nobody else. Like I told him, 'You ain't my father. You're nothing to me. You're just an assistant principal.'"

"You said that to him?"

"Yeah. He said that to me and I told him he had no right to say that to me."

"He must have been very frustrated. Not that I'm excusing it, but it sounds like this is a man who does care for you on some level and then he just lost it."

"I don't think he cares for nobody. Because if he cares, he wouldn't scream at students. He likes cursing at students. He likes telling them they're stupid. No teacher, not even an assistant principal, has the right to call nobody stupid."

"The thing that's really upsetting, though, is that after he said it, and even though you fought back, you still went ahead and took the razor and cut yourself. Why did you do that?"

"I don't know. I was like out of my mind at that moment. It was like I was in a different place. I really felt like dying. I didn't care about anything. I didn't think of friends or family. I didn't think of my sister, and I love my sister. I would die for her. But I wouldn't even go to her. I didn't talk to anybody. Like I got myself on the floor when I was just bleeding and I looked at everybody and it was like everybody just stared. I was like, *What did I just do?* But before I did that I didn't think about nothing else."

"How were you feeling in the weeks leading up to this?"

"I don't know, pretty depressed. I broke up with my boyfriend." She acknowledged having suicidal thoughts, and said she'd had a drop in appetite and trouble concentrating and sleeping. Some days she felt hopeless.

And yet, I was convinced that depression alone did not explain Angela's behavior or her history. It may have been depression that made her take all those pills and lash out in the assistant principal's office. But why did she have so much trouble attending class, following instructions, and doing her homework? Angela had symptoms of ADHD, and she was impulsive like a lot of teens. But ultimately it was the symptoms of her failing grades, her listlessness, her problems eating and sleeping, and her rejection sensitivity that made depression the primary diagnosis.

Angela's hospitalization serves as an excellent illustration of how bad things can get when depression is unrecognized and left untreated. Not only does depression put a young person into a hole both academically and socially, but it also greatly increases his or her risk for suicide.

Fortunately, most adolescents, with or without depression, never experience such a severe crisis. But those who do often reach that point because they haven't received the treatment they need—treatment that in all likelihood could have prevented things from getting out of hand. In a study of randomly selected Oregon teenagers conducted by Dr. Peter M. Lewinsohn and his colleagues at the Oregon Research Institute, among the most important findings was that 80 percent of depressed teenagers do not get psychiatric treatment and that these overlooked teens are likely to experience a recurrence of their depression. Moreover, they not only suffer through current predicaments that might lead to thoughts or even acts of suicide but also are at far greater risk of leading troubled lives as adults. In following their subjects through age 24, the Oregon researchers found that three-quarters of those who had bouts of untreated depression as teenagers had continuing problems into early adulthood. About a quarter had another period of major depression. Another quarter had other problems such as substance abuse, anxiety, or eating disorders. And another fourth had both depression and other psychiatric problems.

Other studies indicate that African-American and Hispanic youth are at particular risk of having their mental health problems go untreated. While 31% of white children and adolescents with emotional problems receive treatment, only 22% of African-American and 14% of Hispanic children and adolescents get the care they need.

There is no guarantee, of course, that even those who do get help won't relapse and find themselves in a crisis. But certainly they stand a better chance of not getting to that point. That was our challenge with Angela. We needed to both treat her depression and make sure she had appropriate outpatient treatment, so that there wouldn't be another crisis.

Angela's mother played a key role in the events that led to her suicidal behavior, and she had to be a big part of Angela's treatment. Ivet had done well in seeing the crisis, but now she would have to reestablish her relationship with Angela. I sat in an empty lounge at the hospital with Ivet, a short, stocky woman dressed in jeans and a plain blue blouse. I asked her to tell me more about her own background. She revealed to me that her life had been filled with tragedy. Her father had been murdered when she was three, and she had lost two of her children, Angela's siblings—one to a congenital heart defect, the other to a drowning accident. In fact, that child, who was 15 months old when she died, had also been named Angela. "She fell into a pail of water and no one paid attention," Ivet said, starting to cry.

The accident had occurred while Ivet was away from home, working at her job in a coffee factory, and her absence made her feel responsible for the death of her baby girl. She became almost obsessed with having another baby, another girl. Her husband would only go along if Ivet agreed to stay home and take care of the baby. She agreed, and the following year the second Angela was born. Ivet bonded much more quickly and closely with this baby.

Ivet told me that she felt that she had overindulged Angela. "I spoil her in many ways," she said, through the interpreter. "I buy her whatever she wants. She wants a computer, I buy her a computer. She has all the labels. She has so many clothes, her friends come to borrow them. But I am also very strict with her, very hard on her."

For her part, Angela described her relationship with her mother as very close. "We had been best friends always," she said. "We talked about everything—the funniest things, the stupidest things. It's like two little girls just talking about anything. And I love talking to her. But for the past four or five months we stopped talking like that. And things just changed. My mother, to me she means a lot. She thinks I don't listen to her, but I do. It's just that sometimes she says things that I can't stand hearing. It's like, 'Get away from me.' And that's when the problem usually starts."

"What do you argue with your mother about?"

"About everything. Boys mostly."

Angela's newly acrimonious relationship with her mother is hardly unusual for a teenage girl. What was unusual here was the interplay of hostility with Angela's acute sensitivity to romantic setbacks and rejections. The deterioration of her once close relationship with her mother was a stressor that triggered depression.

We had hospitalized her primarily for safety. But now that we had assured her short-term security, we wanted to form a solid plan for her long-term treatment. Angela was diagnosed with major depressive disorder and placed on the SSRI Celexa, which she agreed to continue taking once she was released.

"I have a question," I said to Angela. "I understand you cut classes about three hundred times. Now, you impress me with your verbal ability and your presence. You have a sense of yourself. But *something* keeps you from going inside the classroom. And I can't figure out what that is. What makes it possible for you to attend school, but not get into that classroom? We need to solve this, because when you go back to school that same barrier will be there."

"Okay, I'm a very verbal person and I don't like nobody swearing at me or talking to me in a bad way. Because I have a very bad temper. And I feel that if somebody's disrespecting me I don't talk back to them with nice words. I just curse at people. And I just walk out of the class and then I never go back. The teachers put me down. They disrespect me."

It seemed that what Angela interpreted as disrespect from her teachers was their frustration that she wasn't doing her work, or even showing up. And it was clear she was extremely sensitive to rejection, a key symptom for teenagers who have "atypical" depression. (This is a type of depression, common among teenagers, where the primary symptom is an exquisite sensitivity to rejection and in which patients tend to sleep too much and eat too much. By contrast, in classic or "melancholic" depression, patients lose their appetite, have severe insomnia, and are intensely agitated.) When someone said something Angela didn't want to hear, she took it hard and didn't recover quickly. I also wondered if Angela had a learning disability, or perhaps ADHD, that had never been diagnosed. (Her mother's description of Angela's behavior in school at an earlier age suggested that.)

"I talk a lot in class, and I never do my homework," Angela volunteered.

"Why? Is the work too hard?" I asked.

"No, it's not that hard. It's so boring. Why are you going to do homework when the next day you're gonna discuss the same work. That's how I feel."

"But isn't that a vicious cycle? If you don't do your homework, the next day the teacher will say something bad or negative. Or she might say 'Angela, stop talking so much.' And you seem supersensitive. So then you leave the class."

It's sometimes hard for adults to give credence to kids who complain about school—how mean a teacher is, how hard a subject is, how much work there is to do, how boring it is. We have to remember that school is a young person's workplace. If every day that an adult went to work she was bored, and her performance was criticized—and if she felt inadequate compared with her coworkers—eventually she would quit. So academic failure—whether it's caused by ADHD, a learning disability, or depression—increases the chances that a student will drop out. And dropping out of high school is a crisis. High school dropouts are more at risk for antisocial behavior and problems with the law. They are also more likely to have job dissatisfaction and be unemployed. And those failures will lead to less satisfaction in relationships, which often will also lead to teen pregnancy. All of these are stressors that can contribute to depression. Angela's school difficulties had to be addressed in the hospital or during her outpatient treatment. Otherwise, it was another crisis waiting to happen.

In the rather more restrictive environment of the hospital, Angela stood out among the dozen other teenagers. She was charming and engaging and much more expressive than the others. It was easy to imagine her being attractive to boys, more for personality than looks.

I asked Angela, "Do you practice safe sex?"

"Not always," she said.

"What about birth control?"

"I thought I got pregnant a few times," she admitted.

"How did you feel about that?"

"Scared. But now I feel like I want a baby so I can have somebody to love who's gonna love me back."

At one point during her time in the hospital, she and her group were asked to write letters to their unborn children. It had nothing to do with Angela's fantasies, nor with out-of-wedlock pregnancy per se. Angela loved the assignment, and wrote convincingly of how much she would love her baby. She was clearly invested in the fantasy. It was her escape from the life she really had.

Clearly, Angela had a good chance of actually becoming pregnant. She had an inability to see how having a baby would truly affect her life. It could potentially become another negative event that would increase her risk of developing a chronic depression. Pregnancy is not uncommon for depressed teenage girls who have low self-esteem, poor judgment in choosing boyfriends, and who do poorly at school, and have tension at home. A recent study that offers some insight into this phenomenon found that anxious adolescent girls had earlier initiation of sexual activity. For Angela, poverty was an additional risk factor. It's hard to say which leads to which, but teen pregnancy and dropping out of school are negative events that are definitely linked.

Angela also used sex and the threat of pregnancy to gain emotional advantage over her mother. She gained that power when she hit puberty, telling her mother about the unprotected sex she was having, knowing it was her mom's button and relishing how easily she could push it. She would stay out late, far past her supposed curfew. When she came home, she would find her mother on the roof of their apartment building, peering down the street. Ivet did this because she cared, of course—she was more involved than many parents we've seen—but in the end it was just one more standoff in a classic power struggle between a rebellious teenager and her single, poor mother.

And yet, it was remarkable how attached Angela was to her mother when she wasn't depressed. When I saw them together in the hospital, it was almost as if they had come back to each other. They were both smiling and playful. Clearly the hospital had brought her around, but for how long? I was concerned about how she would do in school, and the possibility of her getting pregnant before too long—obviously a bad idea, regardless of her fantasies.

Angela needed cognitive behavioral therapy, in which patients are taught to understand and change their negative and distorted thoughts. There was no quick fix. Being able to stay in the hospital, although necessary and helpful, was only a great first step. Angela needed help with life management—she needed to be enrolled in a pregnancy prevention program. She needed a better understanding of her depression, of the role her low self-esteem played in it. And it was crucial that she continue her medicine for a sustained period of time. Antidepressants aren't like antibiotics that you take for ten days, after which you're cured. No one has clearly established the long-term effectiveness of any depression treatments; what we do know is that just being supportive is not enough. "Psychoeducation" is particularly important in this regard. Nobody likes taking medicine long-term. But the chances of carrying out a treatment are better if the patient and parents recognize the illness and understand what has to be done.

I had other concerns as well. Angela and her mother needed specialized individual and family therapy. They had very poor coping skills. This wasn't a problem when Angela was young and compliant, but now

Angela needed more than what her mother could offer in the way of guidance.

We referred them to a mental health clinic near their home, where Angela's medication would be followed, and she would receive cognitive behavioral therapy, while her mother would receive parent training to give her new skills in dealing with any crisis points that emerged.

Ivet had a tough job. She was a single mother, she wasn't well educated, and she had a sick daughter. While both Angela and her mother wanted to believe that everything would continue to be fine once she left the hospital, we know that the best predictor of future behavior is past behavior. We knew that boys like Eduardo were out there, and chances were the assistant principal wouldn't be the last insensitive educator Angela would encounter. In addition, no matter how hard Ivet tried, she was going to lose her patience and her temper occasionally. But she was capable of learning valuable techniques that would help her daughter deal with the stressors—rejection, disappointment—that triggered her self-destructive behavior. It would take work. Learning these techniques isn't easy for a mother with a college education and a great marriage, let alone one with fewer resources. But Ivet was willing to take on the challenge. I asked Angela how she felt about leaving the hospital. She had done so well and seemed to actually like being there.

"Are you nervous about going home?"

Angela fidgeted, almost answering without speaking. "A little," she said. "I'm scared of walking out of here and turning back and having arguments and fighting again. And things will start all over the same way and end up basically the same way. I'm scared of walking out to the real world and seeing everything is the same."

"How committed are you to taking your medication?"

"Oh, I'm definitely committed!" she exclaimed. "I know I'm going to take the medication and I'm going to try to change myself. I'm not even thinking about anybody else because I've made mistakes and I've tried to commit suicide for something that basically wasn't worthy. It's like life is going to be hard, but you all got to take steps. And we all got to try to make things work. As hard and as much as we can. I think, my opinion now, I've been here for like almost three weeks and it has helped me in a lot of ways. Because I'm taking medication, I'm with people, I'm with the staff. And when I have problems, I just go to talk to one of them. Like when I'm feeling sad I tell them. And I have my roommates and I talk to them. We stay up very late and just talk."

A few months after Angela went home, she wrote me a letter saying she was spending the summer before her senior year working as a junior counselor at a day camp. She was proud that she hadn't been late for work once. When I spoke to her on the phone, she said she had started counseling with a social worker. Meanwhile, she had received a lot of attention when she returned to school, kids talking about her and asking to see her wrist. "I tell them it's none of their business," Angela said. "The teachers were glad I was back." She added that she had seen the assistant principal a few times in passing but he had said nothing to her. "He owes me an apology."

Things were apparently fine at home. "I'm listening to my mother," she said with a laugh. "We're perfect." It seemed Ivet was less hostile and more direct in what she expected of Angela.

"Are you still with your boyfriend?"

"Yeah, we talk every day but I don't see him."

"Why not?"

"Because I don't want to have sex."

"Why not?"

"Because I don't want to get pregnant. I'm too young. I don't have enough experience. I'll need money and a profession."

It was great to hear Angela talking that way. It was the medication, the CBT, and the parent training that her mother was receiving that were holding things together. Surely, at 16, Angela had miles to go on the treacherous road of adolescence, and the treatment couldn't guarantee there wouldn't be crises. It was just that Angela and her mother were getting better at coping with their lives, a day at a time.

8

BEYOND THE DOCTOR'S OFFICE

For a doctor, diagnosing and treating a mood disorder in an adolescent is often a major challenge. But for a teenager, the process can be frustrating and confusing. And for a parent, agonizing—especially when the symptoms are so severe that the teenager, for all intents and purposes, stops functioning. Or worse—becomes suicidal.

Many of the parents whose children I have either treated or interviewed for this book have described themselves as frightened, exhausted, and bewildered. First, they are overwhelmed by the complex process of dealing with their children's behavior and trying to figure out if it is so amiss that it needs professional attention; and second, when they decide that it does, they are usually frustrated by the less-than-surefire diagnoses and treatments they have received from the psychologists, social workers, and psychiatrists they've dragged their child to in search of answers. I've encountered a number of cases in which young people have essentially shut down, refusing to attend school, existing day to day with seemingly no purpose or hope. Eventually, their parents face a terribly unsettling, almost inconceivable, question: Are their children so nonfunctional at home that they need to be sent to a residential school, or even to a hospital?

One of the hardest things a parent ever has to do is consider putting a child into the hospital for a psychiatric illness. There are, first of all, visceral barriers to taking such a dramatic step. Many people get their images of a psychiatric facility from movies like *The Snake Pit, One Flew Over the Cuckoo's Nest,* and, more recently, *Girl, Interrupted.* They might think they are somehow giving up, dumping their child in an institution from which he might not be able to escape any time soon. Try as they might, parents may not be able to get that mythology—and the traditional cultural stigma attached to it—out of their minds. But it is indeed mythology. Today's inpatient facilities for adolescents are staffed by specially trained professionals and they are closely monitored by public and private agencies. Patient rooms are apt to be reminiscent of the accommodations in one of the better motel chains. The availability of better medications and more effective treatments decreases the length of stay in the hospital. And one of the silver linings of our current HMO "managed care" environment—which is really "managed cost"—is that psychiatric hospitalizations today, like all inpatient stays, are much shorter and more focused than in the past. Hospitalizations are used to make sure the patient is safe and not a threat to himself or others, and to facilitate a rapid, comprehensive evaluation. The result is that doctors can swiftly make a diagnosis and lay out a treatment plan. The average duration of adolescent hospitalizations has decreased dramatically, from nearly six months in the 1980s to less than two weeks in 2002.

Sometimes a teenager is hospitalized after a crisis, such as a suicide attempt, in which school administrators, police, and other outsiders have become involved, perhaps even before the parents. But other times, parents themselves might realize their teenager is out of control, at risk of hurting herself or others. When this occurs, the obvious first line of attack is to contact the psychologist, psychiatrist, or other clinician who is already involved in the child's treatment and request help from them to have the child hospitalized. But if there is no clinician involved, or they are not affiliated with a hospital and can't provide this service, one of two options should be considered. One is to ask relatives or friends who are strong and sensible to come to the house and help to safely take the child to the emergency room of a facility that has a psychiatric inpatient service. The other option is to call 911. Be aware that the police will only take a teen if it appears that he or she is out of control, or if a parent voices definite concerns of the child's suicidal or homicidal risk. This scenario is unsettling and disturbing, but it is very often absolutely necessary. The image of a teenager being wrestled to the floor by policemen and being taken against her will, or strapped down by emergency health workers, is a nightmare to most parents. Nevertheless, the alternative might be worse: leaving the teenager inadequately treated could lead to tragedy.

Just as common as an emergency situation is the teenager whose parents have admitted him because he has virtually stopped functioning and is resisting any kind of outpatient treatment. But even in that scenario it's usually something acute, a breaking point, that precipitates dramatic action. The father of a teenager who has been refusing to go to school for a month, won't come out of her room, and won't see a therapist has had enough. He tells his daughter, "That's *it!* Tomorrow you're going to school even if I have to drag you there myself." The teen threatens to kill herself or physically attacks her father. The next thing you know someone is calling 911—either the teenager or her parents.

Some parents use this kind of incident to break the impasse. Going into the hospital is not only an immediate safety measure, but often the only way to jump-start treatment. In the hospital, a depressed and uncooperative adolescent can be shown that her symptoms are being taken seriously, and that her family recognizes the need for treatment.

One thing that should be obvious, but needs to be said nonetheless, is that hospitalization should never be used as a threat or as punishment. It should only be invoked to protect the child. It's not very likely, though, that the teenager will see it this way. She may be pleading, per-

haps convincingly, that she is fine and promising to comply with anything that's required, as long as it means not going into the hospital. It
takes strong parents to stick to their guns in a situation like this, which
may very well include a guilt-laden tirade— *"I'll never forgive you for this!
I hate you! You're the worst parents in the world!"*—from their ill teenager.
This is all the more difficult when they're still wrestling with the decision
in their own minds. Parents in this position have to come to terms with
the severity of their child's illness. They have to accept that they will be
giving up control, both figuratively and literally. They will be required to
sign a document agreeing that their teenager will stay in the hospital until the doctor—not them—decides that she can be discharged. But the
alternative is putting her back at square one—potentially a very dangerous place to be.

Even after everyone has accepted the need for hospitalization, there
are daunting obstacles ahead. Typically, a recommendation for hospitalization is made by a clinician, who may not be able to see the process
through. This is because most child psychiatrists, unlike internists, who
routinely take care of patients in the hospital, find it impractical to have
both outpatient and inpatient practices. Therefore, when a child psychiatrist has a patient who requires hospitalization, he or she will more than
likely have to make a referral to a hospital that has the appropriate inpatient unit. The adolescent and his parents will be seen in an emergency
room, where the first thing they will be asked for is an insurance card.
The teenager will then have to wait, sometimes for hours, until a psychiatric resident is available. (Residents are medical school graduates who
have completed a year of internship and are receiving specialty training.)
After evaluating the patient, the resident will decide whether she agrees
with the recommendation of the outpatient physician to admit the
teenager. If she does agree, then a vacant bed must be located. If none is
available, or if the family doesn't have the correct insurance for that hospital, they will hold the patient in the emergency room until a bed becomes available elsewhere.

If it's not an out-and-out emergency, there are ways for parents to ju-
diciously choose the right place for their child. But finding the right

place for such an "elective" or "voluntary" hospitalization—one with qualified staff, including board-certified child and adolescent psychiatrists—requires some work. (To be board-certified, a physician must have completed a general psychiatry residency and an additional two-year residency in child and adolescent psychiatry, and have passed demanding examinations, first for general psychiatry and then for child and adolescent psychiatry.)

The best way to find an appropriate facility is to call a hospital affiliated with a medical school. Ask to speak to the office of the chairman of the department of psychiatry or of the division of child and adolescent psychiatry, and for a recommendation. An alternative is to contact the American Academy of Child and Adolescent Psychiatry through its website (www.aacap.org) and request the names of child and adolescent psychiatrists in your community who can refer you to an excellent facility and perhaps help you with the process. Many university-affiliated hospitals have general or child and adolescent psychiatry residency programs, so that the primary doctor for your teenager in the hospital will be a resident, supervised by a senior faculty member. In private institutions, the primary doctor is an attending physician in private practice or on the staff of the hospital. In that case, this physician might also provide follow-up care for your child after discharge if the hospital is not too far from your home.

The essential goals of hospitalization are to clearly define and clarify the diagnosis and to establish a treatment plan for both inside and outside the hospital. Parents need to be active in learning about the diagnosis, the prognosis, and the treatment options—just as they would want to know as much as they could if their child had diabetes or were in a serious car accident. To start, here are some questions to ask:

- What is the average length of stay?
- Where do patients with similar diagnoses receive their follow-up care?
- What role will the family play in the hospitalization?
- What role will the family play in follow-up treatment?

Though psychiatric hospitals will not permit you to spend the night with your child, as you would be able to if your child was in the hospital for a physical illness, your participation is still essential. If medications are suggested, you should understand why they are being prescribed, what the potential positive effects are, how long they will take to have an effect, and what the side effects might be. Most important, if you feel that your child is not ready to be discharged, say so. For instance, if you feel your son or daughter might still not comply with treatment, or is still potentially suicidal and you are incapable of providing the required supervision, you must voice these concerns and, if necessary, refuse to take your child home. Typically, hospitals will tell you when your insurance company will refuse to pay for further hospitalization. You know your child best, and if you have grave concerns about the life-threatening possibilities of your child leaving the hospital prematurely, it is crucial that you share those concerns, and your reasons for them, with the hospital staff. That's the only way that you'll be able to get your teenager's clinicians to convince the insurance company that continued hospitalization is necessary.

There are not enough specialized psychiatric beds available for adolescents in the United States; so young people are likely to be seen on the same inpatient units as adults. All this can be quite daunting for parents, but as anxious and out of your league as you may feel, this is not the time to be passive. Even though you might be relieved that your teenager is in the hospital and is safe, it's vital to understand why he is there, what he needs to get out of it, and to be proactive in the process. Understand the treatment options, and make sure that the discharge plans are realistic and reasonable for you, your adolescent, and your family. It is better to have a comprehensive and perhaps longer hospitalization than to need a second one.

REACHING KENNY

I first met Kenny Leone on the inpatient psychiatry unit of the New York University Medical Center. He had been admitted by his parents, who had spent the last few years trying to deal with a son whose struggle with life had become torturous. Their bright boy had become almost nonfunctional. He was now 14, and should have been in ninth grade. But he had fallen way behind his peers because he had not consistently attended school for two years. It seemed inconceivable to the Leones—as it would to any parents—that their son had refused to go to school for such a long time. They had gone for all kinds of help, but nobody had been able to tell them what was wrong with Kenny, much less make him better. Eventually, they had to acknowledge that fixing their child's life was beyond them, and they were faced with the prospect of taking radical action—first, putting him in the hospital for an extended period, and later sending him to a residential program 2,000 miles from home.

When I first talked to Kenny in the hospital, I found a pudgy, obviously self-conscious boy who seemed unable to say much that might offer some insight into what was troubling him. The psychiatrists on the unit who were treating him were still trying to figure out a diagnosis. After thorough interviews with both Kenny and his parents, it seemed he had social anxiety disorder and, more recently, a double depression: a major depressive episode superimposed on dysthymia (a chronic low-grade depression).

How did Kenny arrive at this low point in his young life? Sitting in her living room one day, Dawn Leone, Kenny's mom, seemed unclear in her own mind about the significance of Kenny's behavior and personality as a toddler. Everything she reported indicated he was a normal if somewhat shy preschooler. She remembered that Kenny was always very bright, a quick learner, but socially a little uncomfortable. He didn't like to be with a lot of friends. He was all right when he had one friend at the house, but he really preferred to be by himself.

"I remember we'd go to a Mommy-and-Me program at the Y when he was about two," recalled Dawn, a petite 36-year-old who had just come home from a workout at the same gym. "All the mommies would be in a circle with their kid's in their laps, singing and playing games. Kenny wanted no part of it. He'd be off by himself, playing with blocks or something. When he got to nursery school and kindergarten, teachers loved him because he was so easy. He was smart, he was neat, he wasn't rambunctious. A kindergarten teacher's dream. The teacher had the kids write their names and draw pictures on paper and tape them to the floor. That was their spot to sit. I went to parents' day and all the other kids' placemats were torn and tattered. I looked at Kenny's and it was perfect. He would just sit there."

"So was he happy?" I asked.

"He was a happy kid, I guess, but moody," Dawn said. "If he didn't want to do something, he wasn't going to do it. And he wasn't very nice about it."

I asked her to give me an example. She remembered the day of his First Communion, when he was seven years old. "He thought I was taking too many pictures," she said.

"Was he nasty about it? Irritable?"

"Irritable and glum. Not to the point that I thought anything was wrong. It's funny, though. My memories are different from my mother's. She told me the other day she remembers Kenny being difficult. And I guess I've been thinking about it more lately, and maybe she was right." Kenny's grandmother always saw Kenny as more grumpy than her other grandchildren. "He always seemed to be tired and crabby," she had told Dawn. It was around this time that two things seemed to coincide: the beginning of his weight problem and the start of a perennially negative assessment of his abilities. He was also hypersensitive to perceived slights from family members, peers, or teachers.

A lot of hard stuff happened in Kenny's life when he was about eight. First, his best friend moved away. Kenny and Chad were born a day apart, and their two mothers were close friends, so the boys had spent nearly as much time together as if they had been brothers. When Chad moved all the way across the country, the separation was traumatic. But it was just the beginning. Kenny's father, Will, lost his job, forcing the family to sell their house and move in with Dawn's mother. That was another jolt to Kenny. The family had lived in a beautiful house in an upscale neighborhood. They belonged to the yacht club. Kenny was proud of the house. Now he was too ashamed to invite anyone over. Dawn and Will sent Kenny to the school psychologist, just to help him through the turmoil, but Kenny didn't have much to say to her, and she said it appeared to her that he was handling things as well as might be expected.

As you might imagine, the situation caused an enormous amount of tension in the family and in Kenny's parents' marriage. They began fighting a lot, often in front of Kenny and his younger brother, Adam. Eventually they separated and divorced. As is often the case, the separation did not make Kenny sad—it made him happier. It meant the end of all the fighting. "What's happened to Kenny?" his teacher asked Dawn soon after the separation. "It seems like a weight's been lifted." Kenny was in third grade, and he had a great year in school after his father moved out. Kenny seemed to blame his mother for the overall situation and, in her view, punished her by refusing to be cooperative. One weekend Dawn decided to take the boys to the shore, but when they got there Kenny didn't want to go to the beach. He wanted to stay in the room. "Just to be difficult," Dawn said to me. It's understandable why it would feel that way to her, but in retrospect it seems that Kenny wasn't really trying to cause problems. He simply didn't have the motivation or ability to enjoy an activity that most kids love.

On the first day of fifth grade, his last year of elementary school, Kenny came to school without all the notebooks the teacher had posted on the supply list on the windows of the school. The teacher, a woman with a reputation as a tough taskmaster, announced to the class, "You're expected to be prepared in my class." According to Kenny, she added, "You're not babies anymore, like Kenny Leone." Kenny cried, and when he came home and told his mother about the incident, she was furious. He was so embarrassed by the episode that it seemed to taint the whole year. It's unclear—and ultimately unimportant—whether the teacher's words were really that harsh. Kenny said that's what he heard, and he reacted as though he had been physically wounded. By December, he was refusing to go to school.

Kenny's mom didn't know what to do about this. Unlike millions of parents who deal with their kid's fever or stomach ache, she didn't have an objective standard to help her decide when Kenny was sick enough to stay home, or when he needed to see the doctor. All parents have certain personal guidelines when their kids aren't feeling well. One parent might consider a fever above 99 degrees grounds for staying home; another might insist that anything short of 100 means a day at school. But there is no thermometer for psychiatric symptoms. And while a parent may take a child with a low-grade fever to the family doctor if it persists for a week, a parent whose child simply refuses to go to school might be more inclined to fight it out at home than bring him to a doctor.

"He wouldn't come out of his room," Kenny's mom recalled. "There were fights every day. His father started getting physical with him, he was so frustrated. That made it worse. Kenny would stay in the basement. We would find yellow Post-it notes about the teacher all over the basement, saying 'Fuck you bitch.' It was really scary." Besides refusing to go to school, Kenny had no desire to participate in sports, school plays, or any other activities he had once enjoyed.

After Kenny had missed two months of school, the school psychologist advised the Leones to call the crisis center run by the child and adolescent psychiatry department at a nearby hospital. "Two people came and went down to the basement," Dawn said. "Kenny refused to go. He said there was nothing wrong with him. He just hated his teacher. But they told him if he didn't come with them they'd have to call 911."

They finally convinced Kenny to go to the hospital, but this marked the start of his parents' frustration with the medical establishment. Kenny saw a psychiatrist at the hospital who told Dawn and Will, "He's fine. He may benefit from some group therapy. But don't worry about him.'"

Kenny told his parents, "See? I told you there's nothing wrong with me." Dawn told me it made Kenny feel like he had won. "It empowered him," she said.

How could this happen? Unfortunately, there are too many physicians working too many hours and seeing too many patients, some of whom might claim that everything is fine. However, Kenny's experience at the crisis center is a good example of a physician making an assessment without listening and giving credence to the history provided by the parents. Clearly, Kenny wasn't fine.

As baffling as the doctor's evaluation was, the intervention with the crisis center did mobilize Kenny to return to school. But it was short-lived. He refused to do his homework or study. And then he stopped going again, returning to the basement and spending the last month of school playing video games. He couldn't even go to his favorite grandfather's sixtieth birthday party. Dawn had been working three jobs, but quit the steadiest one to stay home with Kenny.

Dawn is a devoted mother trying to do her best for her troubled son, but she's a good example of what happens to parents who have a chronically ill child. Exhausted, they unintentionally avoid making a big deal about little things. Insidiously, the little things turn into big things. "I don't want to do my homework" becomes "I don't want to go to school." A teenager's refusal to eat dinner with his family turns into isolating himself in the basement. Similarly, parents become intimidated by the medical experts and feel impotent to challenge their diagnoses and recommendations. Dawn had the right to ask the physician at the crisis center what her child's diagnosis was, and for assistance in implementing the recommendations. Inasmuch as Kenny had to be physically forced to go to the crisis center, how was she supposed to bring him to group therapy? For that matter, what was group therapy going to treat, how long was it going to last, and what were the other treatment options? Still, it's hard to imagine how overwhelming this situation must have been for the Leones. It's also very difficult to admit that you don't have enough control over your child to get him to therapy. But it's essential to recognize one's own limitations in intervening with a seriously psychiatrically ill child or teenager.

Clearly, Kenny's behavior and functioning deteriorated after the incident at the beginning of fifth grade. Even if the teacher ridiculed him with the exact words he quoted—versus the possibility that Kenny distorted the incident and then believed his own version—it shouldn't have incapacitated him. We all have embarrassing moments when we're young: we forget a line in the school play, someone makes a cruel comment, we say the wrong thing, or kick the soccer ball into the wrong goal and lose the big game. But we go to school the next day and we show up for the next soccer game. We keep the painful memory, but it doesn't stop us from functioning, and it doesn't pervade our lives. But for Kenny, who is pathologically self-conscious, it was magnified into the Big Mortifying Moment, and it became impossible for his family to get him past it. By the time I met the Leones, it had become central to the family mythology—one of the defining moments of their lives. It had been mentioned prominently in every first conversation with every clinician Kenny had seen. The irony here is that by validating Kenny's feelings about an admittedly difficult teacher, his parents were not really helping him learn how to cope with a kind of situation that everyone experiences throughout life.

Dawn could not get Kenny to leave the house and go to school or social functions. He was becoming increasingly isolated. Though he still had a couple of good friends, he wouldn't call them, and when they called him, he wouldn't get on the phone. Once when his friend Justin called and Kenny wouldn't talk to him, Dawn told the boy to come over. She thought maybe he could coax Kenny into playing. But when he arrived, Kenny refused to come out. Dawn wound up driving the boy home. Like many siblings of young people with depression, Kenny's brother Adam also suffered. Anytime Dawn wanted to do something as a family, Kenny didn't want to go. One day when Kenny ruined the family's weekend once again, Adam just sat down and cried. Inevitably, parents spend more time with their ill child, often at the expense of their other children. This is the case with all illnesses, physical or mental. But a child with a mood disorder can contaminate the entire family environment.

When Kenny was brought to the school psychologist at one point that year, she found him to be a boy in a shell. "He is very controlled, extremely compliant, and anxious to please," she wrote. "Kenny sits upright, in a tight constricted posture, with his arms crossed and his right hand on his mouth. When questioned, he looks up with a serious expression, rubs his chin and, like a little professor, says 'hum . . . hum . . .

hum . . . let's see.' He responds to instructions with 'all right' and nods his head in a rigid, compliant manner that reveals his anxiety and his attempt to maintain control. Kenny is obviously very insecure and unsure of himself. His extraordinarily long response delays reflect his lack of confidence in his abilities and his fears of being wrong. He repeats questions aloud and provides precise responses in full sentences."

Kenny moved on to middle school, and almost from the first day there was more trouble. He couldn't get his locker open, so he walked around the school all day with his jacket on, carrying all his books. Other kids picked on him—to the point that Kenny started staying home again, first a day or two a week, then three or four. The principal was very compassionate and took an interest in Kenny. He took to following him around school to see what was going on. On the days when Kenny was absent, the principal would come to the house and try to get him to come to school. "He must have come to the house 20 times," Kenny's mother said. The absences made things worse when Kenny did go to school. The kids would ask him where he had been, and he felt humiliated, unable to answer. The next day, Kenny stayed home again and slept the day away.

Once when the principal came to the house, Kenny crawled underneath his bed. The principal talked him into coming out from under the bed and drove him to school. But Kenny wouldn't go to any of his classes. "Okay," the principal said. "You can sit in my office." And Kenny did—he stayed in the principal's office and drew pictures. After several days of this, teachers would come by to give him work to do. The teachers, too, tried to persuade Kenny to come to class. The principal, whether by design or accident, had happened upon an appropriate behavioral approach for a school-refusing preadolescent. This way, Kenny was encouraged to develop a normal routine for going to sleep, getting up in the morning, and getting to school on time. He was gradually being exposed to what was making him anxious. This technique can work, especially with a motivated and compassionate group of teachers such as those in Kenny's school. Unfortunately, they went too fast for Kenny, and without a mental health professional directing the intervention and modifying it when he stopped making progress, everyone got frustrated. The plan fell apart, and the vicious cycle continued.

Kenny had another psychiatric evaluation early that year. But he was uncooperative, virtually mute, and the psychiatrist lost his patience and precipitously diagnosed him with oppositional defiant disorder (ODD), which is defined as a recurring pattern of defiant or hostile behavior toward authority figures. He advised Kenny's parents to take a tougher stand. Unfortunately, the doctor didn't ask enough questions of Kenny and his parents, and he misread the symptoms. With teenagers with internalizing disorders, it's difficult but essential to find out what the adolescent is thinking and feeling to accurately diagnose him. In this case, Kenny's oppositional-defiant behavior was a symptom of his depression and anxiety disorders.

In the summer of the following year, Dawn's boyfriend and his two sons moved in, and Kenny didn't like that a bit. That turned the stress up a couple of notches. Kenny had been chronically irritable for years, but now he was clearly more angry, even to the point of breaking things. One day he "tore up his room," Dawn later said. And the next day she came home and found Kenny sitting with a Swiss army knife. "I'm going to kill myself," he told her. Dawn sensed that Kenny was expressing his desperate unhappiness, but that he wasn't really intending to hurt himself. But she couldn't take a chance. She had him admitted to the adolescent unit of a psychiatric hospital. "It was disgusting, dirty, and depressing," she remembered. "I had to leave him in this hellhole." The doctors there put him on Prozac. Dawn was nearly at her wit's end and feared what might happen when the summer ended and school resumed. "I'm afraid he won't get out of bed in September," she told the doctors. However, they discharged Kenny nine days later with no significant improvement and no after-care plan. All Kenny had to do was promise the doctor that he wouldn't hurt himself.

In September, Kenny tried to go to a therapeutic day school for ninth grade. He went the first two weeks, then started missing days again. As he later explained, each day would begin with "a nervous feeling in the pit of my stomach." His parents arranged for him to spend the day either in the principal's office or in his therapist's office. But after a while that didn't work, and Kenny once again refused to go to school altogether. This principal, like the other one, came to the house, along with Kenny's therapist. But Kenny would not go back to school. Some days he would get so angry he would tear up his bed sheets (not an easy thing to do), books, and clothes. One day while watching the news on TV, Dawn saw a story about two teenage boys who wouldn't go to school. She wrote down the name of the psychiatrist who was featured and called him. He, in turn, recommended she call me. But when Kenny refused to come to the appointment his mother had made, she and her ex-husband came without him. They sat in tears telling the awful story of their son's home-bound life. From the history I obtained from them, it seemed that Kenny was suffering from social anxiety but also from a mood disorder. I told them it was impossible to treat him as an outpatient. He had failed so many times before, and his symptoms were getting worse. They couldn't even get him to come to my office. I told Kenny's parents they really needed to put him in the hospital, but they were hesitant. "Is he really that sick?" his mother asked.

Kenny's parents' hesitance may seem baffling, considering how chronic and severe his illness had become. But their reluctance is understandable and quite common. Besides all the usual barriers, the Leones had the traumatic memory of Kenny's previous hospitalizations, which were unpleasant and discouraging. Each time he went home, nothing changed. I sympathized, but I told the Leones that they really had no choice.

Kenny was admitted to our young adult service, which consists of a six-bed section of the 22-bed general psychiatry inpatient unit. The young adult service is designed for those between 14 and 22 who have depression, schizophrenia, or bipolar disorder and have not been re-sponsive to outpatient treatment. The average stay is about two weeks, though some patients leave after only a day or two, while others stay for months.

The unit is clean, bright, and modern, occupying the entire tenth floor of a building on the East River. The patient rooms, with either one or two beds, resemble Marriot Courtyard hotel rooms, with carpeting, desks and chairs, and private bathrooms. The patients on the young adult service are assigned to rooms in one section of the floor, near the nursing station at the center of the unit. There is a dining room, a conference room, a lounge with video and stereo equipment, an art room, and a computer room that also serves as the site for one-on-one school instruction.

The young adult service is headed by Dr. Naomi Weinshenker, a child and adolescent psychiatrist. It includes two psychiatric residents on six-month rotations, a social worker with family therapy expertise, a part-time teacher, and round-the-clock psychiatric nursing staff. All the therapists have their offices on the unit. Unlike this facility, there are many psychiatric units throughout the country that treat adolescents exclusively. There are clear advantages to this design. The numbers are sufficient to allow local school districts to provide a full-time educational program, and the entire milieu is geared to adolescent struggles. However, many of these units primarily serve teenagers with severe behavior disorders, which can be very intimidating for a depressed adolescent. My preference for Kenny would have been an inpatient unit specializing in severe adolescent mood disorders, but there are few of them because they are expensive and difficult to maintain. They require specially trained staff and referrals from a large geographical area to stay financially viable.

At the young adult service at NYU Medical Center, Dr. Weinshenker interviewed Kenny about his mood, his sleeping and eating patterns, his energy level, concentration, and fatigue—all important components of depression. Kenny wasn't very forthcoming—that's not unusual—and in fact, he told Dr. Weinshenker that her questions were "stupid" and dismissed most of them with perfunctory, monosyllabic replies: *How's your sleep?* Fine. *How's your appetite?* Okay. *Are you having difficulty concentrating on school work?* No. *Are you feeling tired and lethargic during the day?* No. Nor did he admit to feeling worthless or hopeless. But it was clear that this was a boy who hadn't been functioning for a prolonged period of time. Since Kenny denied symptoms that his parents reported, the question of whether he was depressed had to be determined by our observation in the hospital. Both his parents felt that his mood had been depressed for more than a year.

Kenny and his parents were given a specialized interview, the Anxiety Disorder Interview Schedule (ADIS) for Children and Parents. Asked to rate how stressful various aspects of Kenny's life were, the Leones reported that many situations involving "teachers, other kids, having to talk in front of the class, writing on the board, gym class, and eating in the cafeteria" were severely distressing and interfering in Kenny's school life. Kenny, though, agreed with only some of his parents' observations. In his ADIS interview, he said he had no anxiety concerning teachers or eating in the cafeteria. And he said that writing on the chalkboard was only mildly distressing and didn't interfere with his school life. In any event, it was significant that many of the school-related concerns were social in nature.

Like many adolescents, Kenny downplayed his symptoms when asked to report them on the questionnaire. Kenny rated "talking to unfamiliar people," "answering or talking on the telephone," and "using a public restroom" as somewhat distressing—all situations he avoided whenever possible because, he explained, he was *afraid* of getting nervous. What if he couldn't avoid these situations? What if he absolutely had to use a public bathroom? "I do it with a pit in my stomach," he wrote. (His anxiety was so severe that he was known to hide under his bed for hours to avoid these situations, behavior that might not seem so strange for a four-year-old; but Kenny was 14.) Kenny and his parents considered his social anxiety a long-standing problem that had intensified when he began middle school—not surprising, considering that even the most well-adjusted kids have some social anxieties in those years.

The fact that Kenny's social anxiety was very pronounced made it painful to watch him interact with peers. "He's tense, stiff," his father said. "He's only able to say the bare minimum." Here again, Kenny disagreed. He insisted he had no trouble making or keeping friends, that he had as many friends as other kids, and that he had a best friend "who's into the same stuff I am. Video games, computers, dogs." The friend he was referring to was Justin, the boy Kenny's mom had to drive home after Kenny refused to open the door for him. Kenny did acknowledge that one of his main complaints about school was that there were "too many people around . . . it feels cramped." He said he preferred to spend most of his time either alone or with his pets. "It's hard to hate an animal because they can come up and sit in your lap," he said.

So what *were* his complaints? "Anxiety and the whole school thing," Kenny said. Taking these answers at face value, he didn't seem to fit a diagnosis of major depressive disorder. However, Dr. Weinshenker based her diagnosis not on Kenny's report but on the history she obtained from his parents, his school, and her own observations during the interview. While Kenny wasn't talking very much, beyond saying he was fine, Dr. Weinshenker deduced that this was his *modus operandi*—to bury his symptoms because he wanted out of the hospital. And in the short term, hiding his depression wasn't too hard. However, after a few days in the hospital, the demands placed on him, and his inability to meet them, made his diagnosis clear. Kenny had to wake up in the morning, attend an hour of schooling with a tutor, and participate in at least two groups, including recreational activities and therapy groups devoted to adolescent and individual issues. The topics of discussion ranged from accepting their illness to understanding their behavior on the unit and at home. In addition, there was daily individual therapy, in which a psychiatric resident tried to engage Kenny and encourage him to discuss his refusal to go to school and his reclusive behavior at home.

These sessions were frustrating for the resident because Kenny was virtually mute. There were also twice-weekly family therapy sessions with the resident, along with the unit's social worker. The family sessions turned out to be the most difficult moments of the week, because Kenny's parents were presenting facts about his life that he refused to acknowledge.

The consensus among the staff was that Kenny had very low self-esteem and was extremely sensitive. During one morning meeting, another patient, a Yankee baseball fan, made fun of the Mets cap Kenny was wearing. Kenny stormed out of the room and refused to return. He was lethargic, fatigued, and seemingly unmotivated. Repeatedly during the day, the nursing staff would find him alone in his room, lying in his bed. When the nurses told him a group activity was starting—whether it was a computer lab or a therapy group—Kenny would curse at them and refuse to go. He refused to take showers, and his body odor became so strong that his roommate asked to be moved. This behavior in the first few days helped Dr. Weinshenker confirm her initial impression based on the history. She was able to make a definitive diagnosis: Kenny had social anxiety disorder that had started when he was a small child, dysthymia (chronic mild depression) that had begun at least two years earlier, and now a major depressive episode. The combination of dysthymia and major depression is termed "double depression" and is usually more difficult to treat than either condition alone.

My own impression when I met Kenny a few days after he arrived on the unit was that he was uncooperative and seemed surprisingly dull. I questioned whether depression was concealing his intellectual ability, and checked the chart to see what his IQ was. It turned out that he was actually very bright. I was particularly impressed by his performance on the Wechsler Individual Achievement Test that had been administered to Kenny by the school psychologist in seventh grade during an earlier attempt by his parents and school officials to deal with his poor academic performance and his refusal to attend school. The test confirmed that Kenny was very intelligent and creative, and that he had a grasp of the world that was impressive for his age. But the psychologist had found a striking discrepancy between Kenny's written language skills and his verbal expression. He could write but he couldn't talk. And he seemed to be unable to bridge the gap. "He often perceives himself as powerless and ineffectual," the psychologist wrote. "He lacks the stamina or energy to push himself to achieve at a level commensurate with his intellectual capacity. While he feels guilty and annoyed with himself for his failure to follow through, he lacks the motivation and confidence to take control and make things better." In effect, Kenny's psychiatric illness made him appear to be either learning disabled or dumb. His social anxiety made it impossible for him to speak out, and his depression sapped his energy.

In the hospital, Kenny had a team of people trying to help him. Dr. Weinshenker increased his dosage of Prozac, and the nurses made sure he took it. Eventually, Dexedrine (a stimulant typically used for ADHD) was added to bolster the effectiveness of the Prozac. This is known as augmentation: for a variety of reasons some medications can enhance the potency of others. Within two weeks, Kenny responded. He was more energetic, cooperative, and he started talking in therapy.

But it took Kenny awhile to get used to the rewards and consequences of the behavioral therapy program that was part of his treatment. He couldn't obtain privileges—whether it was a video game, candy, or a pass off the unit to visit the gift shop or go out for a meal with his parents—without meeting the requirements.

"So how's it going?" Judith Freedman, the unit's social worker, asked Kenny one day at the start of a family therapy session.

"I've taken the shower," Kenny said. "Can my parents take me out for dinner?"

Eventually, Kenny did get to go out for dinner. It was obvious that he had improved, but it had been because he was in a structured, controlled environment with strangers who monitored his medication and made all of his privileges contingent on his behavior. But the hospital was only temporary; the real question was where he would go from there. Kenny's previous hospitalization had been short and ineffective. When he went home, his parents had still had an uncooperative, symptomatic teenager and unrealistic treatment recommendations. This history made our discharge recommendations more obvious: this time, Kenny couldn't just go home. He needed a residential school that specialized in psychiatrically ill adolescents. There he would be in the care of people who would not be as easily manipulated as his parents might be, and that would force him to learn a more appropriate way of managing the stresses and struggles of his life. They would make sure he took his medicine, went to school, and complied with his therapy. Eventually, we hoped, he would accept that he had an illness and take responsibility for getting better.

We recommended starting with a six-week "therapeutic adventure program" in Idaho run by CEDU Family of Services, a California-based organization with residential schools for young people who have serious emotional or academic difficulties. Kenny's parents were ambivalent. Though they more than welcomed a new approach, they were reluctant to send their son so far away, and they weren't sure their local school district would pay for it. Kenny, meanwhile, was more than reluctant. He was fiercely opposed. "Why can't I be home-schooled?" Kenny asked. That response was a red flag that if he were allowed to go home he would revert right back to refusing to go to school and being noncompliant with treatment.

To demonstrate his resistance to leaving home, or even to going back to his own school, Kenny announced that he would hurt himself if forced to go. This threat was typical of what he did when he wanted to avoid stressful situations. The problem was that it made his parents feel guilty and scared. But the hospital was the best place for this to happen. Dr. Weinshenker was able to evaluate whether Kenny was truly suicidal. She was convinced that he didn't have a plan or any real intent, except getting his parents not to send him away.

At the family therapy session that week, the staff tried to get Kenny to talk about why he didn't want to go and what he might do if he were forced. But Kenny refused to speak. He sat in the room with his arms folded, shrugging at the questions. He didn't seem so much defiant as simply bottled up, almost paralyzed.

"I'll be straight with you, Kenny," Judith said. "You can sit here all day, but we need to talk about this." But no matter what tack she took, Kenny did not speak. A tear rolled down his cheek. He didn't wipe it away. He kept his arms folded.

At the end of his month's hospitalization, Kenny's mood was better, and he had more energy. Not only was he feeling better, he actually looked better; he was on his way to losing thirty-five pounds. However, he still did not accept that he had an illness and that he needed help. Perhaps one of the most important outcomes was that Kenny's parents accepted that they weren't capable of helping their sick son at home, and that he would need to be away for an extended period of time. With that, even Kenny loosened his opposition to going to a residential program.

With schools in California and Idaho, CEDU Family of Services is the country's leading program for children and adolescents with learning disabilities and/or emotional and behavioral problems. The name is derived from the program's guiding principle—"See and Do," or "See yourself as you are and do something with it." It was founded in 1967 by Mel Wasserman, a Palm Springs businessman who wanted to establish a place for young people to learn and grow. He sold his business, bought a ranch, and began what has become a major educational alternative for young people with psychiatric disorders.

The program that we thought was right for Kenny is called Ascent; it is designed for teenagers between 13 and 17 who have emotional difficulties but are not suicidal. Situated in Idaho's Selkirk Mountains, the program seeks to change negative behavioral patterns, enhance feelings of self-worth, foster introspection, and improve family relationships. It helps kids accept that if they have a psychiatric disorder, they have to do something about it, including taking medication and participating in therapy. The message is that their psychiatric problem is not an excuse to stay away from school. They have to take responsibility for their lives. At the conclusion of an intensive six-week introductory therapeutic program, they can move on to the CEDU residential school.

Though its goals are lofty, the place is something of an emotional boot camp. Kenny would be sleeping in a large tent with other boys, and doing a lot of Outward Bound–type activities to build self-esteem and create a sense of accomplishment. He would work with other kids and learn to rely on them and in turn be relied on. There would be no TV or video games. Getting to read a magazine was a special privilege. Some "boot camp" programs are pure tough love, with little regard for understanding psychiatric illness. They can be abusive, and some young people have died during the experience. But programs like CEDU reflect a much more sophisticated approach. It is neither a mean place nor an undemanding one. It tells the kid, "We're taking this very seriously. We're getting you on a regular schedule. We're going to help you fight this depression."

Part of the idea was to take Kenny away from his parents, out of the environment he had found so accommodating—something like the old idea of sending severely asthmatic children to Arizona. It is akin to sending a child who's been in a terrible accident to a rehab facility for intensive therapy after surgery. We wouldn't expect the child to be able to talk his parents into keeping him home when that wasn't what he needed for his health.

The roots of residential schools for troubled kids go back to the late 1940s, when Bruno Bettleheim, the controversial psychiatrist, assumed that the problem was toxic parents. Today, however, well-run residential programs like CEDU recognize that parents don't create these disorders. Rather, children with psychiatric disorders require superparenting, and when they don't get such extraordinary attention, their illness frequently leads them to manipulate their parents, which makes their condition worse.

The problem for Kenny's parents was paying for it. The Ascent program alone was $15,000. And then the residential school would cost $60,000 for a year. Dawn went to her local school district to see what could be done. By law in New York State, the district had to provide for alternative education if the regular local program was deemed inadequate or inappropriate for his needs. The school district said at first that it paid for education, not therapy, but with our support the Leones fought and won. Kenny agreed to go. But the program turned out to be a little too much for him. On the third day, Kenny's mother got a call that Kenny had hurt his leg during a log-rolling activity; X-rays showed that Kenny had stress fractures in both legs. "He gave it his best shot," Dawn said. "But this is a kid who hasn't moved off his bed in two years." She felt she had no choice but to bring him home.

It was all too familiar. Kenny went back into hibernation. He was nasty to his family, and he resisted and then stopped taking his medications, which Dawn felt had been having a definite positive effect. Now what? We recommended another residential school, closer to home. It was less structured than CEDU, and the academic program was looser, at least for the summer. Kenny could also come home on weekends if he met the weekday requirements. He agreed to give it a try. If things went well, they could consider having him stay there for the day program in the fall. But Kenny was soon making things difficult. Dawn got a call from the school saying Kenny was refusing to take his medication. I took a hard line with Dawn, hoping she would do the same with Kenny.

"There shouldn't be any discussion of taking the medicine," I told her. "Would you ever discuss taking medicine if Kenny had a physical illness?"

I asked Dawn what Kenny's day was like at the school. "The summer program is a joke," she said. "Nothing is forced. They can sit in their room all day if they want to. So what do you think Kenny does every day? I don't know how much to push. Maybe he's in the wrong program." Like many parents in this situation, she was concerned about whether her child was in the wrong program. But in this case, she had a point. This program did not seem to be what Kenny needed.

Home on the weekends, Kenny was back to his old ways. He refused to go to a christening, which led to an argument, which led to Kenny crying and saying, "I hate myself."

Even so, even after the failure at CEDU and the trouble at his new school, Dawn felt that Kenny's mood was actually better. The combination of Prozac and Dexedrine did seem to lessen his depression. He looked better, he seemed less pessimistic. One weekend, Kenny appeared almost happy, even as he prepared to go back to the residential school. "Hey, Mom," he said brightly, "let's go early and stop at that big mall." His mother was thrilled to hear any glimmer of excitement in Kenny's voice.

But, of course, once the depression lifts, there's still reality. And Kenny's reality was this: he was still weighed down by social anxiety, and he was now two years behind in school. I was reminded of another adolescent with major depression who was being followed by a colleague at the Child Study Center. He was a teenager who had stopped going to school or even leaving the house at 14. By the time his depression finally remitted, he was under a mountain. Being a teenager is hard enough. Add severe, debilitating depression and it can be a tremendous challenge to recover completely. At its worst (short of suicide) if an adult slips into a depression, she might have to stop going to work. But when it finally lifts, she can return to her life. She will still have her friends. Someone becoming depressed during the teen years, though, might find herself lost. She has to go back and learn algebra. She still hasn't had her first kiss. She's isolated from her peers. Kenny's illness was all the more difficult because it was so insidious. His dysthymia had been impairing him for years, and when he also had depression it incapacitated him.

Eventually, Kenny got into the swim of day-to-day living at the residential school. He started to understand that he was in for a long-term struggle, and it wasn't just his parents, teachers, and therapists who had to fight the battle. He couldn't do it alone, but he had to be an active participant. He would have to learn new skills for dealing with his social anxiety, and he would have to start trying to make up for all the time he had lost. It would definitely be a year before a decision could be made about when he could go back to living at home.

Getting to this hopeful point was a feat in itself, and took a very long time—too long. It was years before anyone considered that Kenny was depressed, or that he might be helped by medication. His parents were initially advised to put him into basic talk therapy. But neither individual nor group therapy has ever been shown to be effective in treating depression or dysthymia. The Leones lived in a wealthy, suburban community. Yet, Kenny was absent 48 days from a special school before there was any intervention by the school. There were diagnoses that seemed incomplete, treatment plans that were ill-conceived and unrealistic, and poor compliance with treatments that could have been effective.

Teenagers like Kenny Leone are not exactly common; nor are they rare. Which means that there are many parents like the Leones, trying their best to deal with a frustrating, demoralizing situation. Kenny's case shows how important parenting is—not that bad parenting causes kids to be depressed, but that it takes *exceptional* parenting to deal with it. It's not easy keeping your own sanity and tending to your spouse and your other children—all the while trying to navigate the mental health and educational systems for your ill teenager.

As the Leones can attest, parents have to be armed for the challenges of having a psychiatrically ill child. That may mean accepting when a child can't be treated as an outpatient and continue to live at home. Moreover, as intimidating as it might be, it's essential to ask the professionals to explain their thinking, and at times to question it and get second opinions. Here are a few questions that parents should always ask clinicians:

- What is the diagnosis, and how did you arrive at it?
- What is the success rate of the treatment you are recommending?
- How long will it take before we can expect to see results?
- What kind of patients typically attend the program you are recommending? (For inpatient and residential programs and special schools.)
- How do you know when my child is finished with treatment (or is ready to be discharged from an inpatient program)?

When I last saw Kenny, I thought he had a chance. I don't always feel that way. He's out of the house, and he has parents who aren't giving up. It was their recognition of the severity of their son's illness, the limitations of their ability to help him, and the need for intensive residential treatment that turned the tide.

For Kenny, every day is like a building block. Every time that he has a positive encounter with a peer, every time he accomplishes something in a class, he is adding to the foundation. Self-esteem is built on real events. The jury is still out on whether Kenny rises above his long and debilitating illness, but at the very least his parents can know that they are giving him his best chance.

9

YOUNG AND BIPOLAR

One of the raging debates in psychiatry is over how common bipolar disorder (BPD)—more traditionally known as manic depression—is among children. The root of the question is the difficulty, familiar to any parent of a child with any sort of mental handicap, of diagnosing psychiatric disorders in the young. As any number of teenagers described in this book demonstrate, so many things are happening—or may be happening—all at once in the young, developing brain. And that includes a lot of *normal* things. So giving a meaningful and satisfying diagnosis to whatever's wrong, something that many parents search for, is a real challenge.

Perhaps nowhere is this dilemma more striking than in the case of bipolar disorder, which in adults is characterized by episodes of extraordinary energy and racing and grandiose thoughts, alternating with peri-

ods of deep, sometimes paralyzing depression. The classic form of the illness typically emerges in late adolescence or early adulthood. The question is whether behavior marked by irritability and rapid mood swings in
children is a juvenile form of the disorder that continues into the classic
adult form. If you are the parent of a teenager, you can be forgiven for
being puzzled by the phrase "rapid mood swings." Isn't that, you might
ask, the very definition of normal teenage behavior? Actually, no. To be
sure, teenagers have mood swings. But for a person with bipolar disorder,
these swings are extreme and potentially self-destructive. The debate
centers on whether, or at what point, we can be confident that a child has
developed lifelong bipolar disorder. It is a vital question. Though it is
highly treatable, if left unattended, classic bipolar disorder is a very dangerous illness. A staggering 80 percent of adults with BPD have suicidal thoughts, and 15 percent of those with the disorder do eventually
commit suicide. Among adolescents, clinical samples suggest that the
suicide-attempt rate for bipolar disorder may be as high as 40 percent.
Meanwhile, nearly one quarter of adolescents who do commit suicide
have bipolar disorder.

Doctors have for many years considered children with explosive personalities to be good candidates for a diagnosis of attention deficit hyperactivity disorder. Children with ADHD are hyperactive, impulsive,
inattentive, or easily distracted (as distinguished from attention deficit
disorder [ADD], which has the attention problems without the hyperactivity). Now, there is a school of thought that as many as one in five
preadolescent children diagnosed with ADHD is really suffering from
"juvenile BPD," with some overlapping symptoms of ADHD. But many
clinicians and researchers disagree with this estimate. In two studies that
followed ADHD children for nearly twenty years, there was no greater
prevalence of bipolar disorder or any mood disorder than there was with
control subjects. Moreover, bipolar adults rarely report that their mood
and behavior swings began in childhood, and few parents of children diagnosed with ADHD describe their children as manic or euphoric.
There is a small group of children who are chronically difficult—hyper-

sensitive, explosive, and impulsive. Whether this is a variant of ADHD or some type of mood disorder is still an open question.

While some of the symptoms of ADHD can resemble those of bipolar disorder, a young person's history should help distinguish the two. The fundamental difference is that bipolar disorder is episodic, while ADHD is chronic. Adults with classic bipolar disorder will have mood swings that run in cycles—distinct periods of mania or depression, each lasting weeks to months, with the possibility of returning to "normal" mood states that can also last for prolonged periods. When medications called mood stabilizers work effectively, this normal state can last for years.

In the manic state, a person with BPD will feel as though his thoughts are racing, he will be expansive and talkative, and he may go through many wild mood swings in a fixed period of time before the symptoms all but disappear or give way to depression. In contrast, someone with ADHD is impulsive, inattentive, and hyperactive nearly all the time, in most situations, and his behavior is driven by impulsivity, not mood.

Another difference between the two disorders is that children with ADHD generally don't start exhibiting symptoms out of the blue when they become teenagers. Their parents usually notice their hyperactivity, inattention, and impulsivity from an early age, before age six. Manic depressives, meanwhile, don't exhibit their illness until much later—in some cases before puberty but most often in adolescence.

The controversy lies in the contention by those who recognize "juvenile BPD" that preadolescent children have a different type of manic episode, one marked by irritability and extremely rapid cycling of mood, with episodes lasting as briefly as hours or even minutes. To date, we have not been able to sort this out. Eventually, when long-term, or longitudinal, studies are done on a group of children who are diagnosed with "juvenile BPD," we will be able to have a more definitive answer.

Unfortunately, as is the case with all psychiatric disorders, there is no brain scan or blood test that makes the diagnosis of bipolar disorder a hard science. And because "unipolar" depression is vastly more common than bipolar disorder, in adults as well as in adolescents, most child and adolescent psychiatrists and psychologists have limited experience diagnosing and treating bipolar disorder. To complicate matters, it's estimated that half the children who are diagnosed with bipolar disorder may *also* have ADHD. Making the right diagnosis is of paramount importance because it will determine the treatment. Medicines are used to treat both disorders, but failing to take the right one can deprive someone of the proper treatment.

Since this is a book about teenagers, I will happily step back from the treacherous (and at the moment wide-open) question of how prevalent bipolar illness is in preadolescence. There is plenty to be said about the disorder in the teen years. Of central importance is that the condition frequently begins with a depressive episode during adolescence, and that teenagers with major depressive disorder are at increased risk for bipolar disorder. Factors that seem to predict which adolescent depressives will become bipolar include the age at which the first episode of depression occurs (the earlier the depression, the higher the chances); whether the initial depression has any psychotic features; whether symptoms of mania develop during treatment with antidepressants; and a family history of bipolar illness.

Several major events associated with late adolescence can be triggers for bipolar disorder, just as they can be for unipolar depression: going away to college, separating from parents and family, adjusting to new social demands, and sexual and academic pressures. And any of the classic triggers for major depression—a serious loss or setback, chronic illness— can also activate bipolar disorder in vulnerable individuals. It's not known what causes either bipolar or unipolar depression, although most researchers believe that they are the result of an imbalance of brain chemistry. Insufficient serotonin and a dysregulation of norepinephrine are likely associated with manic episodes. Lithium, the most commonly prescribed medication for bipolar disorder, affects both brain chemicals.

There is strong evidence of a genetic predisposition to bipolar disorder. More than half of all people diagnosed with the disorder have a relative who has either bipolar disorder or depression. Studies of identical twins—who share all their genes—have found that when one has bipolar disorder the other will also have it 65 percent of the time. In contrast, this occurs only 14 percent of the time with fraternal twins. Other studies have found that adopted children whose biological relatives have the disorder have a 31 percent chance of having it themselves. If the biological relatives do not have it, the child's chances are only 2 percent.

Though bipolar disorder tends to begin with an episode of depression, manic symptoms can also be the first sign. These include:

- Abrupt or gradual changes in mood, which can include unrealistic highs in self-esteem or delusions of grandeur (for example, a teenager who feels all-powerful or like a superhero with special powers); great increase in energy and the ability to go with little or no sleep for days without feeling tired; increased talking and rapid speech (the adolescent talks too much and too fast, changes topics too quickly, and cannot be interrupted); and uncharacteristic engagement in activities or projects to the detriment of usual relationships.
- Marked increase in sexual interest and activity that may include masturbating multiple times a day and having indiscriminate, risky sex that is out of character.
- Abuse of alcohol or drugs, reckless driving, or other dangerous behaviors. (This doesn't mean that a teenager who does these things has bipolar disorder, only that these behaviors can be part of the package.)

Some of these symptoms of mania—as well as the symptoms of depression discussed throughout the previous chapters—can be signals of other problems, such as substance abuse, delinquency, ADHD, and even schizophrenia. And it may very well be that a patient has both bipolar and another psychiatric disorder. The vast majority of adolescents with

BPD—between 70 and 90 percent, according to various studies—also
have a comorbid mental disorder, such as disruptive behavior, anxiety
disorder, or substance abuse. In fact, it's the rare adolescent who has
"pure" bipolar disorder.

This strong tendency for bipolar illness to be accompanied by another disorder complicates treatment decisions and is one of the reasons
that those with BPD are at such high risk of attempting suicide. It's also
why a correct diagnosis can be made only with careful observation over
an extended period of time. Though there is vigorous debate about the
prevalence of bipolar disorder among children, in adolescents and adults
it seems clear that BPD is generally undertreated. Studies of "psychological autopsies"—examinations of suicide victims' mental history and state,
based on health records and interviews with family members and friends—
show that among adult suicide victims who had symptoms or even a diagnosis of bipolar disorder, a very small percentage were being adequately
treated. This is even more commonly the case with adolescents because of
the problems with diagnosis. The bottom line is that a parent of a young
person exhibiting the warning signs of bipolar disorder should not hesitate to seek help in trying to clarify the diagnosis and develop an effective treatment plan.

In adults with BPD, the best and most common way to treat the disorder is still with the mood stabilizer lithium (sold both as generic
lithium chloride and as the brand names Eskalith or Lithobid, which are
longer lasting). For the majority of patients, it offers the most effective
long-term prevention of manic episodes and suicidal behavior, as well as
an effective treatment of a first episode of mania after it has begun. Anticonvulsant medicines such as Depakote and Tegretol are also used to
treat manic episodes, though there is no evidence that they are as effective as lithium at *preventing* mania and suicide. (For a more extensive
look at the treatment of bipolar disorder, see chapter 12.)

PAULA'S BREAK

Early in my career, when I was still a resident, I had a patient named Paula, a 19-year-old sophomore at a small college in Virginia. She came from an upper-middle-class home, had gone to a Catholic high school, and had always been a "good girl." She was friendly, sweet, and compliant with her parents. She had adjusted nicely to college and was doing well academically and socially during her first three semesters.

Toward the end of her sophomore year, Paula decided she would spend the first semester of her junior year in France. But that spring, a couple of months before she was to leave, out of nowhere Paula's sleep became erratic. Her parents started getting phone calls from their friends and relatives saying they were receiving "weird" letters from Paula. I later saw the letters. Paula rambled on about how she wanted to get in touch with the recipients to tell them how much she wanted "to be me." But besides the content of the letters, what was alarming was how many of them she wrote. There were 60 in all, to friends, neighbors, and even distant relatives, each one handwritten.

When Paula's worried parents called her, they found her sounding very "pressured," in her mother's words, and tearful. They remembered that earlier in the semester, she had seemed sad when they talked to her during their regular Sunday night phone call. Now they wanted her to come home; they decided they needed to go get her. When they arrived at Paula's dormitory room, her roommate told them that Paula hadn't slept in four days, she was hardly eating, and she was unbelievably stressed. "She's constantly talking about how nobody's letting her be the way she wants to be," the roommate said. Just then, Paula came into the room. She was wearing a miniskirt and a tight halter top that she had borrowed from a girl in her dorm. Her long brown hair was a mess, she looked pale and thin. Her mother later told me, "With the sexy-looking clothes and being so thin, I barely recognized her."

Paula's parents hugged her and sat down to talk.

"We think you should come home for a few days," her mother said.

"No, that wouldn't be the right thing," Paula said. "I've got to be myself and the only place I can do that is in France."

All Paula's mother could think was that her daughter was having some kind of "nervous breakdown." They managed to persuade her to come home for the weekend. But at home, Paula got one phone call after another from young men. At one point, her mother eavesdropped on a conversation and was shocked at the lewd talk. It sounded as if Paula had had sex with two or three men at once. When she confronted her, Paula began screaming and smashing things. Her mother called the police, and in the emergency room of the local hospital a doctor noted "confused, delusional thinking." Taking a family history, he learned that Paula's father had been diagnosed with schizophrenia. He put her on the psychiatric unit with an admission diagnosis of "psychotic—rule out schizophrenia." She began taking Haldol, an antipsychotic drug.

After two weeks, Paula was transferred to New York Hospital, where I was serving my residency in general psychiatry. She walked into my office, and I saw that she had all the major side effects of Haldol. She shook my hand almost robotically, and her Parkinson's-like body movements, unnatural gait, and constricted affect suggested a person trapped inside her body.

"I'm Paula," she said. "I have to be me, who else can I be?"

Paula's mother looked calm, but her father seemed sheepish. "Schizophrenia," the mother whispered to me, indicating her daughter.

After a few preliminaries, I asked Paula about the letters she had written. "I was telling everyone I love them and I needed to make sure they knew how I felt," she said. Within this single conversation, she was up and down, alternately smiling at me and then crying.

"Ask her about the boys," her mother said. When I did, Paula told me that all the boys at school loved her. She was floridly psychotic, talking about how important she was and how everyone wanted to know about her. Obviously, the Haldol was doing nothing for Paula's thinking. I temporarily added another medication, Cogentin, to counter the Parkinson's-like effects of Haldol. I reduced and then discontinued the Haldol. At the time of Paula's hospitalization, in 1979—a different era in health-care management—it was routine to place patients in the hospital and take the time to discontinue medications and then assess the patient's symptoms and make a diagnosis. Today, we don't have the luxury of keeping a patient in the hospital for observation to clarify a diagnosis. Patients are admitted to the hospital only when they are a danger to themselves or others or have failed at outpatient treatment and are not functioning. And they are discharged as soon as it's no longer medically essential to keep them.

A few days after her admission, Paula wasn't sleeping, and we discovered that she had been offering and performing oral sex to several of the adolescent male patients. When I talked to her in a small room on the ward later that day, her speech was rapid, she expressed a special connection to God, and she was rubbing her legs together, apparently trying to sexually stimulate herself. Then, suddenly, she stood up, threw the chair to the side, and lay down in the manner of Christ on the cross. Then she started screaming, "Take me!" along with many expletives about sex, me, and my religion.

Still in training, I was taken aback by the intensity of her behavior. Though it helped clarify her diagnosis, I was struck by how out of control she was. As a doctor, I was able to maintain my composure and call for a nurse to give Paula an injection of Haldol to give her immediate relief. (Lithium would have taken a few weeks to become completely effective.) But as a human being, only half a dozen years older than Paula, I found her behavior frightening. It wasn't that I felt personally threatened, but that I realized how completely a person with bipolar disorder could act on impulse with none of the barriers that normally protect us. All adolescents think about sex and have a desire to break rules, but they struggle with right and wrong. Paula at this moment did not have that ability. What I saw playing out in front of me were her conflicting sexual and religious impulses. Her inability to have any control over her words and actions was also why she had been having so much indiscriminate sex, accompanied by the grandiosity of her perception that it meant that everyone loved her and wanted to be with her.

The clinical thinking at that time was that we all have the ability to become psychotic. So seeing such a dramatic episode was unsettling. Now, though, we recognize that we are *not* all capable of such a breakdown. A predisposition for an imbalance of brain chemistry has to be present. It's a common refrain to hear a parent say: "She was normal until she went to college." That's because 18 and 19 are typically the ages of onset of serious mental illnesses such as bipolar disorder and schizophrenia. A huge difference between these two illnesses with similar symptoms is that people who develop schizophrenia rarely recover completely. Some do better than others, but it's infrequent for someone with schizophrenia to be able to pick up where he left off. John Nash, the mathematician whose story is told in the book and film *A Beautiful Mind,* received the Nobel Prize for research that was done before his first psychotic break. He never returned to the same level of brilliance or productivity. For average people, if they did not learn to drive before the onset of the illness, it's difficult if not impossible to do so afterward. By contrast, the prognosis for those with bipolar disorder is optimistic. As long as they are on the proper medication, they can reconstitute and live normal, productive lives. For instance, Dr. Kay Redfield Jamison described her struggle with bipolar disorder in her memoir *An Unquiet Mind.* Diagnosed as a teenager, she went on to become a psychologist, a professor of psychiatry at Johns Hopkins University School of Medicine, and a bestselling author and internationally renowned authority on manic-depressive illness.

After a few weeks on lithium, Paula was basically fine, back to the way her parents described her before the episode: self-possessed, sweet, and respectful. She was extremely embarrassed about the sexual incidents in the hospital and particularly about having propositioned me. By then, every other patient and doctor on the unit had heard that she'd been caught in bed with another patient. When she said goodbye, she apologized. "I hope you know I didn't mean what I said," she said timidly. I assured her that it wasn't her; it was the illness.

The likely scenario was that when Paula's parents first noticed that she sounded sad and listless earlier in that semester, what they were hearing were symptoms of depression. What followed was consistent with what we know about the common course of bipolar illness: that it often develops from an episode of depression during late adolescence, and that the first episode sometimes has psychotic features.

With her lithium levels normalized, Paula continued as an outpatient. She didn't go to France, but she did go back to school in Virginia in the fall. That Christmas I received a letter from her. She included a copy of her grades, which were stellar. Twenty years later, I still get Christmas cards from her family. Paula, now in her early forties, has stayed on lithium, as she will have to for the rest of her life. She has not had another break. And there is another happy ending to this story: Her father was eventually rediagnosed as having bipolar disorder rather than schizophrenia. He, too, began taking lithium, and is now nearing retirement after many successful years as an executive at a major corporation.

In the two decades since I met Paula and her family, the field has come to understand that schizophrenia had been overdiagnosed. Like her father, Paula very easily could have fallen into that category, presumed to have schizophrenia based on the psychotic features of her episode and the reported family history (that included her father's own misdiagnosis). But there were some key reasons why bipolar illness made more sense. Paula's personality before she became ill was friendly and outgoing, and she possessed very good social skills. And once she was ill, her delusions of grandeur and her lack of need for sleep were also classic symptoms of bipolar disorder.

In addition, it's very difficult to follow a line of thought from a patient with schizophrenia; there are pieces missing, and it's almost impossible to discern any sense of logic. This phenomenon is called "looseness of associations." Many patients with schizophrenia also exhibit what is called "poverty of speech"—they are unable to initiate and maintain conversations—and they tend to take things literally. But being with someone who is bipolar and in a manic state can be a bit like watching a Robin Williams routine: his thoughts are flying around the room, but you can follow and delight in where he's going, which is why it's called "flight of ideas." Being around someone in a manic state can be genuinely frightening, but it can also be strangely enjoyable, particularly in the early stages of the manic episode. This improved understanding of the two disorders has undoubtedly allowed untold numbers of young people to be properly treated and, like Paula, to survive a hellish episode in their lives with nothing more burdensome than a daily pill.

Andrew's Lost Summer

One day in the summer of 1989, I received a call from one of my junior high school teachers. Two days earlier, she and her husband had gotten a baffling and disturbing phone call from their 15-year-old son, Andrew, who was on a camp trip to Niagara Falls. "It's really great here! I'm drinking coffee! I'm buying a lot of cool things!" When his mother told him, "But you don't *have* money," he said, "I'll *get* money." Andrew went on and on in what his mother considered a bizarre euphoria.

Andrew's father, Roy, felt there was something wrong and wanted to bring Andrew home. As a child, Roy had had problems himself and had been diagnosed with separation anxiety disorder and later, as a teenager, with panic disorder, as well as "agitated depression," a form of the disorder characterized by restlessness. As an adult, he had also been treated for depression. "I immediately felt panicked," Roy said of Andrew's phone call. But his wife, Elaine, told him not to overreact. They argued about it, and she prevailed. They would leave Andrew at camp. But two days later, they got a call from the camp director, saying that Andrew had to go home because he was "sick" and couldn't be controlled.

Andrew's parents were jolted and terribly frightened by the camp director's words. This was unbelievable to them. Two years earlier they had taken him to see a psychologist because he seemed more distant and spacey at times. The therapist had a simple explanation: "He's 13."

The psychologist was right, but incomplete, in his assessment. Andrew *was* an adolescent, and he didn't have any symptoms of bipolar disorder at the time. But signs of depression were not so hidden. Andrew remembered being miserable in seventh grade and teachers tossing him the worst adult cliché: "You're 13 years old—what do you have to be depressed about?" Andrew's track coach commented that he always walked around with a glum face. But Andrew felt his face was more glazed than glum. He'd go home crying many days. "I wanted a way out," he says now, "but I was too wimpy to commit suicide."

Unfortunately, the psychologist didn't ask enough questions, or the right ones. And, as is typical of depressed teens, Andrew wasn't supplying any unsolicited information.

Andrew was happier in eighth grade, or so it seemed. He became uncharacteristically uninhibited. He joined the drama club, and loved the spotlight. Nothing wrong with that, of course, but then a teacher called home and said Andrew was speaking out of turn a lot in class. Meanwhile, he seemed just as spacey, his mother recalled. One night, she learned that he hadn't done a paper that had been assigned weeks before. That was not at all like Andrew. Another time, he sat at the dining room table, just staring at his work. Elaine, though upset, thought it was just another "he's 13" thing. Roy, whose eyes were always open to any symptoms that suggested his own disorders, thought it might be more than that. But if it was, it was much more subtle. After all, the class in which he was speaking out of turn was a politics course. Andrew's father was a criminal attorney, and Andrew was an avid follower of current events and had some strong opinions. As for his lapses of concentration, they seemed to be only occasional.

When the camp director called to tell Andrew's parents that they had to come get him, it was clear that whatever was going on was much more serious than they had previously suspected. Elaine asked if there had been any earlier indications that something was wrong. The director said that earlier in the summer Andrew had seemed to isolate himself. Then came Niagara Falls. His strange behavior had continued when the group returned to camp. The night they got back, Andrew went on the roof of the bunk house and was rifling through the Bible and talking to himself.

Elaine was in tears as she and Roy drove up to the camp. She wondered if illicit drugs were involved.

When they arrived at the camp, the director met them in the parking lot and told them she would bring Andrew down to them. Roy turned to Elaine and told her to be calm when she saw him. "Be very strong," he said. "He's not in his right mind." When Andrew appeared, his parents simply hugged and kissed him.

Elaine drove home, and Roy sat in the back seat with Andrew. Their son was delusional. He was talking to people through his watch. Elaine was silent, trying to keep Andrew from knowing that she was driving in tears. Roy, meanwhile, just nodded and rubbed his son's shoulders. "Whatever it took to keep him calm," Roy recalled. "I just wanted to get him home. At one point, Andrew started to get panicky and said he was going to be sick. We stopped the car and we all got out."

Andrew's parents didn't know what they were facing, much less what they were going to do about it. "My biggest fear was hospitalization," Roy said. "When I was 16, with untreated panic disorder, I remember calling my doctor, an internist, and telling him I felt so bad I thought I was going to die. The next thing I know two cops are at the door and they're grabbing me by the arms. I'm saying, 'I don't want to go!' Just then my father drove up, and he didn't allow them to take me to the hospital." Now, 30 years later, he was terrified that his son would have to be put in the hospital. "I was afraid he would have a record," he said, as if it were comparable to going to jail. "What if he wanted to run for office some day? I was also afraid that we would lose control of our son. I thought of the movie *The Snake Pit*."

They were up all night with Andrew when they got home. "He became very paranoid, he was hearing voices," Elaine recalled. "He wasn't connecting with us. It was as if he didn't even recognize us. Then he got so tired. We found out he hadn't slept in a week and a half."

Roy called the psychiatrist who had treated him as a teenager 35 years earlier; he now was semiretired. He said that from what he was hearing, Andrew clearly needed to be hospitalized. "I put down the phone and started to cry," Roy said. That's when Elaine thought of calling me, her former English student. She reached me late on Friday as I was about to leave for a month's vacation. I told her to bring Andrew in right away, and an hour later they were sitting in my office. Before they arrived, I asked my colleague Dr. Glenn Hirsch to attend the meeting and then take care of Andrew.

Andrew had dark, curly hair, dark eyes, and an athletic build. He was very fidgety, and had poor eye contact, seeming to look everywhere but at my face. His mother, Elaine, had been the prettiest teacher in my junior high school, and she was still a beautiful woman; like Andrew, she had dark hair and dark eyes. Her husband, Roy, had sandy brown hair and a beard. He seemed nervous, even more than most other parents I had seen; he was a chain-smoker.

From everything Elaine and Roy told Dr. Hirsch and me, it was clear that Andrew was psychotic. They thought—hoped—he had experimented with some bad drugs. That, they could deal with. But it wasn't drugs. Though he was a little young for the usual first onset, it was my initial impression that Andrew had bipolar disorder. He was agitated, talking very quickly, as if trying to say a lot in very little time. The best course, I thought, was to put him on Haldol, to calm him down quickly, and lithium, the gold-standard medication for bipolar disorder.

"Haldol?" Roy questioned. "I was given that mistakenly in 1965 for panic attacks."

"Let's be optimistic," Dr. Hirsch suggested. "By Sunday he'll probably start to come out of this."

Relieved but still frightened, Elaine was confused about the tentative diagnosis of bipolar disorder. They had seen mania, but hadn't recognized depression. But when Andrew recalled his early adolescence for me years later, he described a cycle of ups and downs that no one had ever picked up on. "All of a sudden I'd feel stupid, cloudy-headed," he said. "I'd feel like the teacher would be speaking, but I wouldn't really be com-

prehending what she was saying. I just kind of wanted to hide and not
talk to anyone. I felt awkward, and it seemed to me that everyone knew
that I was feeling like that. But you don't expect a 13-year-old to be depressed. And that is really what happened in camp. For a week or two I
wasn't myself. My friends would notice but no one really paid much attention to it because, I guess, at 13 or 14 or 15 years old, they don't expect it. It's like an adult thing to be depressed."

Andrew didn't understand it at the time, either. "I thought at camp I
was just homesick, you know, missing Mommy and Daddy. Or I'd feel
down if I didn't do well in a soccer game. Things that you would expect
a 13-year-old to be upset about, but not to the extent that I felt my personality change." He did recognize that his personality was subject to a
roller-coaster pattern of spiraling down into a depressed state, and then
shooting up to normal; down and up, depressed and normal. "When you
snap out of it, it's almost like you have perspective," Andrew recalled
years later. "You say, 'Wow, I was depressed.'" The depression would
come maybe once every couple of months, lasting only a week or two
each time.

The common perception of bipolar disorder is of high highs and low
lows, constant ups and downs like a seesaw. What it is, actually, is a cycle
of discrete episodes of significant duration, which by definition must last
at least a week. We all go up and down, but for most of us our range is
only a little above and a little below our baseline. Someone who is bipolar will go higher and lower than the norm. It's a common misconception that it will always be either sky-high or rock-bottom. Some people
with bipolar disorder will cycle from manic to baseline, and others will
shift from depression to baseline, again and again. Others will go from
high to low, without stopping at baseline. Bipolar young people also tend
to be more rapid in these cycles than adults with the disorder. They are
up or down for only a few days. When someone has four or more episodes
of alternating mania and depression within a twelve-month period, she
is said to have rapid cycling. (In adults, this is more common in women
than men.) There is also something called a "mixed state." This is when

symptoms of mania and depression occur at the same time—any combination of agitation, trouble sleeping, change in appetite, psychosis, and suicidal thinking.

Andrew's parents never knew about his depressive periods because he never told them. So when we saw them that Friday, they were in shock. What Elaine wanted to know was this: If Andrew did have bipolar disorder, did that mean it was going to be a chronic or permanent condition? Wasn't manic depression an endless seesaw of highs and lows? Let's get through the weekend, Dr. Hirsch told them again. Once we know for sure what we're dealing with and how he responds to treatment, we can start talking about the future. What he didn't say was that her question was right on the money. It was unlikely this was a single, isolated episode. Odds were good that Andrew would need medication to maintain his balance, maybe for the rest of his life.

I agreed with Roy's old psychiatrist that Andrew was probably best served by putting him in the hospital until he calmed down. My main worry was that he would run away if he was at home. But his parents were very reluctant to admit him, and promised they would stay right near him, all night if they had to. And Dr. Hirsch was willing to give them his beeper and home phone number in case there was a sudden change, with the agreement that if Andrew's condition deteriorated, he would be hospitalized immediately.

◆

When Andrew came to my office 12 years later to talk with me about his recollections, he was a 27-year-old lawyer, about to be married. I hadn't seen him since the day he came to the hospital—Dr. Hirsch had been treating him since then—and he was quite a contrast to the manic, disjointed teenager I had seen that day. He came from work, dressed in a dark business suit and a maroon tie, his black shoes impeccably shined. He was poised and gave me a firm handshake. He had become a very handsome man, tall with wavy black hair, and he made strong eye contact. Though the topic was difficult and he was a little reserved at first, he seemed to get comfortable as he brought himself back to that time and place.

"I remember my depressive episodes as a teenager as periods of, I would say, flatness," he said. "I wouldn't be able to converse well. My head would be clouded, and my concentration would be very poor." I mentioned that his parents had recalled his sitting at the table with a paper he was supposed to be writing, and all he could do was stare at the work. "Yeah," Andrew said, nodding. "It would almost be like I didn't know how to read. And they didn't know what was wrong. They would tell me I was spacey, which offended me. They made it seem like I was doing it, like it was my fault. And I knew this was something that was just not right. It didn't feel like me. It felt like I was another person."

It's easy to imagine Andrew's parents, or any parents in that situation, thinking that what they had on their hands was a *teenager*. After all, how many parents of adolescents in perfectly normal mental health have thought, "Who *is* this kid?" Even today, parents are not prepared to recognize depression in their teenagers; in the 1980s, it wasn't anywhere on the radar screen.

In retrospect, summer camp for Andrew was both a vacation and a prison sentence. "I felt exposed," he said. "At home, there's school for six hours and I could run home and be my depressed self. Whereas at camp, I'm living in a bunk with 20 people, kids my own age, counselors who were 19 or 20. And you can't hide. So it's much more disturbing, because you want to be social and for one or two weeks of the eight, you can't. And you don't know when the depression is going to come." Still, Andrew never exercised his option *not* to go to camp. He considered it, but balanced it against the fun he knew he would have. He had a group of friends at camp that he liked very much and looked forward to spending the summer with them. He never shared any of this with his parents.

Andrew remembers the summer before the beginning of high school all too well. "Visiting day was three weeks into camp, and I was fine," he recalled. "And then I went into a depression that lasted a long time. It really was a bad one. I wasn't participating in activities. I would hem and haw. I wasn't fun to be around."

"Was this your opinion or other people's?" I asked.

"Mine. My friends were not really cognizant of what was going on. A few of the close ones would say, 'Andrew, why are you like this? What's wrong?' Because I guess I'd mope, my face would be long and really tell a story. But the depression built and built and built and eventually I began to get agitated and angry. And I'd want to leave my bunkmates and go somewhere else."

"Did you talk to anyone about it?"

"I talked to my counselors, but I wasn't getting anywhere. I just remember feeling angry and depressed. And then we went away to Niagara Falls, and that's when something in me crossed the line from being normal. Over the next week or so, I started to lose touch with reality."

Andrew's memory of the details at this point was hazy, so I told him what his parents had told me, both back then and also during our more recent conversation, when they had the benefit of hindsight. They remembered Andrew calling from Toronto and sounding exuberant. "They really weren't worried about you at that point," I told Andrew. "They thought you were so upbeat, though in retrospect they say they should have been worried because that just wasn't you. You were calling them a lot, and calling very late, which was also unusual."

Being joyful seemed to ring no bells with Andrew. What he remembered was fighting with people. "Everyone else was wrong, I was right," he said. "I felt everyone getting angry at me, which made it even worse because I became paranoid. And I couldn't talk to *anyone.* I was on my own at fifteen. Part of me knew something was wrong. I was staying up all night. One of my friends hit me in the face because I was being so annoying, behaving so strangely. We went to an amusement park in Toronto, and we were supposed to stay in groups. But I walked off on my own and took my shoes off and wandered around. Everyone was looking for me frantically. The camp owner was so mad she wanted to send me home on a plane right then and there."

But she calmed down, and Andrew returned to the camp with everyone else. When he got there, his mania was unleashed. He became hypersexual, masturbating four or five times a day. (Bipolar people in manic states often lose their social judgment and inhibition.) He couldn't sleep, and he stayed outside all night. The camp director found him on the roof of the bunk, talking to himself and reading the Bible he had taken from the hotel room in Toronto. A minute later, she was on the phone with Andrew's parents.

"What do you remember about your behavior that night?" I asked.

"The scary part of the whole thing was that part of me knew what was going on was wrong. I had the feeling of being trapped inside my own head, my own mind. It was so scary. You don't know how to react. You think the whole world doesn't believe you, and you don't even know yourself if what you're saying is true or not. Reality is just warped."

Andrew felt as if his mind was divided into two parts, one side playing out this bizarre, frenzied behavior; the other standing aside, appalled and bewildered. On some level, Andrew said, he was aware that a kind of switch had been flipped, and that he had somehow taken a trampoline bounce from depression to exhilaration. But while his parents remember him sounding almost euphoric on the phone, Andrew's memory was that he felt like a caged animal. Whereas before he had been angry at everyone, now it seemed everyone was also angry at *him*. "I was getting violent, fighting with people physically and yelling," he said.

I asked Andrew if he was glad when his parents came to get him. "Not really," he said. "I was kind of relieved that I was getting away from camp, because no one was appreciating me. But at the same time, I felt, 'Hey, I can handle this. I'm fine. You don't have to take me home.' And then on the car ride home, after about three and a half hours—I remember it was pouring rain—it just hit me. I felt like my life was going to be over. Like I had just ruined my life. I felt I had alienated everyone, all my friends that I'd had for the past five years. Five years is a long time in a 15-year-old's life. I started to get very upset. And then I started having delusions and hallucinations. We passed a truck, and I thought that the reason my parents were taking me home was because everyone I knew was going to throw a party for me. Everyone I went to elementary school with, everyone from junior high, was on this truck, following me home from camp. And when we passed the truck, I would hear, like, crowd noise. Not any discernible speech, but just people I knew, talking."

But even as he had these auditory hallucinations, Andrew said, he knew they were just that, which didn't make the experience any easier. In fact, it made it even more frightening to be aware that what was going on was wrong, even as he was experiencing these delusions. It was akin to a person with Alzheimer's disease putting his underwear in a microwave oven (a common sort of thing with that disease) and knowing, as he was doing it, that it was wrong and that it meant he was losing his mind.

When Andrew reached his low point during the car trip home—when it seemed to him that he had ruined his life—he told his parents he felt sick and wanted to stop and get out of the car. Andrew's mother recalled that she thought he might run away, though his father thought he just needed to get some air and stretch his legs.

"So what was it?" I asked.

"Somewhere in between," Andrew said. "The best way to describe it is being trapped, stuck inside a safe. I needed to get out of the car. But even once I got out of the car, there was no relief. I still felt still trapped. I was still having these racing thoughts and these hallucinations and these feelings of self-deprecation. I was also upset because I had lost my friends. So I got mad: *Why are my parents taking me home?* But somehow they got me home."

Elaine and Roy had told me that they didn't do everything well as parents, but that when this kind of emergency occurred, they responded and worked well together as a team. "Sort of unconsciously," Andrew agreed. "They did it when my brother broke his arm. They were just—boom—let's go to the hospital. No hysteria. And I give them a lot of credit for the way they got through that week. They saw it at its absolute worst. At camp, I was just doing weird stuff, totally unusual for me. I was obsessively reading the Gideon's Bible I had found in the hotel room. I was looking for an answer, some sort of comfort. Some help. But at home, it's ironic, I had all the comfort and all the help, and I was much worse. I got home and I started to cry. And then I got angry at the whole situation. I started throwing my clothes out of the closet. And then my dad said something very stern. 'Andrew, if you don't stop that, we're going to have to take you to the hospital.' And that scared me, so I stopped. All I could think of in my head was being put into an ambulance and then a straitjacket. It scared the crap out of me. You know, being in people's hands who didn't know me, didn't care about me. I just pictured some big, fat nurse, kind of a Nurse Ratched type. At times I was lucid. And at other times I just couldn't believe what was going on. I was sitting there watching late-night television because I was up all night talking to my watch."

"Who were you talking to?" I asked.

"I was giving directions to Johnny Carson. I would tell him, 'Now laugh,' and he would laugh. I was like the director with the earpiece. I was talking into the mike." He really believed that Johnny Carson was following his directions.

The next day, Friday, was when Dr. Glenn Hirsch and I met with Andrew and his parents and sent them home with Haldol and lithium. The Haldol was prescribed to eliminate the psychotic features quickly, and to let Andrew sleep. It did its job. He was out for most of the weekend. "I was just a wreck," he recalled. "I struggled to keep my head up. My parents actually had to lift me out of bed."

By Sunday night, Andrew was starting to come out of it. And a few weeks later, after careful adjusting of his lithium dose and monitoring its blood level, he was attending his high school's annual end-of-summer marching band camp. He had been through a terrible ordeal, and knew it, but he wasn't talking to his watch or feeling suicidal. He was playing the clarinet.

Andrew started high school that fall with the lithium but without the Haldol. He and his parents also had more than the usual worries. Was he officially bipolar? Would he have to have another episode to confirm the diagnosis? *Would* he have another episode? It didn't help that during a family visit, his grandfather's wife remarked in front of Andrew that she had had a cousin who had been manic-depressive, "and he jumped out the window." "I wanted to kill her," Roy said. Obviously relating to the situation and very sensitive to the embarrassment his son might feel, Roy was also worried about Andrew's friends and classmates finding out what had happened at camp. And not just now. What if he wound up going to college with someone from camp?

Andrew, of course, had enough to handle without his father reliving his own experiences. Based on the one episode, it was hard to know whether Andrew had the more severe form of the illness, known as bipolar I disorder, in which deep depression alternatives with intense mania, or the less serious bipolar II, in which short depressive episodes vary with less severe mania. (There is an even milder condition called cyclothymic disorder, a quick cycling of moods that in many cases does not lead to either major depression or mania.)

Most of that school year was happily uneventful. Andrew continued taking the lithium as he tried to put the summer behind him. His work habits were good, and his grades were what they had always been. But the following spring, Andrew's father got a call from the public library. "Your son is lying on the floor in the bathroom," the librarian said. "I think he's unconscious."

Roy raced to the library. "I jumped out of the car," he remembered. "He was lying in the stall on his stomach. I thought he was dead. I was terrified. *Andrew, talk to me.* I wanted my son to live. I heard a groan and thought, *Thank God.*"

It turned out that Andrew had taken psilocybic "mushrooms," a hallucinogenic drug whose effects are similar to those of LSD. It was not the first time he had used drugs. He later told his father that he had begun smoking marijuana occasionally, once a month or so, earlier in the school year. He had also taken mushrooms twice before, but they were weak and gave him little more than a marijuana high. He and a friend got the drugs from the friend's older brother. But this time, Andrew wound up in an ambulance. At the hospital, his stomach was pumped.

"Not a bright move, the mushrooms," Andrew admitted as we spoke.

"They were really strong, and I took them on an empty stomach. I took them at lunch period and then went to my classes. By eighth period, which was band, I was feeling really sick. I started to hear the sounds again. I was hallucinating in band. The sound was going back and forth and I started to feel in the pit of my stomach that I was going to be sick. I told the teacher I had to go to the nurse and walked outside and threw up. And then I started to really hallucinate and think negative thoughts like, What if I stay like this forever? What if they have to take me away? I didn't want to be on school property, so I went across the street to the library. And I guess I passed out and apparently almost died. It turned out it was a bad batch. My friends got sick, too. But all they got were stomach aches."

"Well, you know, everything may happen for a reason," I observed. "I actually think the bad reaction to the mushrooms frightened you from trying other drugs. It was enough of a scare, having your stomach pumped and freaking your parents out again."

Andrew's parents had had more than the usual number of drug and alcohol talks with him. Given what happened at camp, and the fact that he was taking lithium, he had more reason than most kids to stay away from recreational drugs and drinking. "To you they're poison," Roy told him. He was right. Any mind-altering medicines can make a teenager particularly sensitive to alcohol, and especially to illicit drugs.

"I knew it was a huge deal," Andrew reflected. "Part of me wanted— and still wants—to ignore the fact that I have a disease and that I need to take medicine for it. I want to be normal. I want to drink like everyone else. I wanted to experiment with drugs when I was a teenager. I was with a group of kids that were experimenting, being immature and stupid. And you know what? You're right—it did scare the shit out of me. It proved to me that I wasn't like everyone else. I couldn't be like everyone else in that respect."

After the mushroom episode, Andrew promised his parents he wouldn't take any more drugs. He kept his promise: he didn't drink, smoke, or do drugs for the rest of high school. He stayed with the same group of friends, and would watch while they got high. "I would just stand there being miserable," he said. Meanwhile, he was conscientious about taking his lithium daily, fully aware of the potential consequences if he didn't. His parents were good about letting him develop the routine on his own, rather than constantly asking, "Did you take your medicine?"

When he went off to college, Andrew knew he had no safety net. He pledged a fraternity and was nervous about all the stories he had heard about hell week. Drinking and sleep deprivation were two things on his "can't do" list. He was very worried about doing anything that might cause another break. He sat down with one of his friends, a fellow pledge, and told him his secret. His friend helped him through it, and never mentioned the illness again.

Besides seeing Dr. Hirsch monthly for medication monitoring, Andrew saw a psychologist weekly throughout high school and on vacations during college. They talked about the illness as part of Andrew's psychoeducation, because it was important for him to understand why he was the way he was. "We talked about whether you get biologically depressed first or you get depressed because of anxiety or something. He was more of a listener, so I would end up having to hear myself talk, like I'm doing now. And after weeks and weeks and weeks of doing that, I became more aware and in tune with why I would go into a depression. Because depression was really the battle for me. Not mania. There were times when I was younger when I might be extra talkative and rambunctious, which may have been mania or it may have been puberty."

"Or just your personality," I pointed out.

"Right. But for the most part it's always been depression."

That became most clear toward the end of college. Andrew had experienced periodic depressions throughout high school and his first three years of college. But he had always snapped out of them before too long without antidepressants. But in his senior year, he fell into a deeper and more persistent depression. He was living in the fraternity house—"a dump," he said—and he was lonely. His girlfriend, Tina, who was a year ahead, had moved on to graduate school. Andrew called his parents one night and cried. His father called Dr. Hirsch, who asked him to arrange for Andrew to come down to New York to see him. Andrew was proof positive that successfully treating bipolar disorder is no protection against standard unipolar depression. After seeing him, Dr. Hirsch started him on Prozac, though not before thinking seriously about the possibility that it might push him back into a manic state. But he was confident that Andrew was taking a sufficient dosage of lithium, and made sure the young man was monitored closely. He insisted Andrew call him every few days during the first weeks, until he was satisfied the Prozac wasn't having any adverse effects.

The antidepressant made Andrew feel better after about three weeks, and he has stayed on the medication to this day. He graduated from college and went to law school, and eventually he and Tina moved in together and made plans to get married. He told her about his illness soon after they met, but her parents found out on their own, in an uncanny way. A neighbor of Tina's, it turned out, had gone to camp with Andrew and had been in his bunk. "So he knew 'Andrew went crazy and had to go home,'" Andrew said. "So when he heard that Tina and I were dating, he told his mom and she asked Tina's mom, 'Do you know what happened to Andrew?' But Tina's parents and I have never talked about it directly. I haven't brought it up, and they haven't asked. I think they asked Tina once if I was okay."

"What about Tina?"

"She accepts the disease and she's understanding. She has a lot of questions, mostly about genetics, like what are the chances our kids would be bipolar and would they respond to medication because I responded to medication."

I explained that he and Tina were at greater risk of having a child with bipolar disorder than couples with no family history, but that the probability was greater that their child would be healthy. "How is your relationship?" I asked.

"Well, we're getting married."

"I didn't ask that."

"Well, when we met in college, we were 19 years old, and she was really funny, and we had a great time together. Then she went to grad school, and we were away from each other for a year. Then I went to law school and things started slowing down. And pretty much for the next two or three years, things have been slow."

"How often do you have sex?"

"Two or three times a week, I guess."

"What was it before?"

"Every night."

A decline in sex drive and difficulty ejaculating are common side effects with SSRIs. But Andrew said it wasn't a problem with his medication. He thought he and Tina were both too busy with work, and he still had bouts of depression. "How often do you have them?" I asked.

"I feel like I'm in one right now, actually," he said. "For about three or four weeks, I've felt dull. I've not been able to put a sentence together as well as I would like."

To live with his illness, Andrew told me, he supplemented his lithium and Prozac prescriptions with a bit of self-medication. He said he still smoked marijuana regularly. "I know that once I get out of this little transition period from school to adulthood and get married and have a kid, then I definitely don't want to have it in the house or do it then."

"What does it do for you now?"

"See, Prozac, I feel, keeps me from going to the point where I was in camp, to a really black depression. And lithium I know keeps me from getting to that manic point. However, I still have depression. And I enjoy the feeling of kind of getting out of reality for a short time. I know it's controlled. I know that because I'm on the medication I'm not going to lose control. And I haven't had a great relationship with drinking since I've been on Prozac. Since I started it, if I drank I would start to do crazy things. I've blacked out, or I've felt sick the next day. So to me, marijuana feels a lot safer. I don't do stupid stuff on it. I don't feel sick."

I sympathized with Andrew's desire to unwind, but didn't think smoking pot was a great idea. There's not exactly quality control in the street drug industry, and you can never be sure what's in that little bag. But more than that, I was troubled that Andrew was talking this way. Though I am a firm believer in the positive power of psychiatric medicines, I, like many people, worry about the social and cultural consequences of giving our kids too much medicine. Are we turning them into medicine cabinets, giving them a dependence on pills that will continue into adulthood? I had no doubt that Andrew could not function without medicine, but I needed to work with him so that he understood the delicate balance of brain chemistry at play. For instance, marijuana can actually *cause* symptoms of anxiety and depression. Many people with panic disorder report that they had their first attacks while getting high on pot. And those with depression often feel even more down and unable to function after smoking. The temporary high may provide short-term relief, but the longer-term effect is to exacerbate the depression. I thought Andrew was using marijuana not to treat his own depression, but to avoid dealing with normal, average moods and the stress of everyday life. In other words, he was smoking for the same reason most people do. The difference was that he had more risks than most people. I suggested that Andrew consider starting therapy again, with the specific goal of managing stress. "It may help you stop using pot."

Dr. Hirsch had had similar discussions with Andrew's parents years before. But now that Andrew was an adult, it would be necessary for him to understand the two sides of the coin and take responsibility. Dr. Hirsch could tell him that he shouldn't smoke marijuana. But he wasn't willing to tell him not to come back if he did. Psychiatrists regularly have to make difficult decisions about taking the right approach with a patient, particularly an adolescent.

"So, looking back on this whole experience as an adult," I asked Andrew toward the end of our conversation, "how do you put it together now? How has having bipolar disorder affected your life, your decisions, your view of yourself? Do you see yourself as a man with manic depression?"

"I take my medication because I know I have to," he said. "But I try not to see myself as a sick person. I try to do normal things. And that's really my mom's influence. From that very first weekend when I was 15, she has pushed me out and said, 'You don't have to let this get the best of you. You can still do anything.' Now sometimes I feel sorry for myself, saying, 'Why can't I be normal?' But then I kick myself and think what I've done is actually an accomplishment, considering what happened to me at such an early age."

Andrew went to law school with some trepidation, concerned that he was subjecting himself to a high-stress education followed by a high-stress career. He did fine in law school, and took a job at a relatively low-pressure firm. But now he wants to advance to a bigger firm that would offer more opportunities and better pay. He knows it would also be a lot more demanding. "I'm worried about that," Andrew said.

Andrew knows that he can never put the camp incident completely in his past. In many ways, it was the defining moment of his life. "You know," he said, "whenever I'm anxious about something, or something is weighing on my mind, I have a dream about camp. It's usually me going back there and reconciling with everyone and saying, 'See? I'm all right.' And actually I had that chance a few months ago. At Tina's neighbor's wedding, all our camp friends were there. I went, but I was extremely nervous. They were very nice; they all came up and said, 'How's everything going?' and shook my hand. And they were all in a group because they had stayed in touch over the years. And I hadn't. I lost out on that because they went back and became counselors. And I couldn't go back to that camp. It's really a shame."

When I spoke to Andrew's parents, their perception was that he was less open, tighter than he had been when he was younger. His mother told me: "When I go to kiss him, his body tenses. He doesn't want to be effusive. He's trying to control himself. He's not very physical with his fiancée. It makes me very, very sad that he doesn't let himself go because he's so afraid of what happened to him when he was 15."

"That one episode permeates the rest of his life," Andrew's father added. "He's so afraid he can't control it."

I asked Andrew if his parents' perceptions about the changes in his interactions with them were accurate. Was he holding back? Was it the medications? Was it that he was older? Andrew chose all of the above. "I guess I like to be in control. My parents are very effusive people, and as I got older I withdrew because it seemed overwhelming to me. And it's also maturity, I guess. It's just not my style."

"That's with them. What about the rest of the world?"

"I pick my friends very carefully. I'm not open with a lot of people. Professionally, I feel that—and I don't know if my parents have made me feel this—it would be bad if it got out that I was bipolar. Who would want a lawyer who's bipolar? So I try to keep it under wraps."

It was very hard to know whether Andrew's parents were perceptive or hypersensitive. Did they see their son's life through the prism of his illness, whereas he tried as much as possible, though perhaps not very successfully, to put blinders on? For instance, Elaine noticed that Andrew was not very affectionate with Tina and attributed it to what she felt was his need to be cool and in control. Without telling him what his mother said, I asked Andrew, neutrally, "Are you affectionate with your future wife?"

"Yeah, real affectionate," he said. "Not in public. She doesn't like it." Things are not always as they seem to parents, whether their children have a mood disorder or not.

Andrew is a good example of the secondary consequences of mental illness. He is an accomplished young man from an educated and sophisticated family, and yet he and his parents still feel the effects of what was essentially one episode of psychotic behavior when he was a teenager at summer camp. It is something of a wedge between them. Meanwhile, the shame of that event, the stigma of mental illness, has also kept Andrew from having long-term friendships from his camp days, and now that cloud of shame and fear could affect his relationship with his future in-laws. Bipolar disorder has been publicly acknowledged for 50 years; first the Broadway impresario Joshua Logan and later accomplished celebrities such as Patty Duke and Dick Cavett have stepped forward to say they have the disease, and this has helped destigmatize it. Yet Andrew and his future in-laws have completely avoided the subject. That's the secondary pain of having a psychiatric illness in America. It's still not treated with the same compassion and acceptance as physical illness— even though psychiatric illness is much more common. This is not to suggest that Andrew should be more open about his illness, only that it's too bad that handling it is not enough. Keeping it "under wraps" is one of the dynamics of his life.

Still, ultimately Andrew's story is a happy one. By being diligent about taking the right medicines, by being self-aware and insightful, he has managed to keep a serious mental illness at bay; he has not had another manic episode since that summer when he was fifteen. It was very unusual not to hospitalize a boy in his condition, and his parents made sure we didn't regret the decision. His compliance with medication is also unusual. Lithium to a manic-depressive can be like insulin to a diabetic. It's a lifelong necessity. Yet some people regard the medication's effectiveness as a signal to stop taking it. In the first year or so after diagnosis, many bipolar patients deny their illness—*It was a nightmare, I'm not really sick.* That they don't have another manic episode becomes their rationalization, and the longer they go without one the more they think they can stop taking the medicine. "What would happen if I stop?" they wonder. What happens is usually not good. Sooner or later, the vast majority relapse. One study that followed teenagers for two years found that nearly 80 percent who stopped taking lithium had recurrences of the disorder.

Some patients, meanwhile, find that lithium doesn't work for them, or that its side effects—dry mouth, fatigue, acne, tremor, increased urination, and weight gain—are too severe. Fortunately, many of the medications that have become effective in controlling seizures, such as Tegretol and Depakote, are also effective mood stabilizers. But like all medications, they have potential side effects as well, and also require careful blood monitoring. And they may not be as effective at long-term prevention of mania as lithium.

As Andrew himself now realizes, despite his fairly ordinary struggles with work and love, reaching the place he's in is not an insignificant accomplishment. Bipolar disorder is a serious illness that can be lethal. My friend Danielle Steel, a passionate advocate and philanthropist for child mental illness awareness and treatment, wrote an affecting book, *His Bright Light,* about the suicide of her charming son, Nick Traina, who had bipolar disorder and substance abuse. "His illness killed him as surely as if it had been a cancer," Danielle wrote. "I wish I had known that, that I had been warned how great the risk was. Perhaps then I would have been better prepared for what came later. I'm not sure that in the minds of the public it is clear that bipolar disease . . . is potentially fatal. Not always certainly, but in far too many cases."

Andrew himself had a friend who succumbed to the illness. He was a college classmate who managed to graduate and, like Andrew, was working and planning to get married. The difference was that he hadn't been diagnosed as early as Andrew, and even when he was, he resisted treatment. He was diagnosed near the end of college, but by that time he was used to treating his extremes of mood with illegal drugs and alcohol. He eventually did start taking lithium, but didn't really believe he had the disease, and didn't stay with the medication. He fended off Andrew's many attempts to help him, and had nothing like the parental support that Andrew had received. After college he moved to the Midwest and spiraled downhill rapidly without any treatment. He never recovered, and committed suicide.

In the popular HBO series *Six Feet Under,* a character named Billy Chenowith has been bipolar since adolescence. When he is taking his medicine, he's great—charming, smart, caring. When he stops his treatment, it is as if he turns into a monster. He becomes belligerent, aggressive, and even violent toward his sister, whom he adores. Some of this, of course, is pure Hollywood (in the grand tradition of *One Flew Over the Cuckoo's Nest,* dramatic truth trumps literal accuracy), but the fact is that a manic-depressive off his medication can be a sad and startling sight. "I hate this," Billy tells his sister in the hospital after he's stabilized following a terrifying episode. "I hate that my blood makes me crazy. I hate that I can't function without being chemically altered."

Michael's Return

When I saw that episode, I was reminded of a patient I had seen a few years ago. Michael had the one-two punch—great student, great looks. But everything changed when he was sixteen. During a spring-break trip to visit his grandparents in Florida, he went into a panic, saying he felt like he was losing control. He cut short his vacation and came back home. Michael's mother took him to see a psychologist, whom he visited once a week over the next month or so. But one Friday in May, he broke down crying in school.

Michael's father had had bipolar disorder and had committed suicide when Michael was six. When I first saw Michael the Monday after the episode in school, he was accompanied by his mother, who was frantic. Over the weekend, Michael seemed to have been hallucinating, talking endlessly about hearing and seeing "the devil." Now, in my office, he had a wide-eyed stare and a pained grimace as he answered my questions about the thoughts in his head. He alternately moaned and giggled as he described racing thoughts, trouble sleeping, and worries about being homosexual.

Michael was hospitalized, and after six weeks he was back to normal and discharged on lithium and Trilafon, an antipsychotic medication that has since been replaced by newer ones. In September he was getting back into normal life, going to school, hanging out with his friends, complaining about his mother, and riding his motorbike. By then, he was only taking lithium. He was doing well.

Michael's senior year in high school was uneventful. He decided to go to a college near home. Halfway through his freshman year, Michael had gone more than a year and a half without another episode and decided that he was no longer sick. Therefore, he decided, he no longer needed to take lithium. The decision sent him into a manic meltdown. Within two months he was delusional again—alternately pronouncing he was God and the Devil—and he became obsessed with his own appeal, claiming he could have sex with anyone. He stopped sleeping, and was euphoric, talking rapidly and incessantly. Yet he also thought about suicide. Things only worsened after he was admitted to the hospital. He set off false fire alarms, attacked patients and staff, and had to be put in restraints. Several hospital aides had to be with him at all times to keep him safe. This time, the medications were ineffective. After four weeks they were discontinued, and a new approach was considered. The doctors at the hospital raised the possibility of Electroconvulsive Therapy (ECT). Naturally, Michael's mother had many concerns and questions. ECT has a controversial reputation, largely because of the distorted image—conveyed in films such as *One Flew Over the Cuckoo's Nest,* in which it was used as a punishment—that it is akin to some kind of medieval torture. When first developed, ECT sometimes resulted in medical complications, such as fractures from the intense seizures it induces, and the experience could be extremely frightening. As currently performed, ECT is a safe, effective treatment for both psychosis and unremitting depression. Patients are given general anesthesia and muscle relaxants before ECT is administered, and the electric shock lasts only a fraction of a second. The only physically observable evidence of the induced seizure is a slight, very brief shaking movement of the big toe. The most frequent side effect of ECT is a temporary short-term memory loss. While most people even regain their memories from that brief period, some do not, and find it very troubling. In general, the overwhelming positive effects of ECT far outweigh the negative.

Michael's mother consented to ECT, and after three sessions a week for four weeks, Michael responded. He did have side effects—short-term memory loss that persisted for several weeks after the last session—but that abated, and Michael, finally stabilized, went back on lithium and was discharged. But all of this happened because he stopped taking the medicine that had been keeping him sane. And once he did that, he couldn't recover by simply going back on the medicine.

Unfortunately, this is not an unusual story. Adolescents with bipolar disorder are all too frequently noncompliant with their medication. Instead, they may use illicit substances and, less frequently but more tragically, attempt suicide—and a substantial percentage complete the act. Like Michael, they don't accept that they are ill and need medication.

Thankfully, this was the last time that Michael stopped taking his medicine—the last time his mother had to go through such a horrific ordeal. As she found out, it's trying enough to have to cope with the challenges of a seriously ill child; it's beyond comprehension when the child is refusing to accept a treatment that the parent knows is effective. Michael finished college, and today, at 30, he is a high school phys-ed teacher and basketball coach who is exceptionally keen on keeping his body in shape. For him, this includes a daily dose of lithium.

All of these young people—Andrew and his friend, Paula, Nick Traina, Michael, the fictional Billy Chenowith—had unique and engaging personalities that became masked by illness. Their stories underscore the need to follow the advice of neurologist Oliver Sacks to not ask what neurological disease a person has, but rather, what kind of person the disease has taken hold of. There is no doubt that when it comes to bipolar disorder, medicine is absolutely necessary. Not only can it bring back the person hidden behind the disease, but it can also be the difference between life and death.

10

THE BIG BUMP: COLLEGE

When I was young, I had a friend named Scott. We were close through most of high school, and though we drifted apart a bit as graduation approached, we both wound up going to the University of Maryland. During freshman year, whenever I saw Scott he seemed downcast. He would walk staring at the ground, oblivious to all the energy of our expansive college campus. Pretty girls didn't turn his head, and he was almost invisible to the kids who walked past him.

We drove home together on spring break, and he talked about how he felt it wasn't worth staying in college. This was 1971, and the Vietnam War was still going, so it was definitely worth staying in college. But Scott was unhappy—pretty much with everything. He didn't like his courses, the professors were stupid, he hated his roommate, his girlfriend was three states away. Apparently, he had no friends at school, and he didn't seem all that interested in making any. This was startling to me. Scott had always been one of the friendliest guys I knew, and an extremely engaged student. But now it sounded like he might actually flunk out of college.

When we returned to school after spring break, Scott stopped going to classes. Every time I called his dormitory room, he was sleeping. He didn't make it through freshman year. Adrift, he quit and went home. His parents were shattered. It seemed all their dreams for their only son were evaporating. Their immediate concern was that he would be drafted, but fortunately, he got a high lottery number. His parents persuaded him to try going to the local community college, but that didn't work either. Floundering, he got a job as an editorial aide at a newspaper where his father's friend was an editor. But he couldn't get motivated enough to go to work after the first week.

I didn't see Scott again until three years later, when he came to my house while I was home at Thanksgiving during my first year in medical school. "Is there a disease that causes you to lose your motivation?" he asked me. The last few years had been lost ones for Scott. He had lived at home, working occasionally in jobs he hated. His parents had tried everything. They bought him weights, hoping the exercise would get him going. Scott promised to use them. But they sat in his room, in pristine condition. His parents redecorated his tiny room in bright blue—blue walls, blue carpet, blue bedding. They were that desperate. That Thanksgiving was the last time I saw Scott. He didn't show up at either our tenth or twentieth high school reunions. I heard later that he worked in a supermarket and had never married.

When I was young, someone like Scott was often said to be "finding himself." A generation later he might be called a slacker. But although nobody seemed to realize it at the time, Scott was in all likelihood depressed. Looking back, there were signs of it in high school, but it really emerged during that freshman year in college, when he was both overwhelmed by a big school with huge classes and lonely without his girlfriend. Drugs might have helped precipitate the depression—marijuana doesn't do much for motivation—or it might have been the other way around, depression leading to drug use. But one thing is for sure: Scott was far from the only student at the University of Maryland, or at any college in the country, who found himself in a depression at that point in his life. And he was not the only student who didn't get help and never really came back.

College is tricky terrain for mental health. During the course of working on this book, many people told me about periods of stifling depression that they experienced during those years. One colleague remembered feeling very down in the weeks before leaving home for the first time in his life and starting college in another part of the country. That was "anticipatory anxiety," and it evolved into depression after he arrived at school. Fortunately, the depression eventually lifted on its own, and he was able to get back on track. As any number of cases I've described demonstrate, what happens during a depression can have huge long-term consequences for a young person. A 40-year-old who has already reached at least some of his goals might have a terrible period while depressed, but he can recover and return to where he was. Younger people have a much harder time catching up.

Scott's story is all too common and plays out in every generation; the stresses of one's colleges years are nothing new, nor is the toll they can take on vulnerable adolescents. This is a time of life when several serious psychiatric illnesses tend to emerge, and the pressure of adjusting to college life—leaving home, forming relationships, figuring out one's major, getting good grades—can be a trigger for any one of them. What's changed, though, are cultural forces that have made these stresses more intense for today's students than they were for their parents. College students today are more likely to have grown up in split families than their parents. And they are surely faced with a more complicated world. Every generation worries about joining the "real world," but today's real world is one of information overload, a daunting technological society with more career choices, and increasing pressure to meet expectations, make correct major life decisions, and make them more quickly. Competition begins earlier than ever—in some circles as early as nursery school—so that by the time they reach college, many adolescents feel tremendously burdened by expectations both for present performance and to meet their future goals. Now they also have to worry about terrorism. At Harvard University's mental health service, the number of patients seen in the wake of the 9/11 attacks doubled from about 40 a week to 80.

Reams of statistics cross my desk in the course of a year, but some of the most sobering I've seen come from the National College Health Assessment, a survey conducted in the spring of 2000 by the American College Health Association. The survey asked some 16,000 students, from 28 public and private universities, questions about drinking, sex, nutrition, and mental health issues. Here's what they asked and how students responded (percentages are rounded):

- How many times in the past academic year have you felt intense hopelessness? Only 38 percent said never. Nearly 10 percent said more than 11 times.
- How many times have you felt overwhelming sadness and were so depressed that you couldn't function? More than 15 percent said at least five times, including nearly 7 percent who said more than 11 times.
- Have you ever been diagnosed with depression? Ten percent said yes. Of these, about a quarter said they had been diagnosed in the past year. Twenty-one percent of those diagnosed were currently taking medication.
- In the past school year, how many times have you seriously contemplated suicide? A total of 9.5 percent said at least once, including 1 percent who said 11 or more times.
- In the past school year, how many times have you attempted suicide? A total of 1.6 percent said at least once.

Even accounting for the possibility that some who took the survey were overstating the case, the results indicate that a significant percentage of American college students feel very bad a good deal of the time. What may be most striking is that the *majority* of college students apparently feel "intense hopelessness" at least occasionally, and some feel this way quite often. The results also indicate that most of them are not getting help. If they were, the percentage who said they had been diagnosed with depression would no doubt be much higher than ten.

□

Adolescence always reflects society—and vice versa. In the 1950s, teenagers were the picture of Eisenhower-era innocence, but a decade later it seemed that they were angry, confused, and rebelling against authority. Today, adolescents reflect the pressured, overtechnological world of the new millennium. But while styles, attitudes, events, and other societal forces change, some basic things stay the same. Whatever the era, adolescence can be broken down into three stages—early, middle, and late—that roughly correlate with age. The late phase starts as a teenager is preparing to graduate from high school and extends until he or she is 21 or 22. This is a generality, of course. For some, adolescence continues until the midtwenties or even later. (Note that 25 is often the minimum age for renting a car.) Just as puberty is a key marker in depression in early adolescence—more so than strict chronological age—college is another milestone. The difference is that puberty is a biological factor. College is environmental.

As complicated and difficult as early and middle adolescence can seem at the time, in many ways the college years are a much bigger challenge. These are the key years for reaching career goals and forming a social network. There is more sexual activity and more access to diversions such as drugs and alcohol that can alter brain chemistry and either trigger depression or worsen it. The big issue in all of this, especially for kids who go away to school, is independence: Mom and Dad are no longer on the scene, watching over them. They're no longer in a position to see Jason or Jennifer every day and notice changes in their behavior and habits that might signal trouble. Now it's largely up to the kids themselves to acknowledge changes in their own moods and take steps to ease their stress and get help if they need it. Realistically, this may be too much to ask. Likewise, the parents' jobs change. First, they have to be alert to the special challenges and risks of depression at this unique time of life. Then they have to figure out how to stay engaged in their child's life from a distance. And, potentially most important, especially for parents of kids who are vulnerable to depression, they need to be ready and able to swoop in and get their children the help they need.

The college years as a whole present unique challenges, but within these four years are distinct phases. The trials of freshman year are different from those of senior year. And a student's response to those stressors will be different. An adolescent is not the same person when he's leaving college as when he arrived.

FRESHMAN YEAR

Though he won't think of it exactly in these terms, what the college freshman faces is all those developmental tasks of adolescence coming to a head all at once: separating from parents, figuring out what he wants to do with his life, forming intimate and social relationships, developing his personal ethics. High school was just a prelude; now the pressure is really on, and without the cocoon of home. It's fair to say that among the four undergraduate classes at any university, it's the freshmen who have the most challenges and the least maturity to handle them.

Of all the stressful adjustments confronting college freshmen who go away to school, the most difficult is separating from parents. Sure, they're thrilled to be out of the house and on their own, but just beneath the surface—or maybe right out in the open—is the frightening realization that being on their own doesn't just mean glorious freedom. It also means real *responsibility*. Not responsibilities like taking out the garbage or doing well on a test, but personal accountability. They are now responsible for their own well-being.

I know my oldest son, Josh, was excited when he went off to college—he was going to his first choice of schools, and he was more than ready—but all my wife and I saw and felt as we drove him up to his campus was his anxiety. To say he was prickly would not be doing justice to his apprehension. Arriving at the dormitory, we brought his things into his tiny room and met his roommate, a young man from a rural area whose background was obviously different from Josh's. At a time like this, as a parent you're thinking about how your kid is going to handle living with a total stranger who may or may not be a good fit. You're realizing how far the dorm is from the main campus and thinking about whether he should get a bicycle. And on some level, you're worried about how good a job you did the last 18 years. Will he eat right and get enough sleep? Will he fit in socially? Can he live without us?

Believe it or not, in one way or another your kid is thinking about most of the same things. As much as a teenager hates all the restrictions of home—his parents telling him when to be home, getting on him to make his bed and eat healthy—it provides a structure that he might not even realize is a comfort. The moment your taillights disappear marks the official start of the adjustment process. Tomorrow morning, you're back at work, back in your routine. You may be sad and feeling strange, but you'll deal with it. Two hundred miles away, your child is waking up in what might strike him as someone else's life.

One of the big, unspoken tasks for many college freshmen is reconciling fantasy and reality. To begin with, think about what most teenagers base their choice of college on: maybe a few pages in a college guide, perhaps a visit to campus and a tour conducted by a student who made the place sound like heaven. Maybe they just liked that the school has a great basketball team. They may soon realize that the place is something other than what they envisioned. Or that they really hadn't thought about how hard it would be to live with strangers they had little in common with. A student from a small town may be overwhelmed by the size of a major university, struck by a feeling of insignificance. Some freshmen fantasize about the opportunity college offers to reinvent themselves. They've left behind everyone they know. People they saw every day for 12 years are nowhere in sight. Time to start fresh. Some can pull this off, but no matter what stage of life we're in, most of us find ourselves still dealing with the same assets and flaws we've always had.

I spoke recently with a friend who recalled his first night at college, an Ivy League school with dormitories out of *Architectural Digest.* He lay in bed, peering up at the ceiling 18 feet away. "I felt like a dwarf," he said—a metaphor for his general state of mind as he tried to adjust to his new life. In high school he had been at the top of his class; now he was at an elite college where *everyone* had been at the top of his or her class. It struck him that it was within the realm of possibility that he could now actually be at the *bottom* of his class. Talk about a dispiriting thought.

As mundane as it may sound, sleep deprivation is a big problem for college students. Teenagers are likely to be night owls to begin with, and now they have all those temptations: hanging out with roommates and friends, drinking, drugs, sex. Yet there are responsibilities in the morning. A student with bipolar disorder has to pay special attention to getting adequate sleep. In this case, it might be necessary to request a single room, if the only alternative is a roommate who stays up late and plays music.

All these are stressors that can trip the switch on a depressive episode, especially for a teenager who is vulnerable—one who either has risk factors (such as family history) or who has already had depression. So a parent who sends a susceptible adolescent off to college has to make sure the student is prepared, should she become depressed. This is where psychoeducation is important. A vulnerable individual has to understand the illness, the same way a diabetic knows that she will go into a coma if she doesn't watch her diet. If depression is an issue—as it was for Jesse Altman in chapter 5, for instance—arrangements should be made ahead of time with a psychiatrist on or off campus who can meet with the student before school starts and monitor her medication. It's not enough to send your child off to school with a bottle of pills and casual plans for her to check in with her psychiatrist at home when she comes home for Thanksgiving. Your child lives at school; she needs a doctor there. Facilitate this in advance.

Those with children who already have depression aren't the only parents who need to think about mental health. While it's not necessary to have the name of a psychiatrist at college posted on the refrigerator, every parent should make sure his or her child knows how to get help, if it becomes necessary, from the college health service. It's no different from knowing where to go if you get the flu.

Fortunately, colleges are well aware of the risks of mental illness for their students, and are bolstering their mental health services. Many have made it part of their orientation programs. Dr. Martin E. P. Seligman, a prominent psychologist at the University of Pennsylvania, applies the concept of cognitive distortion in trying to keep new students from becoming depressed. Each spring he sends all 2,200 incoming freshmen his Attributional Style Questionnaire, which is designed to assess whether they tend to be optimistic or pessimistic, and to what they attribute the cause of negative events in their lives. The students who rate in the bottom quarter—those most pessimistic and who tend to believe that the causes of negative events are pervasive and unchanging—are given the opportunity to enroll in a group in which Dr. Seligman trains students how to avoid falling into a trap of negative thought. Similar psychoeducation programs, an important and effective means of early intervention, have been adopted by other universities.

THE MIDDLE YEARS

Having survived the myriad adjustments of freshman year, students will find academics and career goals their primary stressor in their sophomore and junior years. They are forced to focus on where they are headed. They have to declare a major, and realize that it should have something to do with what they're going to do after they graduate. They know that how well they do in these years will have more long-term consequences than their performance in high school did. There is something seemingly irrevocable about these choices, and yet it's an unusually clear-thinking and resolute 20-year-old who knows exactly what he's going to do in life.

Pressures may also be mounting on the social front. To be sure, some students find it easy to hook up romantically with others. Their stressor may be the fallout of a breakup. Others are less comfortable and less adept with the rituals of dating. They can take a pass as a freshman—boys say that freshmen girls want to go out with upperclassmen, and girls feel they just haven't met the right guy—but by their sophomore year, they are likely to be putting pressure on themselves to start a relationship. It doesn't help if their roommate is sleeping with someone in the next bed. Certainly, sexual orientation issues also become prominent.

SENIOR YEAR

Ironically, as uncomfortable and nervous as she may have been as a freshman, a student can be almost *too* comfortable as a senior. This has become her home. She has close friends with whom she has a strong emotional bond, roommates she's chosen rather than had assigned to her. They've shared experiences and spent many late nights talking about life. She feels safe here. But now what lies ahead is not only the separation from these friends, but something much bigger: the great unknown.

It's different from the transition between high school and college. In an article in *The New York Times* about the emotional stress of senior year, Lewis Fortner, an associate dean of students at the University of Chicago, observed: "After all, it isn't just the end of four years. It's the end of 16 or 17 years of education, which is a highly artificial form of existence. At that time in their lives, students can hardly remember a time when they were not in school, so they usually feel some trepidation about this extraordinary change. The abyss of freedom yawns." Most students get through this transition just fine, but it can be stressful—and a potential depression trigger—for even the healthiest person. So students and parents should be aware and open to getting help if symptoms of depression emerge. Again, young people at risk, and their parents, should be especially vigilant.

·

Given that the whole college experience could be viewed as one stress after another, it's remarkable how well the overwhelming majority of students do. A week after my son went to college, he called—just to chat. Frankly, I was stunned. We had left Josh in a state of barely controlled tension. But now, all those daunting challenges he had been anxious about, and that were so worrisome to my wife and me, had somehow become *fun* for him. He was enjoying taking care of himself. He felt liberated. This is not to say that the next four years would be a cakewalk. I thought again of my old friend Scott, whose undiagnosed depression had caused him to suffer through a torturous freshman year before he flunked out and spent the next years floundering.

Curious to find out what mental health services there had been at our university back then, I called the current director of the student health service, Dr. Maggie Bridwell. She told me that mental health services at the University of Maryland in the early 1970s consisted of a couple of psychiatrists who came in for a few hours each once a week. Students were generally referred to these doctors when they were seen as being "too hippie," she said. Dr. Bridwell became medical director in 1975. That year, there was a rash of suicides on campus, and she responded by hiring psychiatrists who helped primary-care physicians recognize and treat minor depression symptoms. But those psychiatrists were from the Freudian school, and their traditional 50-minute sessions of psychoanalysis were not designed specifically to treat depression, the way today's SSRI medications and cognitive behavioral therapy are.

I asked Dr. Bridwell how a student like my friend Scott would have been treated back then. No one would have paid him much attention, she said. "The older and more conservative physicians would write notes excusing students who were missing classes and then tell them, 'Straighten up and you'll be fine,' instead of addressing their problems and recognizing depression."

Since the 1980s, Dr. Bridwell has overseen a student health service that recognizes mental health as one of its most important components. There is a fully staffed counseling center that refers the most seriously ill students to the main health center that employs three psychiatrists (two full-time) and several clinical social workers. During the 2000–2001 academic year, some 1,400 students came to the health center for psychiatric help, nearly half of them because of depression. But treating depression that comes on during college is only part of the story. Dr. Bridwell, like many of her peers, believes that some students would never even make it to college if not for the help they received in their early teen years. Thanks to the development of SSRIs and more effective treatments for depression, as well as better identification and diagnosis of bipolar disorder, many bright young people whose debilitating mental illnesses might have kept them from attending school in earlier eras are now enrolling and succeeding. This is one of the reasons why college health services today are seeing a greater number of patients with depression: more students arrive at college already diagnosed and under treatment.

The increased incidence and awareness of depression at the University of Maryland is mirrored at just about every other major university in the United States. A survey conducted during the 2001–2002 academic year by *The New York Times* found that demand for campus mental health services had exploded across the country, at both intensely demanding private schools and at less competitive public colleges. For instance, Columbia University saw a 40 percent increase in the use of its counseling service between 1994 and 2001. At a nearby public university, the State University of New York (SUNY) at Purchase, meanwhile, there was a 48 percent jump in just three years. And at the Massachusetts Institute of Technology—which has had the highest student suicide rate in the country—50 percent more students were using the mental health service in 2000 than in 1995. There was also a huge jump, 69 percent, in the number of students who were hospitalized for psychiatric illnesses during that period. Nationally, about 8 percent of the general population uses mental health services. Among college students, the figure is 13 percent.

College health centers have traditionally not been set up to provide for the chronically ill, whether it's a physical or mental illness. The psychiatrists or psychologists on staff have been there mainly to help students adjust to college life and to try to intervene in a crisis, rather than to care for a serious, ongoing mental illness. But the increasing demand has led many major universities to expand their mental health services on campus. Depression leads to dropping out, and colleges are interested in retaining their students. So it's in everybody's interest to provide students with access to mental health services. The University of Michigan, for instance, has opened its Comprehensive Depression Center, both to conduct research into depression for all age groups and to treat students. And at the University of Maryland, resident assistants in dormitories are given mental health education as part of their training, which includes talks on recognizing the warning signs of depression. Freshman orientation includes a program of weekly discussions about mental health issues. Dr. Bridwell noted that the last suicide on campus was in 1980, though there are a number of attempts each year. The heightened awareness of depression on campus is also a factor in increased numbers of freshmen making it through that first year instead of dropping out. Only 77 percent of Maryland freshmen completed the year in 1977. In 2000, 91 percent did. The steepest increase occurred since the 1990s, around the time that SSRI antidepressants came into wide use.

The good news in all this is that psychiatric illness in all its forms is being better diagnosed among the young, and that the traditional stigma of treatment means a lot less to the millennium generation than it did to its predecessors. Indeed, a headline in *The New York Times* report dubbed today's college students "the therapy generation." In a conversation about what seems to be an explosion of depression on college campuses, Dr. Seligman of the University of Pennsylvania told me that we have some-

how turned today's young people into an emotionally fragile generation—an inevitable result, he thinks, of a self-centered society that almost celebrates victims. (Tune in to any daytime talk show.) "It's learned
helplessness," he said. "It's the belief that we play no role when something bad happens, that this was something that was done to us." That's
why he gives the incoming freshman the Attributional Style Questionnaire. "Feeling helpless," he said, "is a recipe for depression." He also
wondered if the "self-esteem movement" had caused some young people
to become addicted to constant praise, even the kind of empty kudos
that don't really build self-esteem. "The most important goal seems to be
to make your students feel good about themselves, rather than to improve their commerce with the world. I'm not sure where the self-esteem
movement started but that's where it's gone." Losing that reassurance
when an adolescent goes off to college can amount to a stressor that
could become an ingredient in depression.

These are provocative thoughts, but whatever is to blame, the fact is
that depression on campus is an undeniable and significant problem.
And even with more resources being poured into mental health services,
it has not been nearly enough. Long waits for appointments and referrals
to off-campus therapists or facilities—which may be *way* off campus, in
the case of a rural college—mean that many students are not getting
what they need. "We are drowning here," the director of the SUNY Purchase counseling center told the *Times*. "Right now, if it's not an emergency, it's two to two-and-a-half weeks to get an appointment."

Besides Dr. Bridwell at Maryland, I spoke to several other directors of
mental health services at major universities, and all of them told me the
same thing: that the student population as a whole has much more psychiatric illness than it used to and seems much more comfortable with
getting psychological help. Dr. Paul Grayson, director of the counseling
center at my current home, New York University, told me that the SSRI
generation quickly changed attitudes. "It used to be a hard sell to get
students to take medicines when they needed it," he said. "Today, many
of them come into the center already taking an SSRI, and many of those
who complain of depression very often say they want medication." Re-

flecting society as a whole, psychiatrists at the counseling center were writing more than twice as many prescriptions for antidepressants in 2002 than they were in 1997. The flip side, Dr. Grayson said, is the all-too-common story of a freshman who arrives on campus taking medication but doesn't come to the counseling center to see a clinician who can monitor and look after him. He goes home for the Christmas break and sees his doctor, but by then he may have stopped taking his medication and is relapsing. By March, he has started to fall apart academically and may even have made a suicide gesture or attempt. In the 2000–2001 academic year, less than half of the students at NYU who took medical leaves for psychiatric reasons ever returned.

Dr. Richard Kadizon, a child and adolescent psychiatrist who is the director of mental health services at Harvard University, told me that his center, which serves a population of 17,000 students in undergraduate and graduate programs and 7,000 faculty members, had 22,000 patient visits in 2001. Taking care of these patients is a full-time and part-time staff that amounts to the equivalent of 17 full-time clinicians. Each year, according to Dr. Kadizon, about 30 students at Harvard have to be hospitalized for depression and/or suicidal behavior. Suicides do occur, but the rate has been consistently below the national average.

While all these universities are doing wonderful work to recognize, treat, and destigmitize depression, there is a limit to what they can do. The most important part of the process, getting a student to come in for treatment, is still up to the individual, with the help of her parents and other people in her life. Moreover, students still learn most of what they know about health from their parents. So Harvard, for one, conducts a seminar on depression during parent orientation weekend. The university's freshman deans also send letters to parents of all incoming students, asking them to write personal letters describing their kids and supplying any information they'd like that might help identify whether the student is at risk for depression and ought to be looked after more carefully.

ANNIE GETS HELP

Annie was 3,000 miles from home, but that didn't stop her mother in California from taking the first step to get her some help. Annie's mom was in the entertainment industry, an assertive woman who was used to picking up the phone and making arrangements. I met her while on vacation in California, and soon after I returned home, I found her on the phone. She wanted to make an appointment for her 19-year-old daughter, who had become depressed during her sophomore year in college.

When Annie came to my office one day in spring, she was initially a bit guarded, but soon she became more attentive and engaged. Unlike some young patients I see, she knew she had a problem, and she really wanted help. She had been depressed since the past fall, she said, and felt as though she was "wallowing." She wasn't sleeping well, and felt she had way too much time on her hands. She looked straight at me and said, "I can't fix it." As she said this, tears formed in her bright blue eyes and began to trickle down her cheeks. Annie had a sweet, open face and an engaging manner—she wasn't one of those just-leave-me-alone-I'm-not-depressed sort of kids.

I handed her a tissue and asked her to take me back to the beginning. Annie told me a big turning point in her life had come when she was eight and her parents divorced. "They were fighting like cats and dogs, so when they split up it was much better," she said. "At least it was quieter. But I got really sad about it, and I don't think I was easy to be around. I've always been a sensitive person."

"Sensitive in what way?" I asked.

"News affects me in a big way. It can be anything. If a friend is sick. Divorce, definitely. So I reacted badly to my parents' divorce. I was fighting with my friends all the time."

Life settled down by high school. However, when I asked her if she'd ever felt the same way she did now, she told me that at one point when she was 16 she had fallen into a period of extreme lethargy. It had been diagnosed as chronic fatigue syndrome, a controversial and poorly defined condition that often mimics the symptoms of depression. By her senior year, Annie was looking forward to going off on her own. "I wanted to get out of California," she said. She went about as far as possible, across the country to New York. "But my freshman year here was horrible. I got depressed, and it took me about four months to get out of it. I couldn't concentrate, and my grades were miserable."

"How was your social life?"

"Not good. I had a single dorm room so I felt like I wasn't connecting with people."

"So how do you compare that to the way you feel now? Or to the way you felt when you had chronic fatigue in high school?"

"This feels a lot worse than that," Annie said softly. "It's hard to sleep. I wake up at five in the morning. My mind wanders a lot, which never happened before. I've felt exhausted since last fall and I think it's getting worse. I just feel so terrible."

Annie admitted that she had been drinking a lot—it made her numb, she said—and she had used cocaine and Ecstasy. The drugs made her feel good, but the people she was doing them with scared her.

It was also clear that Annie had a lot of anxieties. Some were reasonable: though she had come from privileged circumstances, she had worked since high school; but now she wasn't working, and she worried that she was being lazy, wasting her time. Other anxieties were less rational. She feared, for instance, that her father, who was not sick, might soon die. (Significantly, she also said that her father and brother had some kind of depression in their histories, though she wasn't sure about the specifics).

Annie seemed to have a prime example of the kind of depression that comes on during the college years. And since this wasn't the first episode, I thought she was a good candidate for medication. I wanted to talk to her mother first, and I asked Annie if that would be okay. She nodded yes.

Later that day, I called Annie's mother in California and told her that

Annie had described two previous episodes, one in high school and the other last year, during her freshman year. I thought both were probably bouts of depression. This would make three. "Oh, she's definitely had three episodes," her mother said. "And I'm worried she's going to become an alcoholic. I know she drinks when she gets depressed."

I asked her how she felt about putting Annie on Prozac. She chuckled. "Where I come from it's hard to find someone who's *not* on Prozac."

Annie was not so glib about taking the medicine. She wanted to know about side effects and, more important, whether it would change "who I am," frequently asked and reasonable questions. She decided to give the medicine a try, and it lifted her. In fact, she blossomed. She cut down on her drinking and became an academic standout, getting straight As, much better than her performance in high school. She became socially much more at ease as well. She had always had a great sense of humor and an unusual ability to enjoy and relate to people of all ages, but now she had a new-found confidence as well. She joined a swing dance class, and made friends there. "That made a big difference," she said. And with renewed energy and motivation, Annie got an afternoon job working for a photographer. She used what she earned to travel during vacations. She had a new sense of independence. Part of it was maturity, and part of it was her renewed ability to draw from her own inner resouces. Without depression, the barriers were down. By her junior year, Annie had decided that she wanted to go on to film school when she graduated, and would spend her senior year making a short film that was the main part of the application.

After Annie had been taking Prozac for a year, we talked about gradually lowering her dosage and then stopping it. To some extent this was a test. With depression, the more episodes a person has, the greater the risk for additional ones. The rule of thumb with SSRI medications is that a patient can stop taking them if he or she has had six months to a year without symptoms after the first depressive episode. But if it recurs, it's advisable to stay on medication for two years. If there is a recurrence after that, it might be a lifelong proposition. The issue with Annie was whether she had been in a depression during high school, rather than having chronic fatigue syndrome. But she had been doing well for a year, and she was anxious to stop taking Prozac. We waited until October, so that if she had a quick relapse, it wouldn't be during the stressful part of the beginning of her senior year.

Annie was fine throughout that year, and I looked forward to our monthly visits. She would talk excitedly about her student film project, about a boyfriend she had been seeing, about her job. But one day in spring she called and said she was depressed again. She hadn't been accepted into film school. "I didn't even get an interview," she said dejectedly. I didn't want her to leap right back to Prozac, just in case this turned out to be a brief and understandable down period from which she would recover. But after several more weeks in a funk, it was clear this was a relapse. She went back on Prozac. Within three weeks, she had fully stabilized.

Annie was remarkable for her maturity and astuteness about her illness. Her father had it, her brother had it, and she took ownership of it as well. She was never pleased to be taking medicine, questioning it all the time and wondering if she would have to take it the rest of her life. But she sensed it would be hard for her to have a fulfilling life without it.

In June, I received an invitation to Annie's graduation and to a party afterward. I was honored and touched, but felt slightly awkward on her behalf. A cancer survivor might invite her oncologist, but did Annie really want her psychiatrist attending a small family party? As unfortunate as it is, I do recognize the stigma of having a mental illness. I told Annie I'd feel more comfortable just attending the graduation. I went, planning to sit anonymously in an aisle seat so she would see me during the procession into the field house. Afterward I would slip out. But at the door I found Annie's mother waiting for me. She had saved a seat with the family, and happily introduced me to her ex-husband, whom I'd never met. "Oh, I've heard so much about you," he said with a big smile and hearty handshake. Afterward, Annie hugged me and thanked me. But I told her she did it herself. So many people have illnesses they do nothing about. But Annie's ability to confront her illness was remarkable.

She still had her share of problems, like anyone else. She struggled with her weight and continued to search for the right boyfriend. After graduation, she was still upset about not getting into film school. She was living back in California and feeling like a failure. Like many people her age, she was in what might be called extended adolescence, that passage to true independence and adulthood. For some people it's a short bridge, but for others it's a long, dark tunnel. Annie found herself in tears just about every day those first few weeks. But she realized that it's possible to be unhappy without being depressed.

Her mother helped get her a job as a television production assistant and set her up in a small apartment. But that didn't help much. Annie hated the job. And she was as lonely as could be. She tried reconnecting with friends from high school and tried making friends with people from work, but she still found herself alone on Saturday nights. "I go to yoga every day at six-thirty, and nobody talks," she told me over the phone. She had huge phone bills. She called her friends in New York almost obsessively.

Annie's mother was impatient. "I don't understand why you're not happy," she told her. She thought Annie was going through some sort of postcollege letdown. Annie was still on Prozac, and her psychiatrist in California raised the dosage and augmented it with Wellbutrin, an "atypical" antidepressant that doesn't affect serotonin but increases two other neurochemicals, norepinephrine and dopamine. (That approach may be more effective than simply increasing the dosage of the SSRI.) And slowly, Annie emerged—and then she had the motivation for a job change. She began working as an assistant for an entertainment lawyer, and loved the job. Her boss was appreciative and thanked her every day for her work. Meanwhile, she looked forward to reapplying to film school.

There had been a very good chance that Annie would have dropped out of college if she hadn't sought and received help, the same kind of help that my friend Scott never got. Though she went off Prozac again after going another six months without symptoms, Annie knows that keeping depression at bay may well be a lifelong struggle for her—but a struggle she can win.

DEAN GOES WEST

Unlike Annie, Dean Wechsler had grown up in a stable and happy home. His parents were happily married, and he had a carefree personality that helped him handle whatever bumps came along. I first met him when he was in second grade and I diagnosed him with ADHD and a reading disability. He responded very well to Ritalin, which he took on and off through high school. But having ADHD and a learning disability had no affect on Dean's happiness. When he came to my office over the years, he was always upbeat. Dean had blond hair, blue eyes, and chiseled features, and was athletic and charming. He had lots of friends and a great family of significant means. "I had it cushy," Dean told me. "I had no right to be depressed."

And he wasn't—until he went away to college in Colorado. He didn't mind leaving his cushy life behind; like millions of other college freshmen, as much as he loved his parents, he was excited about separating from them and being on his own. But at the same time, for the first time in his life he had more than a little trepidation. "I was very close with my friends in high school," he said years later, "and I was unsure of how I was going to adjust to meeting all these new people. I mean, I knew my friends since we were little. I trusted them."

Dean adjusted reasonably well during the first few weeks after he arrived on campus. But after about a month, he began to be bothered by seemingly trivial things. He lent one of his roommates money and never got it back. That would never have happened at home, he thought. He didn't like sharing a bathroom. "I guess I'm spoiled," he said. "And I'm not that great with transitions. I don't adapt right away. But at the same time I didn't think that things would bother me so much. I didn't think I was going to miss my parents and my family that much. I knew I would miss my friends, and I really did. That was tough."

By nature, Dean was socially very relaxed. He made friends easily, and never had problems with girls. They came to him. "But a lot of my college friends were smoking pot. Like all the time. You know, you smoke pot, you sit around. My friends and I in high school were active in athletics. I was on the football and basketball teams. We smoked pot once in a while, not very much. But with these guys, it was really excessive. They'd wake up and go to their car, because we weren't allowed to smoke in the dorms. They'd go to class, then they'd come back and smoke more pot. They bought so much marijuana. I was worried about the situation because I didn't know them that well."

So far, it sounds like homesickness, with some adjustment problems that were a little bit more severe than Dean might have expected. But by the middle of October, he was sinking into something more serious. "I started to realize that I wasn't leaving here," he said. "This is where I am. I got anxious and wanted to come home. I felt like, okay, it's been kind of fun for a month, but I don't want to stay out here." He called his parents and said he wanted to come home.

His father said no. Instead he wanted Dean to talk to me. It's hard to make a diagnosis over the phone, but when Dean called I tried to shape an interview according to what I knew about him in the past and what his father had told me. I asked Dean to tell me about college—how he liked his classes, how he was doing socially, how he was adjusting to dormitory life and being so far from home.

"I guess I was looking forward to a smoother transition," he said.

"How is it going academically?" I asked.

"Okay," he said unconvincingly. "You know I'm not the greatest student, but it's all right."

"And socially?"

"I was joining a fraternity but I dropped that."

"Why?"

"I don't know, the fraternity thing has an image. I didn't like all the business with the hazing." Dean was in great shape, bigger than most of the pledge trainers, and they thought he had a cocky attitude and really came after him. "You think you're hard?" they taunted. So he quit. "I was getting mad and I figured, what do I need this for?" I could hear the resentment in his voice. "My friends are still doing the fraternity thing and I'm not involved anymore, so that's hard."

"Do you think you're more irritable than usual?" I asked. "Because you're the kind of guy who can usually take stuff like that. But now you're refusing to play the game."

"Yeah, I guess."

Though Dean didn't have a great deal of insight at the time, he told me a few years later: "There were definitely things that I would normally have let roll off my back that I couldn't deal with. There were so many things I was uncomfortable with. I was feeling doomed."

One of the key indicators that Dean had a mood disorder was that he had stopped having sex. He told me that he'd always attracted girls; in fact, he had met someone the day he arrived on campus, and she had actively pursued him, appearing at his dorm room two nights later. But things had already begun to change. "I think when you feel good and you have a glow or whatever you want to call it, people come to you, and I used to feel that way inside. But now, I was feeling so terrible that I guess it showed on the outside. You could see that my confidence wasn't where it was. I wasn't working out anymore. I remember when I got there girls would come over to me. And that stopped. I just felt overwhelmed and it showed."

During that initial phone conversation, Dean said he was oversleeping and not leaving his room much. He was cutting a lot of classes. "I want to come home," he pleaded. He told me years later that at the time he had had very little motivation, and escalating self-doubt. He was thinking he might as well quit school and go to work for his father in the family commercial printing business.

Dean's father wanted him to give it more time and tough it out. He emphasized that all this was new to him. Dean hadn't had any anxiety or depressive symptoms growing up. But I told his dad that I thought it was unwise to leave him out there to deal with his problems on his own. Bring him in, I advised, and we'll see what's going on.

Dean came in to see me, and during our conversation he told me that he was feeling uncharacteristically self-conscious, and that he needed to get drunk to be intimate with a woman. This didn't sound like the Dean I knew—nor did the prickliness and sensitivity about his roommates and potential fraternity brothers. This was clearly a mood change. Dean was chronically irritable and hopeless. I prescribed Paxil to treat his depression and his social anxiety symptoms, but Dean was apprehensive about taking it.

"Do I really need this?" he asked. I felt that he was so clearly not himself, and that if let go his depression would become more severe.

Dean acquiesced to his father's insistence that he go back to Colorado. By now, he was pretty sure he had made a mistake in going to a school so far from home. He wished he had chosen a place that was close enough to allow him to come home for a weekend if he wanted. "You're not giving it a chance," Dean's father told him. "You can't feel a place out without being there for a certain period of time. It's a good school. Finish the year, then we'll see."

Dean went back, still not sure he wanted to be there, but willing to consider his father's opinion that he wasn't giving school a chance. "We like to complain a lot in our family," Dean said, chuckling about his memories of that experience. "So I thought maybe I was just seeing the negative. Of course, it was usually my dad who was always picking things apart. 'I don't like this, I don't like that.' So this was a switch."

To me, it was telling that Dean made a lot of late-night phone calls to his parents, and one to me. One night soon after he returned to school and began taking Paxil, Dean called me, sounding very shaky. He had gone to visit a friend at another college in Colorado and felt his legs go numb. He had been drinking the night before and was panicked that it had caused some terrible interaction. When I asked Dean what he was doing when he felt his legs go numb, he said he was in the bathroom, on the toilet. It turned out that he had merely become engrossed in a magazine article and sitting so long that he had cut off the circulation to his legs. His first conclusion was typical: blame the medicine.

What struck me about these calls was that Dean had never been a hysterical kind of kid. It was his easy-going, "What—me worry?" personality that had made him so attractive socially. But this was a very frightened young man. I also noted a change in the way he viewed others. He used to be the kind of person who would weigh someone's good and bad points and always find a way to minimize the deficits. But now he was seeing more of the negatives in his peers. The medicine wasn't working.

I switched Dean's medication from Paxil to another SSRI, Zoloft, and the new medicine did help him get back on track. (Though all SSRIs affect serotonin, they're not identical. But it's unclear why one brand might work when another doesn't.) He began adapting to college life and regained his energy. At the beginning of the second semester he moved into a house with two friends, a more agreeable situation for him. But, of course, antidepressants are not magic. They might treat the depression, but they don't change reality. And Colorado was still 2,000 miles from home. Dean spent the summer at home working for his dad, then agreed to go back to Colorado for his sophomore year. It was a so-so year. He struggled academically and made up his mind that he wanted to transfer to a school on the East Coast, to be closer not only to home but also to a girl he had begun dating during the summer, who was going to school in Boston.

Transferring wasn't easy because Dean's grades were poor. But his mother helped him with applications, and he was able to get into a good school in Washington, D.C., as a nonmatriculating student. It was a kind of probation: if he did well for a semester, he would be accepted as a matriculating student. I was in Washington to deliver a lecture, and Dean attended. Afterward, we went for a cup of coffee, and I was pleased to find him in much better spirits than the last time I'd seen him over the summer. He was doing well academically, getting mostly Bs. "I think guilt is my drive right now," he said. "My parents said, 'All right, you can transfer,' so I better do well."

I expected Dean would finish college in Washington, and so I was surprised to hear a few months later that he was heading back to Colorado. "My friends started calling from Colorado," he explained, "and I was a little lonely in Washington, and I said, 'You know what? I just want to go back to Colorado.'"

If this sounds like a kid who can't make up his mind, it's really not. Rather, it's that he had finally gotten through his adjustment troubles and reached a place of emotional stability. In Washington, it wasn't depression that made him discontent. He had friends there, and he was smiling and talkative when I saw him. He was even flirtatious with the waitress. He was back. But it wasn't enough. He wasn't *happy* in Washington—like Annie, he was restless, but not depressed—and soon after that he was back in Colorado. He thrived there, and he managed to graduate alongside his classmates. All except the pot smokers, who had never made it past their freshman year.

11

THE NIGHTMARE: SUICIDE

I'm surprised I haven't done it yet because I feel really terrible all the time. . . . I just don't have any courage but anyone else in my position would have already committed suicide.

FROM A JOURNAL ENTRY BY RACHEL, 15

Think about this: according to the Centers for Disease Control and Prevention (CDC), 19 percent of teenagers say they have thought about ending their own lives. If that sounds like the CDC is including a lot of teenagers' rash or casual thoughts, then consider this: half of that 20 percent actually make an attempt—anything from taking too much aspirin to slashing their wrists.

This is the most difficult chapter of this book—for both writer and reader—not only because the suicide of a young person is so devastatingly sad, but also because such a balancing act is called for. Depression comes in many forms, and most of them are not life-threatening and in any case are generally treatable. On the other hand, left unchecked, the most serious depressions, whether unipolar or bipolar, can indeed lead to tragedy. This is an important chapter for every parent to read—not with panic, but with the careful understanding that suicide does not just happen to other people's children, and that there are real things you can do to keep your child safe.

This year in the United States we will lose to suicide nearly 2,000 young people between the ages of 15 and 19, and depression will be a factor in most of them. That means that every single day of the year, five more teenagers kill themselves. Only accidents and homicides claim more young lives. The number more than doubles if you extend the age range to 24—and some think that these numbers may actually be an underestimate. When you consider all suicide attempts—not just those that are completed—the figures become even more staggering. A half million young people in this age range attempt suicide each year.

Multiple studies have found that in 90 percent of suicide cases, there is an underlying psychiatric disorder. Depression is by far the most common, the leading condition in half the suicides of adolescent boys and 70 percent of girls. Antisocial behavior is the second leading accompanying condition, followed by substance abuse and anxiety disorders. What many completed suicides have in common is either ineffective treatment or a lack of intervention altogether.

Teenage suicide has become a much more common phenomenon since the 1960s, especially among boys. The incidence in the last 40 years has increased threefold among adolescents and young adults. The reasons for the dramatic increase have long been the subject of speculation on the part of both professionals and the media. Increased substance abuse, divorce and the breakdown of the family, a more pressured world, and the easier availability of guns have all been suggested. These suppositions, which appear routinely in the media, seem logical and may feel satisfying, but in the end none has been scientifically validated as a significant factor on its own.

The only verifiable fact may be that the mass media themselves play an unwitting role. A number of studies have found that suicide among the young is "contagious"; that is, a teenager who is at risk—he is deeply depressed or reacting poorly to negative events—is susceptible to suggestion if there has been a recent suicide in his community or he has read or heard about others his age who have killed themselves. The phenomenon of suicide "clusters"—two or more teen suicides within a geographical area and an isolated period of time—is well established. And it has been documented that TV movies and other dramatizations about teenage suicide have been followed by increases in the number of suicide attempts and completions. It's probably going too far to say it's become trendy, but suicide arguably has become a part of teenage culture.

A form of contagion also is at play closer to home: suicidal behavior runs in families. As with depression and psychiatric illness in general, the reason for this is most likely a combination of genetics and environment. Family dysfunction, abuse, and lack of parental support are associated with suicide. And we know that teenagers with first-degree relatives (parents or siblings) who have had any kind of suicidal behavior are at much greater risk themselves. There is also evidence that aggressive behavior by first-degree relatives may be a factor in suicidal behavior in adolescents who have other risks, such as social isolation or easy access to guns.

Meanwhile, it is likely that genes influence neurobiological differences that appear to affect mood and behavior, including suicide. We know that an imbalance in the level of the neurotransmitter serotonin is associated with depression, and it has also been shown to play a role in suicidal ideation (thinking about or imagining killing oneself). Tests on spinal fluid and brain-image scans of people who have survived medically severe suicide attempts, as well as brain autopsies of those who have carried out their plans, have shown that low serotonin is associated with a lower threshold to acting on both suicidal and aggressive impulses. That's a deadly combination.

Females, who generally have higher levels of serotonin metabolites, have lower rates of both aggressive behavior and suicide attempts that involve the most lethal methods. Perhaps that explains the finding that adolescent girls are more likely to try suicide but less likely to die in the attempt. A goal of future research is developing a test that will chart changes in the response of stress-related hormones to help identify who may be at increased risk of suicide should they become seriously depressed.

Even so, the rise in teenage suicide seems to have abated. The overall rate stopped climbing in the early 1990s and has declined for most demographic groups since 1998. The only exception has been African-American male teenagers, whose rate has increased 105 percent in the past decade. It's not known for sure why rates for the other groups have started to drop, but the widespread use of SSRIs would seem to be a major factor, along with heightened awareness of teenage depression and suicide and the growth of suicide-prevention programs. These advances are the result of the work of many in the mental health field who have been diligently trying to better understand teen suicide and devise strategies for preventing these tragedies. Here is some of what they have found:

- A diagram of suicidal behavior among adolescents looks like a pyramid. In any given year, about 19 percent of American high school students—3 million teenagers—think about or imagine committing suicide. More than one-third of these—more than one million teenagers—make an attempt. Of these, about 400,000 require medical attention. Ultimately, nearly 2,000 teenagers will commit suicide this year. These figures far exceed public perceptions.
- Suicides and attempts become more common at around age fifteen. The peak age for attempts is sixteen. The lower suicide rate for older adolescents may be attributable to maturity: they are more likely to perceive the consequences and the impact their suicide would have on their family and friends.
- Girls are twice as likely as boys to attempt suicide, but boys are ten times more likely to die. Only one out of 3,000 girls who attempt suicide completes it. But one out of 300 boys who attempt suicide dies. This is primarily because they generally use more lethal methods. Girls tend to take an overdose of pills and are often saved, while boys are likely to use guns. (This relationship of method and results is borne out by the dramatic differ-

ence in gender among different countries. For instance, in China more girls than boys die of suicide because lethal pesticides are their method of choice.) In America, the wide availability of guns and the general growth of our gun culture seems to be a factor in the explosive growth of suicide as a male phenomenon since the 1960s.

That suicide rates have stopped climbing is good news, but it has to be viewed in context: there is still vastly more teenage suicide today than 20 and 30 years ago. In that time, the basic formula has not changed. Whether the victim is male or female, old or young, suicide is the result of a convergence of factors and events. Most classically, it happens when someone with an underlying psychiatric disorder—depression, bipolar disorder, schizophrenia, substance abuse, borderline personality disorder—and a predisposition to suicidal thoughts experiences a traumatic or stressful event that causes an acute mood change. This disruption of mood might induce the teenager to feel that the negative event is unbearable or insurmountable. Both main ingredients are necessary—the underlying vulnerability and the triggering event.

Sixty percent of teenagers who commit suicide have a serious mood disorder. But, of course, the inverse is not true. The vast majority of teenagers with depression do not commit suicide. The difference is in the depth of the negative thoughts—how an adolescent responds to the trigger. Those who are impulsive or aggressive by nature and who respond to stressful, perhaps humiliating events with hopelessness, agitation, or anger are at heightened risk. Typically they think that they are the cause of the negative event; that they have no control over what happens to them; that nothing they can do will change things; and that they will never get better.

The most common triggers for teenage suicide are relationship problems (a breakup with a girlfriend or boyfriend, or rejection by a friend); being suspended from school or getting into trouble with the law; a serious school failure; humiliation; and pregnancy. A typical scenario is a teenager with a major depression who has a romantic setback—the kind everyone goes through at one time or another—that exacerbates an already serious, underlying mental condition. "It's often a pathological relationship," says my colleague Dr. Madelyn Gould of the Columbia University College of Physicians and Surgeons. "For instance, a boy has an intense attachment to a girl, while the girl doesn't even realize she has a boyfriend. The boy's perception of the relationship is magnified beyond reality, so when you interview the girl and friends later, you find that nobody realized the boy took the relationship so seriously." Dr. Gould, an epidemiologist who is a leading expert on teen suicide, remembers one case of a 16-year-old who carved his initials into a girl's skin. He pointed a gun at her and then at himself, back and forth several times, before finally pulling the trigger on himself.

What's significant about that case is the boy's aggression—a factor in many suicides by male teenagers. One study in Finland found that bullying increased the risk for depression and severe suicidal ideation—not just for the person being bullied but also for the one *doing* the bullying. Bullies often feel socially inadequate and frequently have been bullied themselves. Though it is not often couched in this term, the shooting rampage by Dylan Klebold and Eric Harris at Columbine High School in 1999 was also a double suicide. These troubled teenagers decided to go out in dramatic, horrific fashion. The anguishing loss of innocent lives at Columbine often clouds the fact that one of the perpetrators was being treated for a psychiatric disorder, and that both boys had just completed a court-mandated counseling program as part of their sentence for vandalism. They were socially isolated "losers" who clearly met the profile of the bullied. It may not be popular to acknowledge, but they were teenagers enduring pain. This is by no means an excuse for their appalling act. But if we as a society fail to acknowledge and learn from the underlying circumstances of the tragedy, then the victims of these boys will have died in vain and we will be doing nothing to protect future students and teachers.

Dylan Klebold and Eric Harris attended a large high school with nearly

2,000 students. This made identifying these high-risk boys more diffi-cult. In late 2001, in New Bedford, Massachusetts, a similar violent plan was orchestrated by a group of high school students with a similar pro-file, but they were stopped by school officials and the police when a pe-ripheral member of the group came forward before the attack. It showed that school-based programs that educate students about warning signs of depression, suicide, and aggression, and that reduce the barriers of com-munication between faculty and students on these sensitive issues, can have a positive effect.

We can only imagine the horror and relief that parents, teachers, and students must have felt when the New Bedford plan was thwarted. And we hold out every hope that these kinds of episodes will just stop hap-pening. But while these incidents are the ones that grab the headlines, and rightly so, they are not really the biggest story. So many more teenagers suffer alone—invisibly and innocently—and their eventual suicides never make the papers. This is not a complaint. Most news media have a pol-icy of not reporting suicides of private individuals, and in the case of eas-ily suggestible adolescents, this is a very good thing. But just because we don't see it or hear about it doesn't mean it isn't happening. So the real issue is whether these thousands of anonymous suicides can be pre-vented—whether parents, teachers, and mental health professionals can search out and identify those who may be at risk, and stop what might be a ticking time bomb.

Such intervention used to be considered the equivalent of searching the North Atlantic for someone adrift in a life raft. But this is no longer true. Researchers have given us a useful profile of the suicidal adolescent, along with screening programs that can make it a little easier to spot a potential victim and pull her to safety. Most obvious is the adolescent who has already made a suicide attempt: this teenager is 100 times more at risk of completing a suicide than one who has not made an attempt. But what about the teen who makes an attempt and doesn't tell anyone? Or the many whose first attempt is fatal?

One promising method is a screening program designed by Dr.

Gould and her colleague at Columbia University, Dr. David Shaffer, in which psychologists go into schools and talk to kids, trying to detect warning signs of depression and suicidal ideation. The program, called TeenScreen, consists of a short list of questions that identifies signs of depression or anxiety. The key is that the questions are highly specific and the information comes directly from the students, not from their peers, teachers, or parents. The teenagers are asked such questions as, "Has there been a time when nothing was fun for you and you just weren't interested in anything?"; "Has there been a time in the last year when you thought about killing yourself?" If the answer to the suicide question is "yes," the teenager is asked if the thought was serious, whether he has thought about how he would commit suicide, and whether he is still thinking about it. If the answer to this last question is "yes," he is asked how many times he has thought about suicide in the last two weeks, whether the thoughts started more than six weeks ago, and whether he has seen a mental health professional in the past three months. The questionnaire is carefully designed to give doctors the best chance to assess the risk of suicide. "Kids are surprisingly honest," Dr. Gould told me. "They will admit to thinking about suicide and will say whether they have a plan."

Screening programs have some drawbacks, as well as some unintended benefits. The shortcoming is that they can yield "false positives," identifying some teenagers as being at risk who are not. But the harm in this seems minor compared with losing the opportunity to identify a potential suicide victim. At the same time, besides spotting a teenager who is in serious distress at the moment, a good screening program can discover kids who are not suicidal but who have depression or other psychiatric problems that might otherwise go unrecognized and untreated.

Most teenagers get through setbacks without thinking about suicide, much less acting on such a thought. But the statistics show that 18 percent of teenagers have thought about it, which means that in a school with 2,000 students, some 360 of them have at least had a passing thought of ending their own lives, and nearly 100 make some kind of attempt, even if it is only a gesture designed to get attention. (There is some evidence that in an unknown number of cases, death is unintended.) What makes the difference between those who do act on their thoughts and those who don't? This list shows some factors that might pave the way to a suicide attempt, or hinder one:

FACTORS THAT FACILITATE SUICIDE

- An impulsive personality
- Biological factors such as neurochemical imbalances
- Lack of strong family ties
- Social factors such as social isolation, a recent suicide by someone close or in the same community, or absence of strong taboos about suicide
- Easy access to and familiarity with guns
- Agitated mental state

FACTORS THAT INHIBIT SUICIDE

- Strong family and social support
- Being around others
- Religious taboos against suicide
- Difficulty of access to method
- Slowed-down, rather than agitated, mental state

This may sound facile and self-evident, but the biggest difference between a teenager contemplating suicide and one who actually attempts it is recognition of problems by his or her parents before it is too late. This challenge can't be underestimated. Identifying an adolescent who may be contemplating suicide is difficult for the same reason that recognizing depression itself is hard. This is a time of life when adolescents are moving away from their parents, and when they tend to be more private and moody by nature. Still, psychological autopsies have repeatedly found that parents are not cognizant of warning signs that are sometimes just beneath the surface. In some cases, they make the connections after the death of their child, but in others they still think "It came out of nowhere," when in fact, it really didn't. Observing changes in behavior and asking direct questions about hopelessness, the future, and even suicide when you have concerns often yields clues that your teenager may be having problems that aren't being addressed. It doesn't necessarily mean that parents, or anyone, can always predict when such problems will lead to suicide. Rather, it means that if symptoms of depression are recognized and treated, or if other psychological problems can be identified and addressed early enough, the suicide might be prevented. As in many other matters of life and death, early detection is paramount.

And, of course, so is taking the right action. If society treated mental illness with the same respect, concern, systematic study, and research that we bring to bear on physical illnesses such as cancer and heart disease, we would have an impact on the suicide rate, particularly for teenagers. Consider that the risk of suicide for young people coincides with the first signs of the most severe forms of mental illness, which generally emerge in the late teens and young adulthood. We still have a long way to go to learn what will be most effective for this group at risk, but identifying them and making effective treatment available are surely the first steps.

Here is a startlingly candid journal entry written by a teenager, Rachel, who was treated by a colleague of mine.

If I'm not doing what I want to do in a few years, then I will commit suicide. I'm surprised I haven't done it yet because I feel really terrible all the time—well, maybe most of the time. I just don't have any courage but anyone else in my position would have already committed suicide.

I would love to drop out of school but I don't think I could do it because then it's final. I wouldn't feel complete. Nothing helps me. I know when people hear this they're going to say that killing yourself is stupid and I feel like they are yelling at me. I think it makes me feel worse—not that anyone will ever hear this because I've written these a million times to tell people how I feel. I am hoping that I would show this to someone today finally to tell how I feel. I'm really confused about everything. Usually my friends can help me but now there is nothing they can do.

I think a lot about omens. I think everything that happens to me is an omen and the sun is now reflecting off the building right in front of me—in my eyes—and I feel that's a good sign, but I still feel really bad.

Rachel was 15 when she wrote that. And though she came from a stable home environment, she was clearly struggling, desperate for help. The pain that she experienced, the feeling of being trapped, and the difficulty she had in asking for help are very typical of adolescents who have suicidal thoughts. Rachel did herself a favor by expressing her suicidal thoughts so openly, even eagerly. With therapy and a course of medication, she improved and went on to college, but continued to struggle with depression. However, contrary to popular myth, teenagers who commit suicide usually do leave significant warning signs. They may not always be as expressive as Rachel, but they are trying to be heard. Suicide rarely comes out of nowhere.

Tim Hudson was a 16-year-old boy who lived in rural upstate New York. He had a difficult relationship with his stepfather, who had little patience for Tim's teenage ways, which included doing poorly in school and drinking. Tim had an awful temper, and reacted badly when his mother and stepfather tried to discipline him. He had a habit of calling himself stupid. "He was sad and lost, and he drank and smoked pot to ease his pain," observed a family friend who took Tim in when things got bad. "He was a hurting boy."

One day, Tim's mother walked into his bedroom and found him with his stepfather's gun in his lap, threatening to shoot himself. She talked him into giving her the gun and brought him to a psychiatrist, who put Tim on an antidepressant. But he didn't stick with it, and he seemed as sad and volatile as ever, given to quick shifts in temperament and extreme reactions to rejection. "He could be loving, respectful, and thankful," said the friend. "Once we spent the day shopping. We went to K-Mart, and I had my eye on a paint gun. It was seventy dollars, and I said I better not. Tim said, 'I'll buy it for you. What color paint do you want?' If you gave him all your attention, he was great, but the minute you paid attention to someone else, he was like another person. He could be happy one minute and pissed off the next. He'd say, 'I'm sick of all the bullshit.' There wasn't a day when he didn't have a period of depression."

Tim had a girlfriend, and he was constantly worried that she would break up with him. If another boy approached her, he would be jumping with jealousy. One day on the school bus, a boy talked to her, and Tim threatened him with a knife. The next day, the girl broke up with him. Tim went to the friend's house, where he had been staying, went into the barn with a gun, and shot himself.

Tim never had a clear diagnosis, and it's difficult to make one after the fact. It's possible he had atypical depression—he overslept, overate, and was very sensitive to rejection. It's also possible he had bipolar disorder. But what is clear is that two things were working against him: he had a difficult family situation and he was difficult to engage. At the same time, he was difficult to *have* in the family—and that's part of the disease. He needed closer supervision and clear demands for him to stay in treatment, because there were few options if he resisted. Tim needed a clinician who was going to engage him and encourage compliance, whether to help him understand his disease or to give him better social support. But, looking back, he had many risks for suicide. His social system wasn't able to handle him; he couldn't get a diagnosis and treatment; and he had access to a gun.

While Tim had all kinds of problems and there were plenty of warning signs that he was unstable, there are other adolescents whose clues are much less obvious. I'm reminded of the suicide of the basketball star of Columbine High School in Littleton, Colorado, a year after the tragic shootings at the school. Nobody saw it coming. "He was bouncing down the halls with that great big grin on his face like he always did," one of the school's coaches told the Denver *Post*. Greg Barnes was an all-state player who was being scouted by major colleges, and he was, said his coach, "an outstanding player but a better kid." How many times have we heard similar words? In almost every case there is an underlying psychiatric problem that either went undetected or untreated. And in this case, a troubled reaction to the deaths of his classmates may have exacerbated whatever emotional problems he was experiencing.

There are no treatment strategies that specifically target suicidal behavior. Rather, the most effective treatments for major depression are also the best defense against suicide. There is intriguing evidence of decreasing suicide rates in white adolescent males in the United States over the past decade, paralleling the increase in prescriptions for antidepressants, particularly SSRIs, over the same time period. There has also been increased use of psychological therapies to address family situations and specific patterns of negative thought that might have otherwise led to a suicide attempt. One leading approach, cognitive behavioral therapy, aims to help the teenager identify negative feelings and correct irrational ideas. For instance, if a young person thinks suicide is the only solution to a hopeless problem, the therapist will balance the reasons for living against those for dying and teach approaches to solving these seemingly insurmountable problems. One session might be devoted to role-playing, in which the patient rehearses strategies that can be used in a crisis situation. (These and other psychological therapies for depression are discussed more thoroughly in the next chapter.)

What parents need to know is that it is not unusual for teenagers to make known their intentions to end their own lives. Whether it is a direct threat, or something more veiled ("I'd be better off dead"), any statement of a desire to kill oneself should be taken seriously. The worst thing to do is downplay or dismiss the statement as a silly overreaction, hoping that will make the thoughts go away. Discussing it will demonstrate that you do take your teenager's problems seriously, and that you want to help. Remember that depression and suicidal feelings are treatable. Again, there is no blood test or brain scan, and there is no guaranteed effective treatment. But we are learning more and more each year about the interplay between pre-existing (and perhaps hidden) psychiatric disorders and family and social circumstances. For now, as with so many other things about raising children, a parent's open eyes and open mind are the best first defense.

THE DEATH OF BLAKE HANSEN

Sometimes, even vigilance is not enough. As any number of cases in the previous chapters clearly demonstrate, the biggest impediment to effective treatment of depression and other psychiatric illnesses in teenagers is noncompliance: the adolescent's failure or outright refusal to acknowledge a problem and accept the prescribed treatment—whether it is medicine, therapy, or a combination of both. Adults are more likely to be motivated to get help and follow through with treatment; they are likely to bring themselves for treatment. But this can be one more struggle, and a mighty one, between parents and adolescents. Exacerbating the situation may be resistance by a managed-care insurance company to pay for the necessary services.

These two factors collided tragically in the case of Blake Hansen, a Kansas teenager whose bright future collapsed under the increasing weight of poorly treated depression. His mother, Connie Masters, wants her son's death to serve as an object lesson that might lead to a system of mental health care that places more emphasis on getting teenagers at risk the help they need than on how much it might cost. To that end, she shared her story with me for this book and allowed her son's name to be used. I found her through Dr. Bryant Welch, an attorney, psychologist, and mental health advocate based in Maryland, who represented her in a successful wrongful-death lawsuit.

"Blake was a model child," Connie Masters wrote in a letter to me. "He never complained, never talked back, never got into trouble at home, school, or anywhere. He had the kindest soul one could have. I misinterpreted those characteristics to mean that he was well-adjusted and having no problems, until junior high age. It was around this time that I realized Blake had great difficulty in expressing his feelings. He always placed extremely high expectations on himself, sometimes unrealistically. He was a friend to anyone and had a wonderful sense of humor and a beautiful smile that would hide all the pain."

While Blake sounds like a wonderful child, it's also very possible he was already suffering from anxiety symptoms that were going unde-tected—even though he seemed to adjust well to his parents' divorce when he was four, and he didn't appear to others as a kid with problems. He was easy-going, compassionate, and never seemed to get angry. He was also brilliant, testing at a tenth-grade math level in second grade. But at 13, Blake's grades began to drop, and he became uncharacteristi-cally sad, somewhat irritable, and generally discontent. He was sleeping more than usual. "I couldn't pinpoint anything," his mother said in a later conversation. "I had become engaged, and thought the problem was that he wasn't used to sharing me, that he didn't like the loss of at-tention. But I wound up breaking off the relationship, and it didn't change much."

Besides his falling grades, Blake was becoming very difficult to con-trol. He began drinking with friends and staying out all night. "He was hard to discipline," Connie said. "If you grounded him, it didn't affect him. He didn't get angry. He would just sneak out. I told him, 'If you don't start going down the right road, you'll have to go stay with your dad.' It wasn't a threat. I thought it was the only alternative. Maybe he needed some male discipline. His dad was saying Blake was taking ad-vantage of me. But I felt helpless." When she tried to reflect on what had come over her model child, all she could think of was the obvious: he was a rebellious teenager and he was getting in with the wrong people.

When he turned 16, Blake moved in with his father and his stepfam-ily, changing schools in the process. "He was very restless and discontent, but quiet about it," Connie said. "It was masked. He didn't have temper outbursts, and he was not especially irritable. He wasn't expressing any problems, and his grades came back up. So the depression wasn't caught."

Blake's grades dropped again his senior year, and he had his first brush with the law, an arrest for driving while under the influence of alcohol. Because it was his first offense, he was put into a "diversion program," an intensive four weeks of outpatient psychosocial group therapy, plus weekly family therapy, at a private psychiatric hospital. "The four weeks stretched into seven weeks, and he got tired of going because he didn't see the light at the end of the tunnel," Connie said. But there were no legal consequences when he stopped showing up.

For Blake, it was the beginning of what was to be an unending up-and-down struggle with depression. For a time he was on Zoloft, but he was also drinking excessively. In his senior year Blake decided to quit school and join the Army reserves. "It was 13 weeks of training, and he did real well," Connie said. "He was happy, his letters home were upbeat. He was staying clean, no drinking or marijuana. With Blake, it seemed he was either really responsible or really irresponsible. There was no middle ground."

Blake came home after the training and got a job as a cook in a restaurant. He wanted to join the Army full time, but was told they weren't accepting any new recruits. Demoralized, he went back to living with his dad, hanging out with his old friends, and drinking and taking drugs again. There was another arrest for driving under the influence, and then he and his girlfriend broke up. That led to Blake's first suicide attempt. He pulled his car into his father's garage, turned on the engine, and sat in the car until he started getting drowsy. At that point he changed his mind and went into the house and lay down on a couch, where he was found by his stepbrother. It was one of the few times that Blake ever cried, "so you knew he was in deep pain," his mother said. When she saw him, she hugged him and asked why he had felt he had to do it. "I don't know, Mom," he said, shrugging his shoulders.

Blake checked into the psychiatric unit of the local hospital and stayed three weeks, during which time he was on Paxil, along with the antipsychotic medication Risperdal. Though he was unable to verbalize his feelings, he offered some hints of his self-image on a form he filled out during his hospital stay. Under personal and social strengths, Blake wrote: "I am a hard worker. I don't have any social strengths." Asked what he would like to change, he wrote: "My personality, my looks, my brains, dealing with other people."

Blake's mother described him as very isolated and paranoid during this time. "He was not capable of getting a job because he felt people were out to get him. At home he'd feel comfortable, but he was afraid of being around people because he thought that they were talking about him. But it was more depression than psychosis."

Blake was diagnosed with schizoaffective disorder. Patients with that diagnosis have psychotic symptoms that are usually accompanied by prominent mood disorder symptoms, but the psychosis persists after the mood symptoms have subsided. I never had the opportunity to meet Blake, and the lack of clarity in his diagnosis and his own resistance to treatment make his case a challenging one to unravel retrospectively. But it seems possible that instead of schizoaffective disorder he had a major depression with psychotic features. A person with this condition would have psychotic symptoms only in the presence of a prominent change in mood. And those psychotic thoughts would rise and fall with his mood.

After his three-week stay in the hospital, Blake was given an outpatient treatment plan that called for him to take medication and come in for therapy sessions every night for two weeks. But again he didn't take the medication and he didn't show up for therapy. Instead, he went back to self-medicating—drinking and smoking pot to ease the pain of his worsening depression. He quit his job and stopped showing up for his monthly weekend of duty with the Army Reserves. He was becoming more despondent. His psychiatrist recommended inpatient care at a state hospital—the first of three times he did so—but each time was overruled by the county agency that provided mental health care for those who couldn't afford it. The agency said Blake could be treated locally as an outpatient. That was the Catch-22: Blake refused to go to outpatient treatment. His mother was desperate for help; at 19, Blake was at that transitional age when he was no longer under his parents' control, yet he was unable to function without their involvement. "I talked to the psychiatrist endlessly, I talked to the outpatient director," Connie said. "They said they couldn't make him go either."

In September 1995, Blake was arrested for possession of a small amount of marijuana and put in jail. To be sure, he was now part of the largest mental health system in the country: our jails and prisons. Young people with serious depression are more likely to drop out of school and get in trouble with the law. And those who are suicidal have impaired judgment; they are more likely to be impulsive and to be aggressive toward others. Again, the young shooters of Columbine come to mind.

In jail, Blake tried to slit his wrists with a razor, which landed him in solitary confinement for four days but still didn't get him any closer to treatment. Blake's mother and grandfather bailed him out of jail, and brought him back to the local hospital. But because he had no private insurance, he was released after three days. Once again, the psychiatrist's recommendation for long-term inpatient treatment was rejected by the county "gatekeeper," a social worker who ordered outpatient treatment once again. And once again, Blake could not bring himself to go, and six days later he slit his wrists again. He called his mother and told her he wanted to go to the state psychiatric hospital in Topeka. "I don't want to die," he said, which Connie took as a hopeful sign that Blake really did want help. "How many 19-year-olds beg to go to a state hospital?" she asked.

But once more she was told the county wouldn't approve it.

"I'll take him to Topeka myself," Connie told the county worker.

"You'll be turned away at the gate," she was told. "There's a protocol you have to follow. He doesn't fit the criteria." Under the criteria, the patient had to have attempted suicide within 24 hours of the admission. Blake had waited a day before calling his mother and telling her what he had done. Now it was more than 24 hours since the suicide attempt. "You can go ahead and admit him but you'll be responsible for the bill," the county social worker told Connie. She didn't know it at the time, but Kansas, like other states, was cutting its number of state-supported psychiatric hospital beds. It was the result of a "reform act" by the state legislature to have people treated at the community level rather than in state mental hospitals.

Connie tells what happened from there. "They kept him seven days at the local hospital, but he made no improvement. He was on the same medication, but he was never on it long enough. He was noncompliant; that's why the doctor and I wanted him in the state hospital long term. And Blake said, 'I don't feel safe doing this outpatient.' But the same gatekeeper said no. She sent him to a group home, but he wouldn't get out of the car. He said, 'I can't do it, Mom. I don't feel safe. I don't trust myself. I want to go to Topeka.' He went in but didn't get any treatment or medication, and he took off from there. I knew he was still depressed. I didn't want to dwell on it, but I asked him, 'Are you having any thoughts of hurting yourself?' He said no."

But Blake *was* having those thoughts. He bought his first gun, a shotgun. Three days before Christmas, he went into his bathroom and shot himself to death.

Connie Masters eventually hired Bryant Welch and won a small wrongful-death judgment against the local hospital and the county agency and, to a lesser degree, two physicians. In a sad and appalling comment to the *Wichita Eagle,* the assistant director of the mental health agency later said: "We cannot capture people and make them come to treatment. If someone doesn't want to go to treatment, they don't go to treament. If someone wants to kill themselves, they'll kill themself." It's true that it's very hard to treat someone who doesn't want to be treated. But with depression, *that's* one of the symptoms, as real as a rash is a symptom of poison ivy.

According to court records cited by the *Wichita Eagle,* the agency's treatment plan for Blake was drawn up by a "diversion specialist" who had completed less than two years of college and whose previous job before joining the agency was as a shift manager for McDonald's. As Bryant Welch points out, managed care has penetrated the public health sector. "There's a lot of pressure in today's health-care system not to give care that patients need," he said. "That means that if you're a parent, you have to advocate like crazy for your kids."

There is a swinging pendulum in play. There was a time in this country when we hospitalized people routinely because we didn't have alternative treatments. With the antipsychotic treatments of the 1950s and 1960s, people who had spent virtually their entire lives in institutions could be let go. By the 1970s, "deinstitutionalization" was the operative word. As a society, we released patients into the community without having built the community-based programs we said we were going to build. It's one reason that there are so many homeless people. In the 1980s, for-profit psychiatric hospitals took advantage of relatively generous mental health insurance coverage, but that was followed by the swing to "managed care," and another round of seriously ill patients going without adequate treatment.

With adolescents who have psychiatric illnesses, there is a serious dearth of the kind of setting and supervision they require to get better. There are usually two extreme alternatives. On one end there might be a weekly one-hour appointment or a three-hour evaluation in the hospital. On the other end is long-term residential treatment for a few. There's not enough in between. Moreover, what is available is not widely accessible. It's never easy to have a sick child, no matter what the illness, but there are too many barriers to getting effective help for kids who have the most serious mental illnesses. And if the problem is not identified early, those who have a long-untreated illness become the most difficult to treat. So we need a mental health system that's more accessible, more flexible, and more comprehensive.

Blake was not one of those whose parents, teachers, and friends failed to pick up on the warning signs. His mother did not avoid the issue. She asked Blake directly if he was thinking about suicide. Connie is a parent who learned firsthand that noncompliance is the biggest factor in treating adolescents with serious mood disorders—especially if that teenager is already out of the house and on his own. She felt helpless and got terrible support from the mental health system.

"If I knew then what I know now . . ." she said. "With deinstitutionalization, they're treating the worried well and the people with persistent mental illness get pushed through the cracks. There's no mechanism for treating noncompliance. They get a referral from the hospital or a court order, and if the patient doesn't come in, they write him off as a noncompliant client and blame it on *him*. But noncompliance is a part of the sickness, and it's being used as a justification for termination of treatment. It's a Catch-22."

Myth Versus Fact

The following are common misconceptions, and the truth, about suicide and teenagers. Separating truth from fiction can make you a better-informed and more vigilant parent.

Myth: Teenagers who talk about suicide *never* do it.

Fact: Most of the time, people who attempt suicide have provided significant clues to their intentions.

Myth: Nothing can stop someone once he or she has decided to take his or her own life.

Fact: Most adolescents who contemplate suicide are torn. They are in pain and want their suffering to end. They don't necessarily want to die to make that happen. But they can't conceive of another way, and too often their cries for help go unheeded.

Myth: Talking about suicide with teenagers may give them ideas.

Fact: While teenagers at risk might follow the model of a peer who committed suicide, talking about it in order to prevent it will *not* encourage him or her to try it.

Myth: Only certain "types" of kids commit suicide.

Fact: There is no specific type. Socioeconomic status, intelligence, and culture don't make a teenager any more or less vulnerable to suicidal thoughts or actions.

12

THE TREATMENT QUESTION

D iagnosis should always drive treatment. This is true whether a disorder is mental or physical. But while the diagnosis and treatment of major depression in adults has evolved over several decades, the child and adolescent versions of the disorder remain less well understood. Anna Freud's presumption that being depressed is normal for teenagers has long since been discarded, but diagnostic tools and treatment approaches have emerged more slowly for them than for adults.

As in most psychiatry, the science on adults leads the way. Testing of new medications is almost universally done first with adults, then with adolescents, and finally with children. We know that as many as 80 percent of adults suffering from major depression will respond to antidepressant drugs, either one medication or a combination of them. The overwhelming success of Prozac, Zoloft, and other SSRI medications has made them the most popular frontline treatment for depression. In fact, to a large extent, major depression in adults has been "medicalized." Primary-care physicians—internists, family doctors, and gynecologists— provide most prescriptions of SSRI medications for adults. This reflects both their high degree of efficacy and their relative safety.

While an adult who visits a psychiatrist and is diagnosed with depression will, in all likelihood, leave with a prescription, this is not the case with young people. This is largely the result of ingrained myths and misconceptions that place a stigma on young people taking psychiatric medicines. A common sentiment expressed by many teenagers is, "If I have to take medicine, I must be really sick." (Though others harbor a related wish: "If I take this medicine for a while, will I be cured, like with penicillin?") Another refrain, from both parents and teenagers, is a concern that they will need to take medicine for the rest of their lives. Many parents understandably worry that taking antidepressants may have an adverse effect on brain development. There is no evidence to date that antidepressants produce toxic effects on brain development, but we still need more research. In deciding whether to use these medications, we need to weigh this uncertainty against the negative consequences we know forgoing treatment has on adolescent brains and lives.

It's good for parents and teenagers alike to ask questions and express their concerns about taking medicine for mental disorders. Only in this way will they learn the facts they need to make an informed decision and to feel comfortable with that decision. Medicine should of course be prescribed carefully and deliberately. Unfortunately, there is an almost universal belief by the public that teenagers should first try psychotherapy, and medication should be considered only after that fails. This idea comes from two mistaken and outdated beliefs: (1) that medications may be addictive or dangerous to teenagers and (2) that depression in young people is caused either by an early trauma or by some intrinsic weakness in the teenager that can be overcome with psychotherapy.

Ironically, something good has come from these misconceptions. Two types of psychotherapy that have been found to be effective in treating adults with mild to moderate depression have in recent years been systematically tried in teenagers. And the results have been encouraging. The leading method, cognitive behavioral therapy (CBT), is based on the idea that depression comes from having negative and unrealistic perceptions about oneself and the world. The therapy is focused on highlighting, exploring, and correcting these mistaken thought patterns. Several clinical trials suggest that CBT may be effective in teenagers.

A second method, interpersonal therapy (IPT), has a different focus. It holds that when people become depressed, their social relationships are affected negatively, and thus they become more disappointed and frustrated with life in general. A therapist using IPT focuses on these key relationships, by examining the patient's conduct and the response to that behavior by close family and friends. The therapist aims to help the patient understand the effects of his behavior, change it, and thus improve his relationships. The hope is that this in turn will help bring him out of his depression. IPT is not as established as CBT, but has been tested in small trials in adolescents, with promising results.

Both these treatments are short-term, symptom-focused approaches with very specific goals. Each requires a skilled and specially trained therapist—first to engage a teenager who is likely to be both uncommunicative and uncooperative, and then to apply the specific principles and methods of the given therapy. These are most assuredly not conventional "talk" or supportive therapies, in which the patient meets with an empathic professional who tries to help her with her problems. Nor is it "dynamic" therapy, in which the therapist tries to find damaging and unconscious feelings toward parents or early events. There is no evidence that either of these therapies has a role to play in the treatment of depression in teenagers.

The CBT and IPT approaches are not for everyone. First, since these are active therapies, motivation on the part of the patient is essential. And while the evidence in adults is good that they are effective in treating cases of mild to moderate depression, more serious cases are better treated with medication (though some respond to a combination of both).

Moreover, the reality is that access to CBT or IPT is limited, even in and around major cities, because relatively few therapists are trained in them. There is also a bias against them when it comes to insurance coverage. Insurance carriers are more apt to pay for a few psychiatric visits and prescriptions than for several sessions with a psychologist conducting psychotherapy.

All things being equal, what's most effective—medicine or therapy? Is a teenager with mild or moderate depression and access to a specially trained therapist better off with CBT or antidepressants? That question is now being addressed in a major, national investigation called the Treatment for Adolescents with Depression Study (TADS). Participants in this multisite study, which is sponsored by the National Institute of Mental Health and directed by Dr. John March at Duke University, are being given either Prozac, CBT, a combination of both, or a placebo pill. With our understanding of teenage depression way behind what we know about adults with the disorder, the results of the TADS study will be a big step forward. Until then, we will continue by clinical experience and theory.

The previous chapters make clear that attacking depression in teenagers can be a fierce battle. Despite the best treatment approaches and the utmost dedication by doctors and parents, sometimes the disorder is a relentless opponent, especially when it is complicated by another illness such as anxiety or attention deficit disorder. The cases in this book were chosen in order to illuminate these issues and struggles. But it's important also to keep in mind that not all cases are so tough. For many teenagers, both the depression itself and the treatment are straightforward, and success comes with relative ease. In the following pages, I outline the various treatment options, and present cases in which they worked like a charm.

THE MEDICINES THAT CAN
RESCUE YOUR CHILD

Pharmaceuticals changed adult psychiatry. The revolution began in the 1950s, when the development of major tranquilizers allowed patients with chronic psychotic syndromes, such as schizophrenia or manic-depressive illness, to live outside institutions, many for the first time in their adult lives. In the late 1970s, tricyclic (that is, conventional) anti-depressants such as Elavil and Tofranil had much the same effect on the treatment of patients suffering from depression. However, these medications, while quite effective in the adult population, were never found to have proven efficacy in young people. This might have been because adults tend to have "classic" depression, while adolescents more often have "atypical" depression. These symptoms include eating and sleeping too much rather than too little, being very sensitive to rejection and more reactive to the environment than patients with classic depression. The earlier generation of antidepressants seemed to have an effect on classic depression but not on atypical depression.

The development of a new kind of antidepressant—the Selective Serotonin Reuptake Inhibitor (SSRI)—triggered a second revolution in psychiatry starting in the late 1980s. Besides surpassing the previous generation of antidepressants in effectiveness, the SSRIs were safer: unlike the tricyclics, they are not "cardiotoxic"—that is, they have no negative effect on the heart. So it was very difficult for a depressed person to use the newer antidepressants to commit suicide. In addition, doctors didn't have to give children cardiograms before prescribing an SSRI, as they did with the tricyclics. The SSRIs also have fewer side effects, which could be reduced even more by taking smaller doses—and it turned out that over time, low doses were as effective as high ones. They were safe and easily available; they could be prescribed not only by psychiatrists but by primary-care physicians as well.

A second factor that carried this revolution was the HMO movement, which forced primary-care physicians to be more conservative in their referral patterns and to treat more patients themselves. In the case of depression, patients who would have been routinely referred to a psychiatrist in years past were now more likely to be treated by a primary-care doctor and receive medication for their depression. In addition, since the Food and Drug Administration in 1997 began allowing pharmaceutical companies to advertise prescription drugs directly to consumers, the public has become aware of specific SSRIs and their effectiveness in treating mood and anxiety disorders. This, along with the casual references to these medicines, particularly Prozac, in everyday life has had the effect of reducing the stigma traditionally attached to taking psychiatric medications.

Though these medicines changed the world for millions and millions of adults, it has been a more nuanced process for adolescents. For one thing, teenagers are rebellious and contrary by nature, so a medicine's wide acceptance is not necessarily a good thing. In fact, it's a good enough reason for an adolescent to reject it and want something new and different. (This helps explain why they are more likely to be attracted to alternative treatments in general.) The other factor is that some parents still hold on to the idea that teenagers shouldn't be "taught" to take medication, even if they are depressed.

Though the practice of prescribing SSRIs to treat depressed adolescents has trailed its use among adults, evidence has emerged that they are effective with teenagers. The first large placebo-controlled study of Prozac in children and teenagers was published in 1997 by Dr. Graham Emslie of the University of Texas. He compared Prozac to placebo and reported that 56 percent of the teenagers with depression had positive responses to the medicine. This was a significant improvement over the earlier tricyclic antidepressants, which several studies, including one that my colleagues and I conducted, found were no better at treating adolescent depression than placebos.

It must be said that the placebo effect is a factor with adolescents; that is, in clinical trials, significant numbers of depressed adolescents improve when all they are taking is ersatz medicine. The best explanation is that teenagers tend to be labile, or highly variable, in their moods. If they're not persistently down, it can be difficult to assess both their depression and the effect of medicine on it. Depression also can be time-limited, and therefore change can occur just with time. This may partially explain why in placebo-controlled studies a certain number are reported to improve even though they are not taking the real drug.

Other factors may also contribute to improvement seen in patients taking only a placebo. Simply having the attention of a trained professional—even if that professional is only dispensing sugar pills—may have positive effects. Another factor is expectancy—the idea that believing you are doing something to help you get well will actually help you get well. This is demonstrated even in kids' movies. In *Space Jam,* for example, Bugs Bunny give his basketball teammates a supposedly magical potion that he tells them will improve their skills. This bogus potion actually helping them win the game illustrates the theory of expectancy. Future investigations of these concepts may help in the development of more effective psychotherapy.

In any event, SSRIs have always been found to be more effective than placebos, and so throughout the 1990s they became an increasingly popular treatment for young people. Here is a striking statistic: between 1985 and 1994, the rate of antidepressant prescriptions of any kind written for people under 17 by psychiatrists leaped from 6 per 100 visits to *30* per 100 visits.

The paradox is that it's not clear that the antidepressants are always prescribed properly. The overwhelming majority of prescriptions are made by primary-care physicians, who are not likely to always be fluent in some of the subtleties of child and adolescent psychiatric problems that often come into play. For instance, complicated cases of depression, including those in which the patient has other disorders, might not respond to an SSRI alone. In my clinical experience, a young person with ADHD often becomes more hyperactive or impulsive on the medicine. Primary-care physicians aren't trained to make psychiatric diagnoses, just as dermatologists aren't trained to make gynecological diagnoses. But dermatologists *are* trained to diagnose cancer—skin cancer. So maybe it's necessary for pediatricians, family practitioners, and internists to be given training that will allow them to make correct early diagnoses of depression. Clearly, with only 7,000 child and adolescent psychiatrists in the country (and those not having parity in insurance coverage) not everyone has access to a specialist.

The current crop of SSRIs includes Prozac, Zoloft, Paxil, Luvox, and Celexa. How they do what they do is still not exactly known, but the working model is that serotonin—a compound distributed widely in tissue—is discharged by neurons in the brain and then reabsorbed to be discharged again. Serotonin is involved in many different aspects of our body's functioning. It affects the regulation of sleep, and it is involved in blood clotting and digestion as well as mood, aggression, and suicide. Serotonin is quickly recycled back into the neuron that released it through an excellent recycling mechanism. An SSRI blocks the reabsorption process and therefore increases the level of serotonin in the synapses. With the serotonin back in balance, mood improves. Interestingly, a new antidepressant, tianeptine, which has not yet been approved by the Food and Drug Administration, acts in the opposite way. It *increases,* rather than decreases, the amount of serotonin that is reabsorbed in the brain. Nobody seems to know why this agent works.

The antidepressants are not a quick fix. Though various studies have shown that SSRIs affect the serotonin receptor immediately, it takes between two and six weeks before a depressed patient experiences any real improvement in mood and behavior. The best theory of why it takes so long for the medication to work is that the effect on the serotonin receptor is only the first step in a complex cascade of neurochemical changes that eventually lead to correcting the mood regulatory system.

Dr. Donald Klein of Columbia University, one of the world's leading researchers on the diagnosis and treatment of depression, suggests the following analogy. If someone is given sugar water to taste but not to swallow, he would find the taste pleasant and would want to repeat the experience. This is called an "appetitive" drive. After a while, this person would want to swallow the sugar water. That's called a "consumatory" action. After the first time swallowing it, he would find that pleasant, too. But after 10 or 15 swallows, he would find the taste too sweet and eventually say he didn't want any more. That's a sign of his blood-sugar level going up and the regulatory system working. A similar system is at play with depression, though it works differently in adults and teenagers.

Adults who have classic depression are impaired in both their appetite for pleasure and their willingness to stick it out, or to "hunt," to fulfill it. But teenagers, who are more likely to have *atypical* depression, tend to have an impairment in their appetite for pleasure. Their ability to enjoy activities when they are engaged is less likely to be affected. A normal teenager who is not depressed has a hearty appetite for pleasure and is willing to hunt for it—whether it is pursuing a romantic interest, chasing a soccer ball, or looking forward to a slice of pizza after school. A healthy teenager can in turn "feast" on pleasure—having sexual contact with the object of his romantic interest, scoring a goal, or savoring a delicious slice of pizza. But with adolescents who are depressed, the mood-regulation system is out of balance, impairing their appetite for pleasure and limiting their opportunity to consume it. Over time, cognition also becomes affected, leading a teenager to be unable to remember the last time she was happy, and eventually to think she was never happy. What an SSRI does is trigger a series of neurochemical events that eventually put the mood-regulatory system back into balance, like fixing a broken thermostat.

This explains why SSRIs are not feel-good medicines. They have no effect on normal mood, and when they are taken by people who do not have a mood disorder they do not produce a "high." So they can't be abused. Medications such as amphetamines will increase a person's energy and arousal no matter what the baseline was, while Valium and other sedatives will make everyone who takes it sleepy. But the SSRI antidepressants only work on mood if the patient is depressed, much the same way that aspirin only lowers body temperature when one has a fever. A higher dosage isn't necessarily more effective than a lower one (though, depending on the patient, a higher dosage may indeed be necessary). It might seem logical to increase the dosage if there is no response after a couple of weeks. But there is a strong chance that all this will do is increase the side effects, which *are* immediate. This may happen when an SSRI is prescribed by a primary-care physician who may not be familiar with the medicine and is responding to a patient's complaint that he's not feeling better. The watchwords for SSRIs are: "Start low, go slow." While there is no strict correlation between dosage and effectiveness, there *is* one between dosage and side effects. And increased side effects lead to decreased compliance.

Though all SSRIs affect the same neurotransmitter, serotonin, one might be more effective than another for a particular patient, but it's not known exactly why. This can lead to a period of trial and error involving several different SSRIs and dosages at the beginning of treatment. Prozac has been prescribed for more people, including teenagers, than any of the other antidepressants, simply because it has been around the longest and it has brand-name recognition that rivals McDonald's. But there is no evidence that it's any better than the other SSRIs. All have the same efficacy and similar side effects. The most bothersome is sexual dysfunction: a decrease in desire, arousal, and ability to have an orgasm. Unlike adults, teenagers rarely have a decrease in libido; the only reported effect has been delay in ejaculation for boys and a delay or inability to reach orgasm for girls. Other side effects of antidepressants may be agitation or sedation, and some initial decrease in appetite. Additional side effects that have been reported with all the medicines are nausea, headache, and slight hand tremors. But even patients who do experience these side effects—and most do not—find that the symptoms are passing and subside with time. Weight gain is one of the few side effects that seems to increase over time. Another long-term side effect is increasing loss of incentive and drive. Why this occurs is not yet clear.

This is not to say that all the SSRIs are identical. Numerous controlled studies and years of clinical observation have given us some indication of the subtle differences among them, in both effectiveness and side effects. Though these studies focused on adults, they may apply to adolescents. The best reason for picking one SSRI over another is a positive response in the past. But for teenagers who have not had depression previously and are going to be taking medicine for the first time, the subtle differences among the drugs might influence the decision to pick one over another.

PROZAC

Positives: Prozac has not only been around the longest of the SSRIs, it is also the longest acting. This means that it stays longer in the system. It also seems to have fewer symptoms associated with its discontinuation. Therefore, Prozac might be a good choice for a patient who is poor in compliance (because it can still be effective even if a dose is missed), as well as for one with a history of symptoms associated with discontinuing an SSRI. Prozac is also available in liquid form, which is easier to take in very small doses and can be taken by teenagers who have trouble swallowing pills. In addition, it has recently become available in weekly dosage, which preliminary data suggest may be as effective as the daily-dose variety. So if you have a teenager who argues about taking the medicine, this might mean arguing only once a week.

Negatives: There has been a higher incidence of agitation, skin reactions, and weight loss (this may not be a negative) reported with Prozac than with the other SSRIs. There may also be a higher incidence of loss of incentive over time. From an emotional standpoint, Prozac's popularity could be seen as destigmatizing—or not. A medicine that makes appearances in Jay Leno's nightly monologue might be an embarrassment to some. I have had parents say to me in the first five minutes, "My son says he won't take Prozac." Such a teenager might be less resistant to a medicine with a less loaded name.

ZOLOFT

Positives: Fewer patients seem to stop Zoloft than the other SSRIs because of side effects. Zoloft also tends to be shorter lasting. This means that a patient could take a "drug holiday," skipping a day, and perhaps have a decrease in the sexual side effects. This is an advantage more for adults.

Negatives: Because Zoloft lasts for a shorter period, compliance is more important.

PAXIL

Positives: Paxil has been shown to be effective in treating anxiety symptoms in adults, so it may also be a good choice for teenagers who have anxiety symptoms as well as depression.

Negatives: More reports of side effects, including nausea, weight gain, sedation, tremors, sweating, sexual dysfunction, and reactions to discontinuation. Paxil should be avoided if there have been previous problems when stopping this type of medication.

LUVOX

Positives: Controlled studies show that Luvox is effective for teenagers with anxiety disorders. Therefore, it's a rational choice for teens who have both depression and anxiety symptoms.

Negatives: Luvox has a higher rate of side effects when stopped suddenly, and these may include nausea, malaise, sedation, and tremors. It should not be the first choice for patients who have had SSRI-related adverse reactions.

CELEXA

Positives: Celexa is the most serotonin-selective of the SSRIs. Stopping abruptly is less likely to induce significant side effects.

Negatives: As with other shorter acting SSRI medications, compliance is more important.

·

It's common for a psychiatrist to prescribe a combination of medicines to get the best result. The second medication is called an augmenter and is used when the first one gives only a partial response. Which augmenter is used depends on what other symptoms the depressed teenager is experiencing: for instance, a patient who is sleepy or lethargic would be likely to receive a psychostimulant such as Dexedrine or Ritalin as an augmenter. For someone with attention and concentration difficulties, Wellbutrin might be a good augmenter. And for the teenager who has agitation, Risperdal. Meanwhile, if a teenager's blood work found that her thyroid functioning was in the low end of the normal range, an augmenter of thyroxine or Cytomel might be helpful. These are synthetic hormones, normally prescribed for hypothyroidism (reduced functioning of thyroid, which is associated with depression), and they might give the teenager more energy.

The SSRIs are just one of three groups of drugs that produce positive antidepressant effects by affecting or increasing the availability of serotonin in the brain. Another group is the monoamineoxidase inhibitors (MAOIs). But these medications have never been investigated thoroughly in teenagers because of the potential for adverse side effects. Foods containing tyramine—aged cheeses, red wine, caviar, pickled herring—can interact with MAOIs to produce high blood pressure. Those products might not be among the four basic food groups of the typical teenager, but young people are considered to be less responsible in adhering to dietary restrictions, no matter how exotic. An even more serious risk—though its occurrence is rare—is the potentially lethal interaction between MAOIs and other drugs, both prescription and illicit. Such a tragedy occurred in New York City in 1984, when a young woman named Libby Zion, who was taking an MAOI called Nardil and was also using cocaine, received the painkiller Demerol in the emergency room of a hospital where she had gone with severe flu symptoms. The interaction led to her death. Nevertheless, MAOIs may be a useful second-line medication for patients who do not respond to the SSRIs and who have "atypical" depression. They just have to be especially careful about what they ingest.

A third group of antidepressants is known as atypical antidepressants. These include Serzone, Effexor, and Wellbutrin. These medications are so-called "dirty" drugs, an unfortunate moniker for medicines that affect multiple neurotransmitters, not just serotonin. They are quite useful; nevertheless, the first line of attack should be the safest medicine and the "cleanest," which would be one of the SSRIs.

Finally, there is the question of "alternative," nonpharmaceutical substances. Both St. John's wort and SAM-e have been highly publicized in recent years as treatments for depression. St. John's wort is an herb that has become extremely popular for the over-the-counter treatment of depression, even though there was no reliable scientific evidence that it is effective. In response to its wide use, clinical researchers at 11 major institutions conducted the first major study of St. John's wort between 1998 and 2000; the results were published in the *Journal of the American Medical Association* in April 2001. The study—one of the most methodologically sophisticated double-blind, placebo-controlled clinical trials ever done—involved 200 adults with major depression who were given either St. John's wort or a placebo for eight weeks. The study found no difference in response rates between the two, and the 16 investigators concluded that the substance is not effective in the treatment of major depression.

S-adenosyl-methionine (SAM-e) is a naturally occurring substance that is present throughout the body, including in the central nervous system. It contributes to the activation, production, and metabolism of such substances as enzymes, hormones, and neurotransmitters. SAM-e has been used in Europe since the 1970s for the treatment of depression and arthritis. Two small studies have found that SAM-e taken orally improves depression symptoms. But no definitive placebo-controlled trials have been done, and there are no studies of any kind on adolescents. Thus, it cannot be recommended as a treatment to be considered.

CAROLINE'S ANSWER

Caroline was a 16-year-old patient who, seemingly out of the blue, had begun having trouble managing her time, staying on top of her schoolwork, and getting out of bed in the morning. Her parents, somewhat alarmed and searching for possibilities, thought at first that their recent talks about potential colleges were causing her stress. Then they became concerned that it was some type of physical illness. They took Caroline to the family physician, a thorough diagnostician who ruled out Lyme disease, as well as mononucleosis and hypothyroidism (underfunctioning of the thyroid gland that can cause lethargy).

Though Caroline was already thin, the doctor noted that she had lost two pounds since her last visit for a physical five months before. When he asked her about this, she said she hadn't had much of an appetite lately. The doctor asked her some other questions that elicited more information than he derived from the blood work and physical examinations he performed. Did she use any drugs? Caroline admitted that she smoked marijuana on several occasions but not regularly. How was school going? She said she felt snowed under by work. And then, when he asked her about her plans for the future, Caroline burst out crying. She said she was lost, didn't know where to go or what to be, and felt completely overwhelmed.

This astute physician, who had been a pediatrician for 40 years, told Caroline's parents that they should see a psychologist. (A noteworthy aside: studies of referral patterns show that pediatricians refer patients to psychologists and social workers more frequently than to child psychiatrists; this is less true of internists.) The psychologist Caroline went to was a seasoned clinician who was trained as a child psychoanalyst and was a supervisor in the department of psychiatry at the local hospital. It was only a week after her initial visit to the pediatrician, but Caroline was already worse. She was having insomnia, taking up to two hours to fall asleep, and then having more difficulty getting up in the morning. She started to miss school and had spent the entire weekend in her pajamas and in bed, only joining the family when she came down for breakfast—at three in the afternoon.

Both of Caroline's parents took time off from work to take her to see the psychologist that Tuesday afternoon. After getting a history from the parents, she spoke to Caroline, who was weepy throughout the interview. She repeated what she had told the family doctor and said she couldn't remember the last time she was happy. The psychologist concluded that Caroline almost certainly had to be put on an antidepressant. She referred the family to me, and called to tell me that she was so concerned about Caroline's presentation that she thought it was essential that I see her the next day. Her fear was that Caroline might hurt herself, even though she denied a suicidal plan. Caroline did admit to having passive suicidal thoughts. For example, she said that lately she had wished she had never been born, and in bed at night she prayed that she would never wake up.

The next day, I reviewed the history and interviewed Caroline and her parents. There was no doubt that Caroline had the symptoms for the diagnosis of major depressive disorder and that the severity of her symptoms made medication the best first choice for treatment. I recommended that she start taking Celexa, the most recently released SSRI and the one reported to have the least frequent side effects. I started Caroline on ten milligrams and monitored her carefully, seeing her four times in the first two weeks, after which time I moved her up to 20 milligrams. An important component of these sessions was psychoeducation: talking to her parents and to her about her illness and impressing upon Caroline that her negative thoughts, her lack of energy and hopelessness, were caused by a biological disorder. She wasn't lazy or worthless or stupid; she had an illness and it was called depression.

After about three weeks, Caroline started to feel somewhat better.

Her sleep improved and her energy level increased, but neither was back to what it had been. She continued to have sleep problems and was feeling very tired in the afternoon after school, which necessitated a nap. Even though Caroline's thyroid functioning was in the low-to-normal range, I prescribed thyroxine and Cytomel in low doses to augment her Celexa. As it often does, augmentation boosted the effect of the antidepressant. Caroline had more energy in the afternoon, and she said the sluggish feeling she was having decreased. About two weeks later, five weeks overall since she began taking Celexa, her parents reported that she seemed like herself again—motivated, engaged, doing well with schoolwork, and back to her sports and piano. Her father said she even looked "different"—and he was delighted to have his "old" daughter back.

Caroline saw me once a week for the next few weeks and seemed to have a good understanding of her illness. She accepted it, as if it were no different from the acne that had started appearing when she was 13. Back then, she had become religious about washing her face, taking her medication, making sure she avoided certain foods, and dabbing her pimples with white goo at night. She took the same attitude toward her depression, carefully taking her medicines, showing up promptly for her appointments, and actually reading up on her disease. After two months without symptoms, Caroline started coming in on a monthly basis, and at the six-month point, I slowly discontinued the thyroid medicines. Finally, at seven months, I started lowering her Celexa. But two weeks later, after the Celexa dosage had been cut in half to ten milligrams, Caroline's symptoms reappeared. Once again, she seemed lethargic, dramatically less confident, and weepy.

Many patients have a relapse of symptoms when the medicine is decreased, which is the main reason why antidepressants should not be stopped quickly, abruptly, or prematurely. It needs to be done slowly. Caroline's medicine was increased back to 20 milligrams, and she actually needed the resumption of the thyroxine and Cytomel to achieve a full recovery. She stayed on the medicine for the rest of the academic year, and only in December of the following year, when she was 18 and had been accepted to college, did we start decreasing the medication a second time. This time around we did it much more gradually, over six weeks. She had no relapse and was able to completely enjoy the second part of her senior year.

Clearly, depression was Caroline's Achilles heel. While others might get a migraine headache under stress or tension, she was more likely to develop mood problems. Therefore, part of her treatment package was psychoeducational, teaching her to identify the warning signs and accepting that she was at higher risk for depression in the future. It didn't mean that she would definitely become depressed at the next major stressor in her life—the start of college, for instance—but that it was a distinct possibility. Ever the conscientious patient, before she left for school Caroline made an appointment to come in on Columbus Day weekend. When she arrived, without her parents, she had nothing but good news. College so far had turned out to be better than she had dreamed. She liked her roommate, the courses were terrific, and she found being independent very exciting. She had no symptoms of depression.

Though Caroline did well on Celexa—albeit with the bump caused by a premature withdrawal of the medication—some teenagers don't respond well to the first SSRI they try, and a second one is sometimes necessary. In some cases, an augmentation with a drug such as Dexedrine or Wellbutrin is also needed. If the second trial of SSRI doesn't work, a second category of medicine should be tried, and perhaps another augmenter such as lithium, though it often causes weight gain or acne. Ultimately, this is far from an exact science, and a certain amount of trial and error is often required to find the combination that works with each individual's biochemical makeup. With more antidepressants in the Food and Drug Administration (FDA) pipeline, the choices will only increase.

COGNITIVE BEHAVIORAL THERAPY (CBT)

Though medication can have remarkable results in bringing a young person out of a major depressive episode, I always stay alert for the teenager who might benefit from therapy, either on its own or in conjunction with medicine.

One such patient was Matt Duggan, a 14-year-old whose parents, Joe and Janine, described him as "our bearer of bad tidings." Since he was in elementary school, they said, Matt was always "the child who saw the glass as half empty." Now a freshman at a Catholic high school, Matt was tall and well-built for his age and handsome, with blue eyes and closely cropped dark brown hair. But his bearing belied his all-American good looks. The first time he came into my office, his shoulders were slumped and he moved slowly. As we began to talk, his demeanor confirmed his parents' description of him. His face was pretty well expressionless, and he looked down at the floor or gazed out the window for most of our hour-long session.

"Why do you think you're here?" I asked him.

"I don't know," he said, mumbling and barely audible. "My parents think I'm not enjoying the so-called best years of my life."

"Can you tell me what it is your parents are concerned about?"

"My brothers are all into sports and stuff going on at school. I guess I'm supposed to be doing the same thing. But I'm just not into that stuff. Hanging out. What's the point?"

Matt said he had friends, but didn't see them as much as he used to. "I'm too tired to go hanging in the park and always trying to find something to do," he said with a shrug. "I just don't see the point."

And so it went for the better part of the hour. Matt said he was holding his own in school, earning mostly Bs, but this was a change from elementary school, where he had been on the honor roll all the way through sixth grade. He said he was "on and off" in seventh and eighth grade, when he had started having trouble paying attention and just "didn't really get into" studying. Matt had played football until eighth grade, but decided against going out for the freshman football team. He reported feeling tired most of the time, and not being interested in the typical teenage activities. Even the effortless act of watching TV didn't do much for him. Although he had not gained or lost weight in the past few months, Matt said he wasn't a big eater and couldn't identify a favorite food for me. This told me that Matt's appetite had probably changed over time and that if this continued he might in fact begin losing weight.

Although most of his friends had started dating, Matt said he wasn't really interested enough in any girl to ask for a date. During homecoming weekend, when nearly every freshman in his school went on their first "formal" date to the school football game and dance, Matt stayed home watching television. Perhaps most telling about his depression was the way Matt viewed his future. When I asked him what he saw himself doing over the next five or ten years, he thought for a while and then, looking down at the floor, told me: "I don't know what I plan to do. I don't think that I'll go to college, because I just don't see the point. My father is a lieutenant in the fire department. My grandfather, my uncles, cousins, they're all firemen. But I don't want to do that either. That's no life with doing these 24-hour shifts and all, and going into fires and stuff where nobody really cares what you do or appreciates it." (This was before September 11.) "I don't know," Matt said finally. "I'll finish school and then try to figure something out."

Matt stood out in his family as "the only sad sack," in the words of his mother, Janine, a bubbly registered nurse who worked the day shift in a cardiac intensive care unit of a private hospital. She and her husband had three older sons, one a freshman at Notre Dame on an academic scholarship, and twins who were high school juniors. They also had a daughter a year younger than Matt. The Duggans described their household as lively and a gathering place for the neighborhood kids. This included Matt's friends, but his socializing had dropped off steadily since seventh grade. He no longer joined in on pickup basketball games in the front yard, nor did he wrestle with his brothers, tease his little sister, or work in the family restaurant with his siblings and cousins. In fact, Janine remarked, many of the relatives had expressed their concern that Matt was changing and withdrawing more and more with each passing year.

The Duggans said there was no history of anxiety or depression on either side of the family, including Joe and Janine themselves and Matt's siblings. They described all their other children as having gone through typical growing pains, but nothing unremitting or interfering with their lives. Matt himself had no history suggesting an anxiety disorder that might have led to the depression. Growing up, he had had no difficulty going to school, doing sleepovers, or staying with baby-sitters. He had been good at initiating and keeping friendships until eighth grade, when he seemed to "just stop being interested in his friends."

I asked the Duggans to tell me about the phrase "bearer of bad tidings," and I learned that his low mood had probably started earlier than they thought. As Janine explained, "Our oldest son started to call Matt 'BBT,' or the Bearer of Bad Tidings, when Matt was about seven years old. He just seemed to be focused on what could go wrong and not be able to see the upside of things. Just before the start of second grade, Matt began talking about what could go wrong for him. 'The teacher will probably be mean. We probably won't win the Little League championship. What if it rains on Halloween?' You name it, he came up with the most dismal predictions for how things were supposed to go for himself."

Joe, a big bear of a man, added his own observations. "It was pretty upsetting over time to see this kid who was happy and healthy as a little guy just become more and more of a sourpuss. I mean, all the kids and I play basketball and baseball together, and it's a pretty fun deal for us with lots of laughing. But Matt kind of just goes through the motions without any real emotion. He's an incredible athlete, especially in baseball and football. You could throw anything at this kid from the time he was a little tyke, and he would hit 'em out of the park!" But according to Joe, Matt could never let himself celebrate his successes. He seemed to just shrug them off and then talk about what he did wrong, instead of what was good about his performance.

"When he won MVP in Little League, and the times he received trophies for football, he went up and accepted these awards with the attitude of someone walking the plank," his father continued. "I don't know, all the kids and I enjoy a good competition, and get into teasing each other like any normal family, but Matt is different about these things. He's not sensitive to criticism, that's not it. He just can't seem to appreciate what's good about himself, his life, or our family. It's really sad for

Janine and me." The Duggans couldn't help but question whether they had done something wrong with Matt. He was so different from their other children.

I arrived at the diagnosis of major depressive disorder for Matt, and I assured the Duggans it had nothing to do with them as parents. It was likely that Matt had the makings of MDD as a younger child, when he earned the nicknames BBT and Sad Sack, but the depression really took hold just as he was entering puberty, a pattern often found in the internalizing disorders (depression and anxiety) but not in the externalizing disorders (ADHD and conduct disorders). Now he was in the midst of a long and steady single episode, one that had begun two years earlier.

When I gathered Matt and his parents together to present this diagnosis, no one seemed at all surprised or questioned the condition. Janine and Joe had spent time reading up on the condition and said they assumed that Matt had depression. But they were surprised when I did not offer medication as the first course of treatment. I explained that while he had several symptoms of major depression—impaired concentration, low energy, lack of interest in pleasant activities, depressed mood—he was maintaining a decent showing in his schoolwork and denied any suicidal ideation, which meant he was not in acute danger of hurting himself or spiraling quickly into a steep emotional decline. If Matt had been suicidal or shutting down and showing greater impairments in school, I would have wanted to start him on an antidepressant, which could take effect within two to three weeks and give his mood a lift. But his relatively moderate symptoms, along with his lack of family history for depression, meant that we had time and biology on our side. Instead of medication, I offered the Duggans a referral for cognitive behavioral therapy.

Taken a bit by surprise—though not displeased—the Duggans naturally were curious about the therapy. Why was I suggesting it, and what did I think it would do for their son? Matt himself seemed to accept my referral without question, but also without enthusiasm, which is not untypical for teenagers. I gave them a brief overview and then brought in my colleague at the Child Study Center, Dr. Anne Marie Albano, a psychologist who specializes in CBT, to describe the finer points of the therapy to the family. I gave her an overview of Matt's history.

"First," she said, speaking to Matt, "we'll begin by helping you understand the depression, what it is, where it comes from, and how it has interfered with your life. It's important to have a good knowledge about depression so you can fight it more effectively." Dr. Albano explained how depression is seen from the CBT viewpoint: depression occurs in vulnerable individuals who learn over time to do a few things differently than their peers who are not depressed. Initially, they learn to view themselves, the world, and their future, as pretty bleak and negative. This was called the "negative triad" by one of the pioneers of this therapy, Dr. Aaron Beck. It's as if the depressed individual sees life through a dark filter, rather than with a clear and objective view. The thoughts of people with depression tend to be focused on what can go wrong, how badly it can go, and how there's nothing they can do to change things for the better. It's something like that old *Saturday Night Live* character Stuart Smalley, who would talk about "stinkin' thinkin'."

In addition to this negative thinking style, individuals with depression withdraw from situations where they may have fun or feel good about things, and so they stop getting positive reinforcement from others. The more they withdraw, the fewer positive interactions they have. The fewer fun things they do, the more miserable they feel. This behavioral pattern comes from another pioneer in CBT, Dr. Peter Lewinsohn, who demonstrated that depressed individuals have a tough time drawing reinforcement from the environment, even when it's right there in front of them (in Matt's case, going up to receive his baseball trophy looking as if he were "walking the plank"). The two things, negative thoughts and behavioral withdrawal, interact to move the depression forward and create the down-in-the-dumps physical feelings and low mood of depression. "So it's important to understand depression as having three parts to it," Dr. Albano explained to the Duggans. "What you *think*, what you *do*, and what you *feel*."

Matt's parents raised a question often asked of CBT therapists: "Isn't depression a result of a chemical imbalance in the brain? And if it is, then how is talk therapy going to help?" The answers to these questions are a bit complex; in fact they aren't even completely understood by the top scientists working in this area.

"The CBT therapist takes the approach, based on scientific evidence, that depression is a result of a number of factors converging over time," Dr. Albano explained to the Duggans. "Some individuals may be born with a predisposition to become depressed, based on their family history. They may have had a parent, grandparent, or other relatives with depression. This doesn't seem to be the case with you, Matt. Next, as Doctors Stella Chess and Alexander Thomas have demonstrated, we know that every person is born with a temperament, that is, a unique personality and way of responding to the world. Some babies have an easy temperament. They can entertain themselves and sleep and eat well from an early age and are generally happy. Others have a more quiet temperament—we call it 'inhibited temperament.' These kids tend to be a bit hesitant to do things, like exploring a new place or separating from their parents. These kids are not likely to be really outgoing and bouncing all over the place; they're more reserved. There are also other kinds of temperaments, too, but the main thing is that there is no temperament that's right or wrong, good or bad. Temperament comes from our nervous system, so it involves our brain and nerves and the way these are put together for us at birth.

"Our temperament leads to our personality as we grow, and you can probably think about family members and friends with all types of different personalities. There's the angry person, the shy one, the jokester and life of the party, and the hyper person. As a baby begins to interact with the world, his temperament determines the way he's going to react to things. So it may be that your temperament was a bit on the quieter side, and as you were growing up, it sort of shaped you into being more reserved and more quiet than kids with different temperaments. And as time went on, your temperament kind of helped your mind in learning to think about things in a negative way, and feel things in a more down and blue way. This is the convergence of your biology, your personality, and your experiences shaping the way you think and feel, and what you do. So, although brain chemicals are involved in the biology of depression, we've learned from our studies that for many people the process of cognitive behavioral therapy can help them to 'unlearn' some of the less helpful thinking styles involved in depression, along with teaching them how to increase their involvement in pleasant activities that will improve their mood. Some people benefit from CBT alone, while others do best on both medication and CBT. We'll be keeping track of your progress as we move along to see if adding medication would be of help."

CBT treatment typically takes 12 sessions, conducted over a three- or four-month period. Most of Dr. Albano's sessions would be one-on-one with Matt, but there might be others that would include his parents, as well as some with his parents alone. Matt, Janine, and Joe agreed to begin with the therapy and see how things went. It was agreed that if, after about five weeks of treatment, Matt had difficulty with the therapy or didn't show any signs of improvement, medication would be considered as an additional treatment to give him a better chance of benefiting from CBT.

CBT begins with learning about the nature of depression and what triggers the thoughts, behaviors, and feelings that accompany depression. So in addition to starting with a more in-depth interview about Matt's symptoms and feelings, Dr. Albano asked Matt to keep a daily diary to track his mood. Initially, all he had to do was record a simple rating for how depressed he'd been that day, from zero to ten, the scale going from no depression to feeling the worst ever. As therapy continued, the diary was used to track how situations increased or decreased his feelings of depression, and to look at what thoughts went along with his feelings. Dr. Albano also wanted Matt to chart how many things or activities he did during the day that he felt okay or good about. "As we uncover these patterns of thinking, feeling, and behaving," she explained to the family, "Matt will learn that he has more control over his mood because he'll be able to predict how he will feel and he'll understand what things can lift or decrease his mood." The education phase of CBT is fairly well packed into the first two sessions but continues throughout the course of therapy. In addition to learning about depression from the therapist and from readings, and taking literal note of his feelings and actions in different situations, Matt would begin learning about the principles and techniques of CBT, and why they are used.

The cognitive part of cognitive behavioral therapy is focused on a process called "cognitive restructuring," which involves identifying and changing negative thinking patterns. In Matt's case, the first phase of cognitive restructuring was focused on identifying his thinking style and finding those "automatic thoughts" that would occur seemingly on their own and lead him to feeling down and needing to withdraw. Automatic thoughts, or ATs, are negative thoughts that fall into a number of forms or types, originally identified by Dr. Beck. Here are some examples of ATs:

- *All or None Thinking:* The belief that things will either go completely right or be completely terrible.
- *Catastrophizing:* Thinking that this is the absolute worst situation or experience that can happen.
- *Mind Reading:* The idea that you know what someone else is thinking, such as "I know those kids don't like me," even though there may be no evidence to support this.
- *Probability Overestimation:* Looking at an event or situation as being nearly 100 percent likely to occur, when in fact there is little chance of it happening.
- *Disqualifying the Positive:* Minimizing one's accomplishments and negating compliments. For example, when someone says, "That was a great play you made out there," you respond, "Well, I should've gotten a double play instead of just getting the runner out at home plate."
- *Fortune Telling:* Thinking that you know the outcome of a situation, when in fact you can't really predict how things will go. For example, Matt's idea that "it will rain on Halloween" or his assumption that "we probably won't win the Little League championship."

- *Can't, Won't, Should've:* Framing responses in negative language that implies that you doubt yourself or want to give up before even trying. For instance, saying "I can't do this" as opposed to "Well this is hard, but I'll give it a try." Or "I won't do this" instead of "I'm afraid I won't get it right, but I'll try." Or the age-old "I should have done this differently" versus the more positive "I did the best I could."

The main problem with ATs is that depressed people take them at face value and believe them without question. Thus, ATs are treated as facts, rather than as guesses or just one possibility of how things may be. Also, ATs lead an individual to think that there is nothing they can do to change or control a situation, so they give up and don't even try to change things. This leads to behavioral withdrawal and feelings of helplessness.

Using a daily diary form, Matt tracked his ATs as they occurred, including when and where they occurred. Once he learned to identify these thoughts, the next phase of cognitive restructuring involved challenging these thoughts with realistic information. Dr. Albano used the Stuart Smalley character to make this point. "Do you remember what Stuart used to say on his television show? 'I'm good enough, I'm smart enough, and doggone it, people like me.' But even though he told himself these things, he usually broke down and cried."

One of the things we've learned in CBT is that merely telling oneself a positive thought doesn't really change things or feelings. That's because ATs are real facts to a person who is depressed. Instead, the patient needs to be trained to see these thoughts as guesses or hypotheses. Simply thinking a positive thought isn't enough. It needs to be evaluated to assess its validity—that is, is it real and supported by evidence? Simply accepting a thought as fact is what leads to feeling helpless. That's why Stuart broke down. "Instead of reciting a positive thought and treating the automatic thought as a fact," Dr. Albano instructed Matt, "look at it as a guess. Ask yourself, 'What is the *evidence* for my thought? Is there *any* evidence to support it? What are the different aspects of this situation? What can I do if things don't go the way I'd like, which happens to everyone? What can I plan on doing to deal with less-than-ideal situations?"

In CBT, this is called developing a "Rational Response" to a negative thought—using a question or statement to challenge the AT with realistic evidence or coming up with a concrete plan for evaluating the validity of the AT. In response to the "Nothing will ever work out for me" AT, the Rational Response can be "I can't know how things will be over the next year or two, but if I try and do things for myself, there's a better chance of things going the way I'd like." More to the point, the CBT therapist assists the patient with focusing on the here and now, taking smaller steps, and working in a progressive, stepwise way on specific goals set up in therapy.

Cognitive restructuring goes hand in hand with the behavioral component of CBT, known as "activity scheduling," "behavioral experiments," or "behavioral activation tasks." In the early stages of therapy for depression, the patient is asked to start keeping track of how many and what types of activities he or she engages in during the day. Activities are labeled "success oriented," such as studying, applying for jobs, or completing college applications; or they can be "social activities" involving peers or family members, such as attending parties and going to the movies with friends. Finally, there are "pleasant activities or relaxation activities" (such as reading for pleasure, playing sports, or just lying on the beach) to relieve stress and lift one's mood. Typically, patients report depressed moods when there is a corresponding infrequency of these three kinds of pursuits. The CBT therapist assists the patient with identifying and challenging the ATs that stop him or her from participating in these activities. Then behavioral experiments are arranged where the patient "tests out" what happens when he or she engages in these activities.

As Matt continued in therapy, it became apparent that his mood and the amount of time he spent in activities were related. His mood was more depressed on days when he did very little except go to school and do his other compulsory tasks. But he started to see a pattern whereby his mood was a bit brighter on days when he played a game of basketball with his brothers, saw a movie with a friend, or took time to read something for pleasure, not just for homework. With the aid of Dr. Albano, Matt began to understand how his automatic thoughts got in the way of getting out and doing things for fun, with his appreciation of his own successes, and with his ability to look forward to the future.

"So, Matt, let's look at your diary and see what you've been up to this week," Dr. Albano said during one session. "Wow, it looks like the weekend was pretty low for you. You've rated your mood on Friday and Saturday as eight each day. So you were pretty down. What was going on then?"

"I don't know," Matt said. "There just wasn't anything going on, so I stayed home and did nothing."

"Okay, let's back up to earlier in the week. Can you tell me what was going on in school last week? Any exams or extra work, any stuff going on with the kids there?"

"It was a crappy week. I had three exams, there was spring football tryouts so nobody was around to do anything, and the weekend was dead. That's all, really."

"Okay, let's start with your exams. What were they in and how did you do?"

"I got an A on my algebra exam, a B on the history test, and a B on the biology test. But I should've aced all of them. I just couldn't study as much as I needed to."

"Wait a minute. Tell me what kind of ATs are going on here. What did you just say about your A and two Bs?"

"All right, yeah, I said, 'I should've aced them all.' I've disqualified the positive."

"Right. And Matt, when you say that to yourself, how you should have aced those tests, how does that make you feel?"

"Lousy."

"So you have three exams all in the same week, plus your regular homework. You get an A and two Bs, despite this grueling schedule. Now, tell me, using a more rational voice, how to respond to this AT?"

"Okay, well, I did really well on one test and got good grades on the others, even though I had all this extra work. And I had one of the best grades in the class in one test."

"What does that kind of thinking do to your mood?"

"I feel better about it. Other kids caved with that schedule, but I didn't."

"Great, that's right. Now, what about the thoughts about football try-outs and nobody being around? What else were you thinking about these things?"

"I should've gone out for football this year, but didn't. So now I've got nothing to do and the guys are all hanging together and stuff."

"Do the guys leave you out of things?"

"Well, they ask me to go do stuff, like there were parties on Friday and Saturday night, but I didn't want to go because I'm not on the team."

"Okay, let's look at this. 'There was nobody around to do anything.' 'The weekend was dead.' 'I should've gone out for football, but didn't.' 'The guys ask me to do stuff but I didn't want to because I'm not on the team.' Wow, that's some string of negative thoughts!"

"Yeah, I think I screwed myself by not going out for football."

"How did you screw yourself? Did you lose your friends?"

"Well no, but I'm not on the team."

"Did they stop calling?"

"No, they call. And they want me to hang out. It's not them, it's me. I feel like I let myself down by not going out for football. I feel like I'm not part of anything. But I guess I'm the one keeping me apart. The guys are always calling."

"What do you tell yourself about going to the parties with the guys?"

"Who's going to want to hang with me? I'm not a part of the team."

"Well, what do you mean? The guys call you, right?"

"Well, yeah. It's not the guys. They're cool. But, you know, the girls there are more into the football players than just any other guy."

"Really? How do you know that?"

"Well, that's what I think."

"Exactly. Do you have any evidence for that thought? Let me ask you this: Have you been to any of these parties and tried to talk to the girls there?"

"No, I haven't gone to anything this year. Okay, I see what you're getting at. This is my thought and I'm looking at it like it's a hundred percent true. But I really don't know if it's true or not, because I haven't been out to one of these parties yet."

"Okay, so let's plan a behavioral experiment for this coming week. What can you do to test out the thought, 'If I'm not on the team, none of the girls at my school will talk to me at these social events'?"

"Well, there is a school dance on Friday. The guys are already talking about it and want me to come with them. I can see what will happen."

"You can go to the dance and just stand there and wait for something to happen, or you can do something else. Do you know what you can do?"

"I guess I can try talking to girls and ask them to dance, and see what happens then."

"And do you think that every girl will say yes to dancing or that they will all be talkative?"

"No."

"Why not? You're a good-looking, smart boy."

"They may have their own stuff in their heads."

"And?"

"And I won't know if there's any girl who may be interested in me if I don't go and try."

"Okay. And with this kind of thinking and planning, how do you feel now on the mood monitoring?"

"Pretty okay. I'd rate myself a three right now. And, I feel like going and doing stuff more than before."

Matt stayed in CBT therapy for 14 sessions and made excellent progress. Dr. Albano showed him how to challenge negative thinking and reverse the inactivity and lethargy accompanying depression with planned pleasant activities and tasks. She also taught him specific skills for relaxation, problem solving, assertiveness, communication, and generally dealing with the problems of everyday life. By the end of treatment, Matt was no longer the Bearer of Bad Tidings. To his and his family's delight, he was free of depression.

Matt is by no means an unusual success story; CBT has long been established as an effective treatment for adult depression, and research by Dr. Lewinsohn and his colleagues Doctors Greg Clarke and Paul Rohde, and independently by Dr. David Brent, have established the therapy as an effective treatment for depressed adolescents. The Treatments for Adolescents with Depression Study (TADS) is the first study of its kind to put CBT and medication to the test at the same time, and to assess them in combination. These types of studies are essential for moving forward in the field and gaining an understanding of what works for the majority of youth, what type of treatment to start with, when to add a second treatment for boosting the chance of gaining a good outcome, and, probably of most importance, what happens to these kids over the long term, after treatment ends. The TADS, begun in 1998 and running through 2004, will follow 430 depressed adolescents through a course of treatment and then for a year afterward.

Matt Duggan was treated three years before the writing of this book, but if he had been part of TADS, his case would have put a solid success story in the CBT column. He responded very well to CBT alone, without medication, over a short-term course of therapy. At this writing, he is enjoying his senior year of high school. He has a steady girlfriend, is continuing to get excellent grades, and is applying to colleges. In tenth grade, he went out for football, and he's been on the team ever since. Though he's done well, he told Dr. Albano recently that he still finds those ATs creeping in at times and turning his mood a bit blue. However, CBT also involves teaching the depressed patient "relapse prevention" strategies: key techniques to implement when facing stressful times, changes in routine, developmental challenges such as transitioning from high school to college, and other issues that may prompt a decline in mood. Checking in with Dr. Albano from time to time and stopping by her office to say hello, Matt reports that he uses the skills he learned in therapy and keeps track of his mood, thoughts, and activities when things start to get rough. One of the best predictors of maintaining a good outcome after CBT is staying with the program. Matt is doing just that, and should continue to have a bright future.

INTERPERSONAL THERAPY (IPT)

Interpersonal therapy was originally developed for the treatment of acutely depressed adults by the late Dr. Gerald Klerman and his wife and colleague, Dr. Myrna Weissman, two of the leading researchers in the treatment of depression. IPT has since been adapted for the treatment of adolescents by focusing on the developmental relationship issues that are most common to young people: separating from parents; dealing with authority issues and parent-child conflict; living in a single-parent family; negotiating peer relationships, pressures, and conflicts; and dealing with transitions between stages of life, social isolation, and first experiences with death and grief. Simply put, the theory behind IPT is that regardless of the origin of the depression, it occurs in the context of interpersonal relationships, which can contribute to and/or exacerbate the depression. By helping the patient look at her own pattern of communication within significant relationships and understand how it affects other people, the therapist hopes to improve the relationship and bring the patient out of her depression.

IPT is designed as a once-a-week, 12-week treatment that is divided into three phases. The initial phase emphasizes psychoeducation about the depression, reviews the patient's significant relationships, and identifies one or two problem areas that will be focused on later in the course of treatment. The middle phase is devoted to helping the patient learn to link her depressed mood to problems in the identified areas, as well as to link *improvement* in mood to constructive changes in communication and problem-solving skills. The therapist offers specific strategies for negotiating interpersonal difficulties. In the final phase, the patient learns to apply the lessons of the treatment to future situations and to identify warning signs of future episodes of depression.

IPT is intended to make a particularly strong connection with the patient and his world. During the first month of treatment, an IPT therapist may supplement the weekly sessions with phone calls to keep the patient engaged in the process. He or she may also become an advocate with the school system, especially in cases where the teenager won't go to school. Together, the therapist and a school psychologist or social worker can come up with an individual academic program to get the patient back into school. Dr. Weissman, who is a professor of psychiatry at Columbia University, emphasizes that IPT for teenagers should be flexible, yet not open-ended. "My feeling is that if you can't come in because you want to go shopping or you have a soccer game, just call me," she said. "There should be a great deal of flexibility." She also takes the view that it's okay for a teenager not to want to come for therapy. "If a kid doesn't come because he's starting to get better, we don't see that as resistance. We see that as a healthy sign. We teach them to communicate clearly about scheduling conflicts and have them reschedule. Meanwhile, we encourage them to return to normal activities. We regularly assess improvement and renegotiate the treatment contract. Patients come in until they make a decision jointly with the therapist about tapering off sessions to a maintenance schedule. If they want to come in once a month or do the work by telephone, it's okay, so long as they're not sitting in their room contemplating suicide. Therapy is not a bad thing if they need it, but it's not normal for a kid to go in and talk to a stranger about their problems. So we try to get them out of the sick role as soon as possible."

Rosa's Rough Relationships

Rosa was a 17-year-old who was referred by her school guidance counselor to a colleague of mine, Dr. Laura Mufson, a psychologist at New York State Psychiatric Institute, who is one of the nation's experts on IPT for depressed adolescents. Rosa came from a single-parent home. Her father died when she was five, and her mother hadn't remarried. Rosa, an only child, became the sole focus of her mother's life. They were Latin American, and like many first-generation Americans, Rosa was her mother's translator and link to the Anglo world. Her mother worked long hours at menial jobs to provide her daughter with a private-school education, and Rosa felt deeply obligated to succeed academically.

Rosa had become depressed, but was still doing well in school. When Dr. Mufson saw her for their first visit, Rosa said she had never been happy. She said she felt depressed every day, pretty much all day. She cried frequently, was irritable, and basically got no pleasure out of life. She felt she had been depressed for several years, but that it had worsened in the past three months. She felt hopeless and had considered a number of plans for suicide, though she denied intending to follow through with any of them. The symptoms added up to "double depression"—major depression on top of chronic low-level melancholy, or dysthymia.

In the early sessions of IPT, Dr. Mufson zeroed in on Rosa's primary problem areas: conflicts with her mother about obligations at home and privacy, as well as recent problems she had been having with friends. She also appeared to be having difficulty with the impending transition from high school to college, which triggered mixed emotions about separating from her mother and from her friends. The early discussions revealed that Rosa had a tendency to hold in her anger toward her mother. Instead of expressing herself directly, she simply didn't do the things her mother relied on her to do around the house. She had similar difficulty talking to her friends when she got mad at them. Instead, she avoided them, which made her feel worse.

Dr. Mufson spent the heart of the IPT sessions on improving Rosa's ability to express her feelings, as well as helping her clarify the expectations she had for her relationships. They talked about how she might balance the conflict between her mother's reliance on her with her own need for independence and privacy. They role-played, practicing ways Rosa could negotiate her obligations or discuss her needs to put some space between her and her mother, techniques that she then used successfully at home. She also practiced ways of discussing conflicts with her girl-friends, and as a result found they were more supportive. Overall, Rosa became better than she had ever been at appreciating other people's points of view and expressing her own in a constructive rather than antagonistic way. By the end of the 12-week course, her relationships improved dramatically, and she felt happy for the first time in years.

As simple and straightforward as Rosa's case sounds, it would be unrealistic to expect such success with IPT, or any therapy, in every case. Each person is different, and there are many views about the value of medicine versus therapy. Whereas I tend to think that antidepressants are a good first line of attack in most cases of serious depression, colleagues who practice behavioral or interpersonal psychotherapy are firm believers in the drug-free approach. "I would try psychotherapy on everyone first, unless it's a recurrent episode and they're suicidal," Dr. Weissman told me during a discussion of treatment. "If they've had recurrences, I'd certainly give them medication. And I wouldn't let them be on psychotherapy indefinitely."

Whatever route is chosen, anyone who is depressed, whether adult or adolescent, should be feeling better in six to eight weeks. If not, it's time to try something else, either increase the dose of medication, add an augmenter, try another antidepressant, or change the form of psychotherapy. That's where both cognitive behavioral therapy and interpersonal therapy differ from more traditional forms of psychotherapy, which do not promise improvement in two months or less.

"We don't cure anybody in six weeks, in the sense that they'll suddenly stop arguing with their mother and begin getting straight As," Dr. Weissman said. "But they should be eating and sleeping better and having a more positive outlook. It takes a while for some of the other things to improve. What we try to do is teach some skills so they can express their wishes better and act in a way that's more constructive."

TREATMENT AND POLITICS: THE ECT QUESTION

The question of medicine versus psychotherapy pales in comparison with the controversy over a second-line treatment: electroconvulsive therapy, or ECT. Though it seems barbaric to some people, the fact is that ECT is a safe and effective treatment for unremitting depression, bipolar disorder, and psychosis in adults and adolescents who do not respond to medication. (The case of Danny in chapter 9 is one such success.) As I discussed earlier, while under anesthesia, patients are given an electric shock that lasts a fraction of a second and induces a small, virtually undetectable seizure that alters brain chemistry and quickly reduces symptoms. Typically, a patient is given a dozen or so treatments over the course of a month. Historically there were adverse effects, including fractures, panic, spontaneous seizures, and headaches, which still contribute to resistance to the use of ECT. But today, anesthesia, muscle relaxation, oxygen, and other measures effectively counter those responses. The only remaining side effect is short-term memory loss, but this usually subsides within a few weeks of completion of a course of ECT.

There is clear evidence that ECT works, but it has been overshadowed by emotional responses to the idea of literally shocking someone—particularly a child or adolescent—out of mental illness. In fact, four states—California, Colorado, Texas, and Tennessee—have outlawed the use of ECT in young people (the proscribed ages vary from 12 to 16). Similar laws are under consideration in Arizona and Vermont. This puts ECT into the realm of assisted suicide and euthanasia. This is not only misguided and unfortunate, but also ironic: ECT can and does *save* lives.

This is not to minimize the serious nature of ECT or to suggest that it should be considered right alongside front-line treatments such as an SSRI or cognitive behavioral therapy. But there is enough case evidence to demonstrate that ECT is safe and effective, and that it should be an option for adolescents with severe symptoms who do not respond to medicine. Certainly it is better to try it as a secondary treatment or even as a last resort than to allow a severely depressed, nonfunctional, or psychotic adolescent to get even worse or become suicidal.

Aside from fear and misconception, one reason ECT has rarely been used with adolescents is that it is simply not on the radar screen of most child and adolescent psychiatrists. They have less awareness of ECT than psychiatrists, who primarily treat adults and so have much more experience with it. Generally speaking, child and adolescent psychiatrists are less apt to prescribe medicine to their patients than adult psychiatrists are. So they would be even less likely to suggest a treatment as unconventional and seemingly radical as ECT. Fears that ECT might damage the developing brain—as understandable as they may be—are ungrounded in science. Studies investigating long-term impairment have all found that even those who had memory or learning problems immediately after treatment had no persistent problems. Unfortunately, the psychological and political barriers have hindered the kind of extensive clinical research that might destigmitize ECT. Instead, we have to rely on case reports. And those have been uniformly positive, so that paradoxically, this long-controversial treatment is now considered at the cutting edge of treatment for mental illness, including depression, in adolescents.

In a 1999 report on pediatric ECT, Dr. Max Fink, of the School of Medicine at the State University of New York at Stony Brook, and Dr. Carmel Foley, of the Albert Einstein College of Medicine, cited a number of studies that support the use of ECT in certain cases. In one study of 60 cases, ECT helped 63 percent of those with depression and 80 percent of patients with mania. In more than 90 percent of these cases, ECT was used as a last resort, after patients had failed many courses of medication and psychotherapy. Clinicians at a number of prominent academic centers—including UCLA, the Mayo Clinic, and the University of Michigan—have reported success in treating adolescents with ECT, particularly those with mood disorders. An obvious question is: On what basis should a clinician decide whether ECT should be considered for a particular patient? Doctors Fink and Foley think the answer is not very complicated: they concluded that ECT should be considered no less legitimate, and should be used no less routinely, than other treatments. They write: "Adolescent patients with clinical features that, had they occurred in adults, would be considered for ECT, warrant consideration. ECT should not be deferred to 'the last resort treatment,' but should be considered when the first therapies have been tried for a reasonable time and failed."

BIPOLAR DISORDER

For such a complicated illness—and an incurable one—the treatment of bipolar disorder is relatively straightforward. Unlike unipolar depression, there is no controversy over the merits of medication versus therapy, and there are no decisions to make about how long to stay on medicine. A person with bipolar disorder will, in all likelihood, have to take a mood stabilizer for the rest of his or her life.

There may be augmenting treatments. With bipolar disorder, other medications may be necessary to treat specific episodes of mania or depression, and psychosocial therapies and psychoeducation are often necessary to help patients understand their illness and cope with the stresses that can trigger episodes. But as the first-line treatment of bipolar disorder, nothing beats the mood stabilizer lithium, which is sold under the brand names Eskalith or Lithobid. While it is the most effective medicine for moderating and preventing mania—a real miracle drug for many people—it also has the most side effects of all the mood stabilizers. These can include slight hand tremors, excessive thirst and urination, memory problems, weight gain, and acne. Patients taking lithium have to be careful in extremely hot weather because dehydration can increase the concentration of lithium in the blood, producing side effects. Lithium can also suppress thyroid functioning.

For these reasons, patients who take lithium have to be monitored with blood tests, especially in the first few months, to make sure the level of lithium in the blood is within a certain range. It has to be high enough to be effective but not so high that it produces serious side effects. These side effects often subside after a few weeks as the body adjusts to the medication. If they persist, other medicines can treat the side effects. For instance, decreased thyroid functioning can be easily corrected with a synthetic hormone. Side effects such as those associated with lithium are commonly referred to as "nuisance" effects because they are benign compared with those that come with more toxic agents such as cancer chemotherapy. And many adult patients with bipolar disorder find lithium so essential to their lives that they are willing to accept a certain level of side effects. Teenagers, however, have different thresholds for enduring side effects, especially those with social implications such as acne, weight gain, and hand tremors. But all the side effects can be kept at bay with other medications.

An anticonvulsant medication, divalproex sodium (sold as Depakote), has been promoted as an alternative to lithium. It seems to be as effective at treating specific manic episodes, and to have fewer side effects. But there is little evidence to support the use of Depakote instead of lithium as a long-term preventive treatment. Depakote has been used to treat epilepsy since 1983, and it was approved as a treatment for mania in 1995. But, obviously, it doesn't have lithium's track record. An extensive literature review published in late 1997 in the *Annals of the New York Academy of Sciences* suggests that lithium reduces by nearly nine times the suicide rate of patients with mood disorders, including bipolar and recurrent unipolar major depression. In addition, that study found that bipolar patients who discontinued lithium had a ninefold increase in suicidal acts and a ninefold increase in fatalities. Researchers don't understand how these effects are produced, but they suspect that lithium decreases the impulsivity that characterizes so many suicidal acts. In adolescents with bipolar disorder, lithium has been shown to decrease the rate of heavy marijuana use.

Still, there are patients for whom lithium is ineffective, or who find the side effects too severe. But Depakote and other anticonvulsants, such as Tegretol, have their own side effects: nausea, drowsiness, dizziness, and tremors, and they can cause problems with liver function and white blood-cell counts. So regular blood tests are generally part of the treatment.

A WORD TO PARENTS

Now that you know how many choices there are in treating depression, it's important to understand your role as a parent and advocate for your child. Once a diagnosis of depression is made, both you and your teenager must understand your clinician's thinking and endorse the diagnosis before effective treatment can begin. That means it's up to you and your teenager to make sure that both of you comprehend the specific symptoms and discuss how each of them impairs your child's functioning. In this way, you will be able to focus on these symptoms as treatment progresses and to know if they are diminishing and your teenager is getting better.

As with any illness, the doctor should go over the treatment options and explain the pros and cons of each: what will happen without treatment, what to expect of a specific treatment, and how soon results can be expected. There are myriad other questions to consider. If psychotherapy is recommended, who will provide it? How long is the treatment plan? How often will the sessions be? When and how will it be determined if medicine needs to be added? If medicine is the treatment choice, what are the various side effects? How long will the treatment take? How long will the teenager be taking the medication? When do we increase the dose and when do we add an augmenter? When do we switch to a new medicine if the first one doesn't work? It's possible to have too much information all at once, so for some people it's probably best for the clinician to give an overview and a timeline and then go into detail a little at a time. Still, as a parent, you want to be as informed as possible so you and your child can make smart decisions about treatment.

From diagnosis to discharge, there needs to be a partnership between you, your teenager, and the clinician. Though certain details of conversations between doctor and patient remain confidential, the doctor has to be able to rely on you to observe and report your impressions of your teenager's behavior. Two leading clinical researchers in adolescent depression, Doctors Adrian Angold and Elizabeth Costello, have concluded from many years of work that parents tend to be unaware of their teenager's mindset and feelings. They are much better at observing specific behaviors, such as sleep, appetite, and social comfort levels. This is a good thing, because these observations are the best way for parents to help the clinician—first to make a diagnosis and then to monitor the effectiveness of the treatment.

▫

Some parents take the position that, as the Beatles famously sang, all you need is love. Or at least the right kind of love—whether it's understanding or tough love. Love surely helps, and as all the parents in this book demonstrate, no matter how irritable and dislikable our children may get, we still love them. Nevertheless, depressed teenagers need parents who are vigilant, aware, and informed about the signs and symptoms of depression.

We don't want Stepford Teenagers. They don't have to be smiling incessantly and getting straight As. But we do want them to truly experience the world and to become independent—whether it's feeling the joy (as well as the sorrow) of a romantic relationship, concentrating on a tough subject in school and making plans for college, getting a good night's sleep, or enjoying the simple pleasures of eating a slice of pizza.

Depression deprives our kids of these experiences, and we may feel helpless to do anything about it. But as parents we *do* have power. We are fortunate that the field of psychiatry has advanced to the point that we have information and tools to help our teenagers that *our* parents never had. We know that depression is a real illness, and that it can be treated.

I feel privileged to be a child and adolescent psychiatrist. Every week, I meet children and teenagers who are interesting and amazingly honest. They are in pain, and I have the opportunity to figure out what's wrong and how I can help them get better. But with every child, I also meet parents, many of whom are heroic in their efforts to save their teenagers. I sit in awe of how these mothers and fathers persevere and sacrifice to free their children of depression and give them back their ability to experience the joys and face the challenges of life. In the end, that's what we all want for our children.

As Carol Altman, Jesse's mom, reflected: "Having come through the dark tunnel, I would say to other parents that there's no difference between your child having diabetes or depression. It can be a long journey, but when you see the light at the end, you realize that you have saved your child."

NOTES

These notes will allow further exploration of the material presented in this book. Source references for the major studies and findings presented are listed, along with expanded commentary for selected topics. The commentary was developed by F. Xavier Castellanos, M.D., Neidich Family Professor of Child and Adolescent Psychiatry at New York University School of Medicine; the references were compiled by Jennifer L. Rosenblatt.

MORE THAN MOODY: AN INTRODUCTION

Page 4: "Upwards of 40 million . . ." U.S. Department of Health and Human Services. *Mental Health: A Report of the Surgeon General.* Rockville, MD: U.S. Department of Health and Human Services, Substance Abuse and Mental Health Services Administration, Center for Mental Health Services, National Institutes of Health, National Institute of Mental Health; 1999.

Page 4: "The studies indicate . . ." Smucker MR, Craighead WE, Craighead LW, Green BJ. Normative and reliability data for the Children's Depression Inventory. *Journal of Abnormal Child Psychology.* 1996; 14:25–39.

Page 4: "Significantly, studies estimate . . ." Anderson JC, McGee R. Comorbidity of depression in children and adolescents. In: Reynolds WM, Johnson HF, eds. *Handbook of Depression in Children and Adolescents.* New York: Plenum;

1994:581–601; Kessler RC, Walters EE. Epidemiology of DSM-III-R major depression and minor depression among adolescents and young adults in the National Comorbidity Survey. *Depression and Anxiety.* 1998; 7:3–14.

Page 4: "... compared with only ..." Murphy JM, Olivier DC, Monson RR, Sobol AM, Leighton AH. Incidence of depression and anxiety: The Stirling County Study. *American Journal of Public Health.* 1988; 78:534–540; Rorsman B, Grasbeck A, Hagnell O, Lanke J, Ohman R, Ojesjo L, Otterbeck L. A prospective study of first-incidence depression: The Lundby Study, 1957–72. *British Journal of Psychiatry.* 1990; 156:336–342; Regier DA, Narrow WE, Rae DS, Manderscheid RW, Locke BZ, Goodwin FK. The de facto U.S. mental and addictive disorders service system. Epidemiologic Catchment Area prospective 1-year prevalence rates of disorders and services. *Archives of General Psychiatry.* 1993; 50:85–94.

Page 4: "Studies suggest that ..." American College Health Association. *National College Health Assessment: Reference Group Executive Summary Spring 2000.* Baltimore: American College Health Association; 2001.

Page 4: "In 2002, some ..." Centers for Disease Control and Prevention National Center for Injury Prevention and Control website; 2002. Available: http://webapp.cdc.gov/sasweb/ncipc/mortrate.html.

Page 5: "The most recent survey on youth ..." Centers for Disease Control and Prevention. CDC Survellience Summaries, June 9, 2000. MMWR 2000; 49 (No. SS–5).

Page 5: "An adolescent with ..." Weissman MM, Wolk S, Goldstein RB, Moreau D, Adams P, Greenwald S, Klier CM, Ryan ND, Dahl RE, Wickramaratne P. Depressed adolescents grown up. *Journal of the American Medical Association.* 1999; 281:1707–1713; Lewinsohn PM, Rohde P, Seeley JR, Klein DN, Gotlib IH. Natural course of adolescent major depressive disorder in a community sample: Predictors of recurrence in young adults. *American Journal of Psychiatry.* 2000; 157:1584–1591; Garber J, Kriss MR, Koch M, Lindholm L. Recurrent depression in adolescents: A follow-up study. *Journal of the American Academy of Child and Adolescent Psychiatry.* 1988; 27:49–54; Rao U, Ryan ND, Birmaher B, Dahl RE, Williamson DE, Kaufman J, Rao R, Nelson B. Unipolar depression in adolescents: Clinical outcome in adulthood. *Journal of the American Academy of Child and Adolescent Psychiatry.* 1995; 34:566–578.

Page 5: "Consider that some ..." Lewinsohn PM, Hops H, Roberts RE, Seeley JR, Andrews JA. Adolescent psychopathology: I. Prevalence and incidence of depression and other DSM-III-R disorders in high school students. *Journal of Abnormal Psychology.* 1993; 102:133–144.

Page 8: "The noted psychologist . . ." Hall GS. *Adolescence: Its Psychology and Its Relations to Physiology, Anthropology, Sociology, Sex, Crime, Religion and Education.* New York: Appleton; 1904.

Page 11: "While 10 million . . ." Shaffer D, Fisher P, Dulcan MK, Davies M, Piacentini J, Schwab-Stone ME, Lahey BB, Bourdon K, Jensen PS, Bird HR, Canino G, Regier DA. The NIMH Diagnostic Interview Schedule for Children Version 2.3 (DISC-2.3): Description, acceptability, prevalence rates, and performance in the MECA study. *Journal of the American Academy of Child and Adolescent Psychiatry.* 1996; 35:865–877.

Page 11: ". . . there are only . . ." American Academy of Child and Adolescent Psychiatry website; 2002. Available: http://www.aacap.org.

Page 11: ". . . and fewer than . . ." APA Research Office. 2000 Directory Survey. Washington, DC: American Psychological Assocation; 2001.

CHAPTER I. DIAGNOSIS: DEPRESSION

Page 14: "But we've known . . ." Klerman GL, Weissman MM. Increasing rates of depression. *Journal of the American Medical Association.* 1989; 261:2229–2235.

Page 14: "It is actually . . ." American Psychiatric Association. *Diagnostic and Statistical Manual of Mental Disorders.* 4th ed., text revision. Washington, DC: American Psychiatric Association; 2000.

Page 15: "Research has also . . ." Garber J, Kriss MR, Koch M, Lindholm L. Recurrent depression in adolescents: A follow-up study. *Journal of the American Academy of Child and Adolescent Psychiatry.* 1988; 27:49–54.

Page 17: "It's no surprise . . ." Fleming JE, Offord DR. Epidemiology of childhood depressive disorders: A critical review. *Journal of the American Academy of Child and Adolescent Psychiatry.* 1990; 29:2989–2995.

Page 17: "Depressed young people . . ." Birmaher B, Ryan ND, Williamson DE, Brent DA, Kaufman J. Childhood and adolescent depression: A review of the past 10 years. Part II. *Journal of the American Academy of Child and Adolescent Psychiatry.* 1996; 35:1575–1583; Birmaher B, Ryan ND, Williamson DE,

Brent DA, Kaufman J, Dahl RE, Perel J, Nelson B. Childhood and adolescent depression: A review of the past 10 years. Part I. *Journal of the American Academy of Child and Adolescent Psychiatry.* 1996; 35:1427–1439; Kovlin I, Barrett ML, Bhate SR, Berney TP, Famuyiwa OO, Fundudis T, Tyrer S. The Newcastle Child Depression Project. Diagnosis and classification of depression. *British Journal of Psychiatry.* Supplement. 1991; 11:9–21.

Page 17: "Also more common . . ." Birmaher B, Ryan ND, Williamson DE, Brent DA, Kaufman J. Childhood and adolescent depression: A review of the past 10 years. Part II. *Journal of the American Academy of Child and Adolescent Psychiatry.* 1996; 35:1575–1583; Birmaher B, Ryan ND, Williamson DE, Brent DA, Kaufman J, Dahl RE, Perel J, Nelson B. Childhood and adolescent depression: A review of the past 10 years. Part I. *Journal of the American Academy of Child and Adolescent Psychiatry.* 1996; 35:1427–1439; Kovlin I, Barrett ML, Bhate SR, Berney TP, Famuyiwa OO, Fundudis T, Tyrer S. The Newcastle Child Depression Project. Diagnosis and classification of depression. *British Journal of Psychiatry.* Supplement. 1991; 11:9–21.

Page 18–19: "One sobering piece . . ." Centers for Disease Control and Prevention website; 2002. Available: http://www.cdc.gov.

Page 19: "We know that . . ." Shaffer D, Gould MS, Fisher P, Trautman P. Psychiatric diagnosis in child and adolescent suicide. *Archives of General Psychiatry.* 1996; 53:339–348; Weissman MM, Wolk S, Goldstein RB, Moreau D, Adams P, Greenwald S, Klier CM, Ryan ND, Dahl RE, Wickramaratne P. Depressed adolescents grown up. *Journal of the American Medical Association.* 1999; 281:1707–1713.

Page 19: "It often follows . . ." Biederman J, Faraone S, Mick E, Lelon E. Psychiatric comorbidity among referred juveniles with major depression: Fact or artifact? *Journal of the American Academy of Child and Adolescent Psychiatry.* 1995; 34:579–590; Kessler RC, Walters EE. Epidemiology of DSM-III-R major depression and minor depression among adolescents and young adults in the National Comorbidity Survey. *Depression and Anxiety.* 1998; 7:3–14.

Page 19: "In all, some . . ." Anderson JC, McGee R. Comorbidity of depression in children and adolescents. In: Reynolds WM, Johnson HF, eds. *Handbook of Depression in Children and Adolescents.* New York: Plenum; 1994:581–601; Angold A, Costello EG. Depressive comorbidity in children and adolescents: Empirical, theoretical, and methodological issues. *American Journal of Psychiatry.* 1993; 150:1779–1791.

Page 19: "The good news . . ." Kovacs M, Feinberg TL, Crouse-Novak MA, Paulauskas SL, Finkelstein R. Depressive disorders in childhood. I. A longitudinal prospective study of characteristics and recovery. *Archives of General Psychiatry.* 1984; 41:229–237.

Page 19: "What, exactly, is . . ." This raises the further question: Why does mood exist? There is a literature on evolutionary psychiatry/psychology that is somewhat well founded. Many subscribe to the notion that mood is part of how we regulate our behavior in generally adaptive ways. If we're stuck in a rut of some sort, then a dysphoric mood may serve as an advantage, in that it might increase the chances that we'll stop the behavior keeping us in the rut and make other choices. For further information on this point, see: Fawcett RG. Is depression adaptive for the human species? *Archives of General Psychiatry.* 2001; 58:1086.

While Nesse enumerates the possible ways in which low mood and/or depression may be adaptive for an individual, another possibility is that depression, with its known increase in morbidity and mortality, may be maladaptive to the individual but adaptive to the species. Cyranowski et al. point out the increase in depression and sensitivity to loss of relationships in females during childbearing years. It may be that in small bands of ancestral human hunter-gatherers, when a member lost her or his mate, the survival of the tribe was enhanced by the reduced food intake of the remaining member of the pair via depression or ultimately death, leaving more food for those who were successfully reproducing. The genes enhancing a depressive reaction to loss would be carried by the close kin of a depressed individual, and the enhanced survival of these kin would promote the increase of depressogenic genes in the population. A similar mechanism has been postulated for increasing the frequency of genes for "altruistic" behavior. See Nesse RM. Is depression an adaptation? *Archives of General Psychiatry.* 2000; 57:14–20; Cyranowski JM, Frank E, Young E, Shear KM. Adolescent onset of the gender difference in lifetime rates of major depression: A theoretical model. *Archives of General Psychiatry.* 2000; 57:21–28.

Page 20 "Clinical studies on . . ." Agency for Health Care Policy and Research. *Treatment of depression—Newer pharmacotherapies.* (Evidence Report/Technology Assessment, number 7, pub. no. 99-E014). Rockville, MD: Agency for Health Care Policy and Research; 1999; American Psychiatric Association. Practice guidelines for major depressive disorder in adults. *American Journal of Psychiatry.* 1993; 150:1–26.

Page 22: "For example, there . . ." Robinson RG, Downhill JE. Lateralization of psychopathology in response to focal brain injury. In: Davidson RJ, Hugdahy K, eds. *Brain Asymmetry.* Cambridge: MIT Press; 1995:693–711.

Page 22: "Similarly, diseases such . . ." Yamamoto M. Depression in Parkinson's disease: Its prevalence, diagnosis, and neurochemical background. *Journal of Neurology.* 2001; 248:III5–III11.

Page 22: "With adolescents, there . . ." Cohen P, Pine DS, Must A, Kasen S, Brook J. Prospective associations between somatic illness and mental illness from childhood to adulthood. *American Journal of Epidemiology.* 1998; 147:232–239.

Page 22: "If it's possible . . ." Larson RW. The solitary side of life: An examination of the time people spend alone from childhood to old age. *Developmental Review.* 1990; 10:155–183; Larson RW. The emergence of solitude as a constructive domain of experience in early adolescence. *Child Development.* 1997; 68:80–93; Larson RW, Richards MH, Moneta G, Holmbeck G, Duckett E. Changes in adolescents' daily interactions with their families from ages 10 to 18: Disengagement and transformation. *Developmental Psychology.* 1996; 32:744–754.

Page 23: "Teenagers distance themselves . . ." Larson RW. The solitary side of life: An examination of the time people spend alone from childhood to old age. *Developmental Review.* 1990; 10:155–183; Larson RW. The emergence of solitude as a constructive domain of experience in early adolescence. *Child Development.* 1997; 68:80–93.

Page 23: "Dr. Larson concluded . . ." Larson RW. The emergence of solitude as a constructive domain of experience in early adolescence. *Child Development.* 1997; 68:80–93.

Page 24: "On the following page are some . . ." Angold A, Costello EJ, Messer SC, Pickles A, Winder F, Silver D. The development of a short questionnaire for use in epidemiological studies of depression in children and adolescents. *International Journal of Methods in Psychiatric Research.* 1995; 5:237–249; Messer SC, Angold A, Costello EJ, Loeber R, Van Kammen W, Stouthamer-Loeber M. Development of a short questionnaire for use in epidemiological studies of depression in children and adolescents: Factor composition and structure across development. *International Journal of Methods in Psychiatric Research.* 1995; 5:251–262.

CHAPTER 2. THE TEENAGE BRAIN

Page 34: "Studies suggest that . . ." Steffens DC, Skoog I, Norton MC, Hart AD, Tschanz JT, Plassman BL, Wyse BW, Welsh-Bohmer KA, Breitner JCS. Prevalence of depression and its treatment in an elderly population. *Archives of General Psychiatry.* 2000; 57:601–607.

Page 34: ". . . studies showing that . . ." Kovacs M, Beck AT. An empirical-clinical approach toward a definition of childhood depression. In: Schulterbrandt JG, Askin A, eds. *Depression in Childhood.* New York: Raven Press; 1977:1–27; Puig-Antich J. Psychobiological markers: Effects of age and puberty. In: Rutter M, Izard CE, Read PB, eds. *Depression in Young People.* New York: Guilford Press; 1986:341–396.

Page 35: "One researcher, Jay . . ." Giedd J. Personal communication; August 20, 2001.

Page 36: "In fact, Dr. Adrian . . ." Angold A. Personal communication; March 4, 2002.

Page 36: "Also intriguing are . . ." Greenhill LL, Waslick B, Chuang S, Shaffer D, Mann J. Neurobiology of suicide attempts in adolescence. Presentation at the American Academy of Child and Adolescent Psychiatry 48th Annual Meeting, Honolulu, Hawaii, October 24, 2001.

Page 37: ". . . although we know . . ." Ormsbee HS, Fondacaro JD. Action of serotonin on the gastrointestinal tract. *Proceedings of the Society for Experimental Biology and Medicine.* 1985; 178:333–338.

Page 37: "An important clue . . ." Hankin BL, Abramson LY. Development of gender differences in depression: An elaborated cognitive vulnerability-transactional stress theory. *Psychological Bulletin.* 2001; 127:773–796.

Page 39: "Studies of animals . . ." Meaney MJ. Maternal care, gene expression, and the transmission of individual differences in stress reactivity across generations. *Annual Review of Neuroscience.* 2001; 24:1161–1192.

Page 39: ". . . humans, stressful events . . ." Lewinsohn PM, Allen NB, Seeley JR, Gotlib IH. First onset versus recurrence of depression: Differential processes of psychosocial risk. *Journal of Aboral Psychology.* 1999; 108:483–489; Olsson G. Adolescent depression. Epidemiology, nosology, life stress and social network. *Upsala Journal of Medical Sciences.* 1998; 103:77–145.

Page 41: "Years later, I . . ." Mussen PH, Jones MC. Self-conceptions, motivations, and interpersonal attitudes of late and early maturing boys. *Child Development.* 1957; 28:243–256.

CHAPTER 3. MORE THAN DEPRESSION

Page 51: "Gather a roomful . . ." Klein RG, Mannuzza S, Koplewicz HS, Tancer NK, Shah M, Liang V, Davies M. Adolescent depression: Controlled desipramine treatment and atypical features. *Depression and Anxiety.* 1998; 7:15–31.

Page 51: "Significantly, of those . . ." Ibid.

Page 51: ". . . Rachel Klein, found . . ." Klein RG. Adult consequences of childhood separation anxiety disorder. In: Macher JP, Crocq MA, eds. *New Prospects in Psychiatry/The Bio-Clinical Interface I.* Amsterdam: Elsevier; 1992:233–244.

Page 52: "Kids who are . . ." Jacobson RH, Lahey BB, Strauss CC. Correlates of depressed mood in normal children. *Journal of Abnormal Child Psychology.* 1983; 11:29–39.

Page 55: "In the other anxiety . . ." Angold A, Costello EG. Depressive comorbidity in children and adolescents: Empirical, theoretical, and methodological issues. *American Journal of Psychiatry.* 1993; 150:1779–1791.

Page 56: "Another condition that . . ." Angold A, Costello EG. Depressive comorbidity in children and adolescents: Empirical, theoretical, and methodological issues. *American Journal of Psychiatry.* 1993; 150:1779–1791.

Page 56: "Posttraumatic stress disorder . . ." Amaya-Jackson L, March JS. Posttraumatic stress disorder in adolescents—Risk factors, diagnosis and intervention. In: Christoffel K, Runyan C, eds. *Adolescent Medicine: State of the Art Reviews.* Vol. 6: *Violence and Injury Prevention.* Philadelphia: Hanley & Belfus, Inc. 1995; 6:251–270.

Page 57: "Two such disorders . . ." Disney ER, Elkins IJ, McGue M, Iacono WG. Effects of ADHD, conduct disorder, and gender on substance use and abuse in adolescence. *American Journal of Psychiatry.*1999; 156:1515–1521.

Page 57: ". . . socially phobic young . . ." Kessler RC, McGonagle KA, Zhao S, Nelson CB, Hughes M, Eshleman S, Wittchen HU, Kendler KS. Lifetime and 12-month prevalence of DSM-III-R psychiatric disorders in the United States. Results from the National Comorbidity Survey. *Archives of General Psychiatry.* 1994; 51:8–19.

CHAPTER 4. THE ODDS

Page 80: "Gender is perhaps . . ." Weissman MM, Klerman GL. Sex differences in the epidemiology of depression. *Archives of General Psychiatry.* 1977; 34:98–111.

Page 80: "This disparity holds . . ." Nolen-Hoeksema S. *Sex Differences in Depression.* Stanford: Stanford University Press; 1990.

Page 80: "This inclination to . . ." Radloff LS. Sex differences in depression: The effects of occupation and marital status. *Sex Roles.* 1975; 1:249–267.

Page 80: "The latest studies . . ." Angold A, Worthman CW. Puberty onset of gender differences in rates of depression: A developmental, epidemiologic and neuroendocrine perspective. *Journal of Affective Disorders.* 1993; 29:145–158.

Page 81: "One study asked . . ." Nolen-Hoeksema S, Larson J. The worries of adolescent males and females. Unpublished manuscript, Stanford University, Stanford, CA. 1992.

Page 81: "According to psychologists . . ." Nolen-Hoeksema S, Girgus J. The emergence of gender differences in depression during adolescence. *Psychological Bulletin.* 1994; 115:424–443.

Page 82: "Statistically, children of . . ." Birmaher B, Ryan ND, Williamson DE, Brent DA, Kaufman J. Childhood and adolescent depression: A review of the past 10 years. Part II. *Journal of the American Academy of Child and Adolescent Psychiatry.* 1996; 35:1575–1583; Birmaher B, Ryan ND, Williamson DE, Brent DA, Kaufman J, Dahl RE, Perel J, Nelson B. Childhood and adolescent depression: A review of the past 10 years. Part I. *Journal of the American Academy of Child and Adolescent Psychiatry.* 1996; 35:1427–1439.

Page 82: "Meanwhile, it's been . . ." Hammen C, Burge D, Burney E, Adrian C. Longitudinal study of diagnoses in children of women with unipolar and bipolar affective disorder. *Archives of General Psychiatry.* 1990; 47:1112–1117.

Page 83: "In studies of . . ." Beardslee W, Bemporad J, Keller MB, Klerman GL. Children of parents with a major affective disorder: A review. *American Journal of Psychiatry.* 1983; 140:825–832.

Page 83: ". . . Columbia University epidemiologist . . ." Weissman MM, Warner V, Wickramaratne P, Moreau D, Olfson M. Offspring of depressed parents: 10 years later. *Archives of General Psychiatry.* 1997; 54:932–940.

Page 83: "In another study . . ." Weissman MM, Warner V, Wickramaratne P, Prusoff BA. Early-onset major depression in parents and their children. *Journal of Affective Disorders.* 1988; 15:269–277.

Page 84: "A particularly interesting . . ." Angold A, Worthman CM, Costello EJ. Puberty and depression. In Hayward C, ed. *Gender Differences at Puberty.* Cambridge, England: Cambridge University Press; in press.

Page 84: ". . . an analysis of . . ." Klerman GL, Lavori PW, Rice J, Reich T, Endicott J, Andreasen NC, Keller MB, Hirschfield RM. Birth-cohort trends in rates of major depressive disorder among relatives of patients with affective disorder. *Archives of General Psychiatry* 1985; 42:689–693.

CHAPTER 5. THE ARC OF DEPRESSION

Page 95: "A childhood anxiety . . ." Warner V, Weissman MM, Mufson L, Wickramaratne PJ. Grandparents, parents, and grandchildren at high risk for depression: A three-generation study. *Journal of the American Academy of Child and Adolescent Psychiatry.* 1999; 38:289–296.

Page 114: "In one study . . ." Harrington L, Fudge H, Rutter M., Pickles A, Hill J. Adult outcomes of childhood and adolescent depression. *Archives of General Psychiatry.* 1990; 47:465–473.

CHAPTER 6. THE STRESS TRIGGER

Page 116: ". . . one quarter of . . ." Brown EJ, Heimberg RG. Effects of writing about rape: Evaluating Pennebaker's paradigm with a severe trauma. *Journal of Traumatic Stress.* 2001; 14:781–790.

Page 116: "A recent study . . ." Kendler KS, Thornton LM, Gardner CO. Genetic risk, number of previous depressive episodes, and stressful life events in predicting onset of major depression. *American Journal of Psychiatry.* 2001; 158:582–586.

Page 117: "In studies . . ." Heim C, Owens MJ, Plotsky PM, Nemeroff CB. Persistent changes in corticotropin-releasing factor systems due to early life stress: Relationship to the pathophysiology of major depression and post-traumatic stress disorder. *Psychopharmacological Bulletin.* 1997; 33:185–192.

Page 117: "In addition, magnetic . . ." Bremner JD, Narayan M, Anderson ER, Staib LH, Miller HL, Charney DS. Hippocampal volume reduction in major depression. *American Journal of Psychiatry.* 2000; 157:115–118.

Page 118: "At the National . . ." Chrousos GP, Gold PW. The concept of stress and stress system disorders. Overview of physical and behavioral homeostatis. *Journal of the American Medical Association.* 1992; 267:1244–1252; Meyer SE, Chrousos GP, Gold PW. Major depression and the stress system: A life span perspective. *Developmental Psychopathology.* 2001; 13:565–580.

Page 118: "We know that . . ." Thase ME, Sullivan LR. Relapse and recurrence of depression: A practical approach for prevention. *CNS Drugs.* 1995; 4:261–277.

Page 127: "A study cited . . ." U.S. Department of Health and Human Services. *Report of the Secretary's Task Force on Youth Suicide.* Vol. 3: *Prevention and Interventions in Youth Suicide.* DHHS Publication ADM 89–1622. Washington, DC: U.S. Government Printing Office; 1989.

Page 128: "In 1998, Garofalo . . ." Garofalo R, Wolf RC, Kessel S, Palfrey J, DuRant RH. The association between health risk behaviors and sexual orientation among a school-based sample of adolescents. *Pediatrics.* 1998; 101:895–902.

Page 128: ". . . it does appear . . ." McDaniel JS, Purcell D, D'Augelli AR. The relationship between sexual orientation and risk for suicide: Research findings and future directions for research and prevention. *Suicide and Life-Threatening Behavior.* 2001; 31:84–105.

Page 128: "One study found . . ." Zucker KJ, Green R. Psychological and familial aspects of gender identity disorder. *Child and Adolescent Psychiatric Clinics of North America.* 1993; 2:513–542.

CHAPTER 7. CRISIS POINTS

Page 136: "It's been said . . ." Some professionals believe that mood in general, and the visceral signals ("gut feelings") that we perceive, are designed to provide us with warning lights. In this view, one of the primary challenges of parenting adolescents is figuring out how/when to take the warnings seriously and when it's best to ignore them.

Page 138: ". . . National Youth Risk . . ." Centers for Disease Control and Prevention. Youth risk behavior surveillance—United States, 1999. *CDC Surveillance Summaries,* June 9, 2000. 49(SS05);1–96. 2000.

Page 142: ". . . Oregon Research Institute . . ." Lewinsohn PM, Roberts RE, Seeley JR, Rohde P, Gotlib IH, Hops H. Adolescent psychopathology: II. Psychosocial risk factors for depression. *Journal of Abnormal Psychology.* 1994; 103:302–315.

Page 145: "... Peter M. Lewinsohn ..." Lewinsohn PM, Rohde P, Seeley JR, Klein DN, Gotlib IH. Natural course of adolescent major depressive disorder in a community sample: Predictors of recurrence in young adults. *American Journal of Psychiatry.* 2000; 157:1584–1591.

Page 145–146: "Other studies indicate ..." RAND Corporation. Mental health care for youth: Who gets it? How much does it cost? Who pays? Where does the money go? *RAND/RB-4541.* Santa Monica, CA: RAND; 2001. Copyright RAND 2001.

Page 149: "A recent study ..." Spencer JM, Zimet GD, Aalsma MC, Orr DP. Self-esteem as a predictor of initiation of coitus in early adolescents. *Pediatrics.* 2002; 109:581–584.

CHAPTER 9. YOUNG AND BIPOLAR

Page 180: "A staggering 80 percent ..." Birmaher B. Suicidality of youth with bipolar disorder. *Research Update on Youth Suicidal Behavior: Good News the Clinician Can Use. Presentations in Focus.* 2001:7–9.

Page 180: "... and 15 percent ..." Simpson SG, Jamison KR. The risk of suicide in patients with bipolar disorders. *Journal of Clinical Psychiatry.* 1999; 60 (suppl 2):53–56.

Page 180: "Among adolescents, clinical ..." Birmaher B. New approaches to identifying and limiting pervasive and devastating suicidal behaviors in adolescents. *Research Update on Youth Suicidal Behavior: Good News the Clinician Can Use. Presentations in Focus.* 2001:2–3.

Page 180: "Meanwhile, nearly one ..." Birmaher B. Suicidality of youth with bipolar disorder. *Research Update on Youth Suicidal Behavior: Good News the Clinician Can Use. Presentations in Focus.* 2001:7–9.

Page 180: "In two studies ..." Mannuzza S, Klein RG, Bessler A, Malloy P, LaPadula M. Adult outcome of hyperactive boys: Educational achievement, occupational rank, and psychiatric status. *Archives of General Psychiatry.* 1993; 50:565–576; Mannuzza S, Klein RG, Bessler A, Malloy P, LaPadula M. Adult psychiatric status of hyperactive boys grown up. *American Journal of Psychiatry.* 1998; 155:493–498; Weiss G, Hechtman LT. Hyperactive Children Grown Up: ADHD in Children, Adolescents, and Adults. 2nd ed. New York: Guilford Press; 1993.

Page 181: "And because 'unipolar' ..." Major depression is subtyped as "unipolar" when episodes of depression alternate with periods of normal mood; depression is characterized as "bipolar" when the depressive episodes also alternate with episodes of full-blown mania, or a milder variant (termed "hypomania").

Page 183: "Studies of identical ..." Berrettini, WH. Linkage studies of bipolar syndromes. In: Young LT, Joffe RT, eds. *Bipolar Disorder: Biological Models and Their Clinical Application.* New York: Dekker; 1997:219–234.

Page 183: "Other studies have ..." Mendlewicz J, Rainer JD. Adoption study supporting genetic transmission in manic-depressive illness. *Nature.* 1977; 368:327–329.

Page 183–184: "The vast majority ..." Birmaher, B. Suicidality of youth with bipolar disorder. *Research Update on Youth Suicidal Behavior: Good News the Clinician Can Use. Presentations in Focus.* 2001:7–9.

Page 184: "Studies of 'psychological ..." Isometsa ET, Henriksson MM, Aro HM, Lonnqvist JK. Suicide in bipolar disorder in Finland. *American Journal of Psychiatry.* 1994; 151:1020–1024.

Page 184: "... the warning signs ..." These warning signs include abrupt or insidious changes in mood; immersion in substance abuse as a partial attempt to self-medicate; expression of profound hopelessness that seems to come from nowhere and that tends to be dismissed as being overly dramatic; dramatic changes in physiologic functions—appetite, particularly loss of weight from high levels of activity; becoming uncharacteristically engaged in activities of projects, to the detriment of usual relationships or physiologic needs such as sleep.

Page 186: "nervous breakdown": "Nervous breakdown" is a lay term and does not refer to any specific psychiatric symptom or disorder. As used by the general public, the term could refer to any of several conditions, such as severe depressive episodes, onset of bipolar disorder, psychotic disorders, or even panic with agoraphobia.

Page 209: "One study that ..." Birmaher B. Suicidality of youth with bipolar disorder. In: Birmaher B, ed. *Research Update on Youth Suicidal Behavior: Good News the Clinician Can Use. Presentations in Focus.* 2001:7–9.

CHAPTER IO. THE BIG BUMP: COLLEGE

Page 217: "At Harvard University's . . ." Kadizon R. Personal communication; September 10, 2001.

Page 217: ". . . National College Health . . ." American College Health Association. *National College Health Assessment: Reference Group Executive Summary Spring 2000.* Baltimore: American College Health Association; 2001.

Page 222: ". . . Martin E. P. Seligman . . ." Seligman MEP. Personal communication; February 13, 2002.

Page 222: "Attributional Style Questionnaire . . ." Peterson C, Semmel A, von Baeyer C, Abramson LT, Metalsky GI, Seligman MEP. The Attributional Style Questionnaire. *Cognitive Therapy and Research.* 1982; 6:287–300.

Page 223: ". . . *New York Times* . . ." Gutmann S. The abyss yawns. *New York Times,* January 13, 2002:32.

Page 225: ". . . *New York Times* . . ." Berger L. The therapy generation. *New York Times,* January 13, 2002:30–42.

CHAPTER II. THE NIGHTMARE: SUICIDE

Page 240: For statistics on suicide contained in this chapter, see the following references. *Research Update on Youth Suicidal Behavior: Good News the Clinician Can Use. Presentations in Focus.* 2001; Brent DA, Perper JA, Goldstein CE, Kolko DJ, Allan MJ, Allman CJ, Zelenak JP. Risk factors for adolescent suicide: A comparison of suicide victims with suicidal inpatients. *Archives of General Psychiatry.* 1988; 45:581–588; Centers for Disease Control and Prevention. Suicide among children, adolescents, and young adults—United States, 1980–1992. *Morbidity and Mortality Weekly Report.* 1995; (44:289–291); Centers for Disease Control and Prevention. Youth risk behavior surveillance—United States, 1999. *CDC Surveillance Summaries,* June 9, 2000. 49(SS05);1–96. 2000; Centers for Disease Control and Prevention website; 2002. Available: http://www.cdc.gov; Garland AF, Zigler E. Adolescent suicide prevention: Current research and social policy implications. *American Psychologist.* 1993; 48:169–182; Shaffer D. The epidemiology of teen suicide: An examination of risk factors. *Journal of Clinical Psychiatry.* 1988; 49:36–41.

Page 241: "... young is 'contagious' ..." Gould MS. Suicide and the media. In: Hendin H, Mann JJ, eds. *The Clinical Science of Suicide Prevention.* New York: New York Academy of Sciences; 2001:200–224; Gould MS, Shaffer D. The impact of suicide in television movies. *New England Journal of Medicine.* 1986; 315:690–694; Phillips DP, Carstenson LL. Clustering of teenage suicides after television news stories about suicide. *New England Journal of Medicine.* 1986; 315:685–689.

Page 242: "... has been documented ..." This phenomenon predates television. The publication by Goethe of *The Sorrows of Young Werther* led to a rash of suicides in western Europe at the birth of the Romantic period.

Page 242: "... suicidal behavior runs ..." Garfinkel BD, Froese A, Hood J. Suicide attempts in children and adolescents. *American Journal of Psychiatry.* 1982; 139:1257–1261.

Page 242: "Tests on spinal ..." Coccaro EF. Central serotonin and impulsive aggression. *British Journal of Psychiatry.* 1989; 155:52–62; Mann JJ, Brent DA, Arango V. The neurobiology and genetics of suicide and attempted suicide: A focus on the serotonergic system. *Neuropsychopharmacology.* 2001; 24:467–477; Mann JJ, McBride PA, Brown RP, Linnoila M, Leon AC, DeMeo M, Mieczkowski T, Myers JE, Stanley M. Relationship between central and peripheral serotonin indexes in depressed and suicidal psychiatric inpatients. *Archives of General Psychiatry.* 1992; 49:442–446.

Page 242: "Females, who generally ..." Raleigh MJ, Brammer GL, McGuire MT, Pollack DB, Yuwiler A. Individual differences in basal cisternal cerebrospinal fluid 5-HIAA and HVA in monkeys. The effects of gender, age, physical characteristics, and matrilineal influences. *Neuropsychopharmacology.* 1992; 7:295–304.

Page 245: "... study in Finland ..." Kaltiala-Heino R. Bullying, depression, and suicidal ideation in Finnish adolescents: School survey. *British Medical Journal.* 1999; 319:348–513.

Page 246–247: "One promising method ..." Shaffer D, Wilcox H, Lucas C, Hicks R, Busner C, Parides M. The development of a screening instrument for teens at risk for suicide. Poster presented at the 1996 meeting of the American Academy of Child and Adolescent Psychiatry, Philadelphia, PA, October 25, 1996.

Page 248: "Still, psychological autopsies ..." Shaffer D, Gould, MS, Fisher P, Trautman P, Moreau D, Kleinman M, Flory M. Psychiatric diagnosis in child and adolescent suicide. *Archives of General Psychiatry.* 1996; 53:339–348.

Page 251: "'He was bouncing . . .'" Guy A, Seibert T. Hoops star's death stuns Columbine. *Denver Post,* May 5, 2000:B01.

Page 252: "There is intriguing . . ." Shaffer D. Suicide attempters and screening for risk. In: Birmaher B, ed. *Research Update on Youth Suicidal Behavior: Good News the Clinician Can Use. Presentations in Focus.* 2001:5–6.

Page 256: "Blake was diagnosed . . ." All psychiatric diagnoses are provisional, because we are still lacking a true understanding of what the fundamental dysfunctions are. Affective disorders are those in which the primary problem is one of mood, either depression, mania, or both. Psychotic disorders, which include schizophrenia, are typified by losing touch with reality, as manifested by symptoms such as hallucinations or fixed bizarre beliefs. Individuals suffering from severe depression or from full-blown mania often develop some psychotic symptoms. The term schizoaffective disorder applies to illnesses in which the psychotic symptoms coexist with mood symptoms but also occur in the absence of prominent mood symptoms.

Page 256–257: "Young people with . . ." We know there is a strong relationship between conduct problems and depression. Therefore, one can reasonably assert that having depression during childhood *predicts* a higher risk for various adverse outcomes, including suicidal behavior as well as school failure and trouble with the law. However, depression does not necessarily *cause* this. The association is likely to be mediated by all of the other "bad" things that go with adolescent depression (such as other conduct problems). Indeed, Fergusson et al. suggest this is the manner in which major depressive disorder relates to such outcomes. See Fergusson DM, Woodward LJ. Mental health, educational, and social role outcomes of adolescents with depression. *Archives of General Psychiatry.* 2002; 59:225–231; Jaffee SR, Moffitt TE, Caspi A, Fombonne E, Poulton R, Martin J. Differences in early childhood risk factors for juvenile-onset and adult-onset depression. *Archives of General Psychiatry.* 2002; 59:215–222; Kasen S, Cohen P, Skodol AE, Johnson JG, Smailes E, Brook JS. Childhood depression and adult personality disorder: Alternative pathways of continuity. *Archives of General Psychiatry.* 2001; 58:231–236.

Page 258: "In a sad and . . ." Painter S. A son's suicide, a mom's crusade. *Wichita Eagle,* June 18, 2000: 1A.

CHAPTER 12. THE TREATMENT QUESTION

Page 261: "Diagnosis should always . . ." Diagnoses allow clinicians to group or classify conditions that are similar along a range of dimensions, including causes, outcomes, associated features, and responses to treatment. In psychiatry, we still know very little about the fundamental causes of the disorders that we treat, but there are exciting developments that suggest some possible pathways. According to this theory, depression can result from disruptions of the hormonal system that is supposed to help us respond to stress.

Imagine what life would be like if we had no way to cope with stress. We would be fine as long as we had all the food, shelter, warmth, and company that we needed, but we would cease to function when any of these were unavailable to us. Even worse, we would be unable to respond to emergencies, whether by escaping from threatening or dangerous situations or by defending ourselves. Thus it is obvious that having a functioning stress response system is of great importance. Individuals who lose the ability to produce stress response hormones are said to have Addison's disease. This affliction affected President John F. Kennedy, who would have died if not for his daily treatment with the stress response hormone hydrocortisone. In most people, cortisone and related hormones are produced by the adrenal glands, in response to signals from the pituitary, which is in turn regulated by a small brain region called the hypothalamus. The molecule at the top of this chain is called corticotropin releasing hormone, so it's always abbreviated as CRH or CRF (for corticotropin releasing factor—the same thing). It turns out that CRH is an important molecule in other places besides the pituitary. In particular, there are large numbers of CRH "receptors" (molecules that act like the lock for which CRH is the key) in an almond-shaped part of the brain called the amygdala (Latin for "almond-shaped"). One of the many functions of the amygdala is to alert other brain regions about frightening or dangerous situations. According to the theory, when stress levels are temporarily higher than normal but then subside to normal (because the stress response—fight or flight—was effective), the CRH system in the amygdala remains stable. If this pattern is repeated, with resolution of the stress, the CRH system may even "desensitize" itself, so that there will be fewer CRH receptors in the amygdala. Thus, the same intensity of stress on the outside produces less of a tendency to be internally alarmed. However, when the stress levels remain elevated, many individuals are susceptible to a paradoxical phenomenon: instead of decreasing the number of CRH receptors in their amygdala (the astute reader will have realized that these findings apply mainly to laboratory rats, but in many respects humans and rats are surprisingly alike), a phenomenon termed "positive feedback" can occur. This means that the number of CRH receptors in the amygdala increases as a result of increased CRH stimulation, rather than decreasing. That produces an even larger internal response of alarm and fear, even when the external stress signals are not as severe as before. Engineers know that positive feedback systems are dangerous. If continued unabated, they eventually disrupt the system completely. Thus, on the outside, the depressed individual (human or rat) can appear paralyzed and numb, but on the inside, he or she (the humans) may be overwhelmed by a vicious cycle of worry, self-loathing, guilt, despair, and dread. Researchers at the National Institute of Mental Health and elsewhere have made the fascinating observation that *all effective antidepressants,* whether SSRI medications, older antidepressants (called tricyclics), or even electroconvulsive therapy, reverse the positive feedback effect on CRH receptors in the amygdala. All these treatments decrease the number of CRH receptors down into the normal range, and they all take two to three weeks to do that, since receptors that are newly created last about two to three weeks before they "wear out." As mentioned, these findings have been confirmed primarily in lab rats, but they are now being tested on nonhuman primates and on humans. New classes of potential antidepressants are being tested that were developed as a result of this theory, and we hope that they will improve our ability to treat these disorders even more in the coming decade.

It's also worth mentioning here that as our understanding of the brain and its functioning improves, we are able to understand how certain kinds of systematic "talking therapies" such as those described later in this chapter may work. Again, our hope is that as we learn even more, we will be able to predict who is the best candidate for which type of treatment without having to take the trial-and-error approach that is still the rule.

See: Caldji C, Tannenbaum B, Sharma S, Francis D, Plotsky PM, Meaney MJ. Maternal care during infancy regulates the development of neural systems mediating the expression of fearfulness in the rat. Proceedings of the National Academy of Sciences. 1998; 95: 5335–5340; Meyer SE, Chrousos GP, Gold PW. Major depression and the stress system: A life span perspective. *Development and Psychopathology.* 2001; 13: 565–580.

Page 261: "... 80 percent of adults ..." Sadock BJ, Sadock VA, eds. *Kaplan and Sadock's Comprehensive Textbook of Psychiatry.* 7th ed. New York: Lippincott Williams and Wilkins; 2000.

Page 263: "Several clinical trials ..." Brent DA, Holder D, Kolko D, Birmaher B, Baugher M, Roth C, Iyengar S, Johnson BA. A clinical psychotherapy trial for adolescent depression comparing cognitive, family, and supportive therapy. *Archives of General Psychiatry.* 1997; 54:877–885; Wood A, Harrington R, Moore A. Controlled trial of brief cognitive-behavioural intervention in adolescent patients and depressive disorders. *Journal of Child Psychology and Psychiatry.* 1996; 37:737–746.

Page 263: "IPT is not ..." Kaslow NJ, Thompson MP. Applying the criteria for empirically supported treatments to studies of psychosocial intervention for child and adolescent depression. *Journal of Clinical Child Psychology.* 1998; 27:146–155.

Page 266: "The first large ..." Emslie GJ, Rush J, Weinberg WA, Kowatch RA, Hughes CW, Carmody T, Rintelmann J. A double-blind, randomized, placebo-controlled trial of fluoxetine in children and adolescents with depression. *Archives of General Psychiatry.* 1997; 54:1031–1037.

Page 266: "... a significant improvement ..." Keller MB, Ryan ND, Strober M, Klein RG, Kutcher SP, Birmaher B, Hagino OR, Koplewicz H, Carlson GA, Clarke GN, Emslie GJ, Feinberg D, Geller B, Kusumakar V, Papatheodorou G, Sack WH, Sweeney M, Wagner KD, Weller EB, Winters NC, Oakes R, McCafferty JP. Efficacy of paroxetine in the treatment of adolescent major depression: A randomized, controlled trial. *Journal of the American Academy of Child and Adolescent Psychiatry.* 2001; 40:762–772; Kutcher S. Affective disorders in children and adolescents: A clinically relevant review. In: Walsh BT, ed. *Child Psychopharmacology.* Washington, DC: American Psychiatric Association Press; 1998:91–109.

Page 266: "... in clinical trials ..." Emslie GJ, Maynes TL. Mood disorders in children and adolescents: Psychopharmalogical treatment. *Biological Psychiatry.* 2001; 49:1082–1092.

Page 267: "between 1985 and ..." Olfson M, Marcus SC, Pincus HA, Zito JM, Thompson JW, Zarin DA. Antidepressant prescribing practices of outpatient psychiatrists. *Archives of General Psychiatry.* 1998; 55:310–316. Not only are psychiatrists prescribing more antidepressants to youth, but a recent study shows that the total number of children 18 and under taking antidepressants has tripled in the last decade and antidepressant use has quadrupled in 15- to 18-year-olds over this period. These rates are even more striking because they account for prescriptions written by psychiatrists as well as those from other sources, such as pediatricians. See Olfson MD, Marcus SC, Weissman MM, Jensen PS. National trends in the use of psychotropic medications by children. *Journal of the American Academy of Child and Adolescent Psychiatry.* 2002; 41:514–521.

Page 274: ". . . clinical researchers at . . ." Shelton RC, Keller MB, Gelenberg A, Dunner DL, Hirschfeld R, Thase ME, Russell J, Lydiard RB, Crits-Christoph P, Gallop R, Todd L, Hellerstein D, Goodnick P, Keitner G, Stahl SM, Halbreich U. Effectiveness of St John's wort in major depression: A randomized controlled trial. *Journal of the American Medical Association.* 2001; 285:1978–1986.

Page 275: ". . . studies of referral . . ." Williams JW, Rost K, Dietrich AJ, Ciotti MC, Zyzanski SJ, Cornell J. Primary care physicians' approach to depressive disorders: Effects of physician specialty and practice structure. *Archives of Family Medicine.* 1999; 8:58–67.

Page 283: "Dr. Peter Lewinsohn . . ." Lewinsohn PM, Sullivan JM, Grosscup SJ. Changing reinforcing events: An approach to the treatment of depression. *Psychotherapy: Theory, Research and Practice.* 1981; 17:322–334.

Page 292: ". . . research by Dr. Lewinsohn . . ." Brent DA, Holder D, Kolko D, Birmaher B, Baugher M, Roth C, Iyengar S, Johnson BA. A clinical psychotherapy trial for adolescent depression comparing cognitive, family, and supportive therapy. *Archives of General Psychiatry.* 1997; 54:877–885; Lewinsohn PM, Clarke G, Rohde P. Psychological approaches to the treatment of depression in adolescents. In: Reynolds WM, Johnston H, eds. *Handbook of Depression in Children and Adolescents.* New York: Plenum Press; 1994.

Page 298: "In a 1999 . . ." Fink M, Foley CA. Pediatric ECT: An update. *Psychiatric Times.* 1999; 16:63–65.

Page 300: "An extensive literature . . ." Tondo L, Jamison KR, Baldessarini RJ. Effect of lithium maintenance on suicidal behavior in major mood disorders. *Annals of the New York Academy of Sciences.* 1997; 836:339–351.

Page 300: "In adolescents with . . ." Geller B, Cooper TB, Sun K, Zimerman B, Frazier J, Williams M, Heath J. Double-blind and placebo-controlled study of lithium for adolescent bipolar disorders with secondary substance dependency.

Journal of the American Academy of Child and Adolescent Psychiatry. 1998; 37:171–178.

Page 302 "... Adrian Angold and ..." Angold A, Weissman MM, John K, Merikangas KR. Parent and child reports of depressive symptoms in children at low and high risk for depression. *Journal of Child Psychology and Psychiatry and Allied Disciplines.* 1987; 28:901–915.

GLOSSARY

affective dysregulation: the inability to effectively control the pattern of observable behaviors that are associated with subjective feelings (affect)

agitated depression: form of depression in which one experiences periods of restlessness and the inability to fall asleep or remain sleeping, as well as being physically agitated; this is often accompanied by anxiety

anticipatory anxiety: an anxious state that typically occurs before or in anticipation of an event

antidepressants: medications used to treat unipolar mood disorders (depression). They include three specific types: selective serotonin reuptake inhibitors (SSRIs), monoamineoxidase inhibitors (MAOIs), and tricyclic antidepressants.

antipsychotics: medications that reduce the intensity of or eliminate hallucinations and delusions

anxiety disorder (generalized anxiety disorder): persistent and excessive worry or apprehension, occurring for at least six months, that is difficult to control and impairs normal functioning

appetitive drive: a key aspect of the pleasure center in the brain that enables the experience of pleasure at the expectation or anticipation of future activities

attention deficit hyperactivity disorder (ADHD): a chronic behavioral disorder with three major symptoms: inattention, impulsivity, and hyperactivity

atypical depression: a type of depression, common among adolescents, that is characterized by lifts in mood in response to positive events or circumstances, an increase in appetite, increased sleep, a feeling of heaviness in the arms or legs, and extreme sensitivity to rejection

behavioral activation tasks: a therapeutic technique used to counteract the lethargy, anhedonia, and loss of interest in activities that often accompanies depression in which the therapist and client collaborate to plan activities that encourage the client to become more active and involved (e.g., a walk in the park, going to a movie with a friend)

behavioral experiments: therapeutic activities designed to test the negative predictions and beliefs common in depression, with the goal of gathering evidence to refute these predictions (e.g., a teen who believes that no one will talk to him at a party might be asked to attend the party and test whether or not this is true)

biological markers: indicators (e.g., hormone response to stress, specific gene clusters, specific brain differences) that enable us to pinpoint certain biological and physiological causes for depression and associated symptoms, giving us more reliability and confidence when making a diagnosis

bipolar disorder: a mood disorder characterized by varying episodes of mania or hypomania, and depression

bipolar I disorder: the presence of one or more manic episodes, often preceding or following a depressive episode

bipolar II disorder: the presence of one or more major depressive episodes and at least one hypomanic episode but no manic episodes

cardiotoxic: exerting a negative effect on the heart's functioning by poisoning the cardiac muscle or its conducting system

cognitive behavioral therapy (CBT): a research-based approach to therapy that is generally short-term and focused on addressing specific thoughts and behavior involved in maintaining an individual's problems

cognitive distortion: inaccurate perception of oneself and how others view one

comorbidity: the existence of more than one disorder at the same time

consummatory pleasure: aspect of the pleasure center in the brain that allows for the ability to experience pleasure when engaged in activities, such as sports, sex, social interactions, and so on

cyclothymic disorder: a chronic but less severe form of bipolar disorder that includes episodes of hypomania and several episodes of depression during a period of two years

deconditioning: reversing a previously established learned association

delusion: an obviously erroneous idea that is firmly believed, regardless of its absurdity or lack of basis in reality

delusions of grandeur: a strong unfounded belief that one possesses special worth, power, or knowledge or is somehow related to a deity

diversion program: a program designed to target problem youth and direct them away from the justice system and into a treatment center or program

double depression: the cooccurrence of dysthymic disorder and a major depressive episode

dysthymic disorder: literally means "ill-tempered"; a minor depression. This diagnosis is given when the patient suffers from a persistent depressed mood, lasting most of the day, most of the time, across the span of at least two years for adults or one year for children and adolescents; a child or adolescent with dysthymic disorder may display a mood that is irritable rather than depressed.

ego: a term initially used by Sigmund Freud to describe one of the central personality structures in his theory. Today the term is more commonly used in reference to a person's self or identity.

electroconvulsive therapy (ECT): the passing of an electrical current through one or more hemispheres of the brain for the purpose of treating illnesses such as severe depression

externalizing disorder: any disorder in which the primary dysfunction lies in outward-directed behavior that directly impacts on others, such as acting out, antisocial behavior, and turning against others; attention deficit hyperactivity disorder and conduct disorder are considered externalizing disorders

first-degree relative: a member of one's immediate biological family; that is, a parent, sibling, or child

flight of ideas: a pattern of continuous and rapid speech marked by abrupt changes in topic

hallucination: a false sensory experience in which one perceives a sight, sound, touch, taste, or smell that is not actually present

hypomania: an episode of increased energy that can last for hours to days but is not characterized by a loss of touch with reality and so is not severe enough to be categorized as manic

internalizing disorders: any disorder in which the primary dysfunction lies in symptoms that affect the child's internal state more than the external world; anxiety disorders and depression are considered internalizing disorders

interpersonal therapy (IPT): a contemporary approach to the treatment of mood disorders that focuses on helping the patient develop a better understanding of how the interaction of important relationships can affect one's mood and affect; this therapy strengthens the person's communication and problem-solving skills

longitudinal studies: research design in which the same subjects are studied over the course of a determined period of time

looseness of associations (LOA): the constant changing of topics in a conversation, with no apparent connection from one subject to the next; common in psychosis

major depressive disorder (MDD): a serious depression that lasts six months or longer. It has many similarities in both adolescents and adults: sadness, pessimism, sleep and appetite disturbances, and decreased concentration and sex drive; in adolescents, however, these symptoms can also be accompanied by anxiety and irritability.

melancholic depression: major depression accompanied by the inability to feel pleasure and the incapacity to feel better, even after positive experiences or events

mixed state: period in which both manic and depressive episodes are present almost every day, with rapidly alternating mood patterns

monoamineoxidase inhibitors (MAOIs): class of antidepressants that work by slowing the elimination of the brain's neurotransmitters

mood disorder: a group of mental illnesses that are characterized by disturbances in mood (the sustained emotional state that affects one's perception of the world)

mood stabilizers: class of medications (including lithium and various anticonvulsants) that are used to control the wide emotional and behavioral swings characteristic of mood disorders such as bipolar disorder

neurotransmitters: chemical agents released by a neuron to send a signal to the neighboring neuron; successive releases by each neighboring neuron allow for communication throughout the nervous system

panic disorder: the recurrence of unexpected, intense anxiety attacks, with physical symptoms such as palpitations, accelerated heart rate, sweating, trembling or shaking, dizziness, and shortness of breath

placebo: substance lacking in medicinal value that is used in research as a point of comparison for active treatments

posttraumatic stress disorder (PTSD): disorder occurring as a result of exposure to a traumatic stressor, characterized by the persistent reexperience of the traumatic event through the recollection of images, thoughts, and perceptions accompanied by intense feelings of distress, lasting for at least one month

poverty of speech: condition in which speech becomes less spontaneous or forthcoming; questions are answered briefly with little unprompted elaboration

psychological autopsy: a process by which an individual's psychological profile is developed following his or her death (often by interviewing family and friends and studying the individual's academic performance and personal writings)

psychopathology: abnormal and maladaptive behavior, cognition, or emotion.

psychosis: the inability to distinguish reality from nonreality and, in particular, the experience of hallucinations and delusions

rapid cycling: form of bipolar disorder in which one has frequent episodes of depression or mania or a shift from one extreme to the other with no interval of normalcy; episodes last at least one week; some have reported that they may be briefer in children, but this is controversial

regulation (emotion regulation): the monitoring and adjustment of thoughts or behaviors that influence the nature, timing, and expression of emotions

risk factor: a variable that indicates a higher likelihood that one will develop a disorder

role-playing: the use of acting in therapy to teach clients alternate ways of reacting to a given situation

selective serotonin reuptake inhibitors (SSRIs): group of medications that have been shown to be effective in the treatment of mood and anxiety disorders; their mechanism of action is believed to be increasing the amount of serotonin available in regions of the brain

separation anxiety disorder: disorder in which a child is preoccupied with threats to the integrity of his or her family and experiences extreme anxiety when separated from home or those to whom he or she is attached

serotonin: neurotransmitter believed to be central to such functions as sleep, sexual behavior, aggressiveness, motor activity, and mood; abnormalities in serotonin have been suggested to play a causal role in psychiatric disorders such as schizophrenia and mood disorders

social anxiety disorder: also known as social phobia; a disorder associated with an intense and persistent fear of social situations in which one is exposed to possible scrutiny

somatic symptoms: physical symptoms resulting from psychiatric illness, such as fatigue, aches and pains, and changes in appetite and sleep patterns

suicidal ideation: any thoughts of suicide or taking one's own life; these thoughts may or may not include a specific plan to commit suicide

synapse: the junction between two neurons (or between a neuron and a muscle or gland cell) through which neurotransmitters travel

temperament: a set of character traits an infant is born with; sometimes thought of as a child's inherent disposition and the foundation of his or her personality

tricyclic antidepressants: class of medications used to treat attention deficit hyperactivity disorder, tic disorders, anxiety, and depression; they are believed to work by increasing the amounts of various neurotransmitters available in the brain

MEDICATION CHART

The following chart provides detailed information on the medications mentioned in the text as well as others used in the treatment of adolescent depression. Parents should note that while all of these medications have been approved by the Food and Drug Administration (FDA), many have not been approved for children and adolescents or for the specific purposes listed here. Pharmaceutical companies must apply to the FDA individually to gain approval for each specific use and age range. In an effort to save time and money, many of these companies choose not to apply for all purposes and all ages. This does not necessarily mean that these uses are unsafe or ineffective, simply that they have not been reviewed by the federal government. However, many of these medications have been studied by independent investigators in placebo-controlled trials and have been found effective. Physicians should use their discretion in prescribing these medications outside of FDA-approved use and do so based on the established scientific data. Parents should ask their children's physicians about the FDA-approval of the medications they recommend and the rationale behind their recommendations.

SELECTIVE SEROTONIN REUPTAKE INHIBITORS (SSRIs)

BRAND NAME	GENERIC NAME	STARTING DOSE	DOSAGE RANGE	FDA–APPROVED AGE RANGE
Celexa	Citalopram	10 mg QD	5 to 40 mg daily	Adults
Luvox	Fluvoxamine	25 mg QD	50 to 300 mg daily	8 & older
Paxil	Paroxetine	10 mg QD	10 to 30 mg daily	Adults
Prozac	Fluoxetine	10 mg QD	5 to 40 mg daily	Adults
Zoloft	Sertraline	25 mg QD	25 to 200 mg daily	Adults (6 & older for obsessive compulsive disorder only)

FDA INDICATIONS: major depressive disorder (Celexa, Paxil, Prozac, Zoloft), obsessive compulsive disorder (Luvox, Paxil, Prozac, Zoloft), bulimia (Prozac), posttraumatic stress disorder (Zoloft), panic disorder (Paxil), social anxiety disorder (Paxil), generalized anxiety disorder (Paxil)

SIDE EFFECTS: anorexia, nausea, diarrhea, akathesia (inability to sit still), insomnia/sedation, sexual dysfunction, hypotension, weight gain, disinhibition

Tricyclic Antidepressants

BRAND NAME	GENERIC NAME	STARTING DOSE	DOSAGE RANGE	FDA–APPROVED AGE RANGE
Anafranil	Clomipramine	25 mg	10 to 300 mg daily	10 & older
Elavil	Amitriptyline	25 mg	10 to 300 mg daily	12 & older
Nopramin	Desipramine	10–25 mg	10 to 300 mg daily	Adolescents/Adults
Pamelor	Norpramin	10 mg	10 to 300 mg daily	Adults
Tofranil	Imipramine	10–25 mg	10 to 300 mg daily	Adolescents/Adults

FDA INDICATIONS: major depressive disorder (Elavil, Norpramin, Pamelor, Tofranil), enuresis (Tofranil), obsessive compulsive disorder (Anafranil)

SIDE EFFECTS: *anticholinergic:* dry mouth, orthostasis, constipation, blurred vision (precipitated narrow angle glaucoma), cardiac conduction abnormalities, cognitive impairment; *histaminic effects:* sedation, orthostasis, increased weight, cognitive impairment, impaired coordination; sexual dysfunction, diaphoresis (perspiration), tremors, anxiety

NOTE: Electrocardiogram (EKG) and blood pressure monitoring are required for patients taking these medications.

ATYPICAL ANTIDEPRESSANTS

BRAND NAME	GENERIC NAME	STARTING DOSE	DOSAGE RANGE	FDA–APPROVED AGE RANGE
Effexor*	Venlafaxine	37.5 mg Q3–4 days BID dosage	25 to 150 mg daily	Adults
Effexor XR*	Venlafaxine XR	37.5 mg Q3–4 days BID dosage	75 to 225 mg daily	Adults
Serzone**	Nefazodone	50 mg BID	50 to 400 mg daily	Adults
Remeron	Mirtazapine	7.5 mg HS (½ tab)	7.5 to 15 mg nightly	Adults
Wellbutrin	Bupropion	37.5 mg (½ tab) QD	37.5 to 300 mg daily	Adults
Wellbutrin SR	Bupropion SR	50 mg (½ tab) QD–BID	200 to 400 mg daily	Adults

FDA INDICATIONS: major depressive disorder, generalized anxiety disorder (Effexor, Effexor XR), nicotine withdrawal (Zyban— an alternative brand name for Wellbutrin SR)

SIDE EFFECTS: *Effexor only:* similar to SSRIs, plus hypertension. *Serzone only:* similar to SSRIs, plus sedation. *Remeron only:* anticholinergic side effects: increased lipids, sedation, weight gain. *Wellbutrin only:* nausea, anxiety, headache, decreased appetite, increased risk of seizures

NOTES:
*Blood pressure should be monitored while taking this medication.
**Liber function (LFTs) should be monitored while taking this medication.

Monoamineoxidase Inhibitors (MAOIs)

BRAND NAME	GENERIC NAME	STARTING DOSE	DOSAGE RANGE	FDA–APPROVED AGE RANGE
Nardil	Phenelzine	15 mg QD	10 to 50 mg daily	Adults
Parnate	Tranylcypromine	10 mg QD	10 to 50 mg daily	Adults

FDA INDICATIONS: major depressive disorder

SIDE EFFECTS: hypertensive crisis, hypotension, sedation, peripheral edema

NOTES: Patients taking MAOIs require a tyramine-free diet. While taking MAOIs, patients must check with their prescribing psychiatrists before beginning any new over-the-counter or prescription medications.

MOOD STABILIZERS

BRAND NAME	GENERIC NAME	STARTING DOSE	DOSAGE RANGE	FDA–APPROVED AGE RANGE
Depakote*	Divalproex	250 BID-TD	max = serum level of 50–125 Ug/ml	2 & older
Depakene*	Valproic Acid	250 BID-TD	max = serum level of 50–125 Ug/ml	2 & older
Eskalith**	Lithium	300 mg BID	max = monitor blood levels, maximum level 1.4 mEq/L	12 & older
Lamictal	Lamotrigine	25 mg QD every day with concomitant divalproex	200 to 800 mg daily	2 & older
Lithobid**	Lithium	300 mg BID	max = monitor blood levels, maximum level 1.4 mEq/L	12 & older

Neurontin	Gabapentin	100 mg BID-TID	300 to 1200 mg daily	3 & older
Topamax	Topiramate	25 mg (½ tab) QD	50 to 400 mg daily	2 & older
Tegretol***	Carbamazepine	100 mg BID-TID	200 to 1,000 mg daily	6 & older

FDA INDICATIONS: bipolar disorder (Depakote, Depakene, Eskalith, Lithobid), affective disorder (Depakote, Depakene) [no psychiatrics conditions for Lamictal, Neurontin, Tegretol, Topamax]

SIDE EFFECTS: *Eskalith and Lithobid only:* GI upset, weight gain, resting tremor, polydipsia, polyuria, cognitive impairment, rashes, acne, headache, reversible hypothyroidism. *Tegretol only:* drowsiness, dizziness, ataxia, nausea, blurred vision, fatigue, GI upset, transient leukopenia. *Neurontin only:* somnolence, dizziness, ataxia, tremor, weight gain, depression. *Lamictal only:* fatigue, headache, dizziness, nausea, rash, cognitive impairment, *rare:* Steven-Johnson syndrome, aplastic anemia. *Topamax only:* fatigue, cognitive impairment, tremor, weight loss, *rare:* nephrolithiasis. *Depakote only:* GI distress, headache, tremor, anorexia, hair loss, increased LFTs, thrombocytopenia, *rare:* aplastic anemia, hepatotoxicity—increased under 2 years old

NOTES:

*Liver function (LFTs) should be monitored while taking this medication.

**Liver function (LFTs), kidney function, complete blood count (CBCs), and thyroid function tests (T4 and TSH) should be monitored while taking this medication.

***Liver function (LFTs) and complete blood count (CBCs) should be monitored while taking this medication.

Augmenters

Psychostimulants

BRAND NAME	GENERIC NAME	STARTING DOSE	DOSAGE RANGE	FDA–APPROVED AGE RANGE
Dexedrine	Dextroamphetamine	2.5–5 mg QD-BID	5 to 60 mg daily	3 & older
Ritalin	Methylphenidate	5 mg BID-TID	5 to 90 mg daily	6 & older

FDA INDICATIONS: ADHD, narcolepsy

SIDE EFFECTS: decreased appetite, GI upset, headache, rebound anxiety, increase of tics, growth deceleration (controversial)

T3s

BRAND NAME	GENERIC NAME	STARTING DOSE	DOSAGE RANGE	FDA–APPROVED AGE RANGE
Cytomel	Liothyronine	25 mcg	25 to 50 mcg daily	Adults

FDA INDICATIONS: thyroid disease

SIDE EFFECTS: palpitations, tremor, insomnia

T4s

BRAND NAME	GENERIC NAME	STARTING DOSE	DOSAGE RANGE	FDA–APPROVED AGE RANGE
Synthroid	Levothyroxine	12.5 to 25 mcg	25 to 100 mcg daily	All ages

FDA INDICATIONS: thyroid disease

SIDE EFFECTS: palpitations, tremor, insomnia

ANTIPSYCHOTICS

BRAND NAME	GENERIC NAME	STARTING DOSE	DOSAGE RANGE	FDA–APPROVED AGE RANGE
Trilafon	Perphenazine	4 mg QD	5 to 60 mg daily	12 & older
Haldol	Haloperidol	0.5–1 mg QD-BID	0.5 to 20 mg daily	3 & older

FDA INDICATIONS: psychosis, schizophrenia (Haldol), Tourette's syndrome (Haldol), ADHD (Haldol), nausea and vomiting (Trilafon)

SIDE EFFECTS: orthostasis, hypotension, dizziness, hyperprolactinemia, sexual dysfunction, weight gain, cardiac conduction changes, increased liver enzymes (primarily a concern for Thorazine, Mellaril, and similar "low potency" antipsychotics), leukopenia, temperature dysregulation, decreased seizure threshold, dysphoria, extrapyramidal symptoms, cognitive impairment, tardive dyskinesia, and very rarely, neuroleptic malignant syndrome. *Trilafon only*: sensitivity to sun

ATYPICAL ANTIPSYCHOTICS

BRAND NAME	GENERIC NAME	STARTING DOSE	DOSAGE RANGE	FDA–APPROVED AGE RANGE
Geodon	Ziprasidone	20 mg QD	80 to 160 mg daily	Adults
Risperdal	Risperidone	0.25–0.5 mg QD-BID	0.5 to 20 mg daily	Adults
Seroquel	Quetiapine	25 mg QD-BID	25 to 400 mg daily	Adults
Zyprexa	Olanzapine	2.5–5 mg QD	5 to 60 mg daily	Adults

FDA INDICATIONS: psychosis of schizophrenia, schizoaffective disorder and associated with bipolar disorder (Risperdal), psychotic disorders (Geodon, Seroquel, Zyprexa), short-term management of bipolar disorder (Zyprexa)

SIDE EFFECTS: extrapyramidal symptoms, tardive dyskinesia, weight gain, somnolence, anticholinergic side effects

BENZODIAZEPINES

BRAND NAME	GENERIC NAME	STARTING DOSE	DOSAGE RANGE	FDA–APPROVED AGE RANGE
Ativan	Lorazepam	0.25 mg BID	0.5 to 6 mg daily	12 & older
Klonopin	Clonazepam	0.25 mg BID	0.5 to 6 mg daily	Adults (for panic; approved for children and adults for seizure)
Valium	Diazepam	2.5 to 5 mg BID	3.75 to 30 mg daily	2 & older
Xanax	Alprazolam	0.25 mg BID	0.5 to 6 mg daily	Adults

FDA INDICATIONS: anxiety

SIDE EFFECTS: sedation, habit-forming (especially Ativan, Xanax), disinhibition, greatly exaggerate the effects of alcohol

RELATED READINGS

A Beautiful Mind: The Life of Mathematical Genius and Nobel Laureate John Nash
Sylvia Nasar
Touchstone Books, 2001
The basis for the Academy Award–winning film; details John Nash's life-long struggle with schizophrenia.

A Brilliant Madness: Living with Manic-Depressive Illness
Patty Duke, Mary Lou Pinckert, and Gloria Hochman
Bantam Books, 1993
The story of Patty Duke's personal fight with manic-depressive illness and her successful treatment; presents important information regarding this illness and its treatment.

Darkness Visible: A Memoir of Madness
William Styron
Vintage Books, 1992
William Styron's chronicle of the years he spent facing depression, his close brushes with suicide, and his eventual path to recovery.

Depression in the Young: What We Can Do to Help Them
Trudy Carlson
Benline Press, 1998
Using the author's personal account of the suicide of her 14-year-old son as context, presents practical information for parents and educators on the nature of child and adolescent depression and its treatment.

His Bright Light: The Story of Nick Traina
Danielle Steel
Delta, 2000
Danielle Steel's story of her son's struggle with bipolar disorder and his eventual suicide, at the age of 19.

Manic-Depressive Illness
Frederick K. Goodwin, M.D., and Kay Redfield Jamison, Ph.D.
Oxford University Press, 1990
Widely considered to be the seminal text on bipolar disorder; geared primarily toward professionals; provides an extensive review of the research in the field.

The Noonday Demon: An Atlas of Depression
Andrew Solomon
Touchstone Books, 2002
Offers an exploration of depression from several vantage points—the author's own experience with the illness as well as others' personal accounts; scientific research from the field; and philosophical discussion of the nature and treatment of mental illness.

Straight Talk about Psychiatric Medications for Kids
Timothy E. Wilens, M.D.
Guilford Press, 1998
Offers detailed and accessible information on medications used to treat depression, bipolar disorder, and other psychiatric disorders in children and adolescents.

Survival Strategies for Parenting Children with Bipolar Disorder
George T. Lynn, M.A., M.P.A., C.M.H.C.
Kingsley, 2000
Presents advice on recognizing symptoms, medication guidelines, strategies for getting support at school, and general parenting tips for those with children who suffer from bipolar disorder.

Understanding Teenage Depression: A Guide to Diagnosis, Treatment, and Management
Maureen Empfield, M.D., and Nicholas Bakalar
Owl Books, 2001
An informative study of the causes and treatment of adolescent depression; discusses the importance of understanding and addressing depression in adolescents.

An Unquiet Mind
Kay Redfield Jamison, Ph.D.
Random House, 1997
Autobiographical account of Dr. Kay Redfield Jamison, a psychologist and one of the world's leading authorities on bipolar disorder, and her own battle with the illness.

When Nothing Matters Anymore: A Survival Guide for Depressed Teens
Bev Cobain, R.N.C.
Free Spirit, 1998
A guide to help teenagers understand and cope with depression; discusses the different types of depression, how and why the condition begins, its links to substance abuse and suicide, and how to get help.

RESOURCES

The following is a list of web-based resources that can be helpful to adolescents with a mood disorder, as well as their parents and teachers. Although most of the information will be found online, you can contact the organizations directly for more specific information.*

American Academy of Child and Adolescent Psychiatry
www.aacap.org
3615 Wisconsin Avenue NW
Washington, DC 20016–3007
(800) 333–7636
(202) 966–7300

Provides information in Spanish. Information on this website is provided as a public service to aid in the understanding and treatment of the developmental, behavioral, and mental disorders. Information on child and adolescent mental disorders, fact sheets for parents and caregivers, current research, and managed care information are available.

---

*While the author has made every effort to provide accurate telephone numbers and Internet addresses at the time of publication, neither the publisher nor the author assumes any responsibility for errors or for changes that occur after publication.

Child and Adolescent Bipolar Foundation (CABF)
www.bpkids.org
1187 Wilmette Avenue
P.M.B. #331
Wilmette, IL 60091

A parent-led, not-for-profit, web-based organization of families raising children diagnosed with, or at risk for, early-onset bipolar disorder. This website provides information for parents of children diagnosed with bipolar disorder (e.g., current
research studies, information regarding social security disability, and an interactive
message board that allows viewers the opportunity to participate in discussions with
other parents, family members, and professionals).

Depression and Related Affective Disorders Association (DRADA)
www.drada.org
Meyer 3–181
600 North Wolfe Street
Baltimore, MD 21287–7381
Baltimore at (410) 955–4647
Washington, D.C. at (202) 955–5800

A community organization; serves individuals affected by a depressive illness and
their family members and health-care professionals, as well as the general public.
Works in cooperation with the Department of Psychiatry at the Johns Hopkins
School of Medicine to ensure that the educational programs and materials produced by the organization reflect accurate and current information.

Juvenile Bipolar Research Foundation
www.bpchildresearch.org
49 S. Quaker Road
Pawling, NY 12564

Raises and distributes funds for the most promising research into the causes, treatment, and prevention of early-onset bipolar disorder. The common goal of both the
scientific and clinical teams is to advance the state of knowledge about this illness so
that more effective treatments can be developed.

National Alliance for the Mentally Ill (NAMI)
www.nami.org
Colonial Place Three
2107 Wilson Blvd., Suite 300
Arlington, VA 22201–3042
NAMI HelpLine: (800) 950-NAMI (6264)
Main office: (703) 524–7600
Fax: (703) 524–9094

A nonprofit, grassroots, self-help support and advocacy organization of consumers, families, and friends of people with severe mental illnesses, such as schizophrenia, major depression, bipolar disorder, obsessive-compulsive disorder, and anxiety disorders. Referrals to local NAMI affiliate groups are available.

The National Depressive and Manic-Depressive Association
www.ndmda.org
730 N. Franklin Street, Suite 501
Chicago, Illinois 60610–7204
(800) 826–3632
(312) 642–0049
Fax (312) 642–7243

A patient-directed, illness-specific organization whose primary mission is to educate patients, families, professionals, and the public concerning the nature of depressive and manic-depressive illnesses as treatable medical diseases; to foster self-help for patients and families; to eliminate discrimination and stigma; to improve access to care; and to advocate research toward the elimination of these illnesses. This website provides support group information as well.

National Foundation for Depressive Illness, Inc.
www.depression.org
P.O. Box 2257
New York, NY 10116
(800) 239–1265

This foundation seeks to educate the public about depressive illness, its consequences, and its treatability; to provide information to physicians and other professionals; and to provide information and referrals to all who make requests. The foundation is committed to an extensive, ongoing public information campaign addressed to this pervasive, costly, and hidden national emergency.

National Institute of Mental Health (NIMH)
www.nimh.nih.gov
NIMH Public Inquiries
6001 Executive Boulevard, Rm. 8184, MSC 9663
Bethesda, MD 20892–9663
Voice (301) 443–4513
Fax (301) 443–4279

Provides information in Spanish. A government agency that conducts and supports research on mental illness and mental health. The information NIMH provides on its website is intended to help individuals better understand mental health and mental disorders.

National Mental Health Association (NMHA)
www.nmha.org
2001 N. Beauregard Street, 12th Floor
Alexandria, Virginia 22311
(800) 969-NMHA (6642)

The country's oldest nonprofit organization addressing all aspects of mental health and mental illness. With more than 340 affiliates nationwide, NMHA works to improve the mental health of all Americans, especially the 54 million individuals with mental disorders, through advocacy, education, research, and service.

New York University Child Study Center
www.AboutOurKids.org
577 First Avenue
New York, N Y 10016
(212) 263–6622

Provides information in Spanish. Provides scientifically based child mental health and parenting information through a continually expanding store of practical and accessible articles based on the latest research in child and adolescent psychiatry, psychology, and development. It is a reliable resource for information about common challenges, such as transitioning to college, and more serious issues, such as substance abuse and mood disorders.

ACKNOWLEDGMENTS

First and foremost, I would like to thank my family for their patience, tolerance, and support while I was writing *More Than Moody*. Like most things worth doing in life, this project took more time and effort than I originally expected. I appreciate that they didn't tell me that *they told me so*. Every day I feel blessed and lucky that I am the father of Joshua, Adam, and Sam. That in many ways is my good fortune. Though I'm sure luck had something to do with it, I can take some credit for choosing Linda, my wife. She is a constant beacon, helping me stay on the path and tireless in her efforts to make sure I balance work and family.

This book would not have happened without my collaboration with Rick Firstman. He is a master wordsmith, a steadfast reporter, and a patient partner.

Every day I come to work at the NYU Child Study Center and I am surrounded by gifted clinicians, brilliant researchers, and a talented staff, all dedicated to helping children and teenagers with mental disorders. These dedicated professionals were incredibly generous with their time and knowledge in giving suggestions, advice, and critiques of the manuscript at every phase. Fortunately for me, Danny Pine, M.D., one of America's most brilliant child psychiatrists, is a NIMH scientist who conducts some of his most important work through the Child Study Center. His wealth of knowledge and insight, and his remarkable ability to instantly cite the perfect pieces of literature for the topic at hand, made it easy for me to make sure that the book was current and accurate. Xavier Castellanos, M.D., the Neidich Family Professor of Child and Adolescent Psychiatry, and director of our Institute for Pediatric Neuroscience, went over this book line by line and developed the footnotes that appear with the references. His clinical skill and research knowledge are awe-inspiring. And he turns out to be a terrific editor. Anne Marie Albano, Ph.D, the Recanati Family Assistant Professor of Child and Adolescent Psychiatry, one of the nation's foremost child clinicians, also read and reread the book and provided valuable information, particularly for the chapter on cognitive behavioral therapy. I am also very grateful to Doctors Gary Gosselin and Eric Teitel, the physicians in charge of our adolescent inpatient unit at Bellevue Hospital Center, who, along with Dr. Greg Berman, one of our senior child and adolescent psychiatry residents, were willing to share their clinical experiences with me. Keith Ditkowsky, M.D., also provided key material about patients whose stories appear in the book. The NYU Child Study Center would not be possible without our amazing board of directors, who have been steadfast in their generosity and advocacy for child mental health. And the board would not be possible without the leadership of our incomparable chair, Brooke Garber Neidich.

My old friends and colleagues Doctors Rachel and Donald Klein provided their usual honest appraisals, encyclopedic knowledge, and wise advice. Dr. Glenn Hirsch, the medical director of the Child Study Center, offered his clinical experience and his calm assurance that what I was doing was important. Dr. Raul Silva, the deputy director for child and adolescent psychiatry at the Bellevue Hospital Center also provided master clinical consultation. Laurie Miller, Ph.D., the director of our Institute for Children at Risk, was generous with her time and her critique of chapters on genetics and other risk factors. Other colleagues, including Naomi Weinshenker, M.D., Melvin Oatis, M.D., Sabine Hack, M.D., Carmen Alonso, M.D., Veronica Rojas, M.D., Richard Gallagher, Ph.D., Barbara Coffey, M.D., Elissa Brown, Ph.D., Linda Carter, Ph.D., and Jonathan Lampert, M.D., make me proud to be part of such an illustrious group of caring clinicians.

I am fortunate to have three supportive bosses: Dr. Robert Cancro, Chairman of the NYU Department of Psychiatry, whose generous spirit has permitted me to create the Child Study Center; Dr. Robert Glickman, Dean of the NYU School of Medicine, who has the hardest job in America yet always finds time to be encouraging of my work; and John Sexton, president of New York University, who is the most articulate storyteller, enthusiastic student, and energetic leader in academia. They make it possible to tackle the impossible—trying to change the lives of millions of children suffering from psychiatric illness.

Outside of NYU, many colleagues were willing to share their wisdom: Doctors Adrian Angold and Jane Costello from Duke University; Dr. Reed Larson from the University of Illinois; Dr. Marty Seligman from the University of Pennsylvania; Doctors Maddy Gould, Larry Greenhill, Myrna Weissman, and Laura Mufson from Columbia University; Dr. Maggie Bridwell from the University of Maryland; Dr. Richard Kadizon from Harvard University; Dr. Paul Grayson from New York University; and Doctors Gaye Carlson and Max Fink from the State University of New York at Stony Brook. Bryant Welch, an attorney, psychologist, and mental health advocate, provided me with several enlightening case studies.

My friends and family also participated by being supportive and tolerant of my constant need to work on this book. I am grateful to Edith Usi Koplewicz, Brian Novick, Arthur Carter, Michael Silverstein, Sally Peterson, Melvin and Doris Sirow, Danielle Steel, Ruth Westheimer, Virginia Anthony, and Sandi Mendelson. My friend Judy Schumer also read the book line by line and told me what I was doing wrong.

Many generous publishing colleagues participated. Cheryl Mercer was very generous with her thoughts and words. Michael Carlisle, my agent, who always thinks what I have to say is important, convinced me it was time to write this book. I thank him and Faith Hamlin, his co-agent on this project, for having the good sense to bring it to Jeremy

Katz, an enthusiastic and skillful editor whose keen suggestions helped transform the manuscript. I also thank Jennifer Repo. Mark Chiminsky provided useful guidance and helped refine this work. Michael Branson and Marilyn Ducksworth are part of the Putnam team—they're the ultimate pros in literary publicity.

I never seem to have enough time in the day to do everything I want to, and I have the amazing assistance of Karen Nappi, who manages to keep me moving on time and accomplishing as much as possible. In addition, Betsy Militello, the administrator of the Child Study Center, not only keeps the place running but is also a fabulous editor. Thanks to Catherine Watts Collier for making sure that our message reaches the world. Kudos go to Jennifer Rosenblatt, who provided all the references for the book. In addition, she took on the painstaking task of going over the book repeatedly to make sure our changes were correct, we were scientifically accurate, and that we made it on time. And a special thank you to Ivet Bandirma-Urioste, my practice coordinator, who was invaluable in making sure that this book was filled with real teenagers whose stories could illuminate the subject of adolescent depression. She also organized the glossary and the resource section. Ivet will make a phenomenal psychologist some day.

Finally, I extend my deepest appreciation to all the young people and their parents who allowed me to include them in this book. All of them were generous with their time and open with their thoughts. In telling their stories, they are helping others, and I hope they found some benefit for themselves in the experience. A special thank you to Connie Masters, who lost her son, Blake Hansen, to depression in 1995 and has since devoted herself to the need for more compassionate and attentive care for young people by the United States mental health system.

INDEX

About the Author

Harold S. Koplewicz, M.D., is the Arnold and Debbie Simon Professor of Child and Adolescent Psychiatry and Pediatrics and the founder and director of the New York University Child Study Center. He also serves as the vice chairman of the Department of Psychiatry and Professor of Clinical Pediatrics at the New York University School of Medicine. In addition, he is the director of Child and Adolescent Psychiatry at Bellevue Hospital Center.

Dr. Koplewicz is the recipient of many awards, including the 1997 Exemplary Psychiatrist Award from the National Alliance for the Mentally Ill, and the 1997 Reiger Service Award for the American Academy of Child and Adolescent Psychiatry in recognition of his work in the development of school-based mental health programs. He has also received the 1999 Humanitarian Award from Marymount Manhattan College, and the 2000 American Grand Hope Award.

Dr. Koplewicz holds advisory positions with several major parenting and mental health organizations, including appointments to the Board of Directors for the National Foundation for Depressive Illness, the National Board of Advisors for *Parents* magazine, and the Professional Advisory Committee of the Mental Health Association of New York City.

He has published more than fifty scholarly articles on child and adolescent psychiatry and is the editor in chief of the *Journal of Child and Adolescent Psychopharmacology*. Named one of "America's Best Mental Health Experts" by *Good Housekeeping* magazine and repeatedly as one of "America's Top Doctors" by Castle Connolly, Dr. Koplewicz has appeared frequently in the media, including *The Oprah Winfrey Show, Good Morning America,* CNN, *Dateline NBC,* and other programs. Dr. Koplewicz is also the author of several books, including *It's Nobody's Fault: New Hope and Help for Difficult Children and Their Parents* (Time Books, 1996), which received the Parent's Choice Award and was a Books for a Better Life finalist. Dr. Koplewicz lives in New York City with his wife and their three teenage sons.